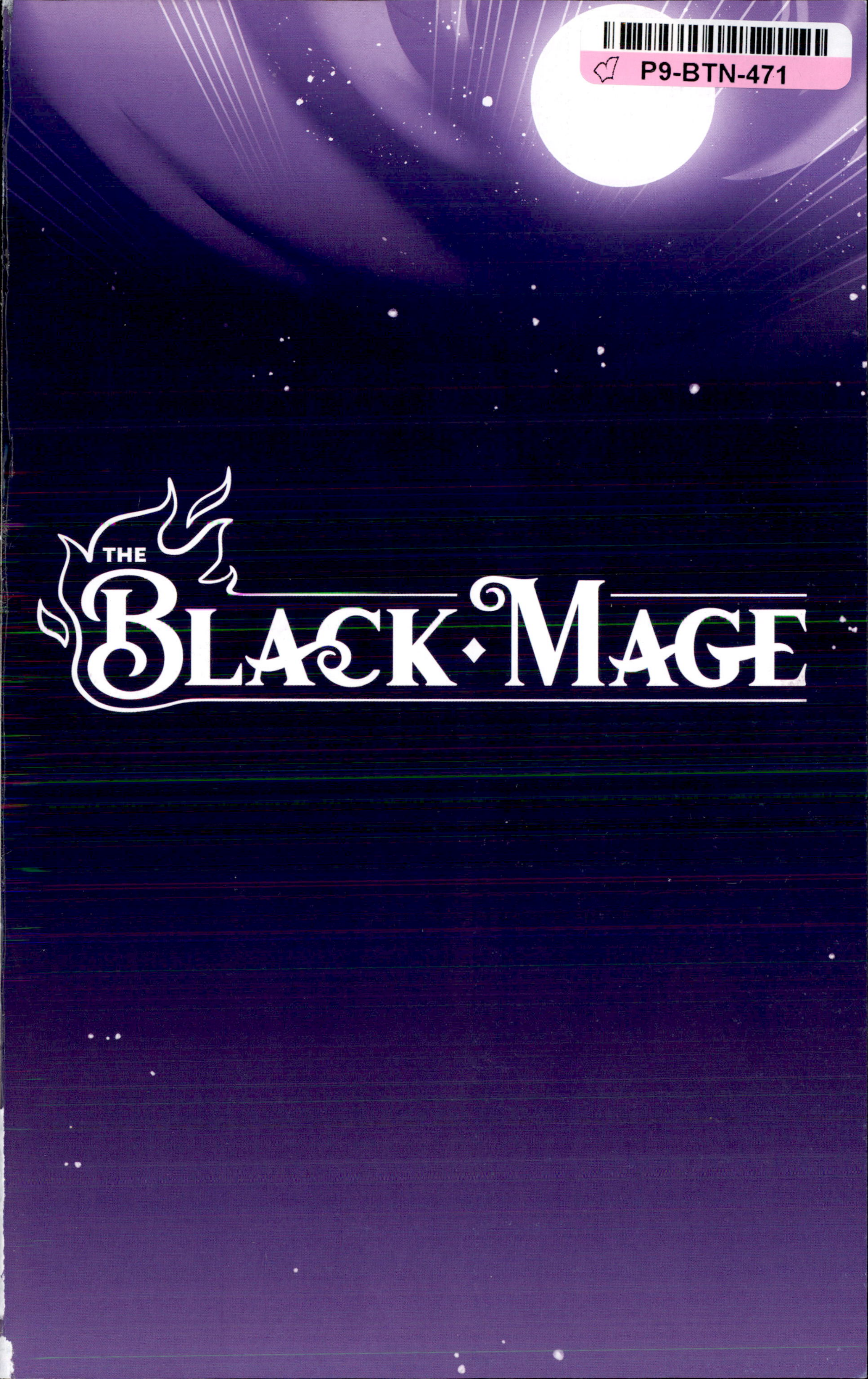
THE
BLACK MAGE

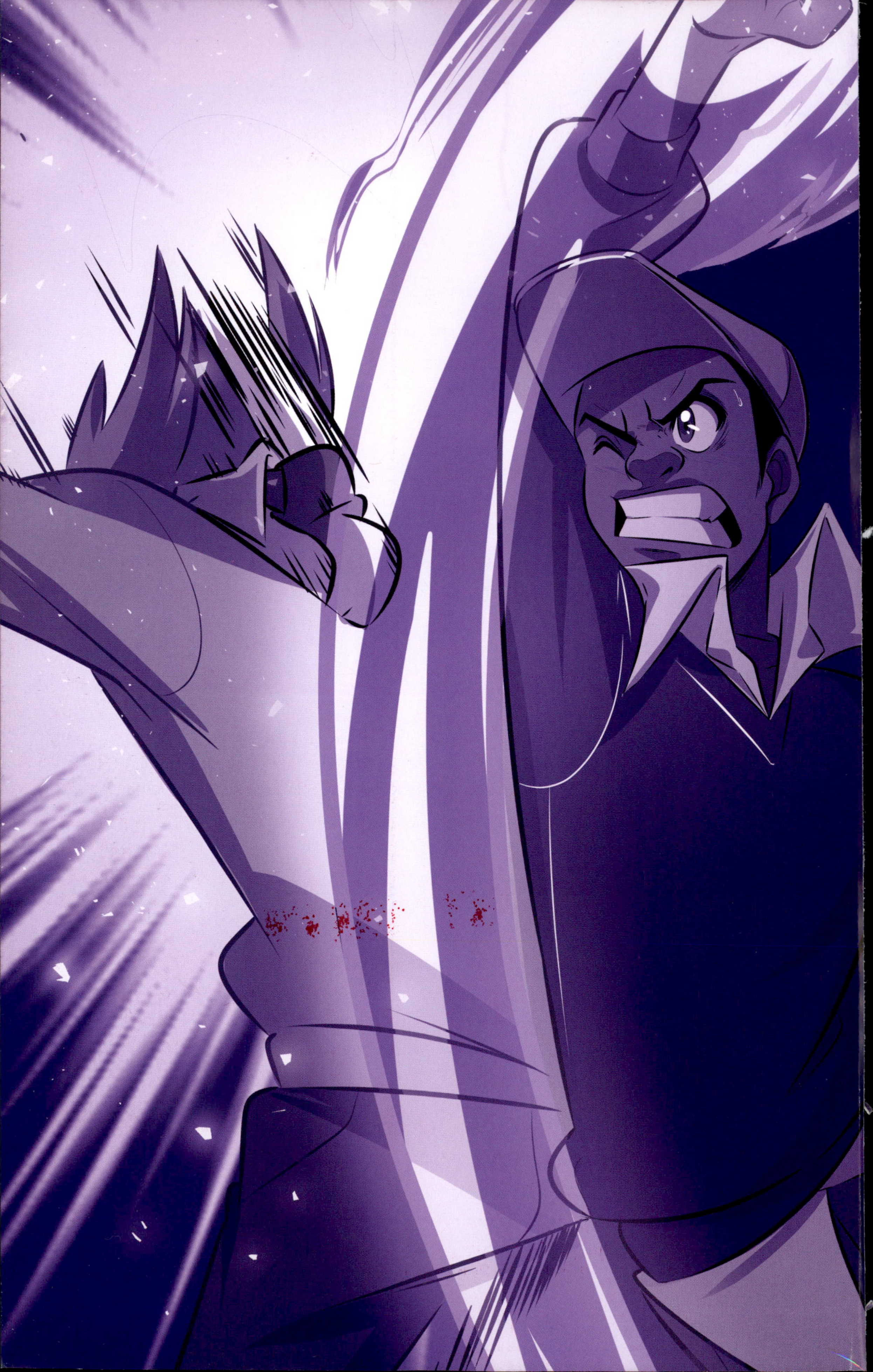

THE BLACK·MAGE

Written by Daniel Barnes
Illustrated and colored by D.J. Kirkland
Lettered by Hassan Otsmane-Elhaou

Layout assists by Tyson Hesse
Chapter 1-4 Flats by Bobby Fasel
Chapter 5 Flats by Alexandra Salas

Designed by Deron Bennett & Kate Z. Stone

Edited by Desiree Wilson
with assistance from Charlie Chu

Published by Oni Press, Inc.

Joe Nozemack, Founder & Chief Financial Officer

James Lucas Jones, Publisher

Sarah Gaydos, Editor in Chief

Charlie Chu, V.P. of Creative & Business Development

Brad Rooks, Director of Operations

Margot Wood, Director of Sales

Amber O'Neill, Special Projects Manager

Troy Look, Director of Design & Production

Kate Z. Stone, Senior Graphic Designer

Sonja Synak, Graphic Designer

Angie Knowles, Digital Prepress Lead

Robin Herrera, Senior Editor

Ari Yarwood, Senior Editor

Michelle Nguyen, Executive Assistant

Jung Lee, Logistics Coordinator

onipress.com
facebook.com/onipress
twitter.com/onipress
onipress.tumblr.com
instagram.com/onipress

@danny8bit
@OhHeyDJ / djkirkland.com

First Edition: October 2019
Paperback ISBN 978-1-62010-652-5
Hardcover ISBN 978-1-62010-707-2
eISBN 978-1-62010-653-2

Library of Congress Control Number: 2019931469

1 3 5 7 9 10 8 6 4 2

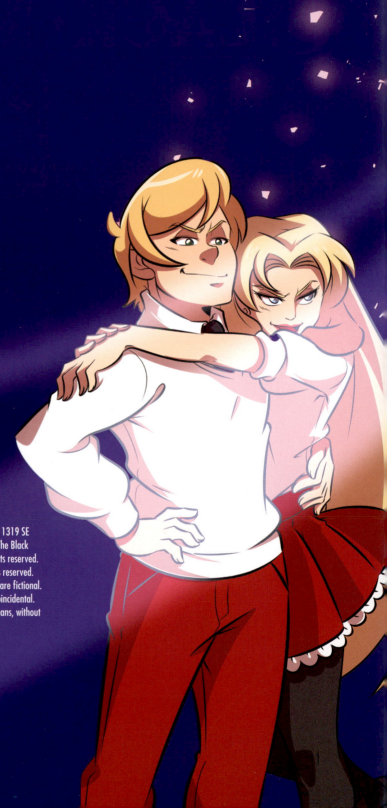

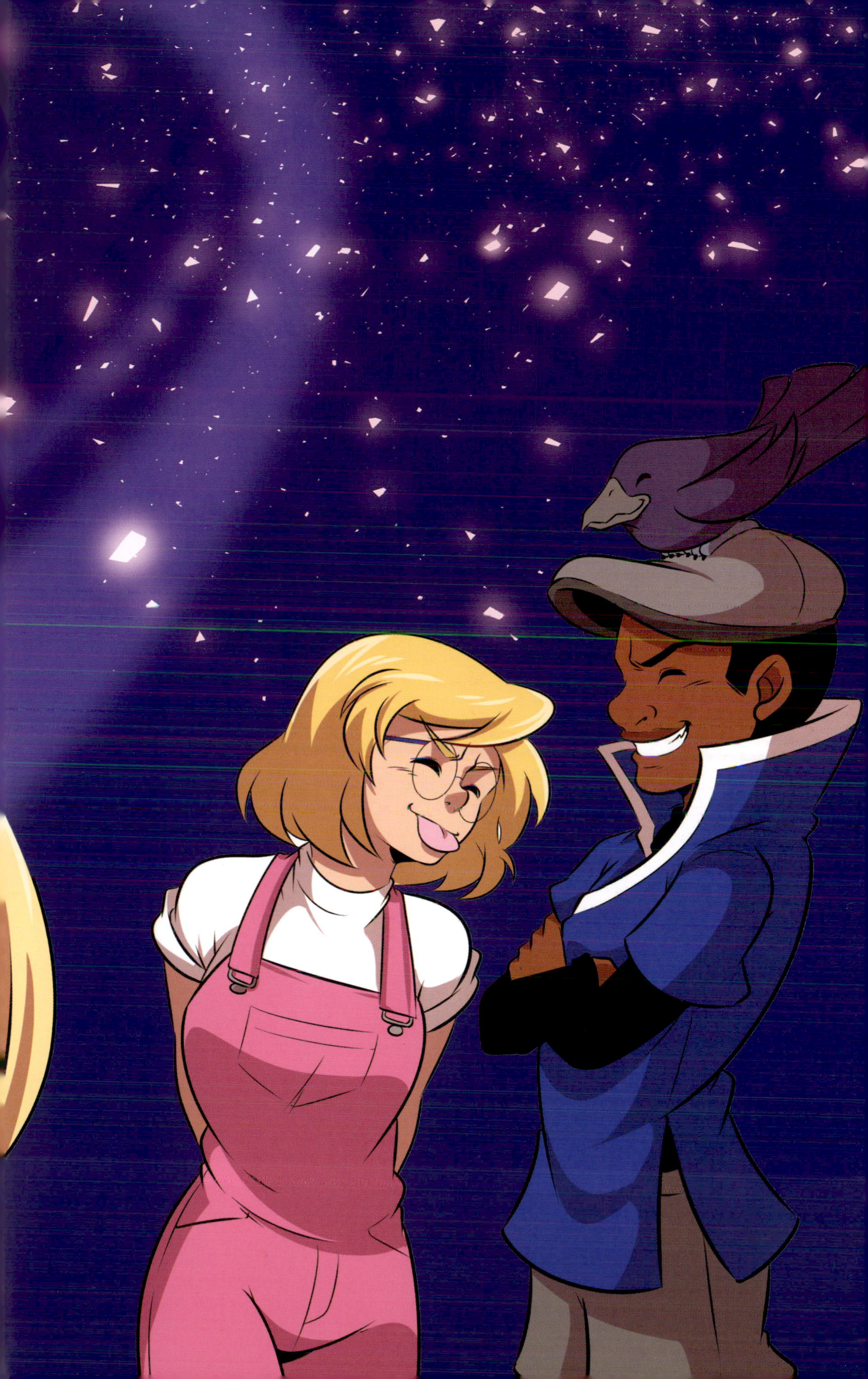

CHAPTER ONE

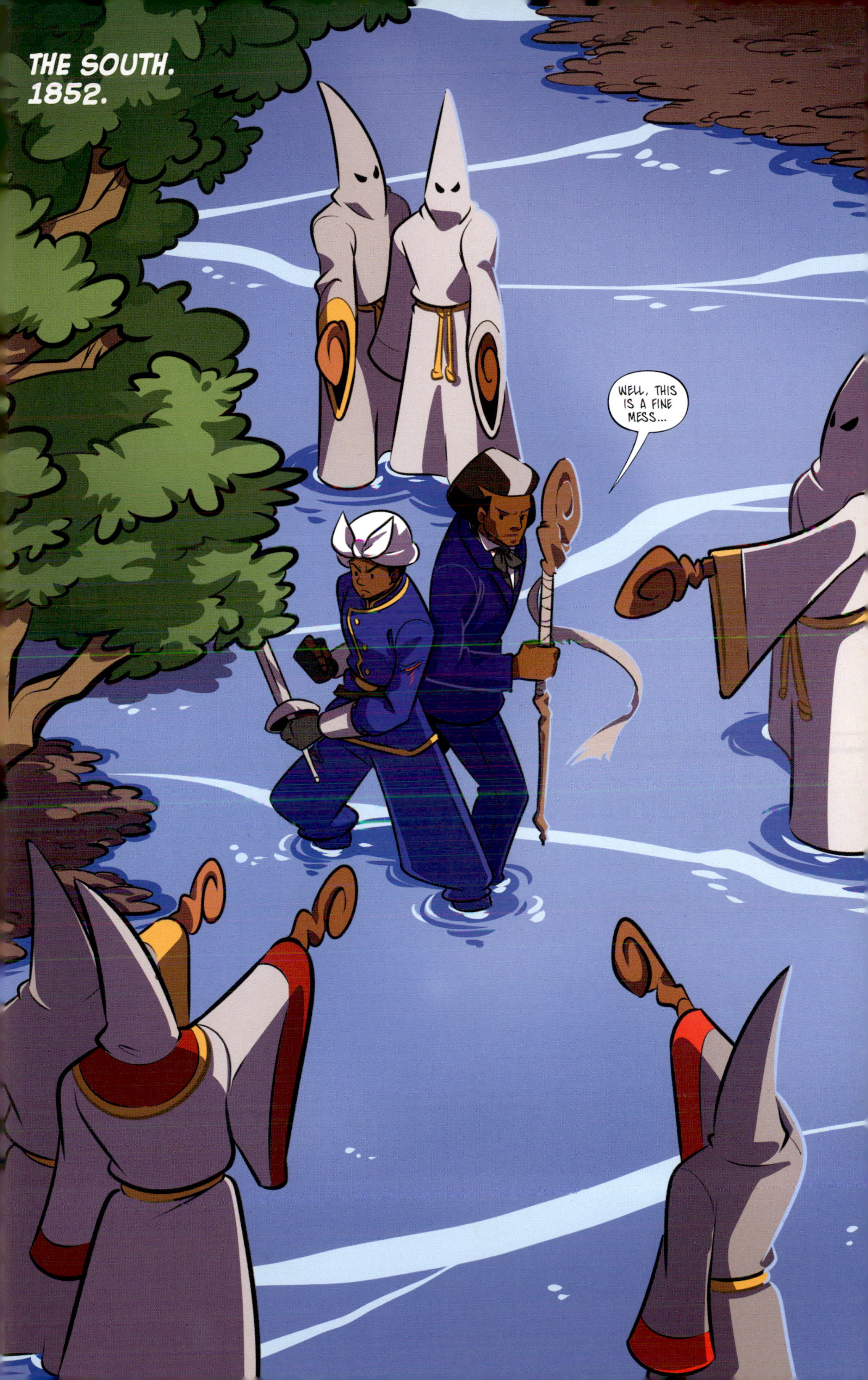
THE SOUTH.
1852.
WELL, THIS IS A FINE MESS...

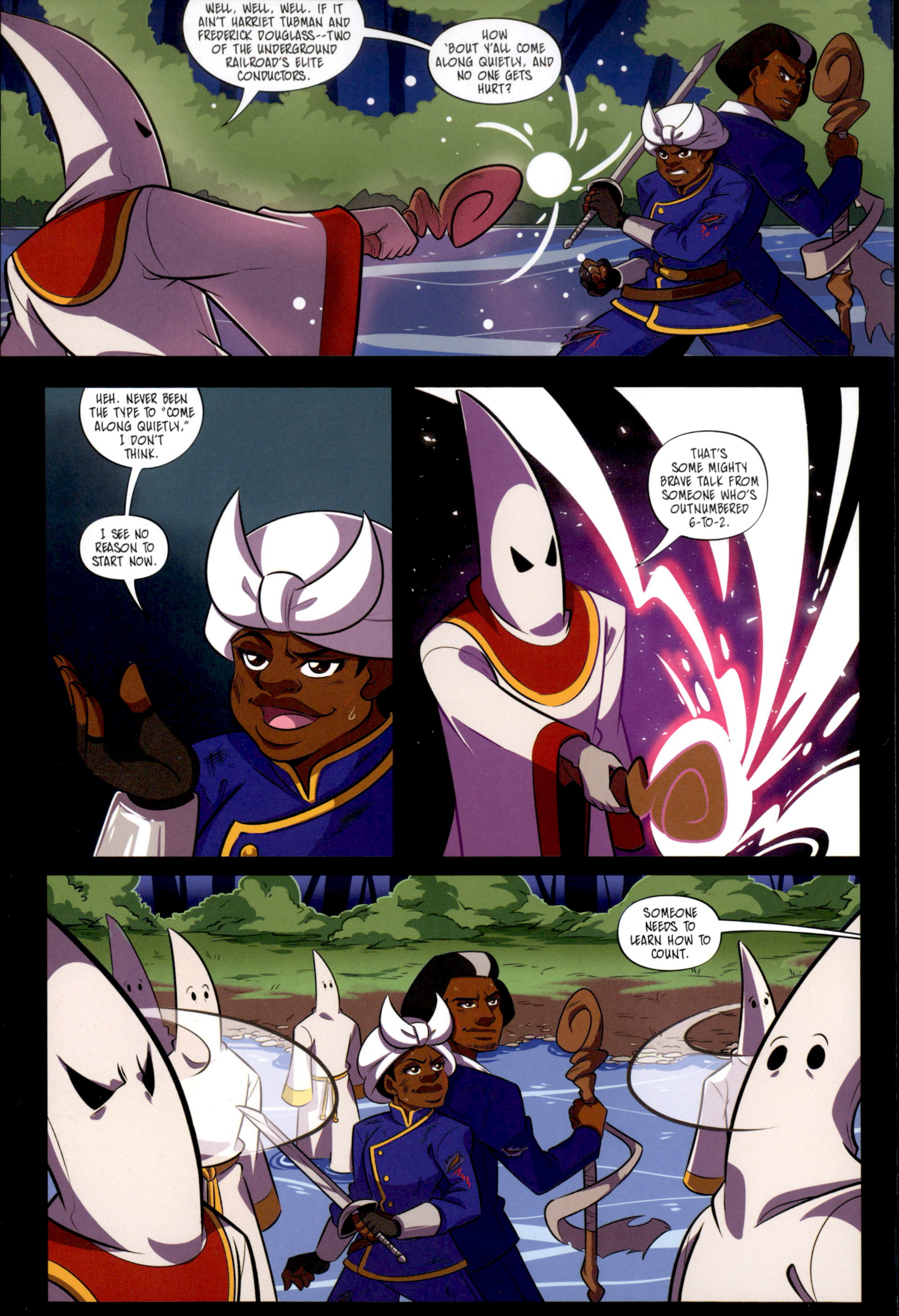
WELL, WELL, WELL. IF IT AIN'T HARRIET TUBMAN AND FREDERICK DOUGLASS--TWO OF THE UNDERGROUND RAILROAD'S ELITE CONDUCTORS.
HOW 'BOUT Y'ALL COME ALONG QUIETLY, AND NO ONE GETS HURT?
HEH. NEVER BEEN THE TYPE TO "COME ALONG QUIETLY," I DON'T THINK.
I SEE NO REASON TO START NOW.
THAT'S SOME MIGHTY BRAVE TALK FROM SOMEONE WHO'S OUTNUMBERED 6-TO-2.
SOMEONE NEEDS TO LEARN HOW TO COUNT.

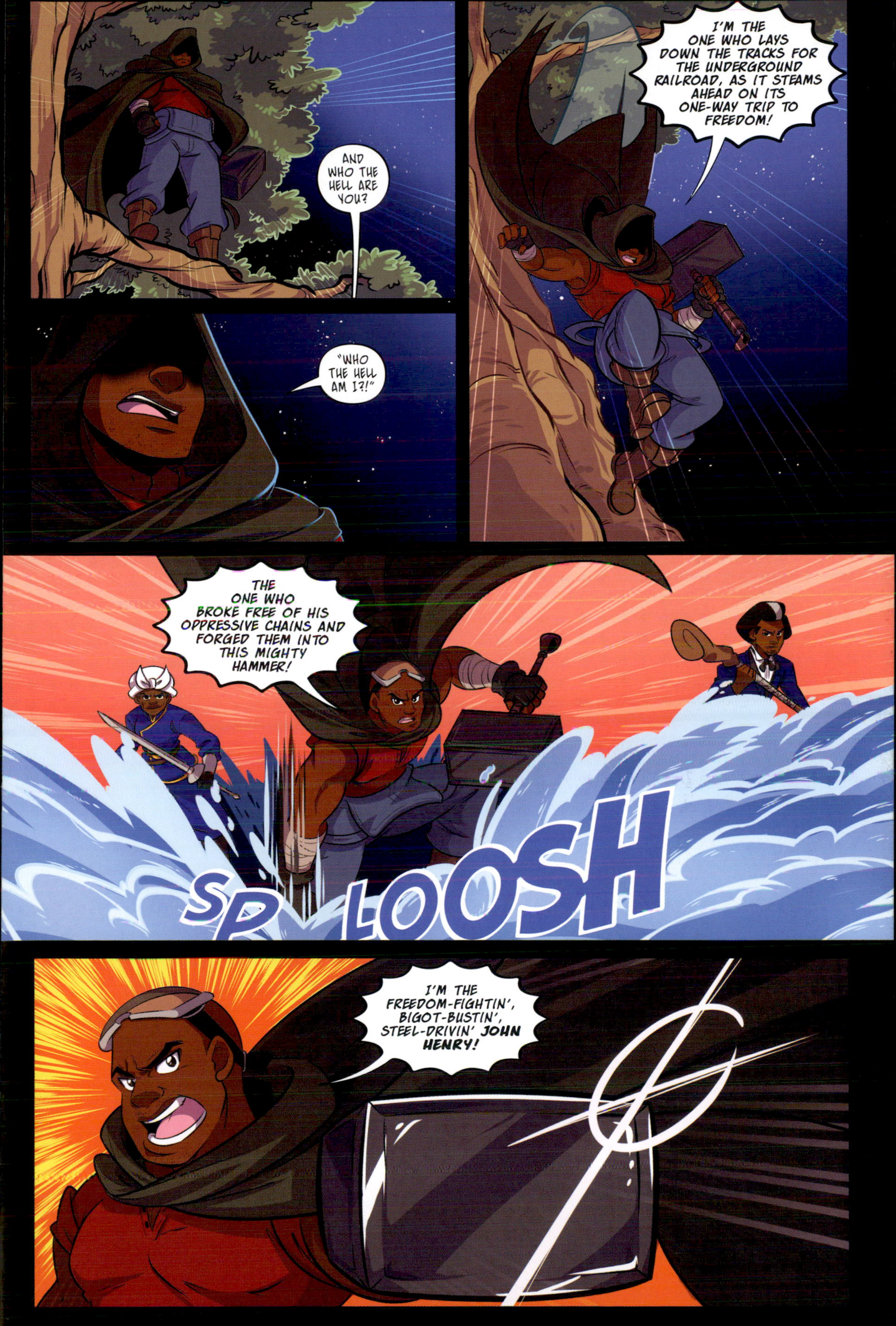
AND WHO THE HELL ARE YOU?
I'M THE ONE WHO LAYS DOWN THE TRACKS FOR THE UNDERGROUND RAILROAD, AS IT STEAMS AHEAD ON ITS ONE-WAY TRIP TO FREEDOM!
"WHO THE HELL AM I?!"
THE ONE WHO BROKE FREE OF HIS OPPRESSIVE CHAINS AND FORGED THEM INTO THIS MIGHTY HAMMER!
SPLOOSH
I'M THE FREEDOM-FIGHTIN', BIGOT-BUSTIN', STEEL-DRIVIN' JOHN HENRY!

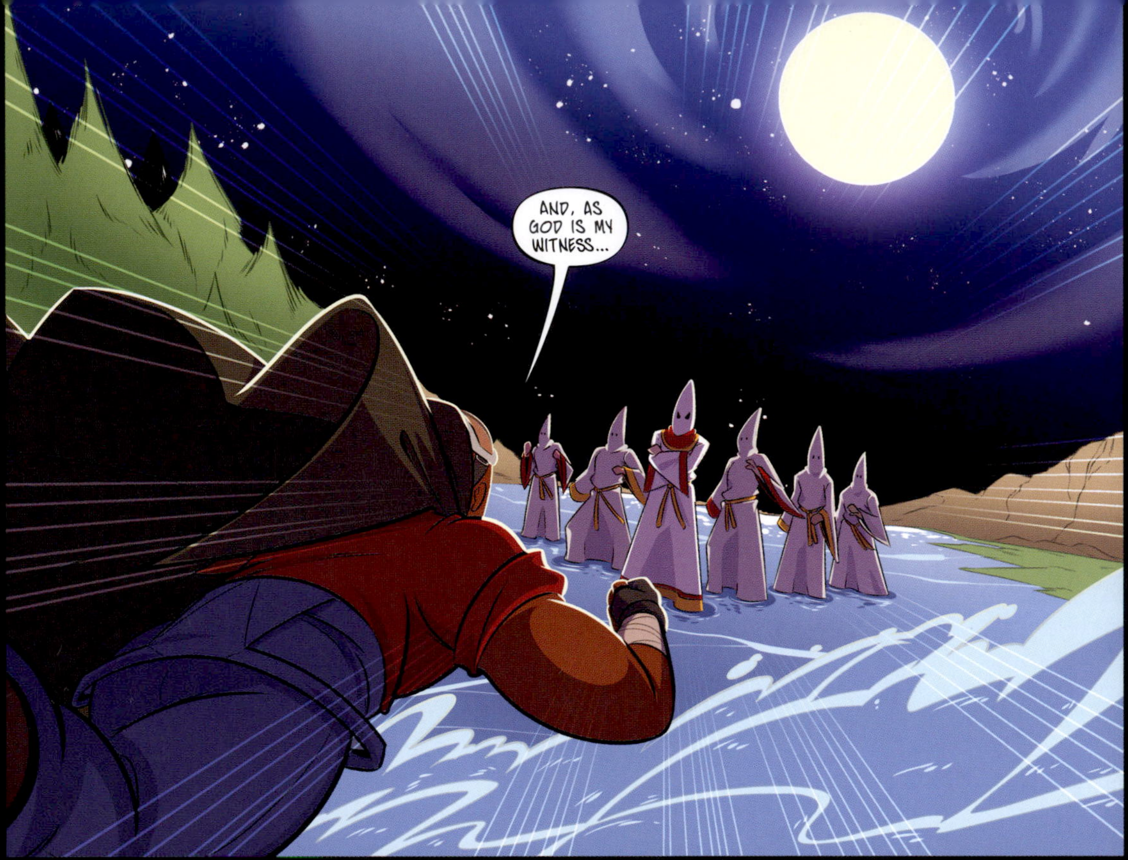
AND, AS GOD IS MY WITNESS...

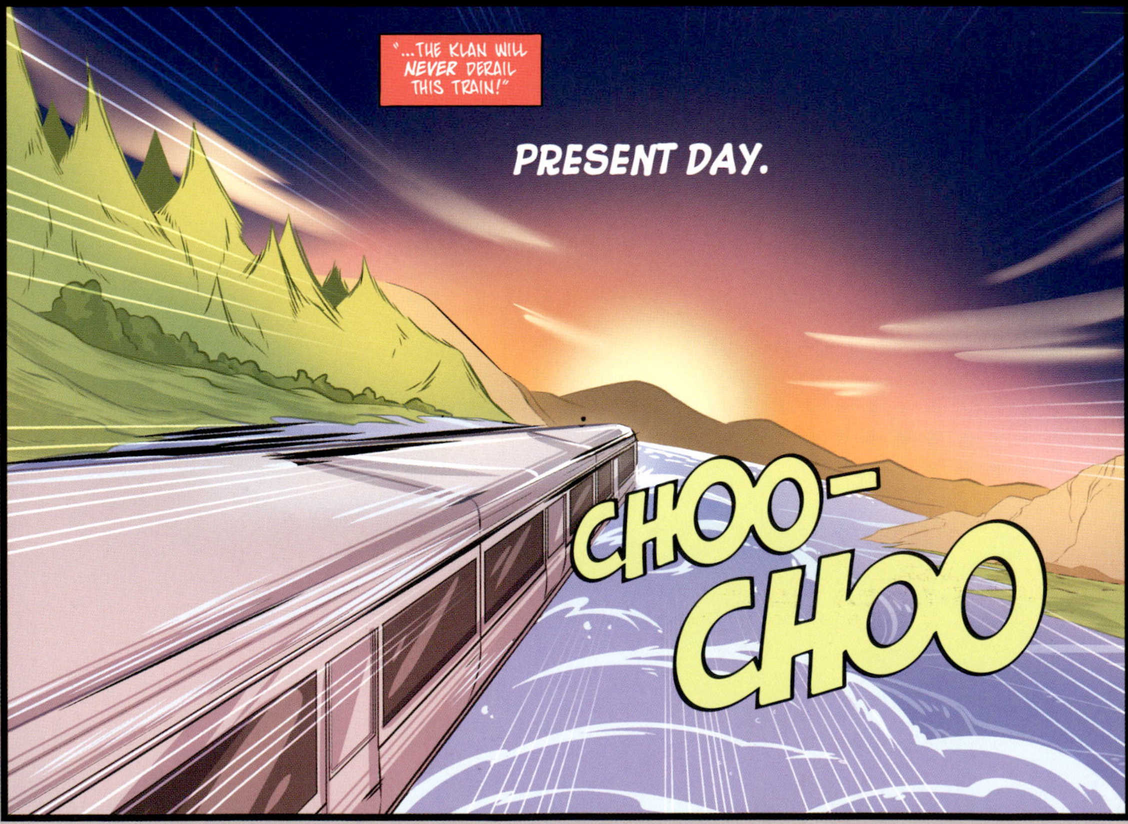
"...THE KLAN WILL NEVER DERAIL THIS TRAIN!"
PRESENT DAY.
CHOO-CHOO

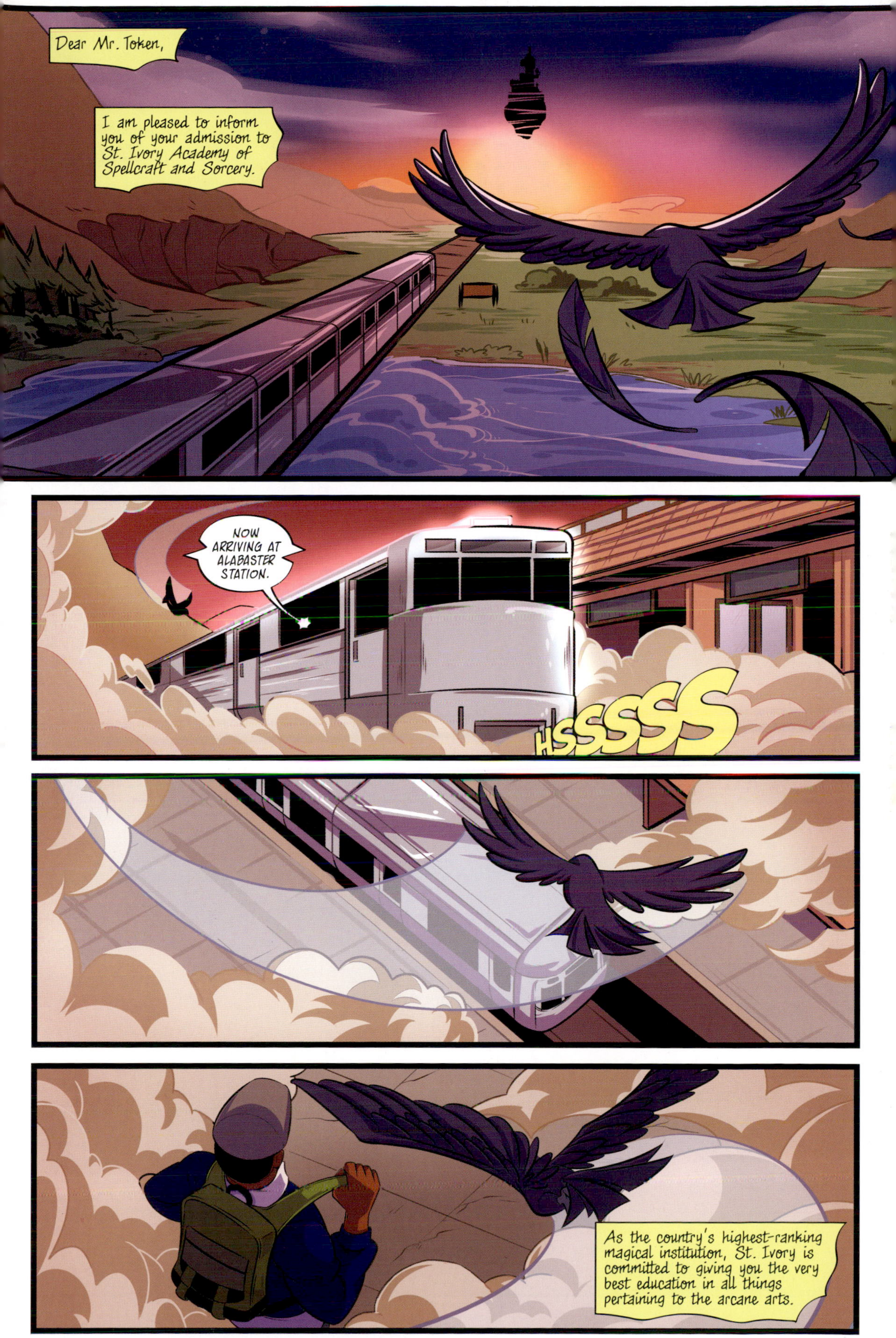
Dear Mr. Token,
I am pleased to inform you of your admission to St. Ivory Academy of Spellcraft and Sorcery.
NOW ARRIVING AT ALABASTER STATION.
HSSSSSS
As the country's highest-ranking magical institution, St. Ivory is committed to giving you the very best education in all things pertaining to the arcane arts.

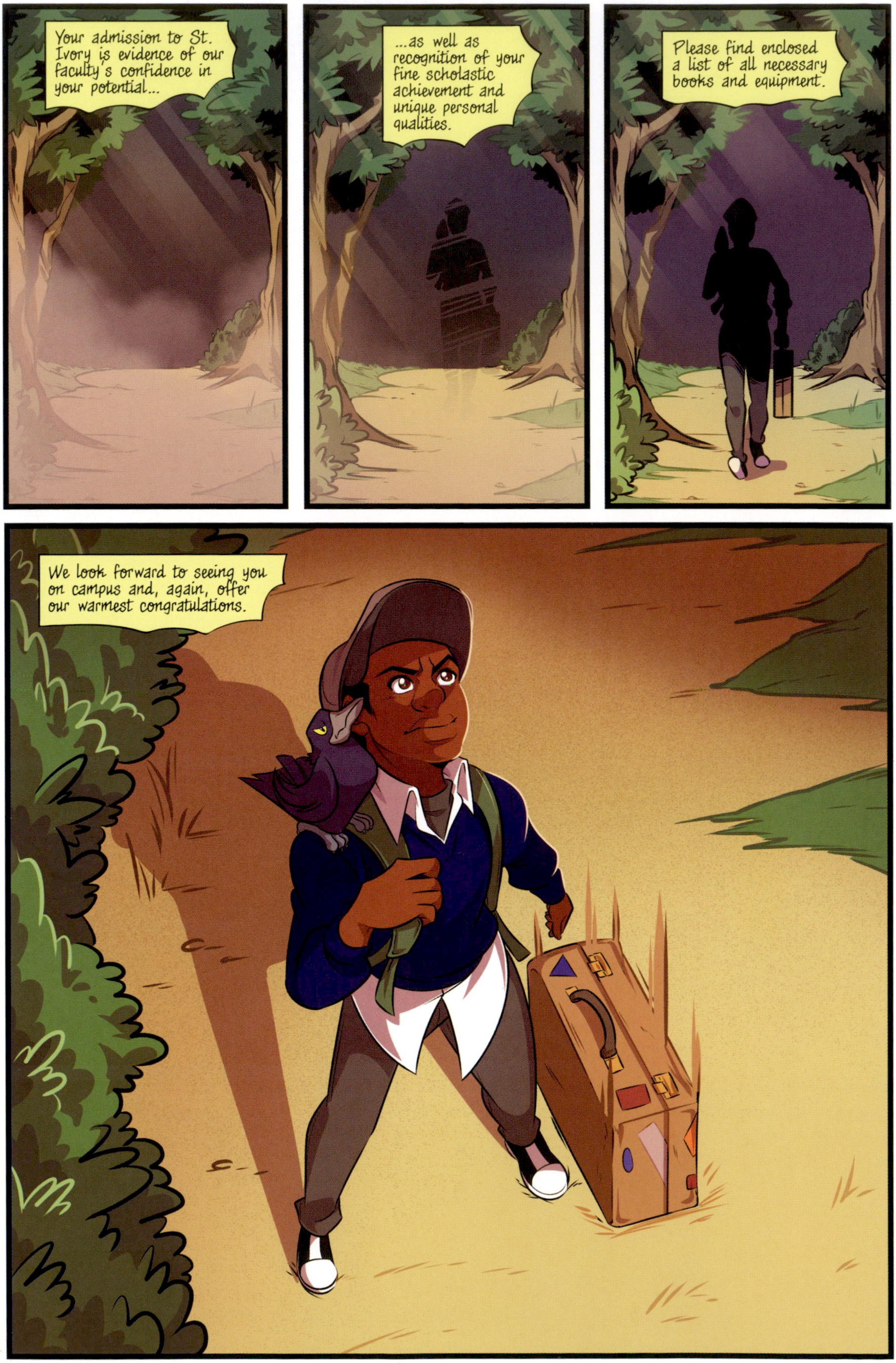
Your admission to St. Ivory is evidence of our faculty's confidence in your potential...
...as well as recognition of your fine scholastic achievement and unique personal qualities.
Please find enclosed a list of all necessary books and equipment.
We look forward to seeing you on campus and, again, offer our warmest congratulations.

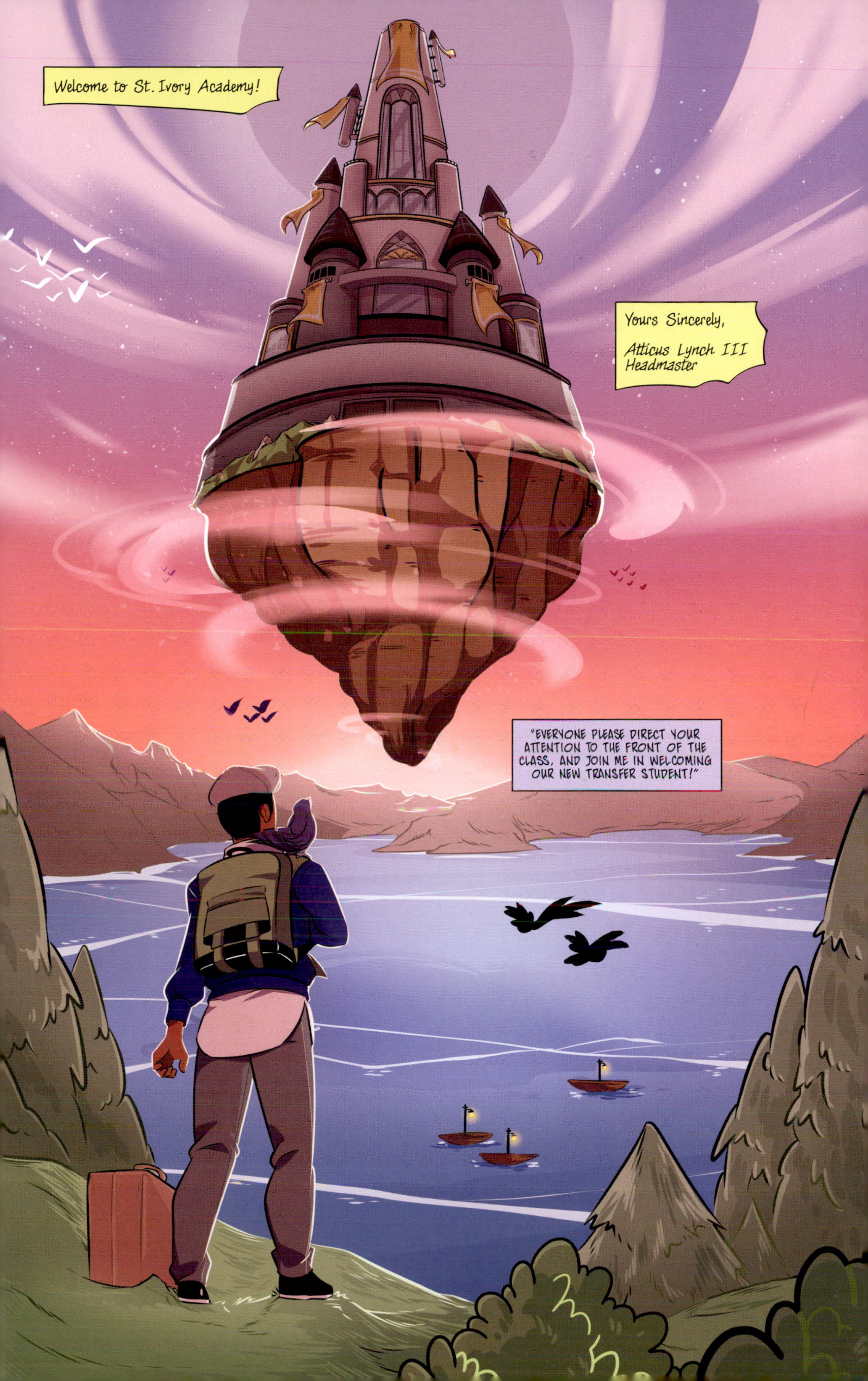
Welcome to St. Ivory Academy!
Yours Sincerely,
Atticus Lynch III
Headmaster
"EVERYONE PLEASE DIRECT YOUR ATTENTION TO THE FRONT OF THE CLASS, AND JOIN ME IN WELCOMING OUR NEW TRANSFER STUDENT!"

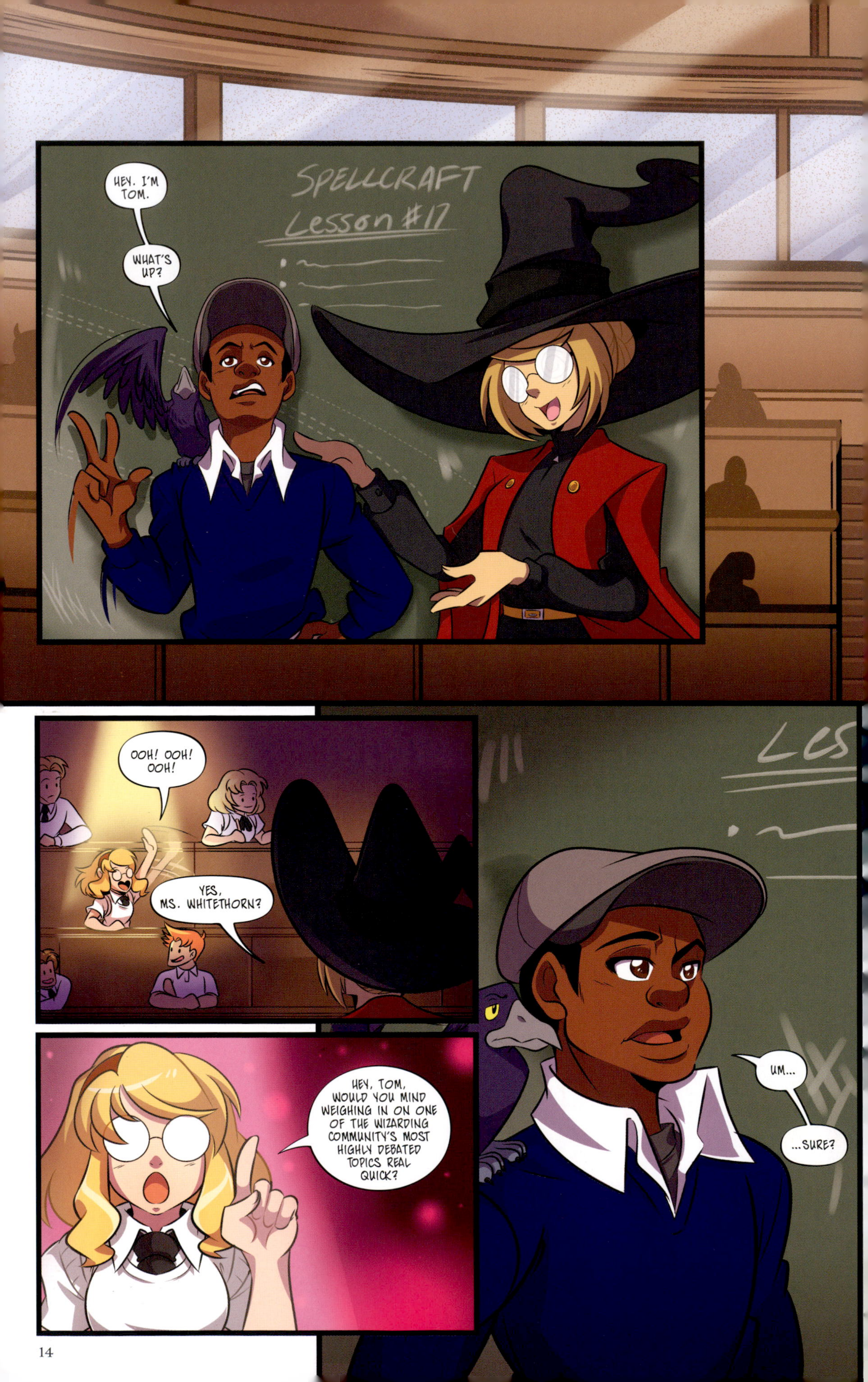
SPELLCRAFT
Lesson #17
HEY. I'M TOM.
WHAT'S UP?
OOH! OOH! OOH!
YES, MS. WHITETHORN?
HEY, TOM, WOULD YOU MIND WEIGHING IN ON ONE OF THE WIZARDING COMMUNITY'S MOST HIGHLY DEBATED TOPICS REAL QUICK?
UM...
...SURE?

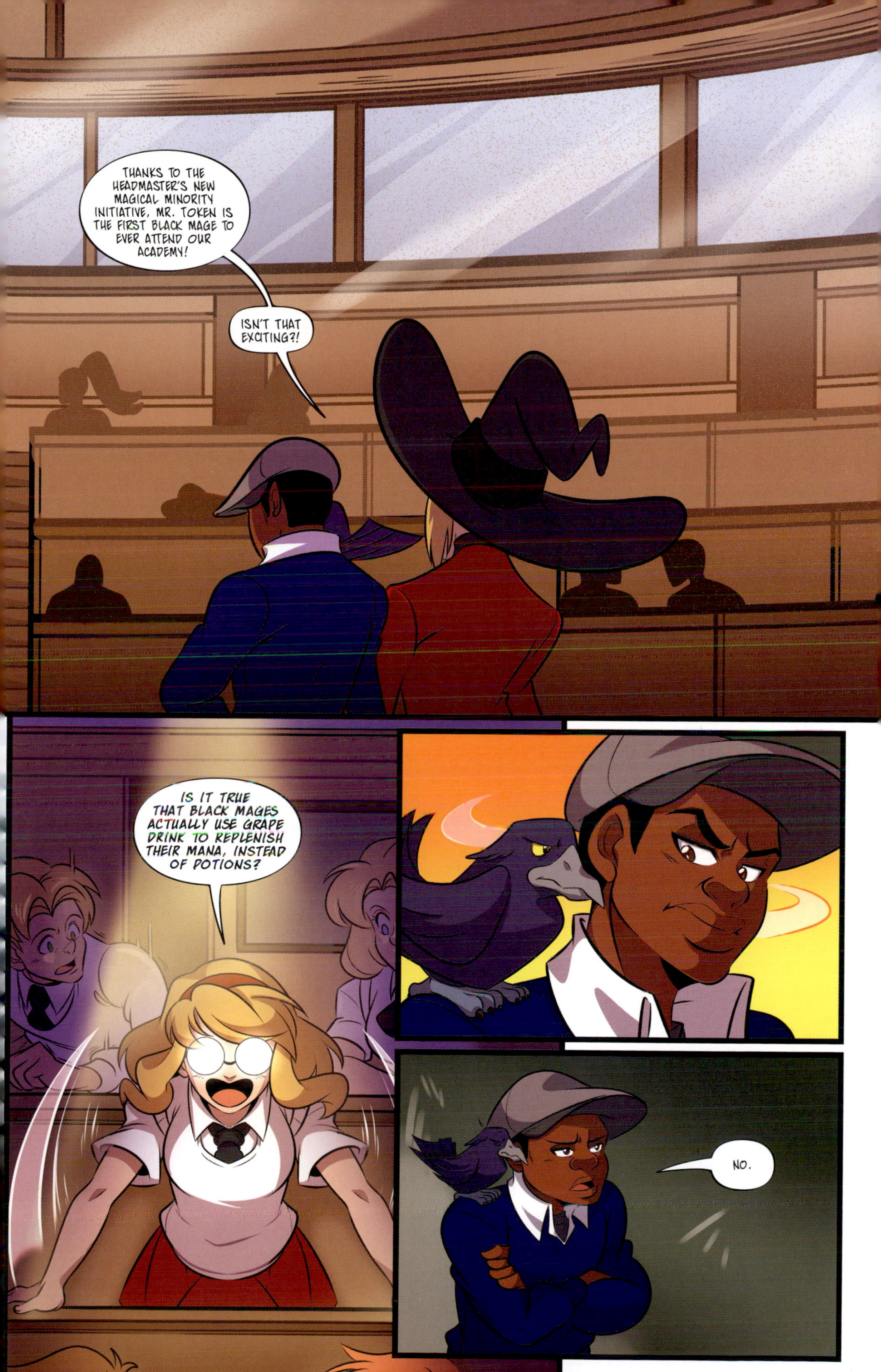
THANKS TO THE HEADMASTER'S NEW MAGICAL MINORITY INITIATIVE, MR. TOKEN IS THE FIRST BLACK MAGE TO EVER ATTEND OUR ACADEMY!
ISN'T THAT EXCITING?!
IS IT TRUE THAT BLACK MAGES ACTUALLY USE GRAPE DRINK TO REPLENISH THEIR MANA, INSTEAD OF POTIONS?
NO.

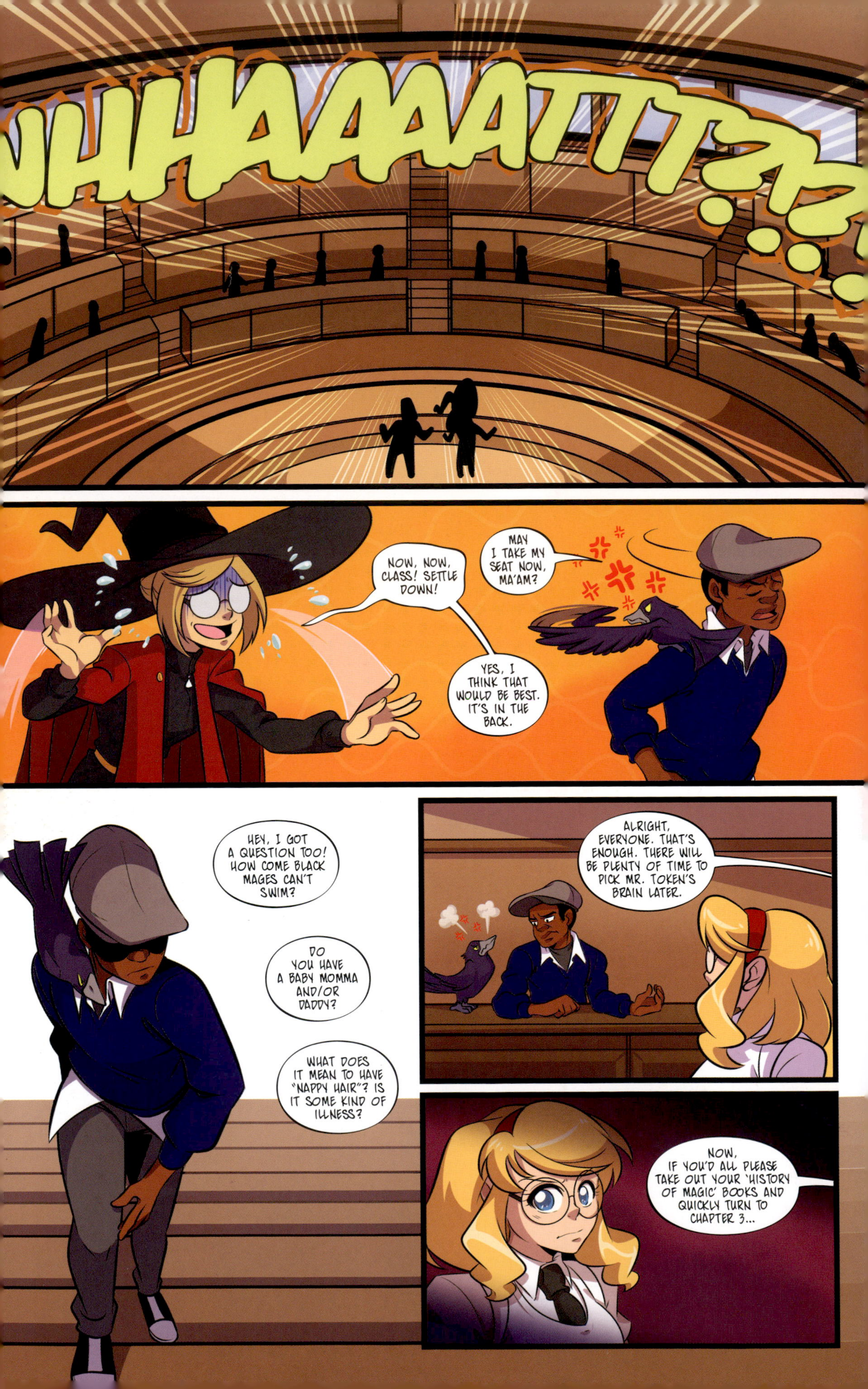
WHHAAAAATTT?!?!
NOW, NOW, CLASS! SETTLE DOWN!
MAY I TAKE MY SEAT NOW, MA'AM?
YES, I THINK THAT WOULD BE BEST. IT'S IN THE BACK.
HEY, I GOT A QUESTION TOO! HOW COME BLACK MAGES CAN'T SWIM?
DO YOU HAVE A BABY MOMMA AND/OR DADDY?
WHAT DOES IT MEAN TO HAVE "NAPPY HAIR"? IS IT SOME KIND OF ILLNESS?
ALRIGHT, EVERYONE. THAT'S ENOUGH. THERE WILL BE PLENTY OF TIME TO PICK MR. TOKEN'S BRAIN LATER.
NOW, IF YOU'D ALL PLEASE TAKE OUT YOUR 'HISTORY OF MAGIC' BOOKS AND QUICKLY TURN TO CHAPTER 3...

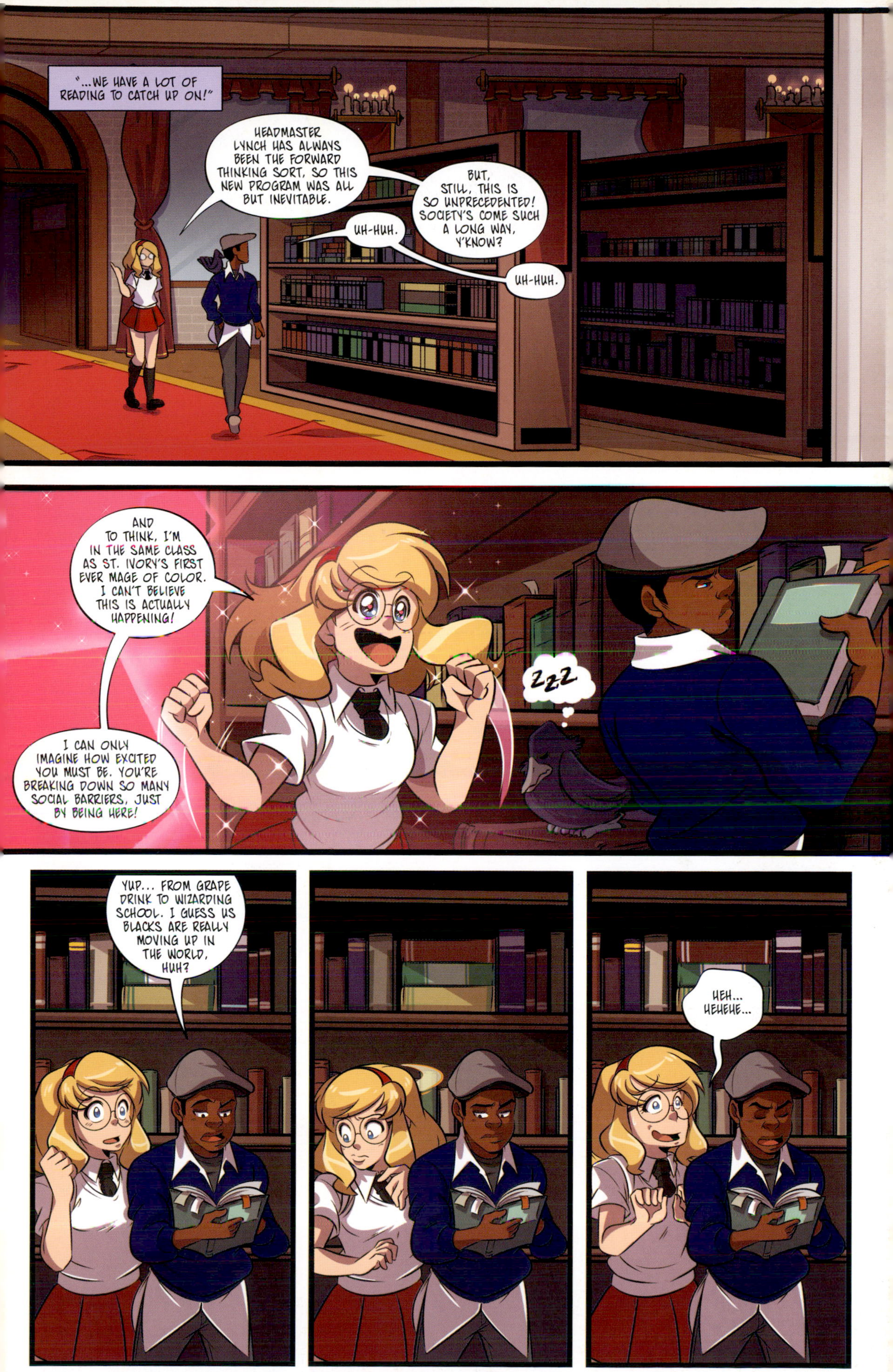
"...WE HAVE A LOT OF READING TO CATCH UP ON!"
HEADMASTER LYNCH HAS ALWAYS BEEN THE FORWARD THINKING SORT, SO THIS NEW PROGRAM WAS ALL BUT INEVITABLE.
UH-HUH.
BUT, STILL, THIS IS SO UNPRECEDENTED! SOCIETY'S COME SUCH A LONG WAY, Y'KNOW?
UH-HUH.
AND TO THINK, I'M IN THE SAME CLASS AS ST. IVORY'S FIRST EVER MAGE OF COLOR. I CAN'T BELIEVE THIS IS ACTUALLY HAPPENING!
I CAN ONLY IMAGINE HOW EXCITED YOU MUST BE. YOU'RE BREAKING DOWN SO MANY SOCIAL BARRIERS, JUST BY BEING HERE!
ZZZ
YUP... FROM GRAPE DRINK TO WIZARDING SCHOOL. I GUESS US BLACKS ARE REALLY MOVING UP IN THE WORLD, HUH?
HEH... HEHEHE...

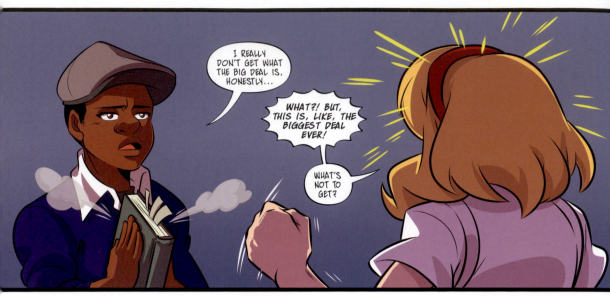

I REALLY DON'T GET WHAT THE BIG DEAL IS, HONESTLY...

WHAT?! BUT, THIS IS, LIKE, THE BIGGEST DEAL EVER!

WHAT'S NOT TO GET?

YOU GUYS LET ONE BLACK STUDENT IN, AFTER SHUTTING MINORITIES OUT FOR CENTURIES.

WHOOP-DEE-DOO.

WHAT DO YOU GUYS WANT, A COOKIE?

I... I KNOW OUR SCHOOL'S TRACK RECORD, DIVERSITY-WISE, HAS BEEN LESS THAN STELLAR, IN THE PAST.

BUT, THAT'S ALL ABOUT TO CHANGE. THIS IS THE BEGINNING OF A NEW ERA!

THE *MAGICAL MINORITY INITIATIVE'S* GOING TO CHANGE THE WIZARDING LANDSCAPE FOREVER, AND YOU'RE ITS FIRST BENEFICIARY!

HOW CAN YOU BE SO INDIFFERENT ABOUT THAT?

OH, PLEASE.

THE ONLY REASON YOUR HEADMASTER EVEN IMPLEMENTED THIS "INITIATIVE" WAS BECAUSE THIS SCHOOL'S ACCREDITATION WAS IN JEOPARDY.

HE DIDN'T DO IT OUT OF THE KINDNESS OF HIS NOW SUDDENLY PROGRESSIVE HEART.

THE WIZARDING COMMUNITY ISN'T ENTERING SOME "POST-RACIAL AGE." I'M JUST A BOX TO CHECK FOR SOME HIGHER-UP.

IT'S AS SIMPLE AS THAT.

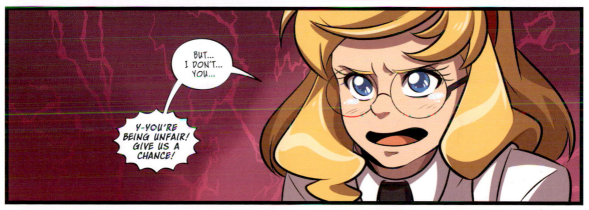

BUT... I DON'T... YOU...

Y-YOU'RE BEING UNFAIR! GIVE US A CHANCE!

GIVE ME A BREAK.

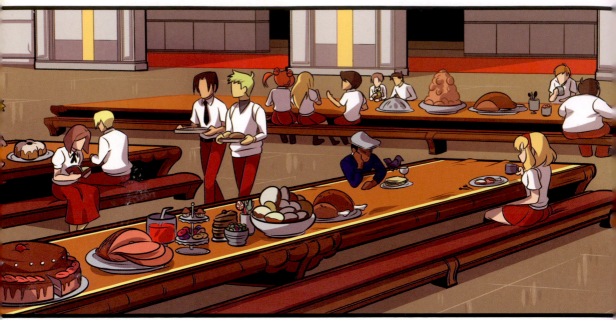

SO... IS THERE A REASON YOU'RE FOLLOWING ME AROUND, OR...?

I'M YOUR STUDENT LIAISON. IT'S MY JOB TO FOLLOW YOU AROUND.

OH....

AAAWWW. WHY THE LONG FACES, YOU TWO?

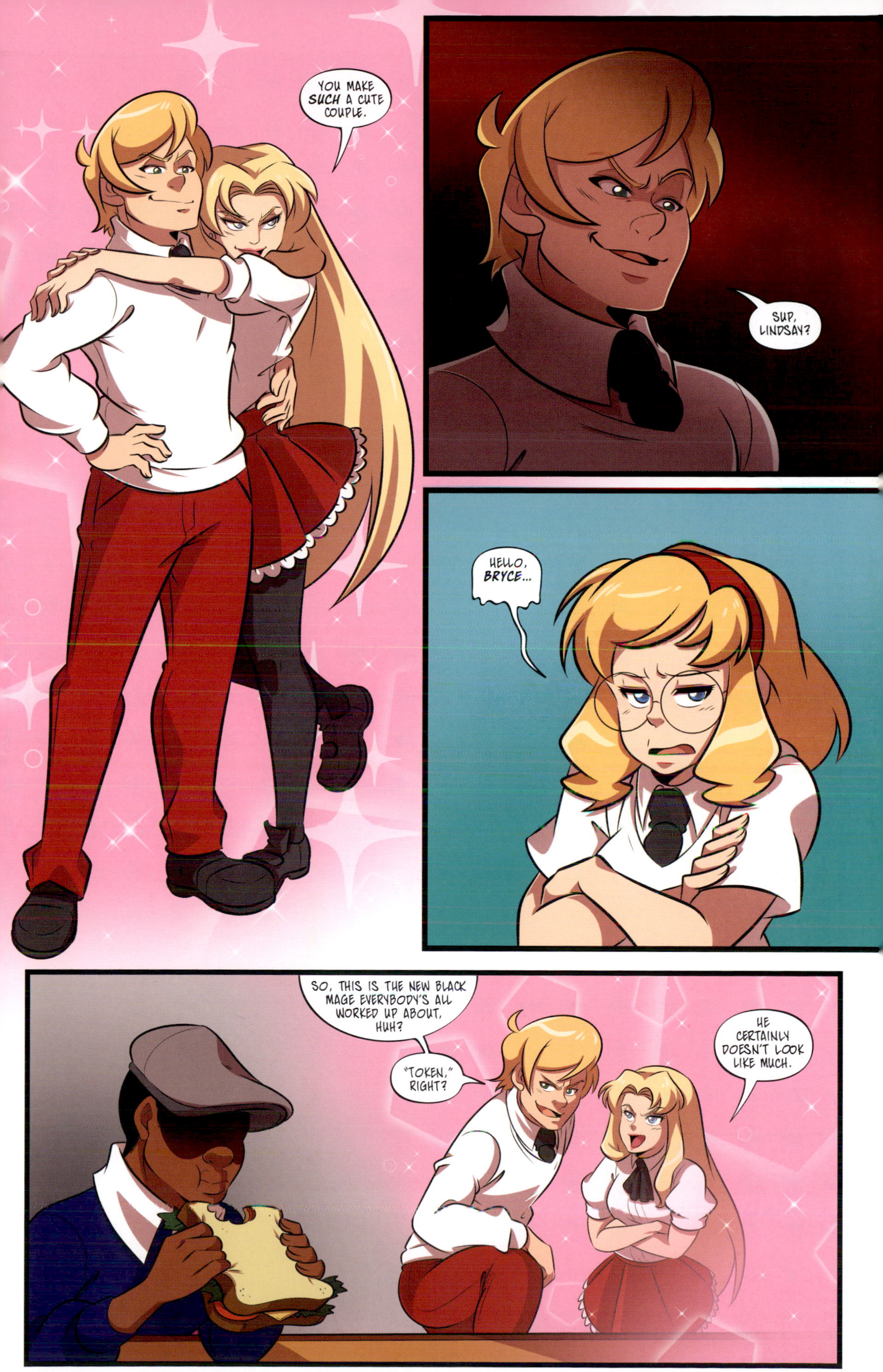
YOU MAKE SUCH A CUTE COUPLE.
SUP, LINDSAY?
HELLO, BRYCE...
SO, THIS IS THE NEW BLACK MAGE EVERYBODY'S ALL WORKED UP ABOUT, HUH?
"TOKEN," RIGHT?
HE CERTAINLY DOESN'T LOOK LIKE MUCH.

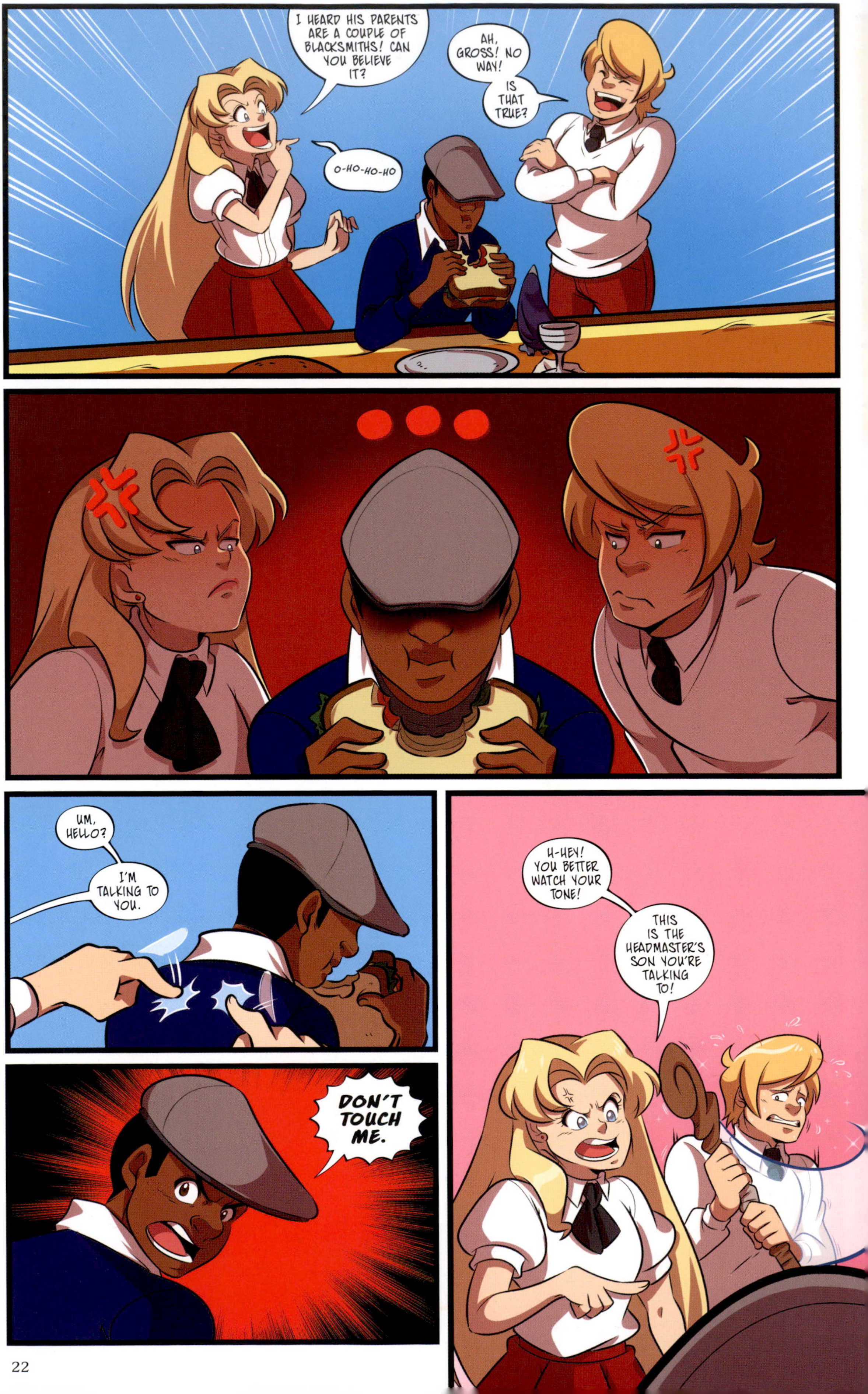

I HEARD HIS PARENTS ARE A COUPLE OF BLACKSMITHS! CAN YOU BELIEVE IT?
AH, GROSS! NO WAY!
IS THAT TRUE?
O-HO-HO-HO
UM, HELLO?
I'M TALKING TO YOU.
DON'T TOUCH ME.
H-HEY! YOU BETTER WATCH YOUR TONE!
THIS IS THE HEADMASTER'S SON YOU'RE TALKING TO!

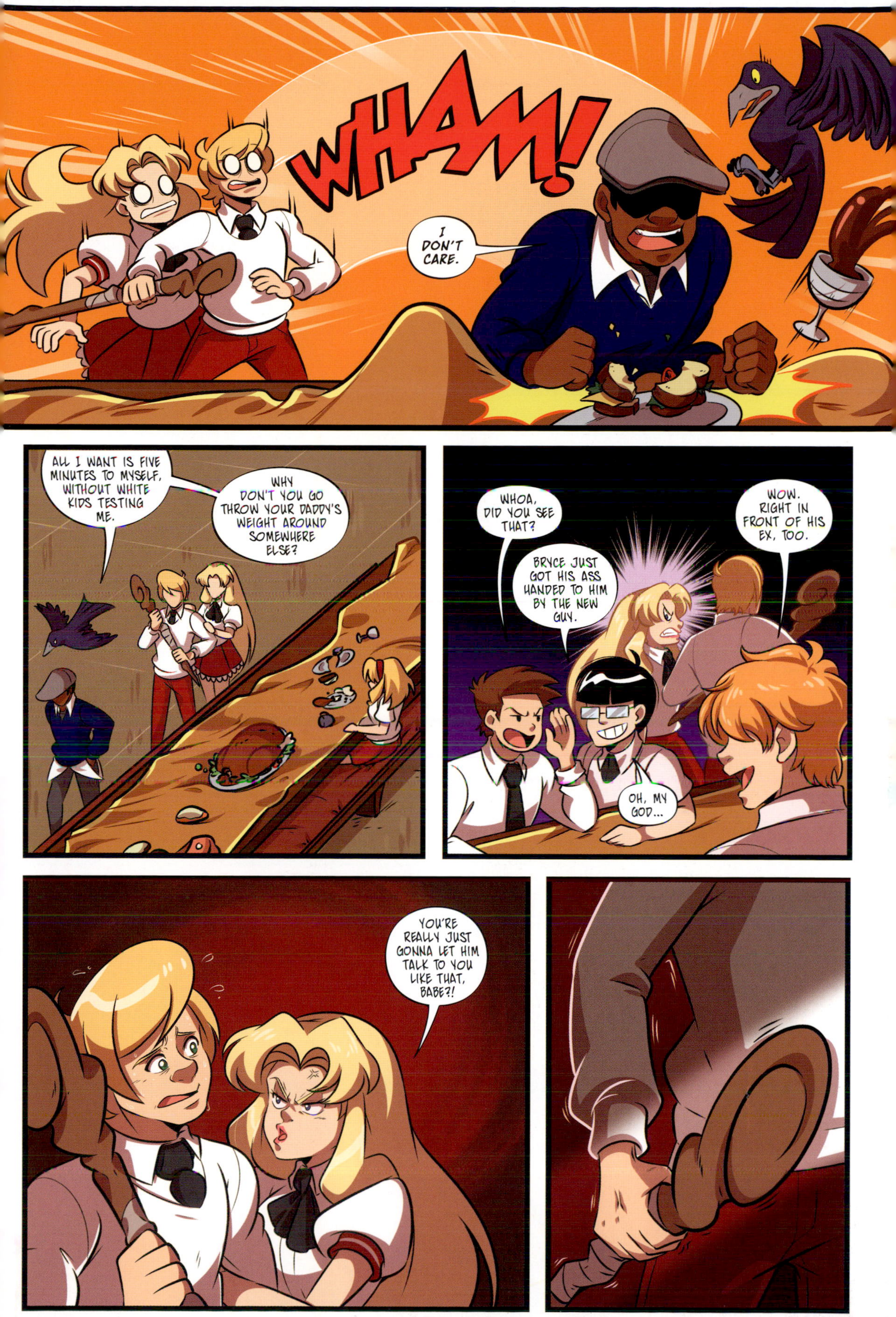
WHAM!
I DON'T CARE.
ALL I WANT IS FIVE MINUTES TO MYSELF, WITHOUT WHITE KIDS TESTING ME.
WHY DON'T YOU GO THROW YOUR DADDY'S WEIGHT AROUND SOMEWHERE ELSE?
WHOA, DID YOU SEE THAT?
BRYCE JUST GOT HIS ASS HANDED TO HIM BY THE NEW GUY.
WOW. RIGHT IN FRONT OF HIS EX, TOO.
OH, MY GOD...
YOU'RE REALLY JUST GONNA LET HIM TALK TO YOU LIKE THAT, BABE?!

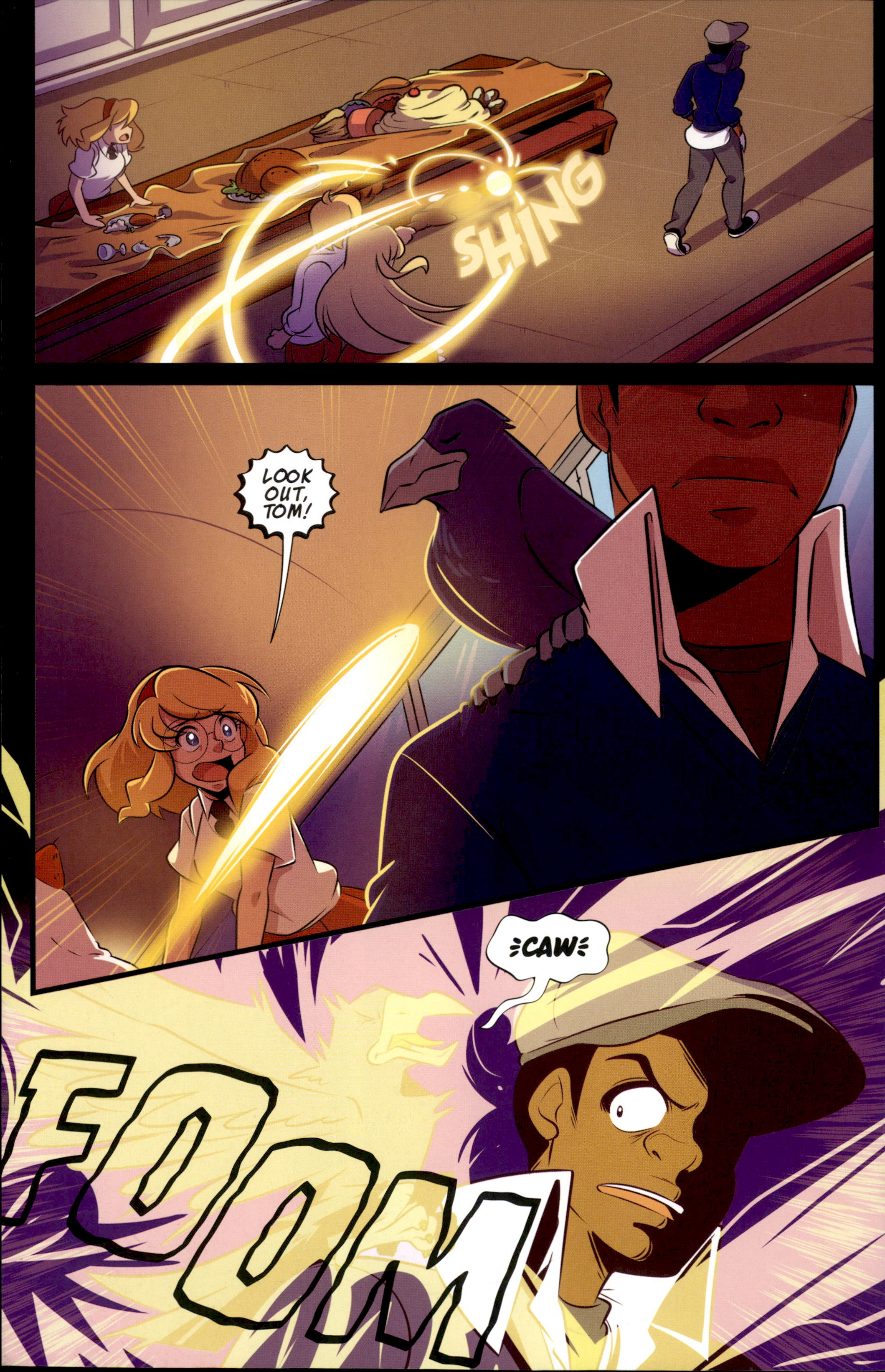
SHING
LOOK OUT, TOM!
CAW
FOOM

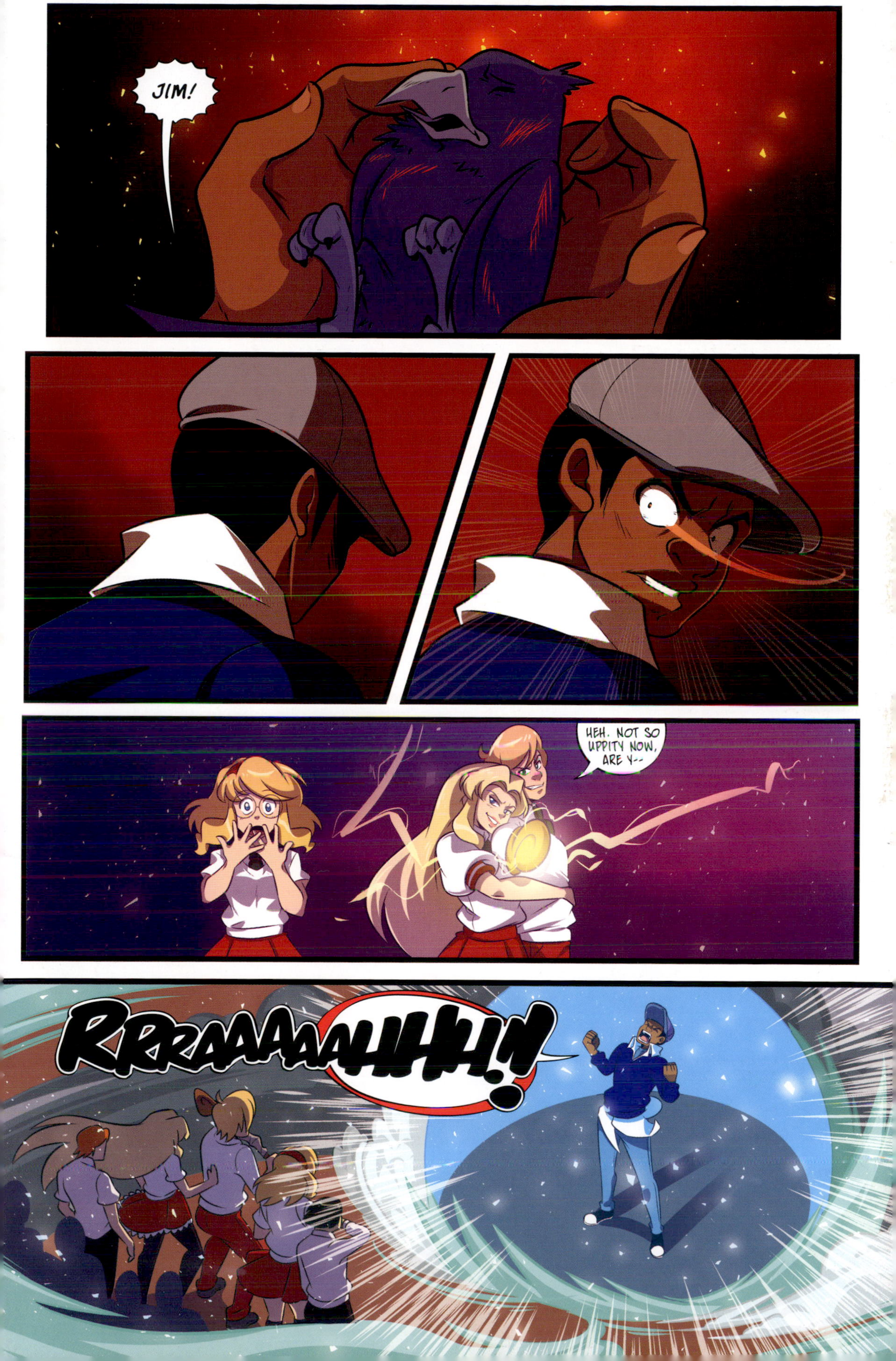
JIM!
HEH. NOT SO UPPITY NOW, ARE Y--
RRRAAAAAAHHHH!!

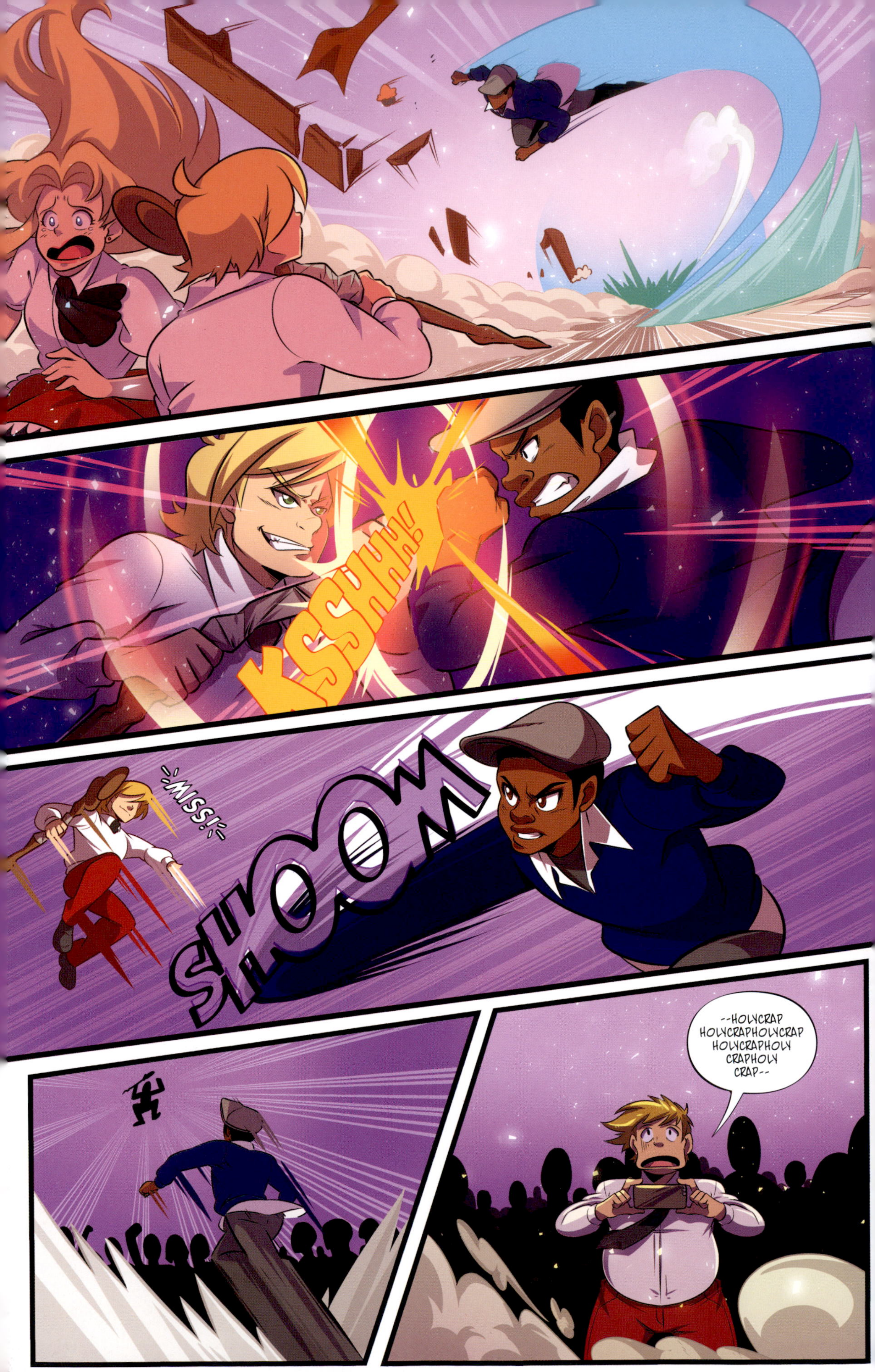
KSSHHH!
-MISS!-
SHOOOM
--HOLYCRAP HOLYCRAPHOLYCRAP HOLYCRAPHOLY CRAPHOLY CRAP--

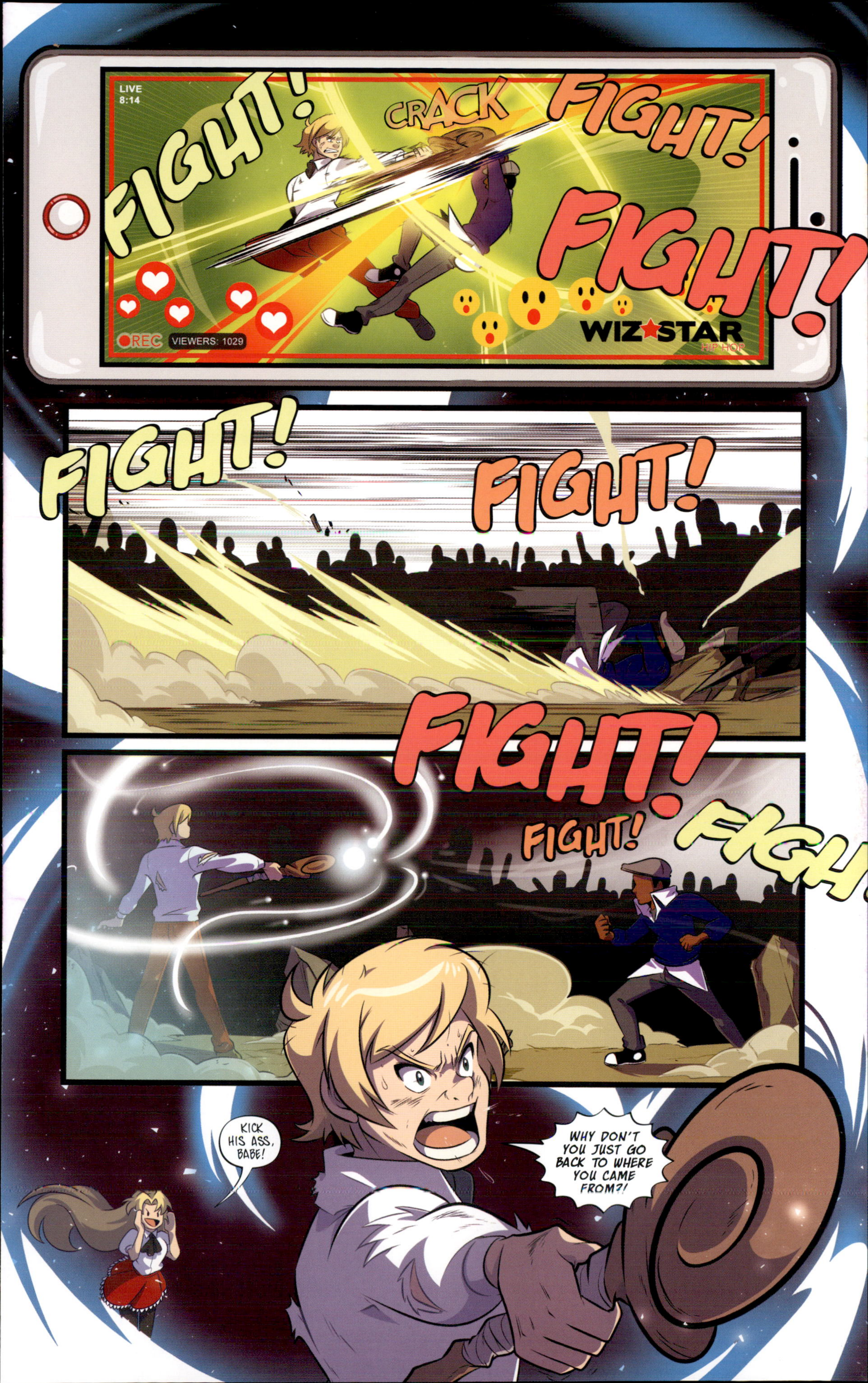
LIVE
8:14
FIGHT!
CRACK
FIGHT!
FIGHT!
REC
VIEWERS: 1029
WIZ★STAR
HIP-HOP
FIGHT!
FIGHT!
FIGHT!
FIGHT!
KICK HIS ASS, BABE!
WHY DON'T YOU JUST GO BACK TO WHERE YOU CAME FROM?!

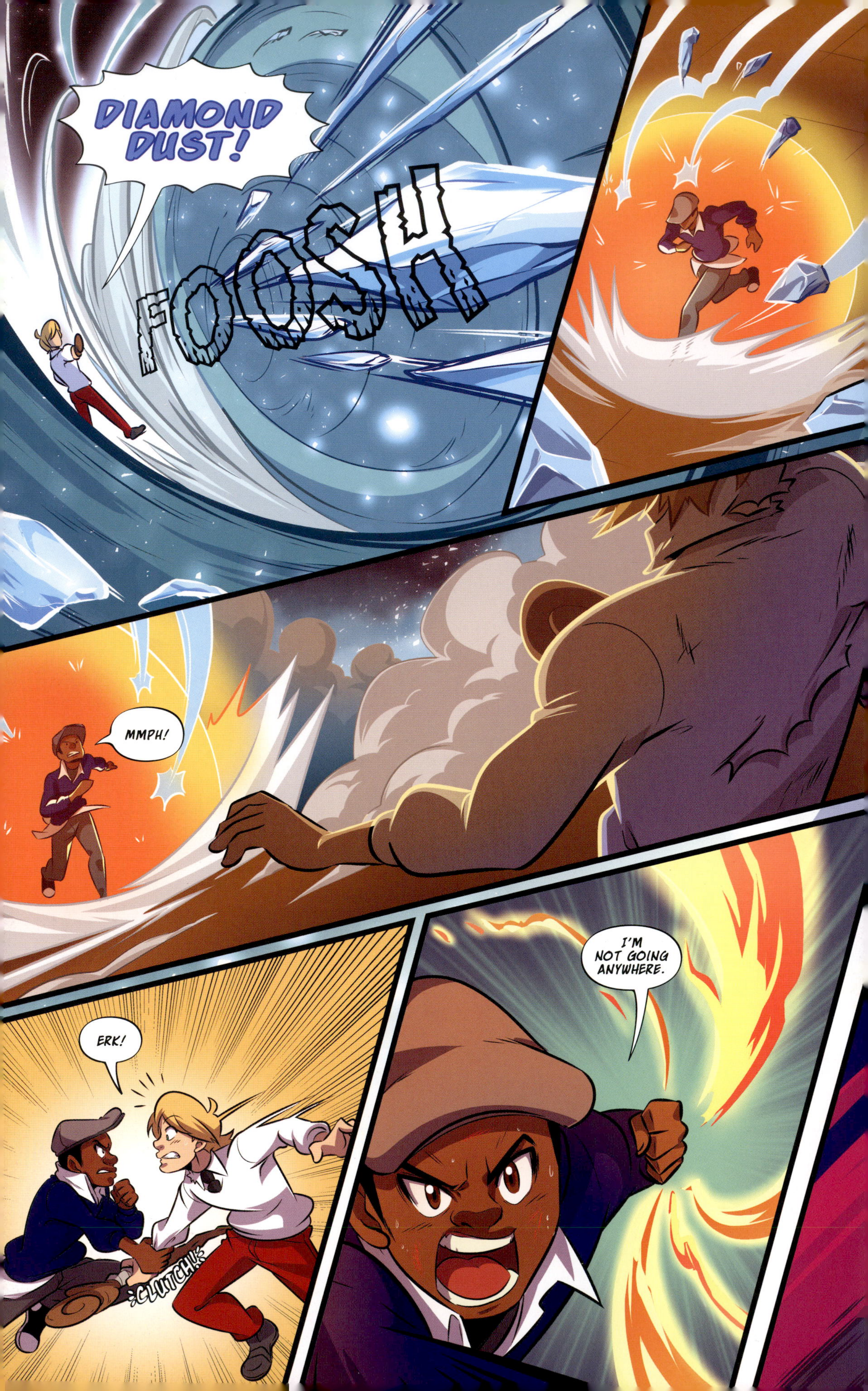
DIAMOND DUST!
FOOSH
MMPH!
ERK!
CLUTCH!
I'M NOT GOING ANYWHERE.

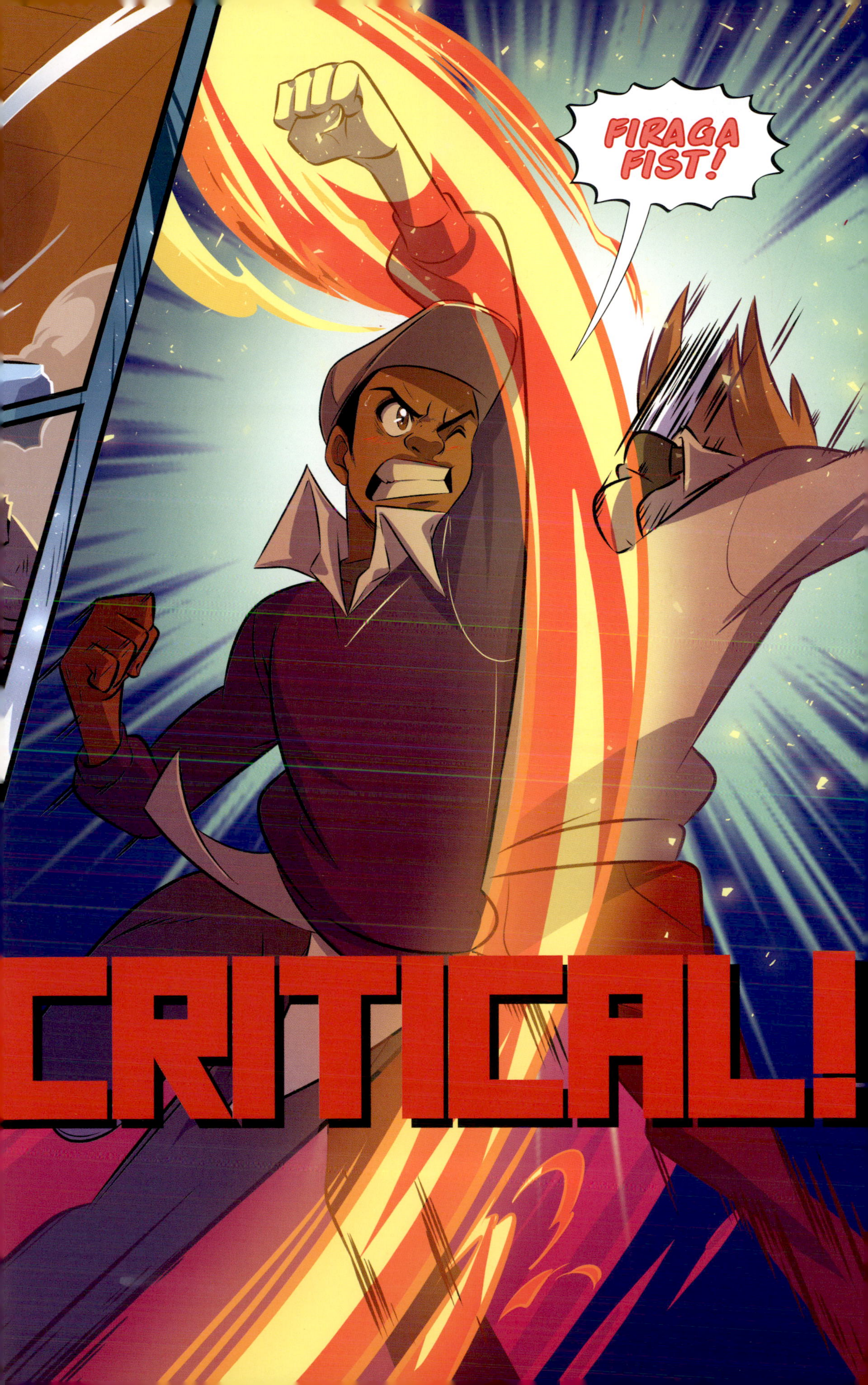
FIRAGA FIST!
CRITICAL!

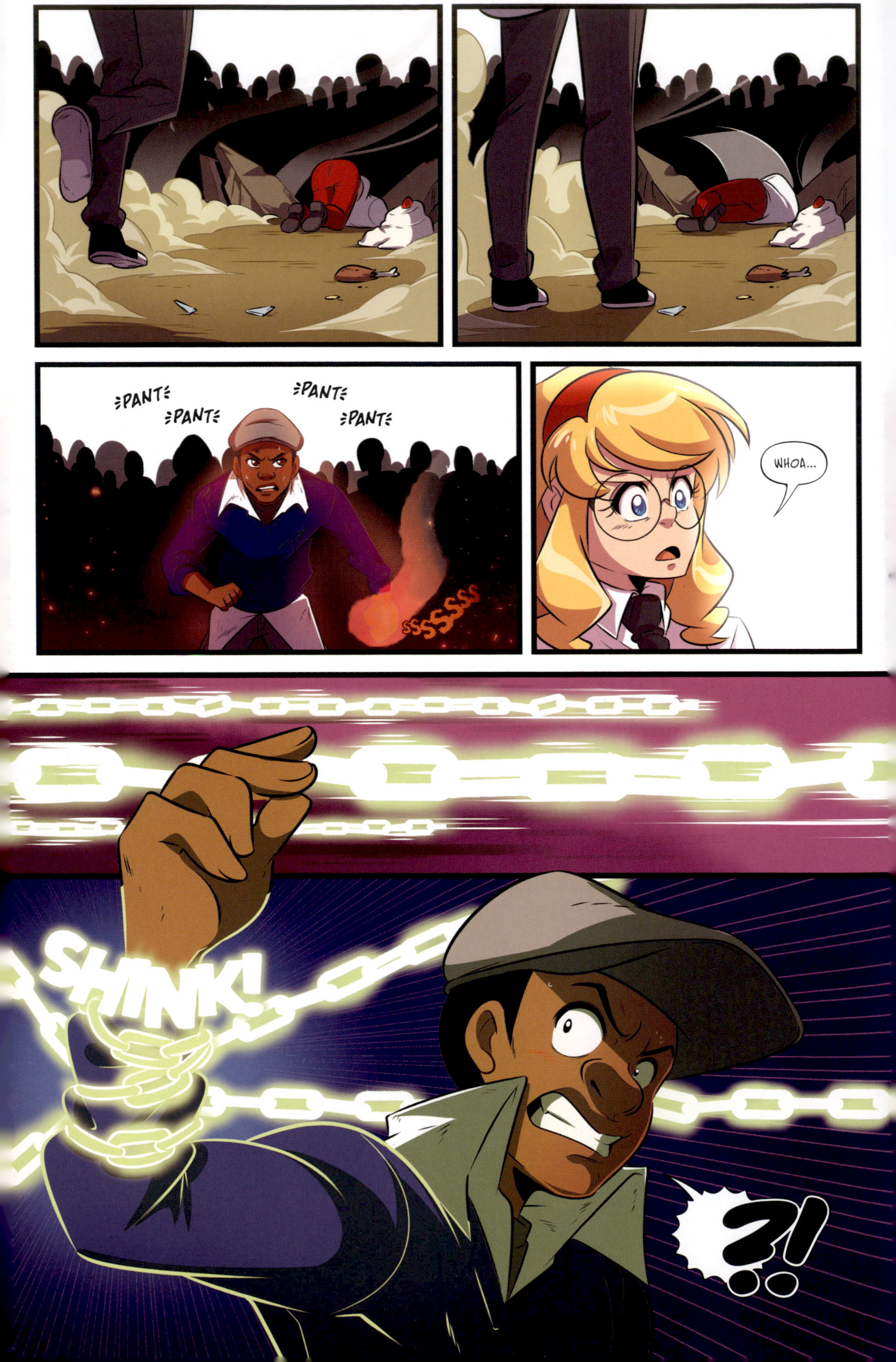

PANT
PANT
PANT
PANT
SSSSSS
WHOA...
SHINK!
?!

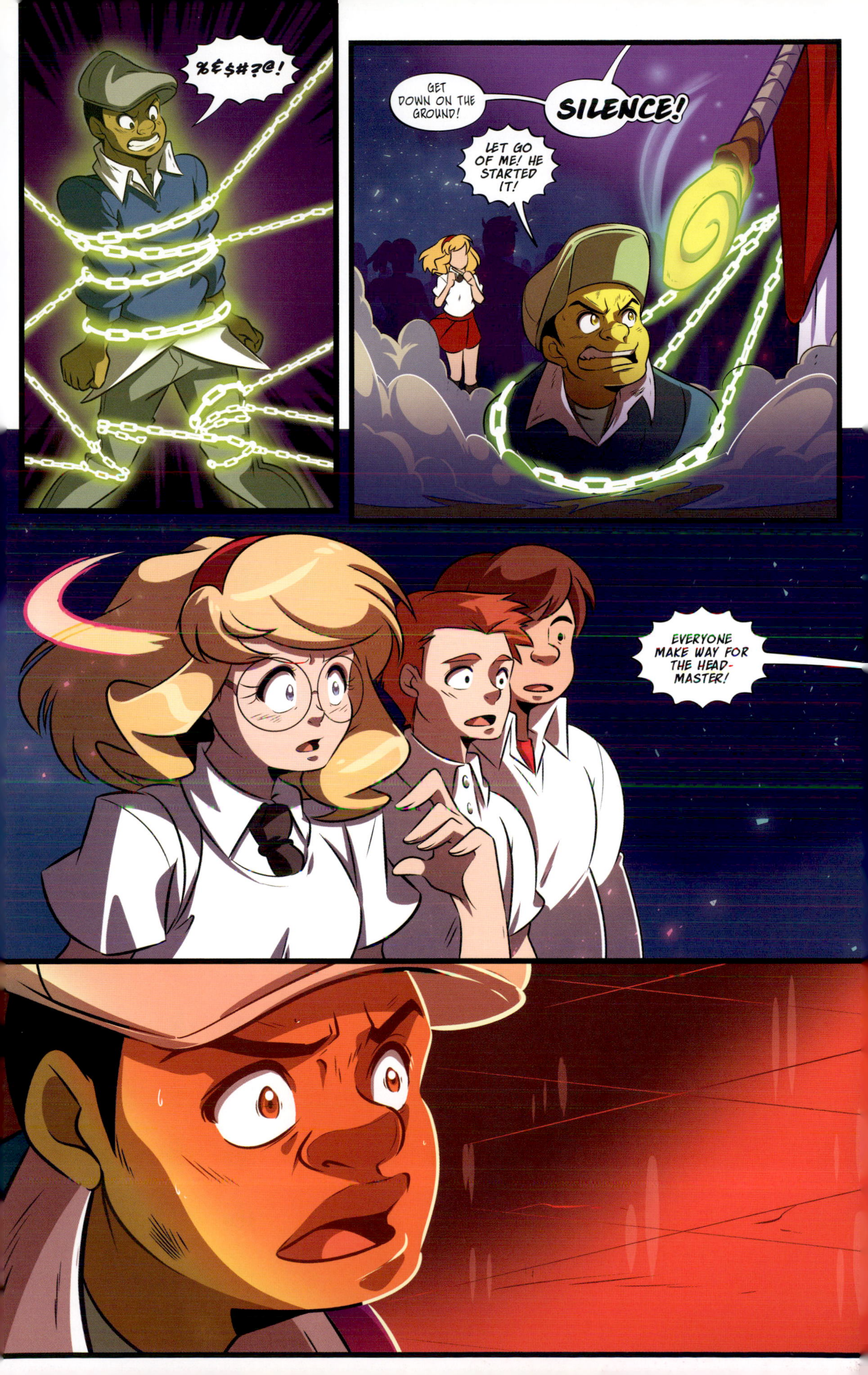
%&$#?@!
GET DOWN ON THE GROUND!
SILENCE!
LET GO OF ME! HE STARTED IT!
EVERYONE MAKE WAY FOR THE HEAD-MASTER!

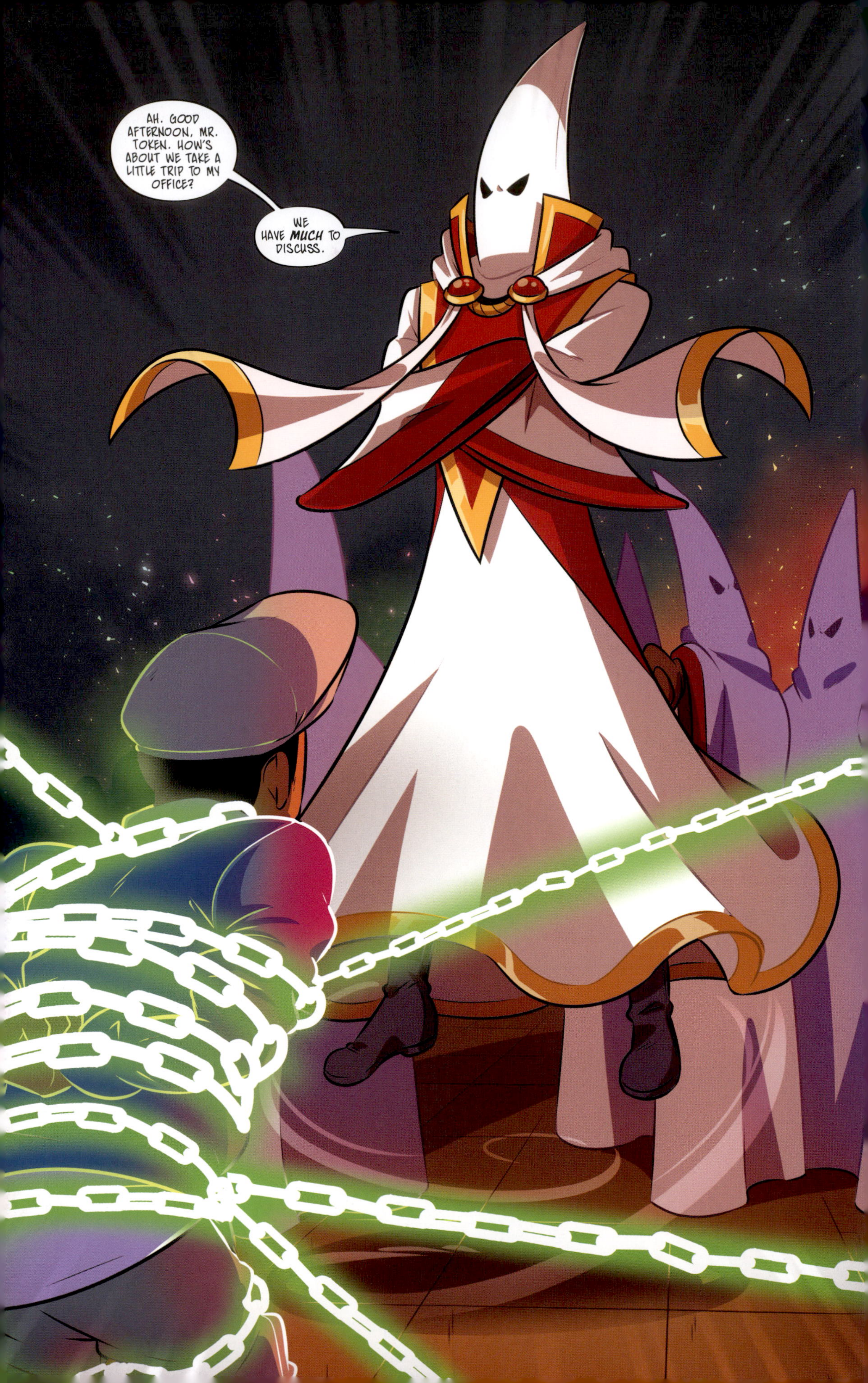
AH. GOOD AFTERNOON, MR. TOKEN. HOW'S ABOUT WE TAKE A LITTLE TRIP TO MY OFFICE?
WE HAVE MUCH TO DISCUSS.

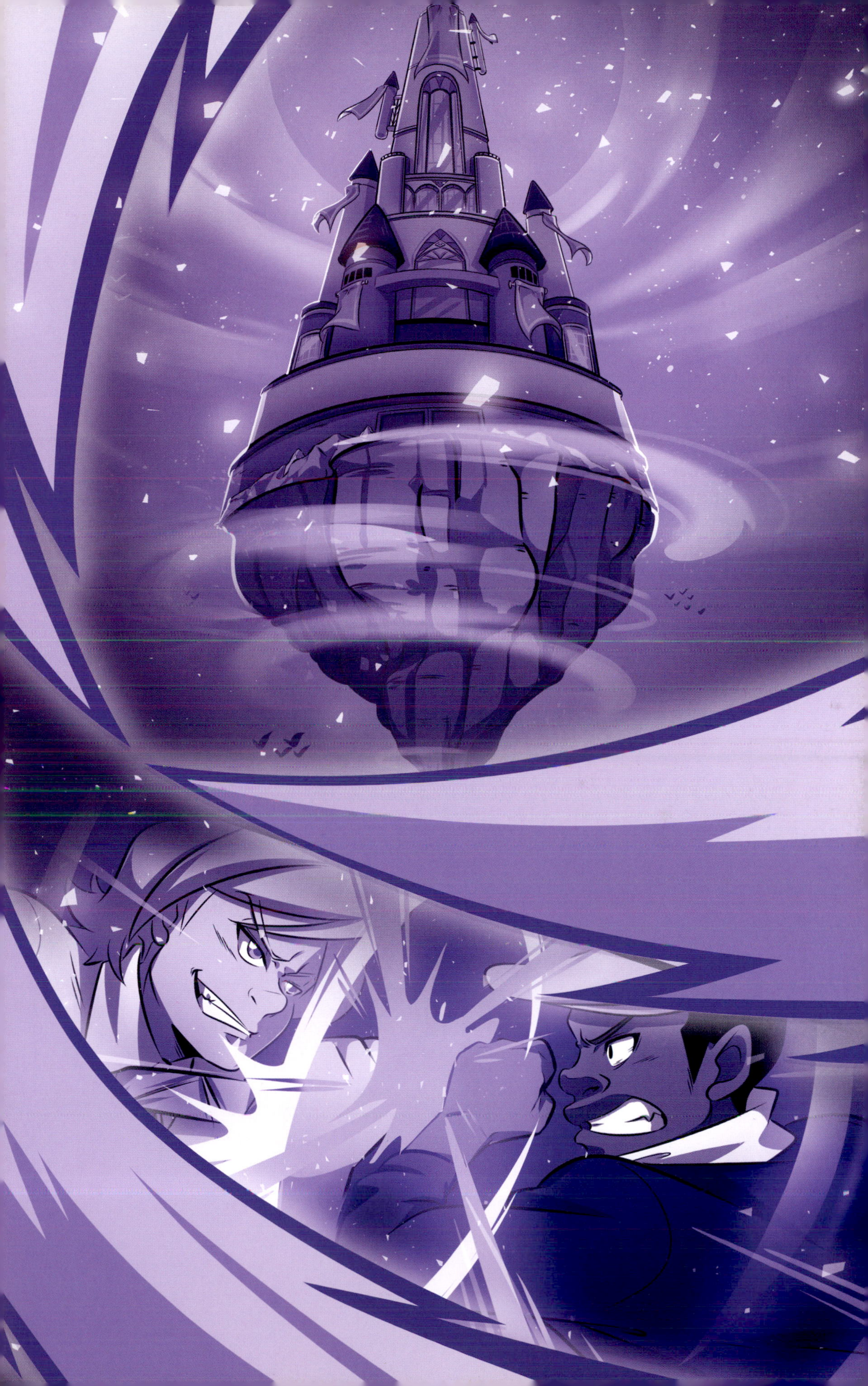

CHAPTER TWO

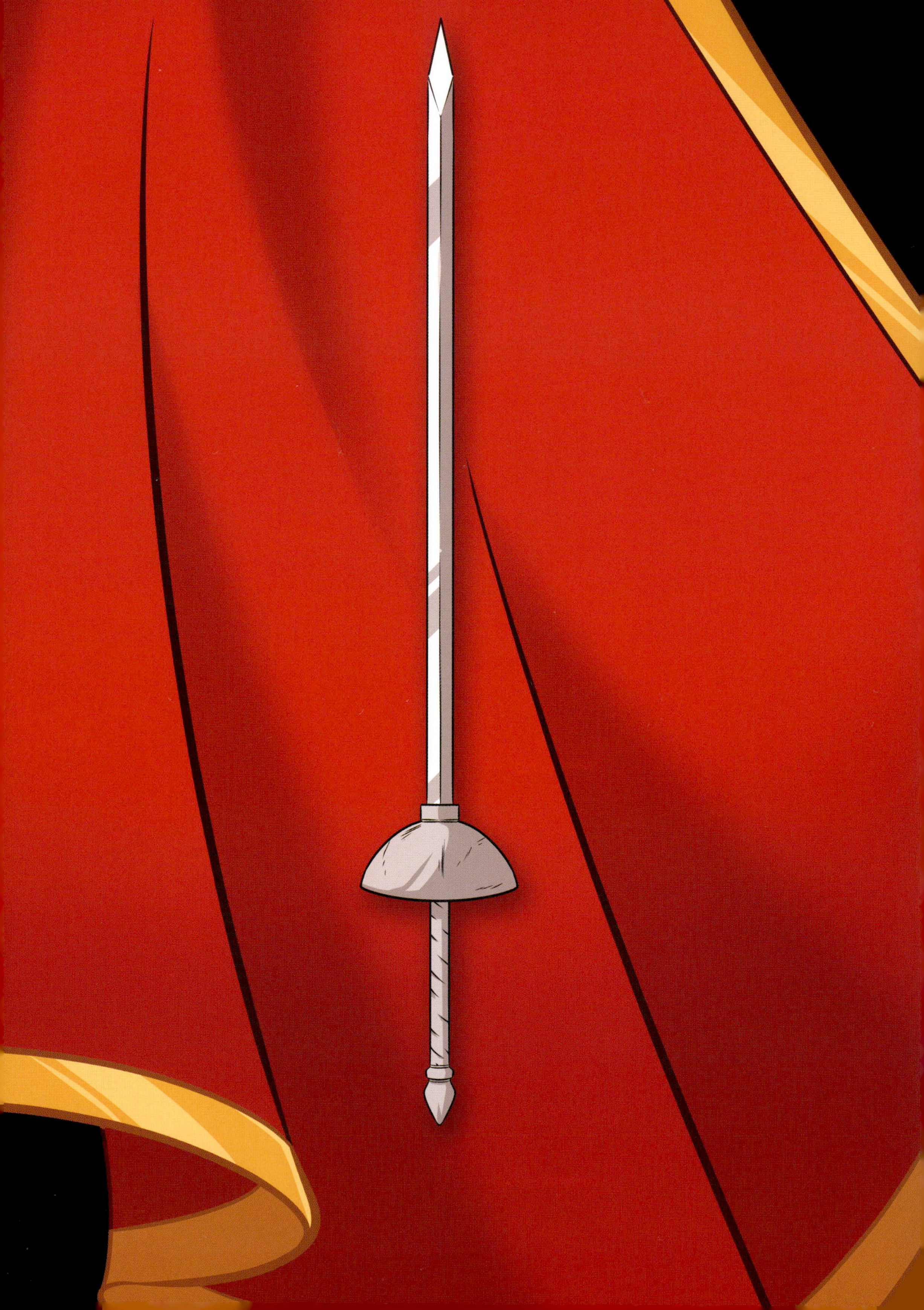

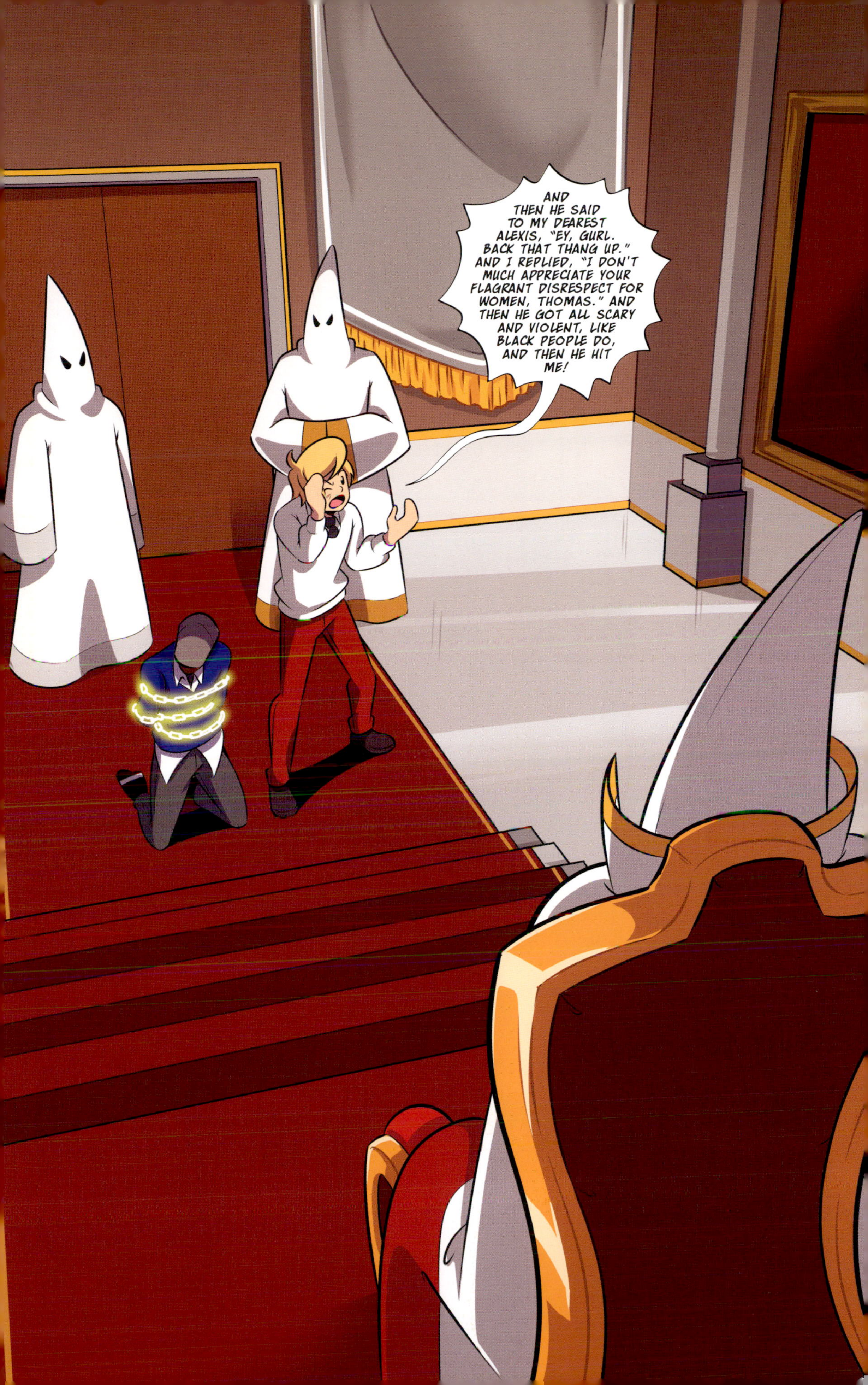
AND THEN HE SAID TO MY DEAREST ALEXIS, "EY, GURL. BACK THAT THANG UP." AND I REPLIED, "I DON'T MUCH APPRECIATE YOUR FLAGRANT DISRESPECT FOR WOMEN, THOMAS." AND THEN HE GOT ALL SCARY AND VIOLENT, LIKE BLACK PEOPLE DO, AND THEN HE HIT ME!

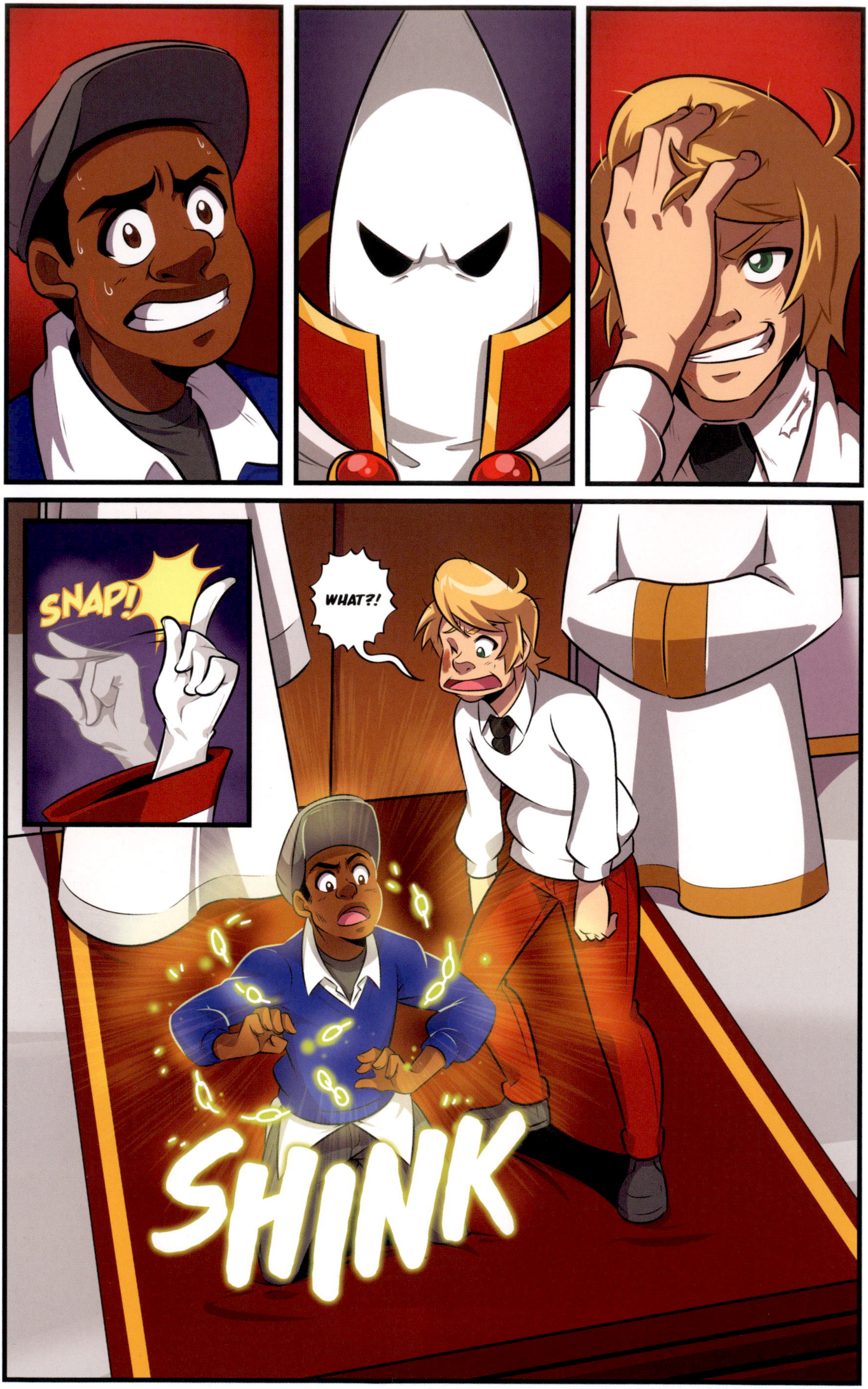
SNAP!
WHAT?!
SHINK

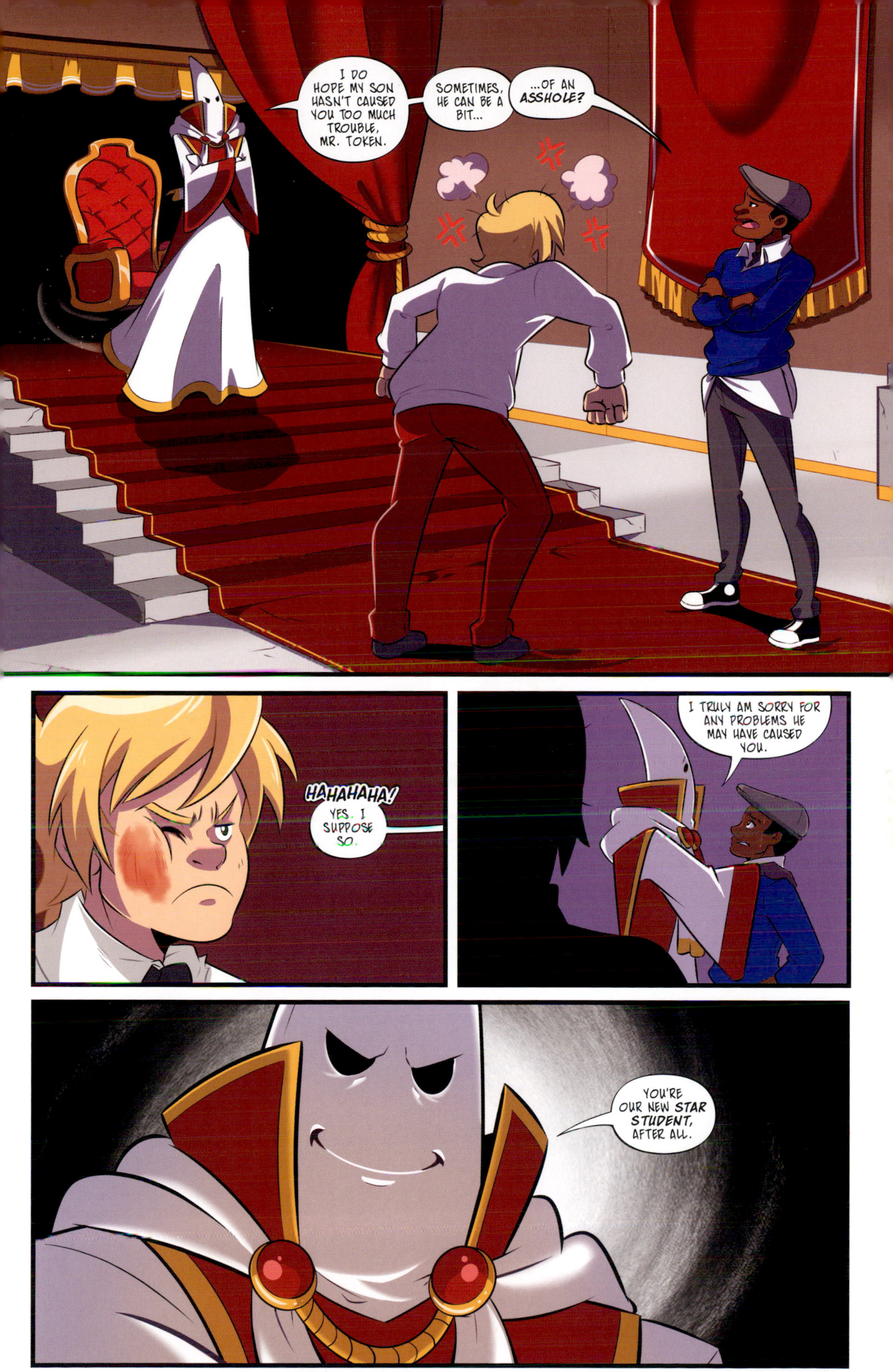
I DO HOPE MY SON HASN'T CAUSED YOU TOO MUCH TROUBLE, MR. TOKEN.
SOMETIMES, HE CAN BE A BIT...
...OF AN ASSHOLE?
HAHAHAHA!
YES. I SUPPOSE SO.
I TRULY AM SORRY FOR ANY PROBLEMS HE MAY HAVE CAUSED YOU.
YOU'RE OUR NEW STAR STUDENT, AFTER ALL.

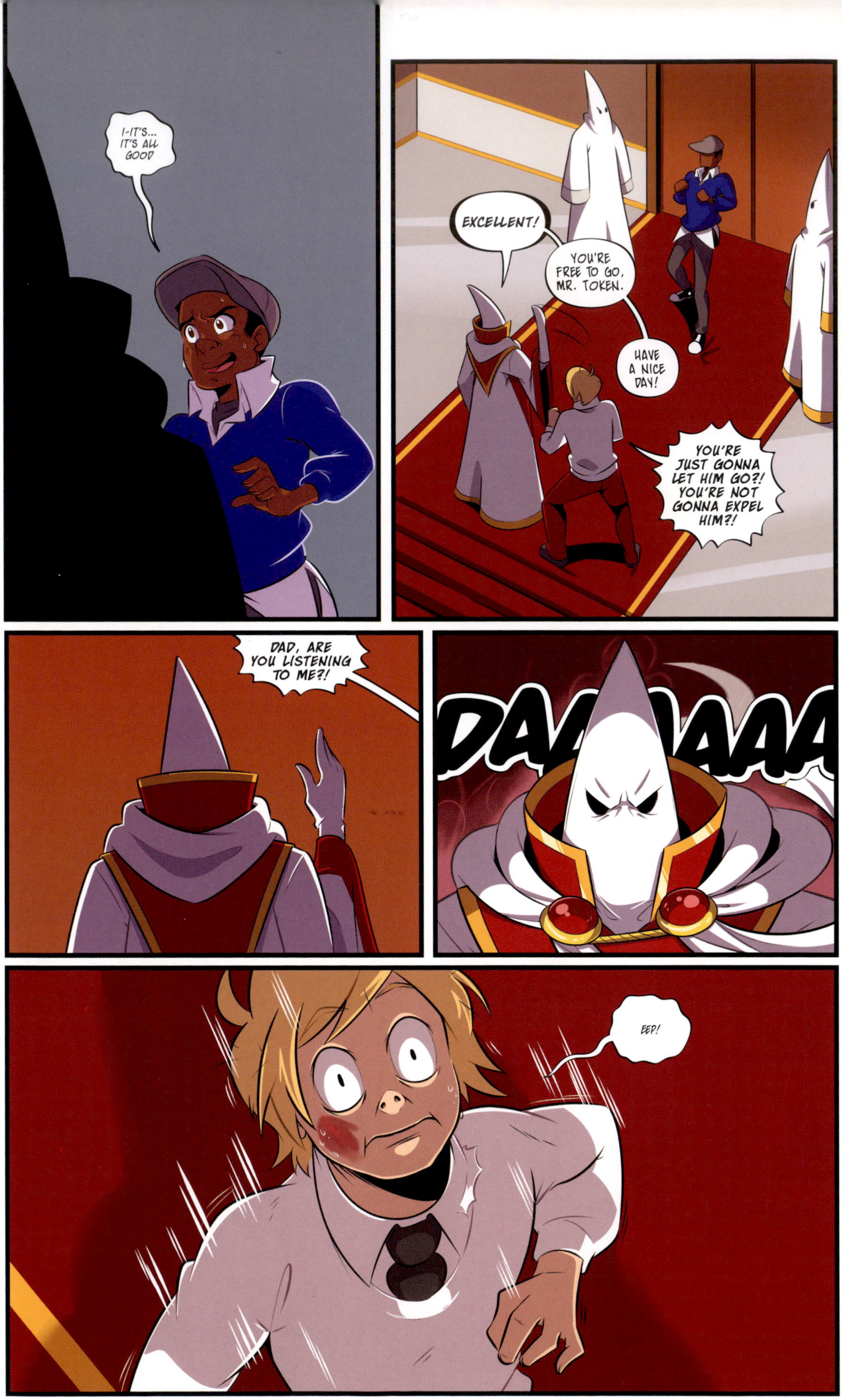
I-IT'S... IT'S ALL GOOD
EXCELLENT!
YOU'RE FREE TO GO, MR. TOKEN.
HAVE A NICE DAY!
YOU'RE JUST GONNA LET HIM GO?! YOU'RE NOT GONNA EXPEL HIM?!
DAD, ARE YOU LISTENING TO ME?!
DAAAAAA
EEP!

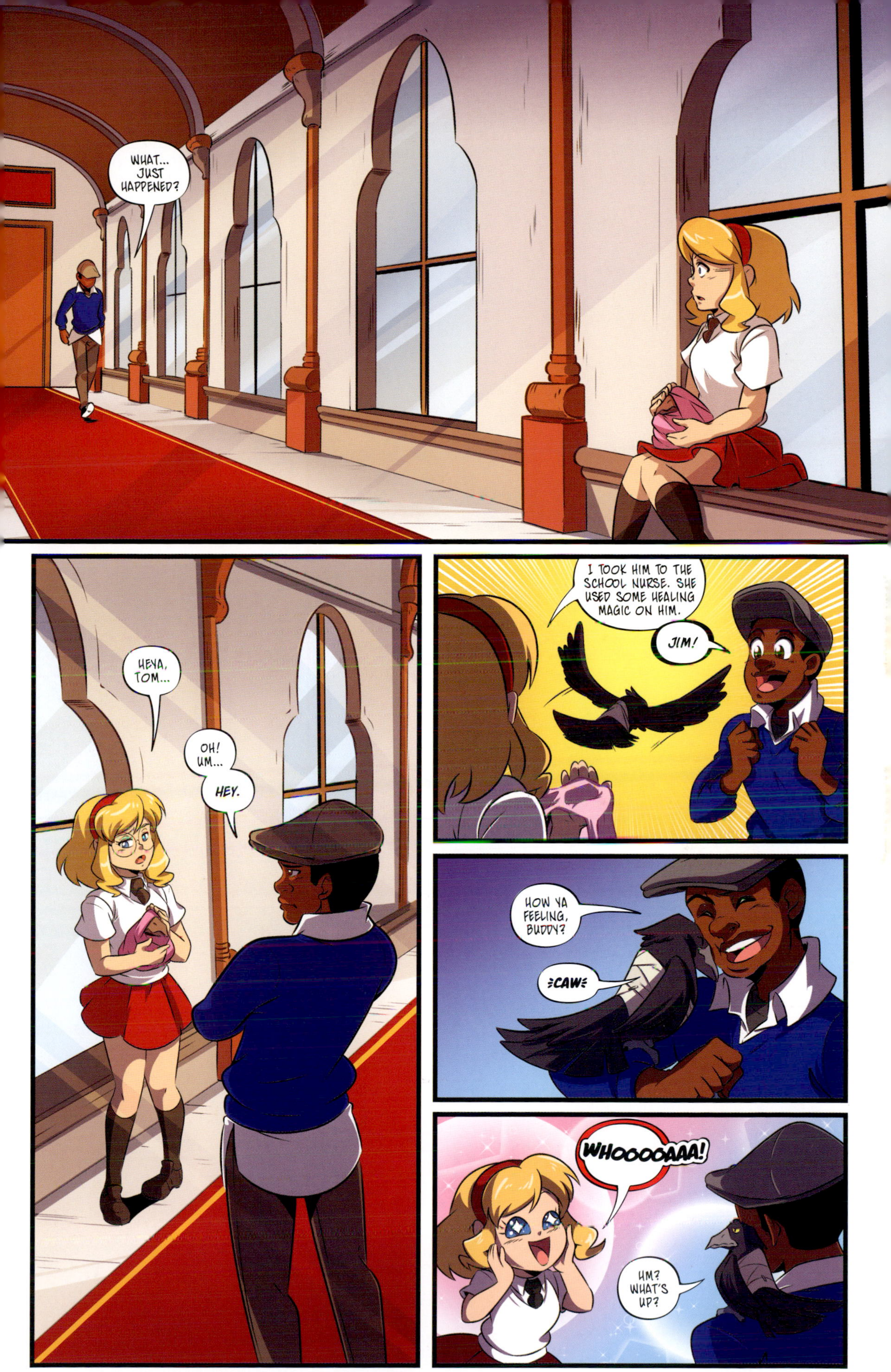

WHAT... JUST HAPPENED?
HEYA, TOM...
OH! UM...
HEY.
I TOOK HIM TO THE SCHOOL NURSE. SHE USED SOME HEALING MAGIC ON HIM.
JIM!
HOW YA FEELING, BUDDY?
CAW
WHOOOOAAA!
HM? WHAT'S UP?

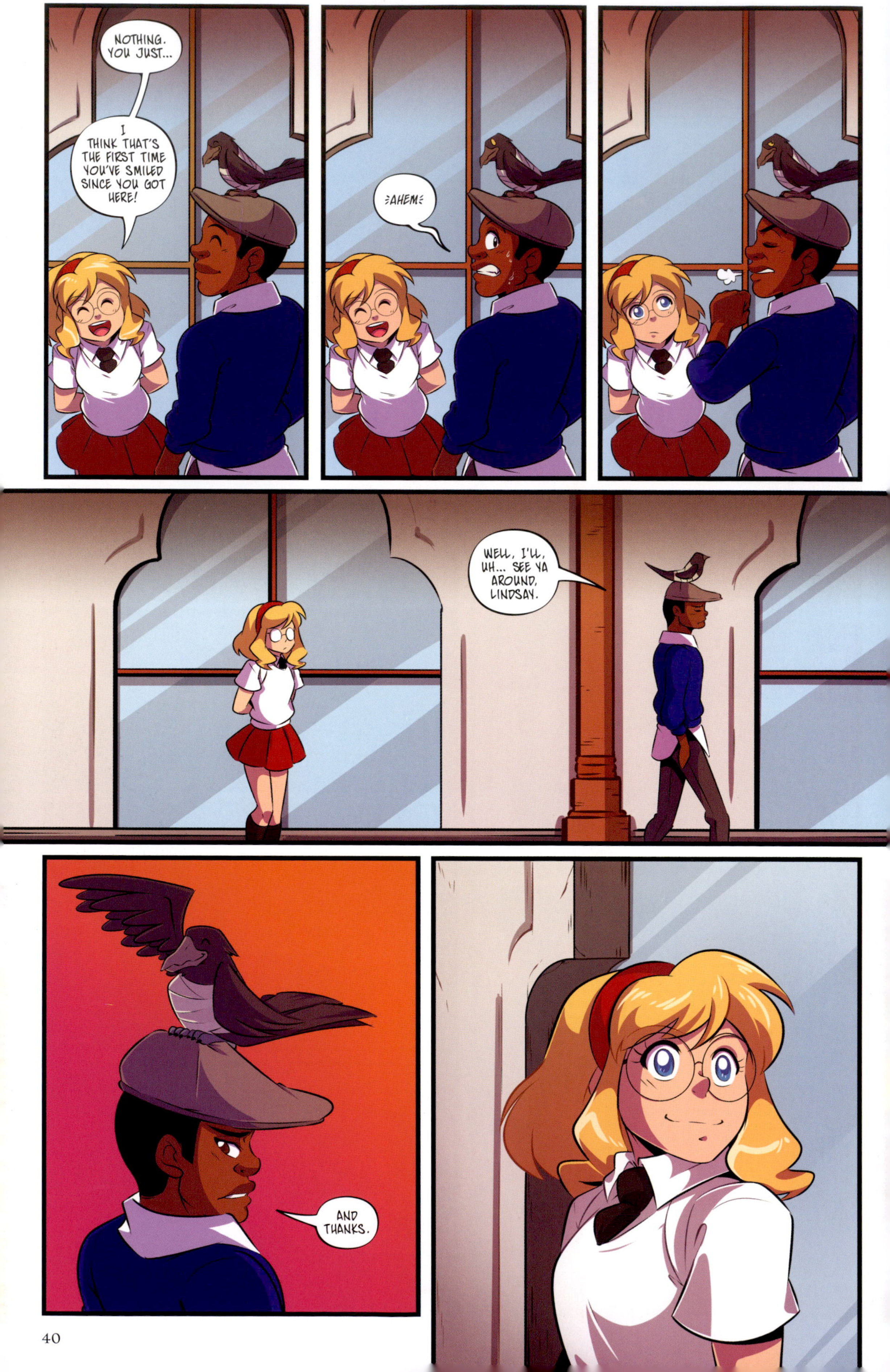
NOTHING. YOU JUST...
I THINK THAT'S THE FIRST TIME YOU'VE SMILED SINCE YOU GOT HERE!
AHEM
WELL, I'LL, UH... SEE YA AROUND, LINDSAY.
AND THANKS.

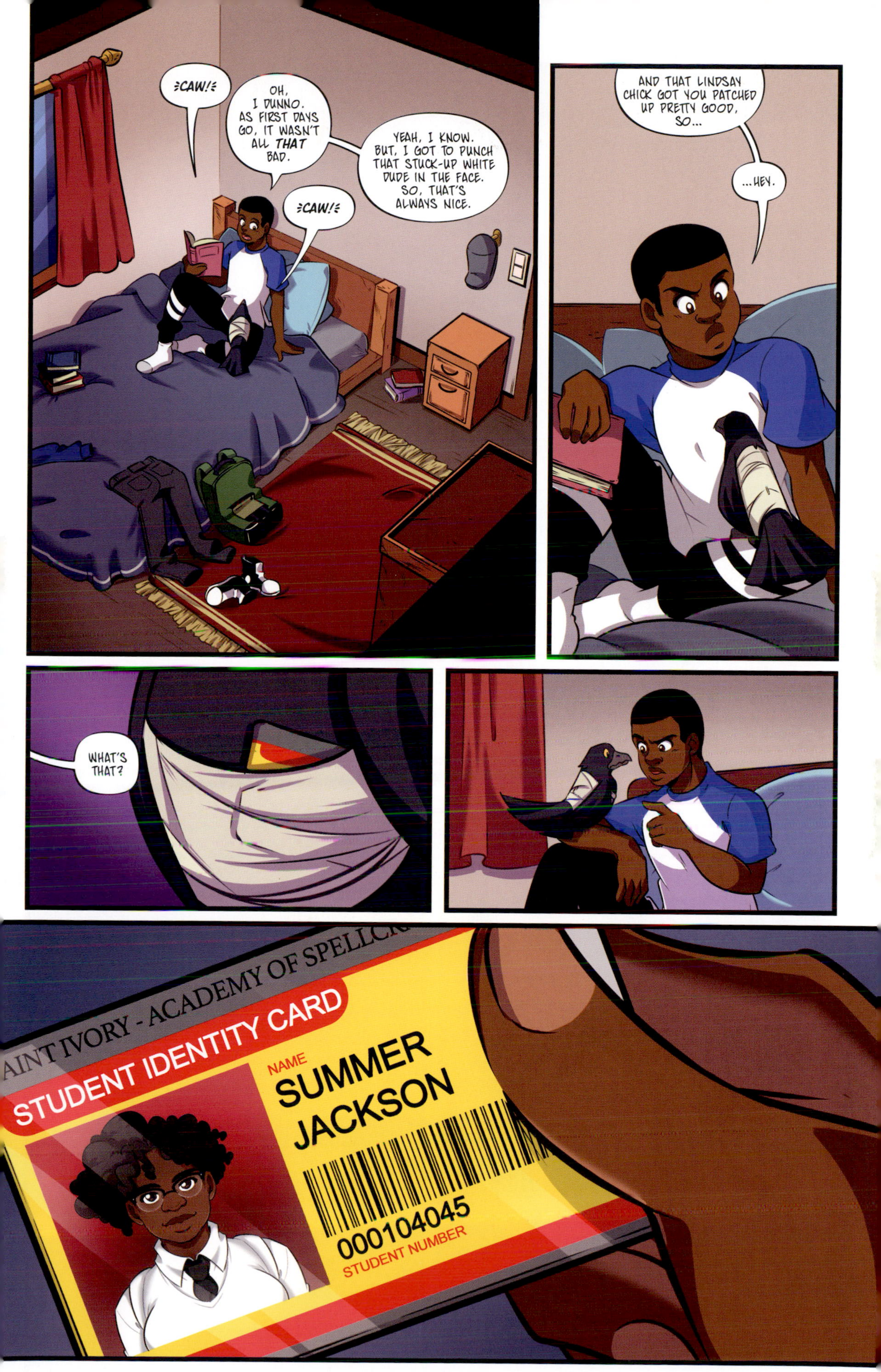
CAW!
OH, I DUNNO. AS FIRST DAYS GO, IT WASN'T ALL THAT BAD.
CAW!
YEAH, I KNOW. BUT, I GOT TO PUNCH THAT STUCK-UP WHITE DUDE IN THE FACE. SO, THAT'S ALWAYS NICE.
AND THAT LINDSAY CHICK GOT YOU PATCHED UP PRETTY GOOD, SO...
...HEY.
WHAT'S THAT?
AINT IVORY - ACADEMY OF SPELLC
STUDENT IDENTITY CARD
NAME
SUMMER JACKSON
000104045
STUDENT NUMBER

FOR GENERATIONS, THE FABLED POWER CRYSTAL OF ST. IVORY HAS KEPT OUR BELOVED ACADEMY AFLOAT, HIGH ABOVE THE EARTH.

FORGED IN A MAKO PIT, DEEP BENEATH THE PLANET'S SURFACE, BY OUR SCHOOL'S FOUNDERS, IT ACTS AS A BATTERY OF SORTS FOR US, GENERATING OUR ELECTRICITY AND HEATING OUR WATER.

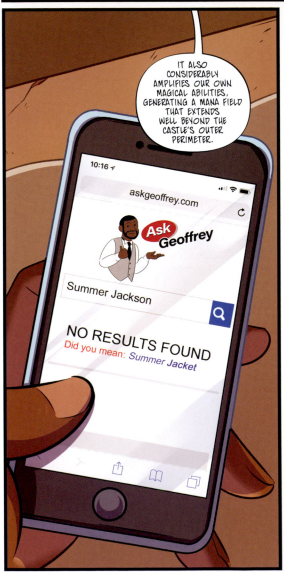

IT ALSO CONSIDERABLY AMPLIFIES OUR OWN MAGICAL ABILITIES, GENERATING A MANA FIELD THAT EXTENDS WELL BEYOND THE CASTLE'S OUTER PERIMETER.

10:16

askgeoffrey.com

Ask Geoffrey

Summer Jackson

NO RESULTS FOUND
Did you mean: Summer Jacket

VRRRT VRRRT

10:16

askgeoffrey.com

Ask Geoffrey

MESSAGES
Unknown Number
Enjoying the gift I left you?

NO RESULTS FOUND
Did you mean: Summer Jacket

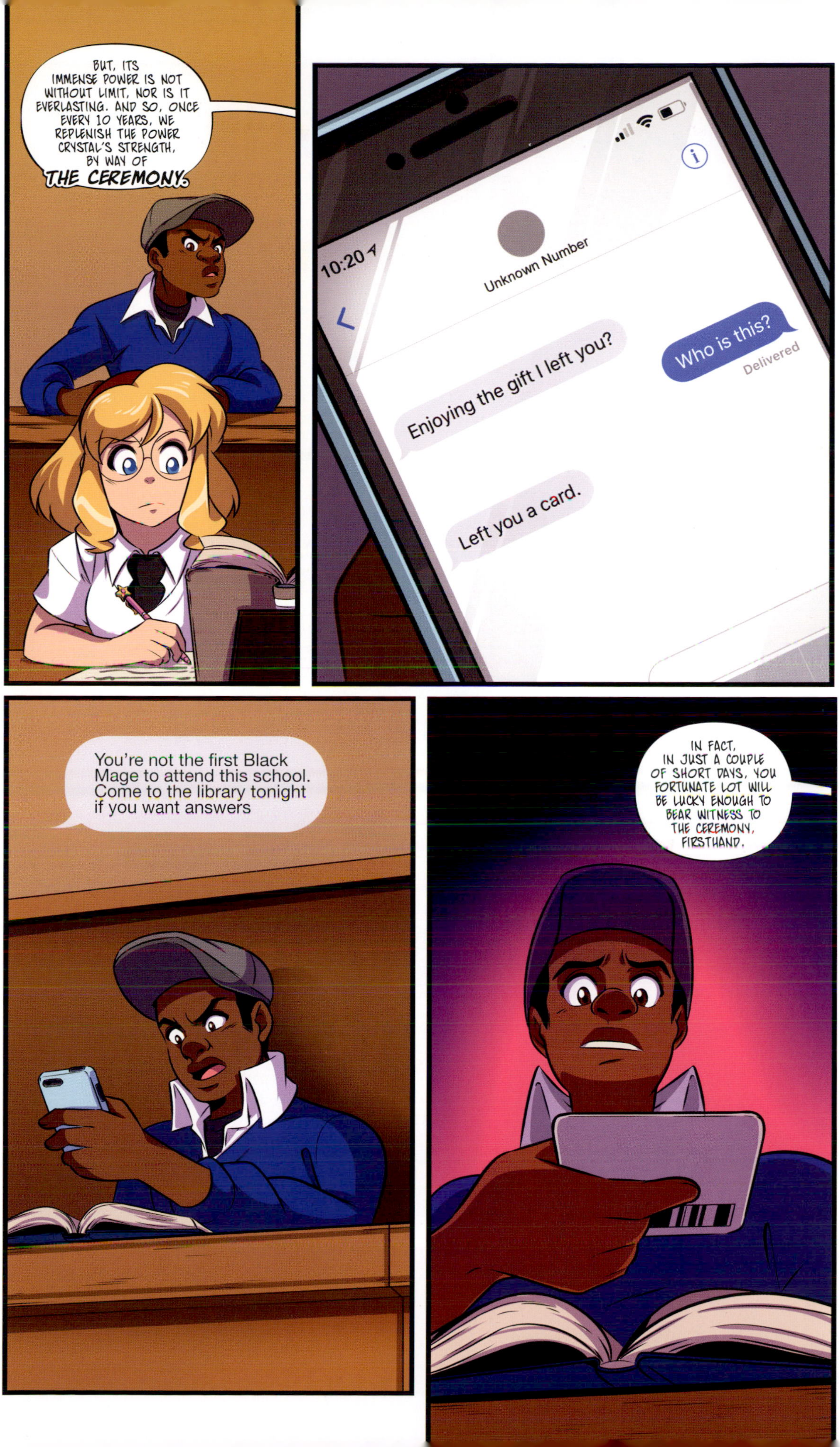
BUT, ITS IMMENSE POWER IS NOT WITHOUT LIMIT, NOR IS IT EVERLASTING. AND SO, ONCE EVERY 10 YEARS, WE REPLENISH THE POWER CRYSTAL'S STRENGTH, BY WAY OF THE CEREMONY.
10:20
Unknown Number
Enjoying the gift I left you?
Who is this?
Delivered
Left you a card.
You're not the first Black Mage to attend this school. Come to the library tonight if you want answers
IN FACT, IN JUST A COUPLE OF SHORT DAYS, YOU FORTUNATE LOT WILL BE LUCKY ENOUGH TO BEAR WITNESS TO THE CEREMONY, FIRSTHAND.

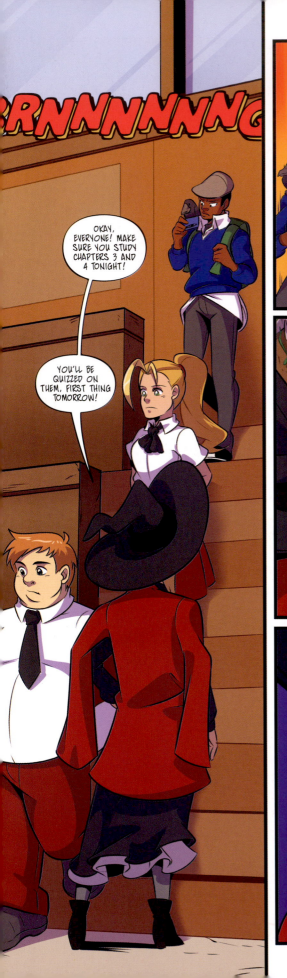

RRNNNNNNG

OKAY, EVERYONE! MAKE SURE YOU STUDY CHAPTERS 3 AND 4 TONIGHT!

YOU'LL BE QUIZZED ON THEM, FIRST THING TOMORROW!

WHAT'S THAT YOU'VE GOT THERE, MR. TOKEN?

N-NOTHING! JUST SOMETHING I FOUND!

I THINK SOMEONE MIGHT'VE LOST IT!

OH, WELL, IF THAT'S THE CASE, I'D BE MORE THAN HAPPY TO RETURN IT FOR--

TH-THAT'S OKAY, MA'AM! I'LL FIND OUT WHO IT BELONGS TO MYSELF!

HA HA HA HA

HA HA HA

THANKS, THOUGH!

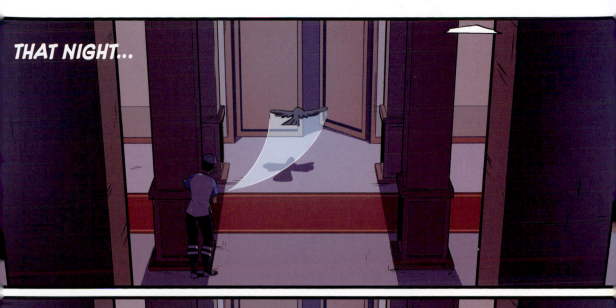

THAT NIGHT...

CREEAAK

HEY!

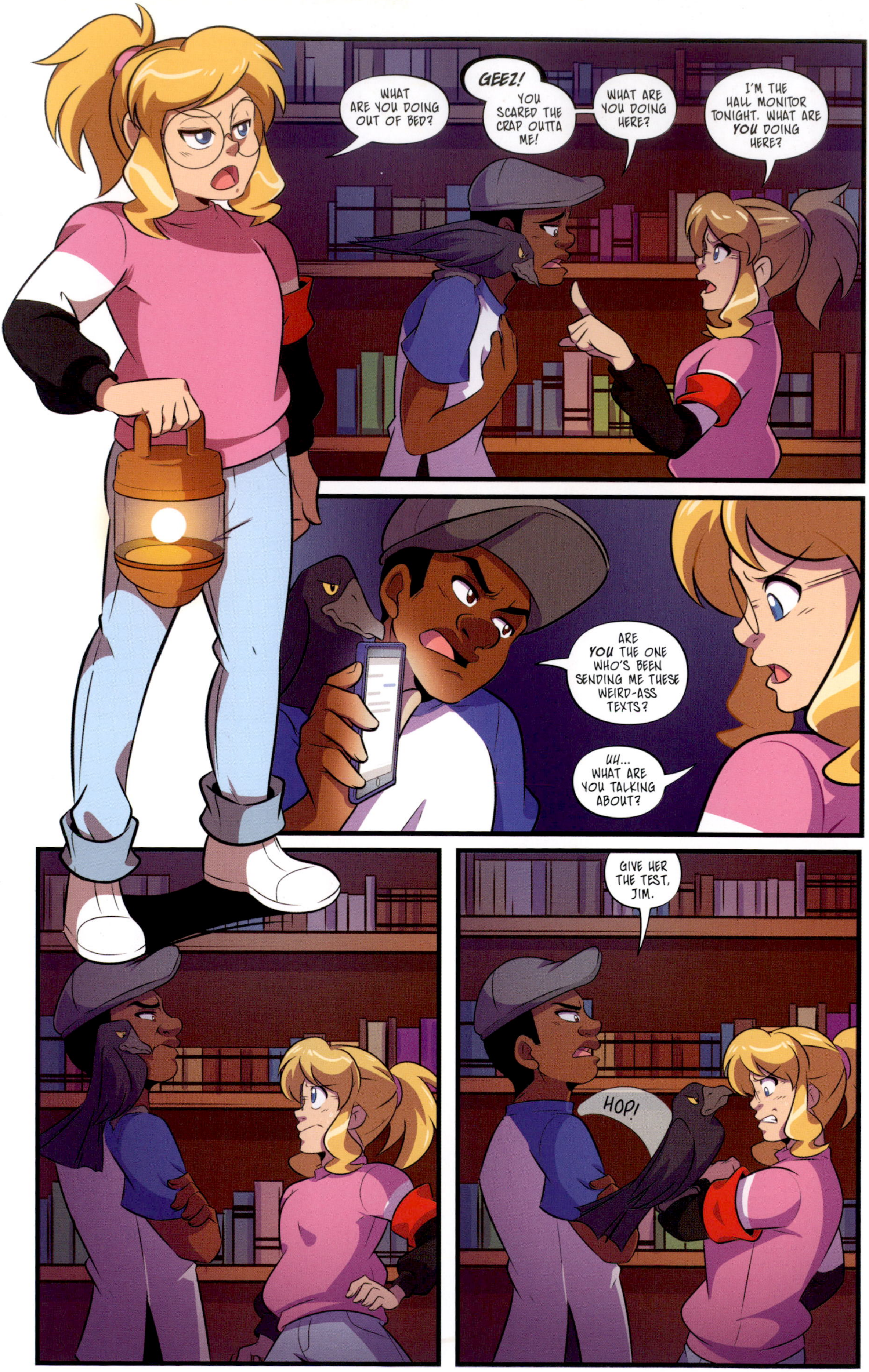
WHAT ARE YOU DOING OUT OF BED?
GEEZ! YOU SCARED THE CRAP OUTTA ME!
WHAT ARE YOU DOING HERE?
I'M THE HALL MONITOR TONIGHT. WHAT ARE YOU DOING HERE?
ARE YOU THE ONE WHO'S BEEN SENDING ME THESE WEIRD-ASS TEXTS?
UH... WHAT ARE YOU TALKING ABOUT?
GIVE HER THE TEST, JIM.
HOP!

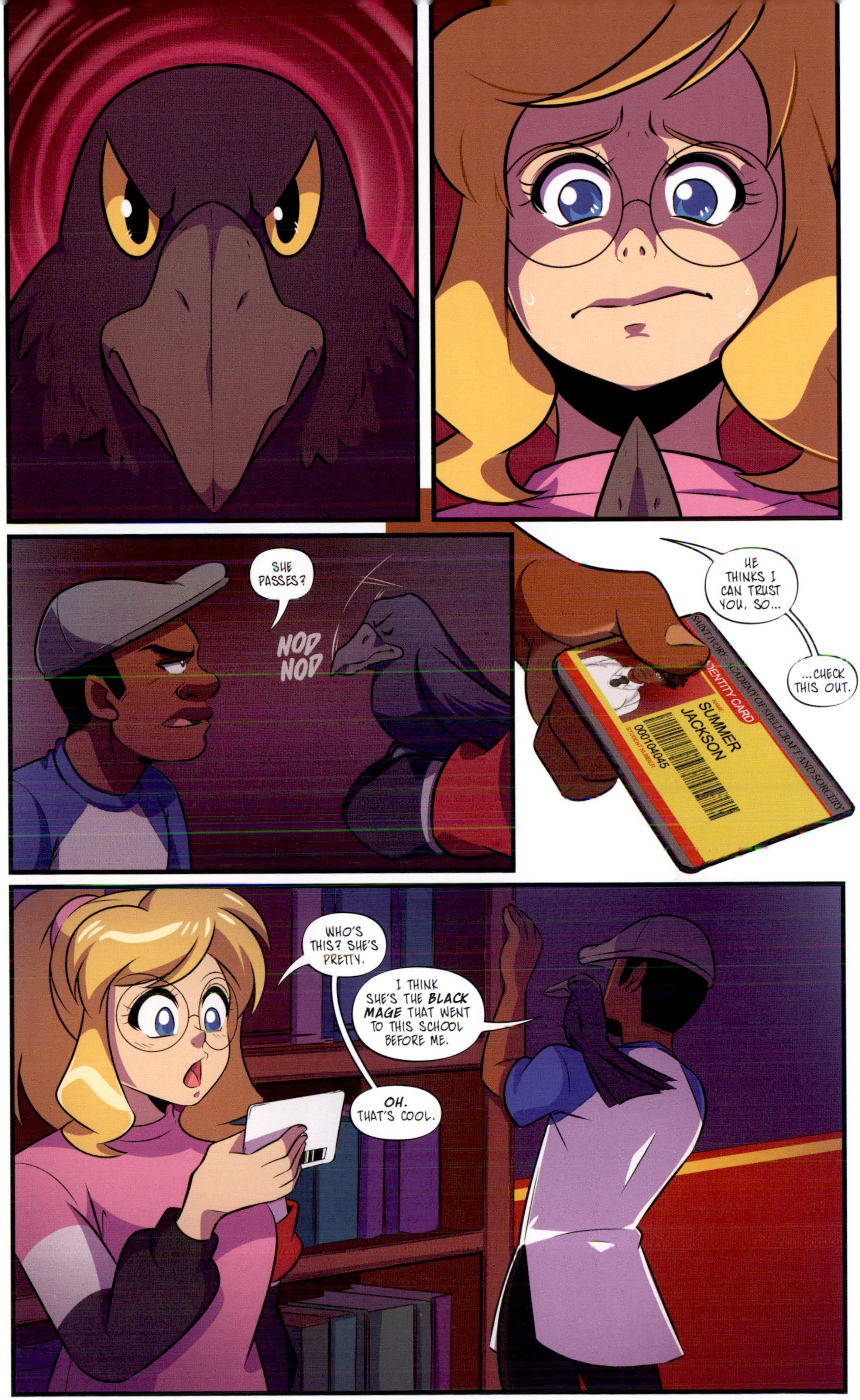
SHE PASSES?
NOD NOD
HE THINKS I CAN TRUST YOU, SO...
...CHECK THIS OUT.
SAINT IVORY ACADEMY OF SPELLCRAFT AND SORCERY
IDENTITY CARD
NAME
SUMMER JACKSON
000104045
STUDENT NUMBER
WHO'S THIS? SHE'S PRETTY.
I THINK SHE'S THE **BLACK MAGE** THAT WENT TO THIS SCHOOL BEFORE ME.
OH. THAT'S COOL.

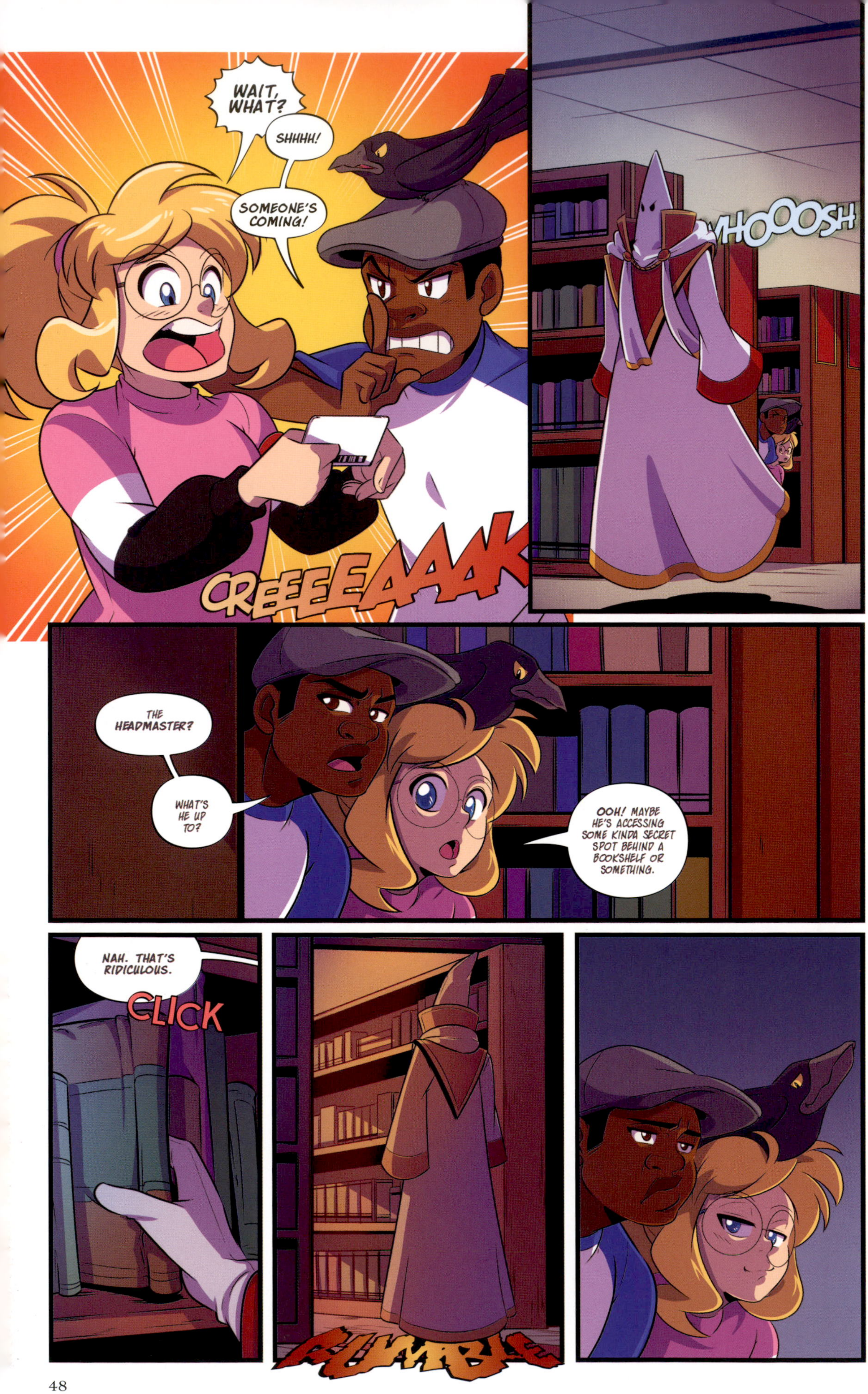
WAIT, WHAT?
SHHHH!
SOMEONE'S COMING!
CREEEEAAAK
WHOOOOSH
THE HEADMASTER?
WHAT'S HE UP TO?
OOH! MAYBE HE'S ACCESSING SOME KINDA SECRET SPOT BEHIND A BOOKSHELF OR SOMETHING.
NAH. THAT'S RIDICULOUS.
CLICK

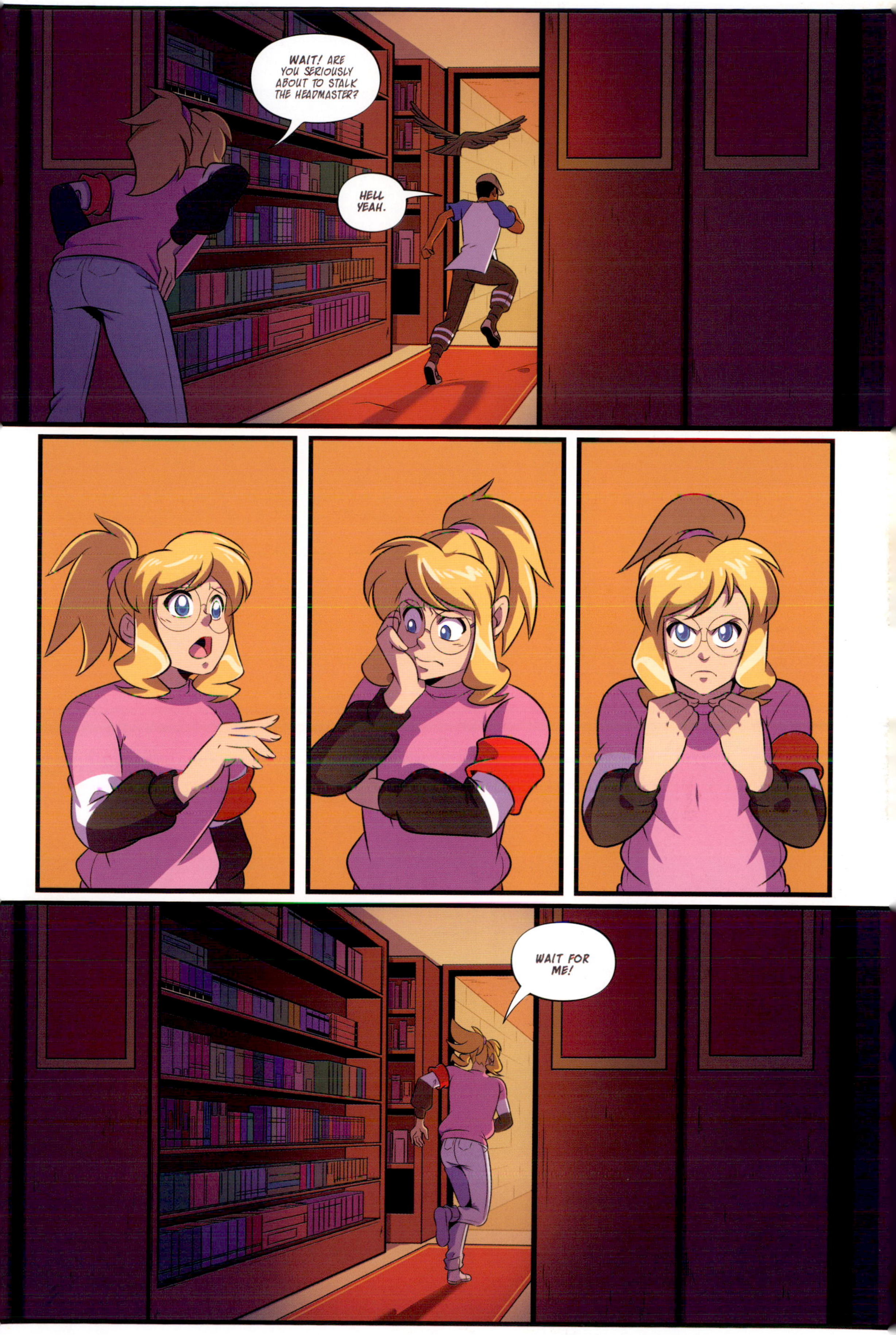
WAIT! ARE YOU SERIOUSLY ABOUT TO STALK THE HEADMASTER?
HELL YEAH.
WAIT FOR ME!

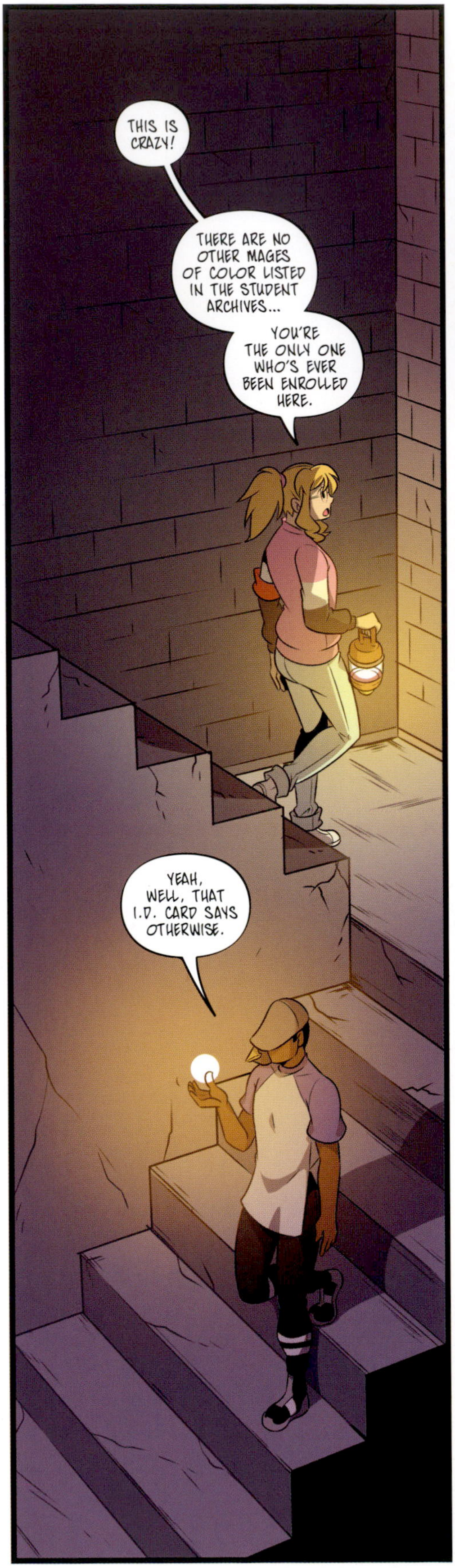
THIS IS CRAZY!
THERE ARE NO OTHER MAGES OF COLOR LISTED IN THE STUDENT ARCHIVES...
YOU'RE THE ONLY ONE WHO'S EVER BEEN ENROLLED HERE.
YEAH, WELL, THAT I.D. CARD SAYS OTHERWISE.
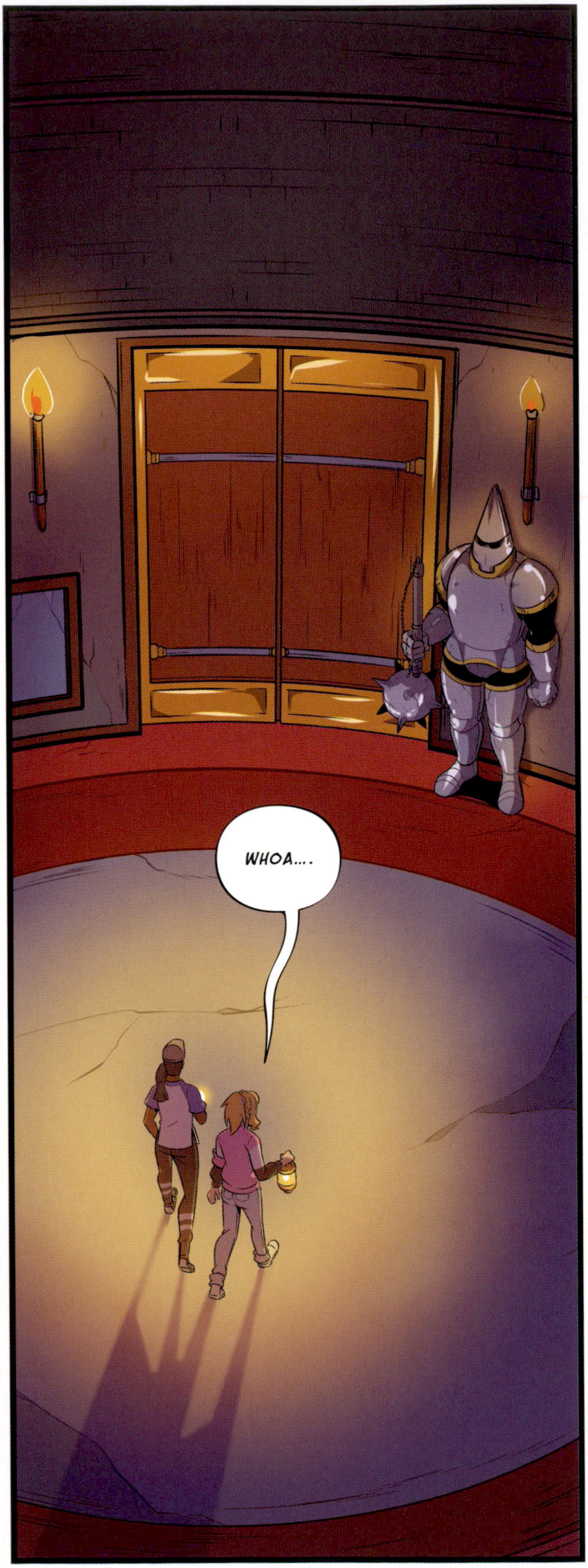
WHOA....

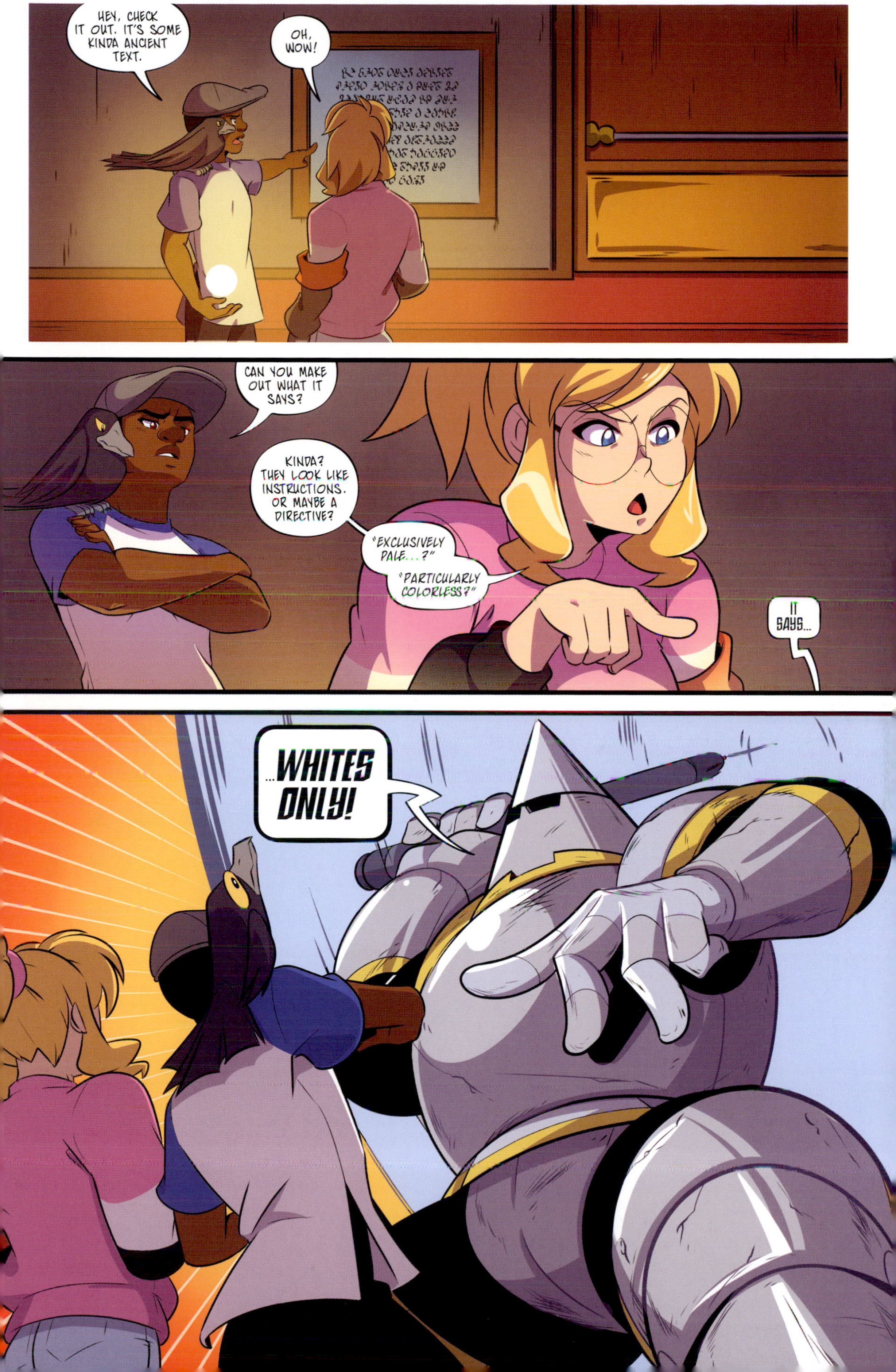
HEY, CHECK IT OUT. IT'S SOME KINDA ANCIENT TEXT.
OH, WOW!
CAN YOU MAKE OUT WHAT IT SAYS?
KINDA? THEY LOOK LIKE INSTRUCTIONS. OR MAYBE A DIRECTIVE?
"EXCLUSIVELY PALE...?"
"PARTICULARLY COLORLESS?"
IT SAYS...
...WHITES ONLY!

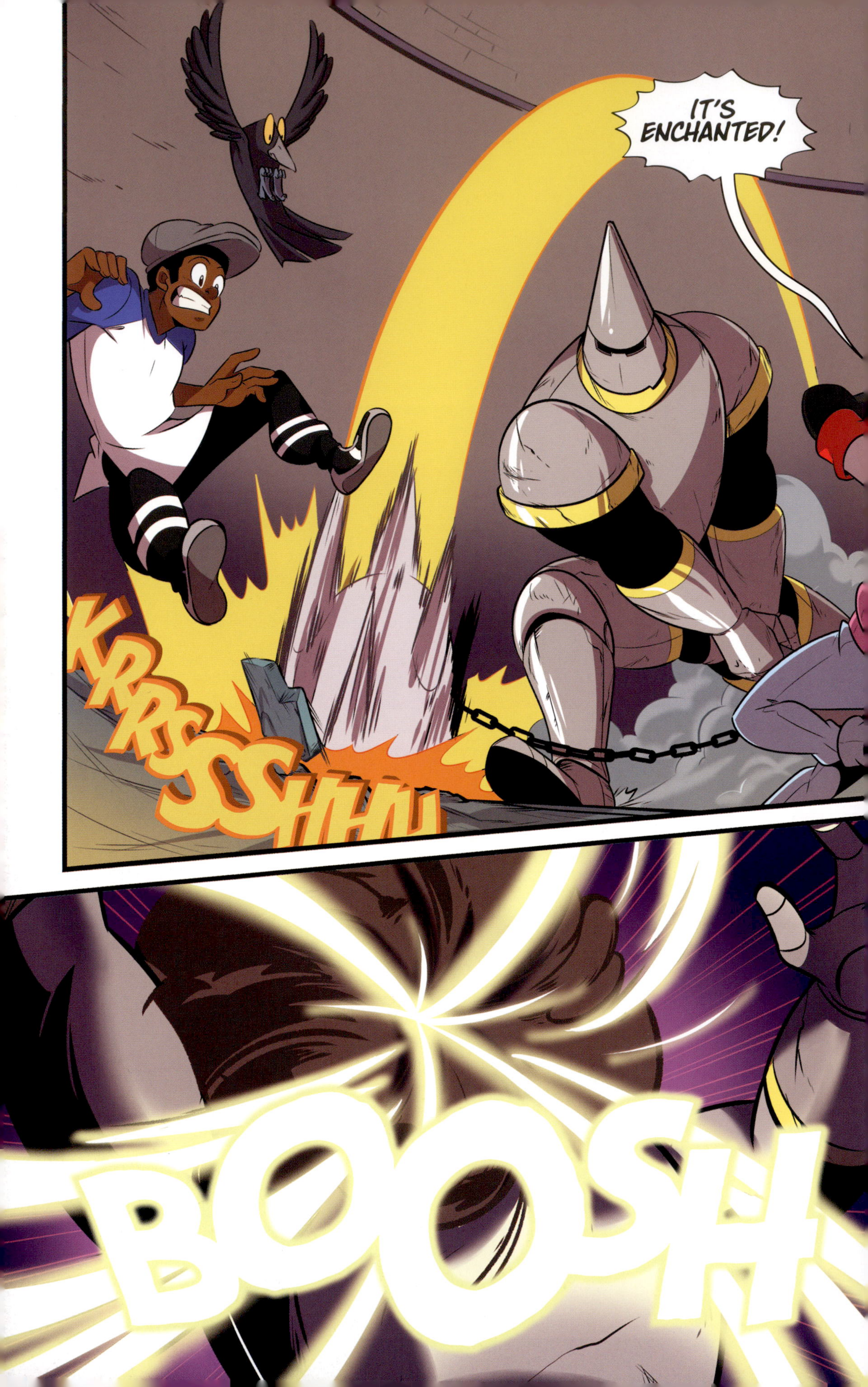
IT'S ENCHANTED!
KRRSSSHHH
BOOSH

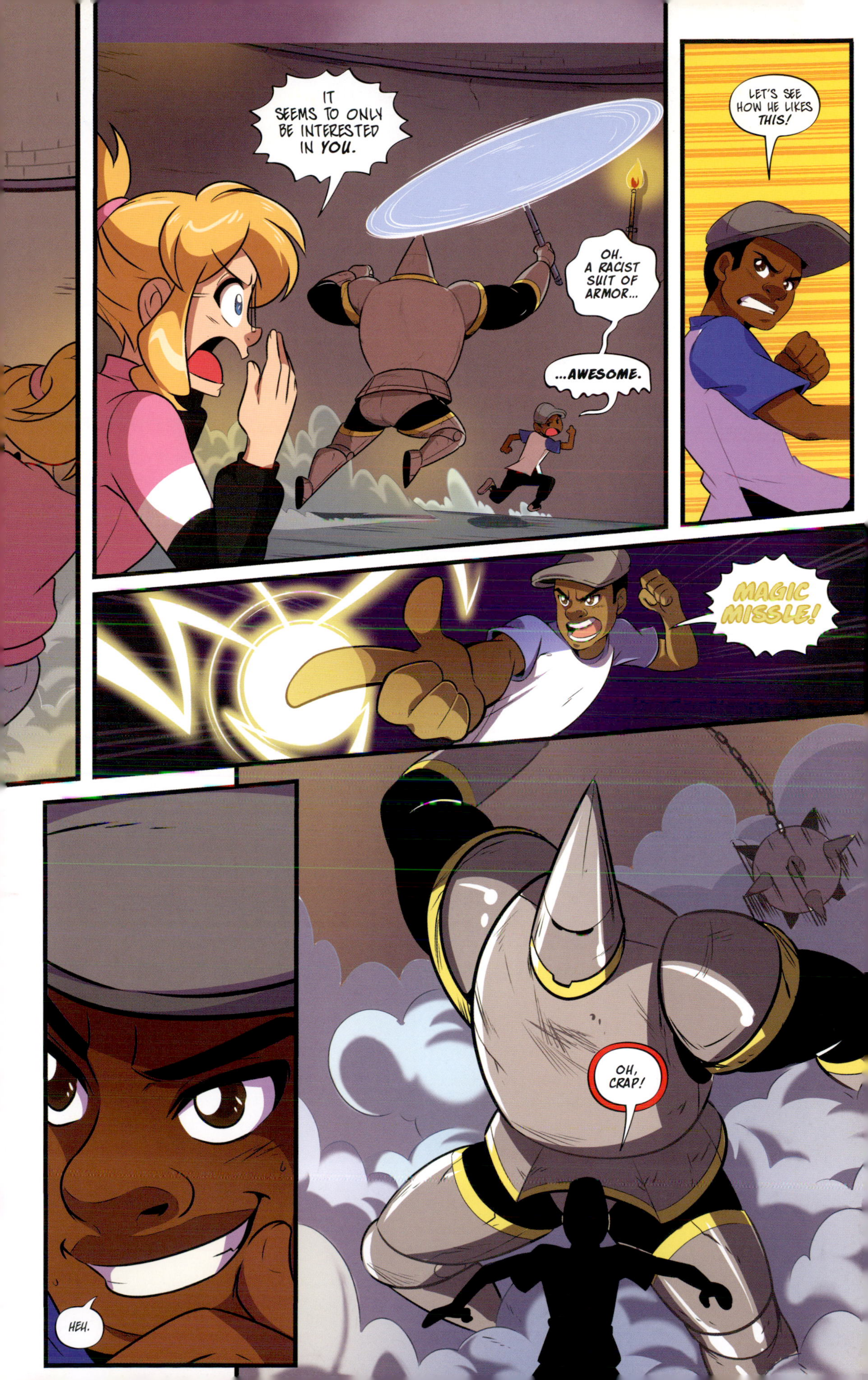
IT SEEMS TO ONLY BE INTERESTED IN YOU.
OH. A RACIST SUIT OF ARMOR...
...AWESOME.
LET'S SEE HOW HE LIKES THIS!
MAGIC MISSLE!
HEH.
OH, CRAP!

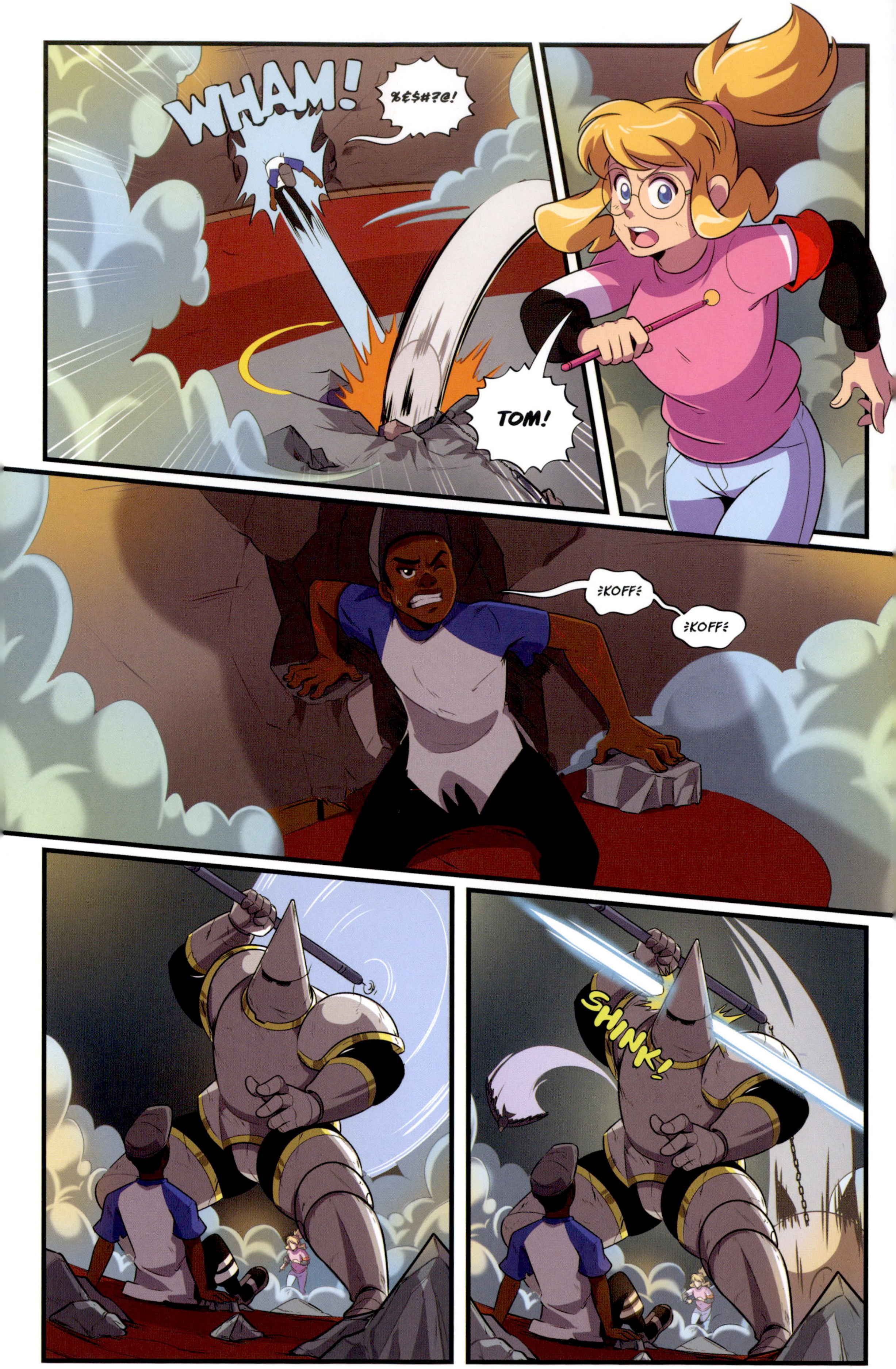
WHAM!
%£$#?@!
TOM!
KOFF
KOFF
SHINK!

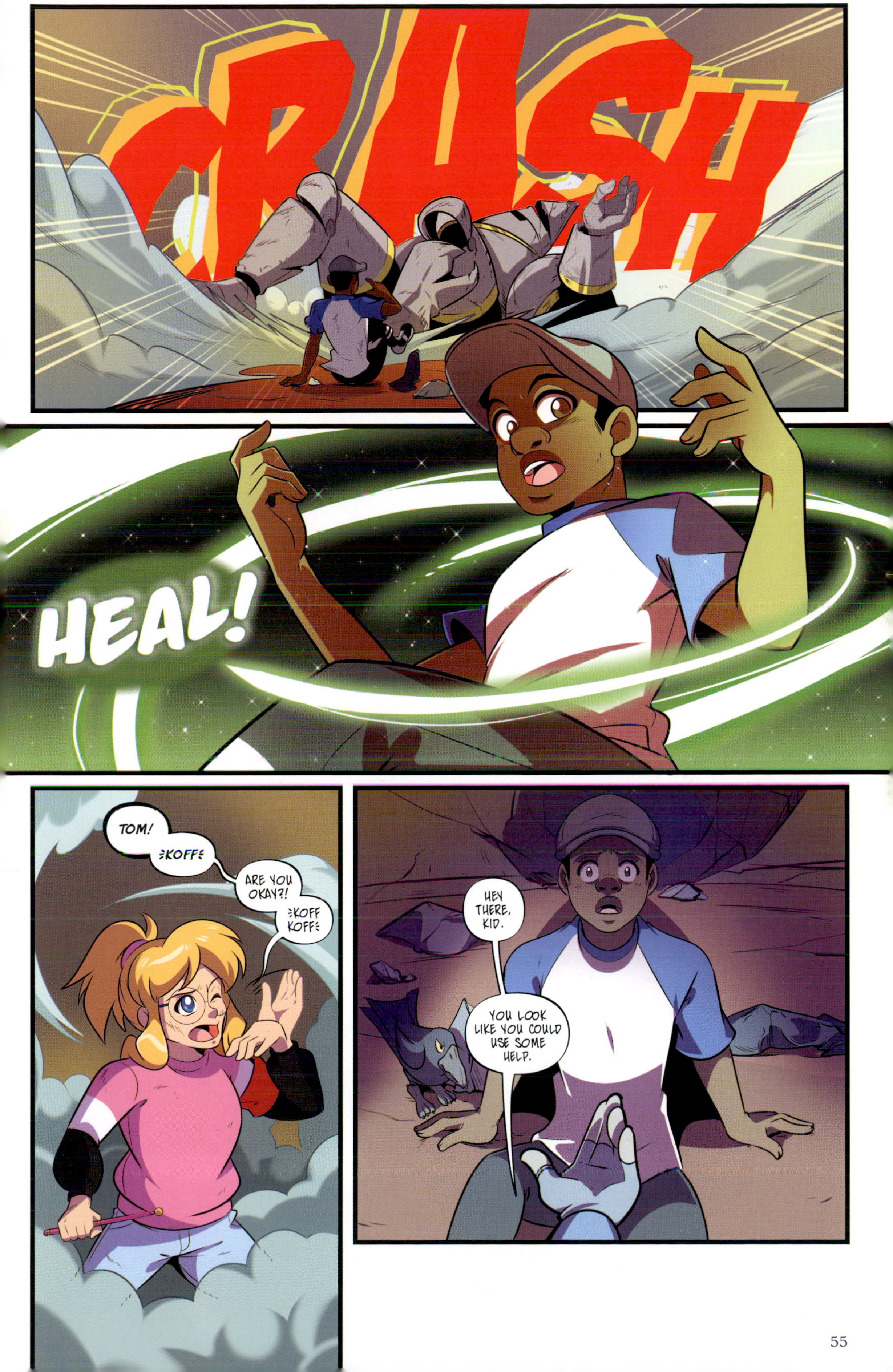
CRASH
HEAL!
TOM!
KOFF
ARE YOU OKAY?!
KOFF KOFF
HEY THERE, KID.
YOU LOOK LIKE YOU COULD USE SOME HELP.

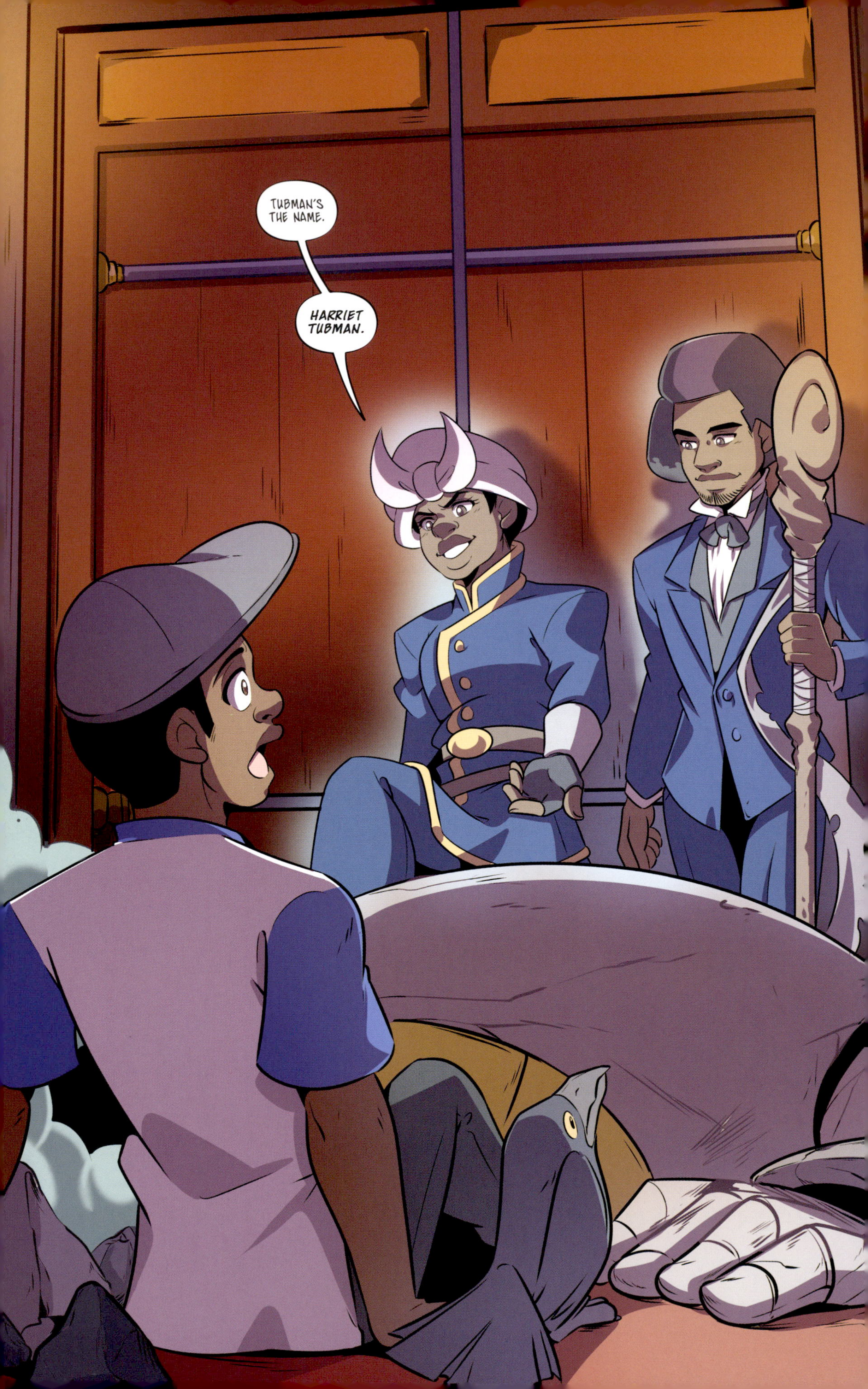
TUBMAN'S THE NAME.
HARRIET TUBMAN.

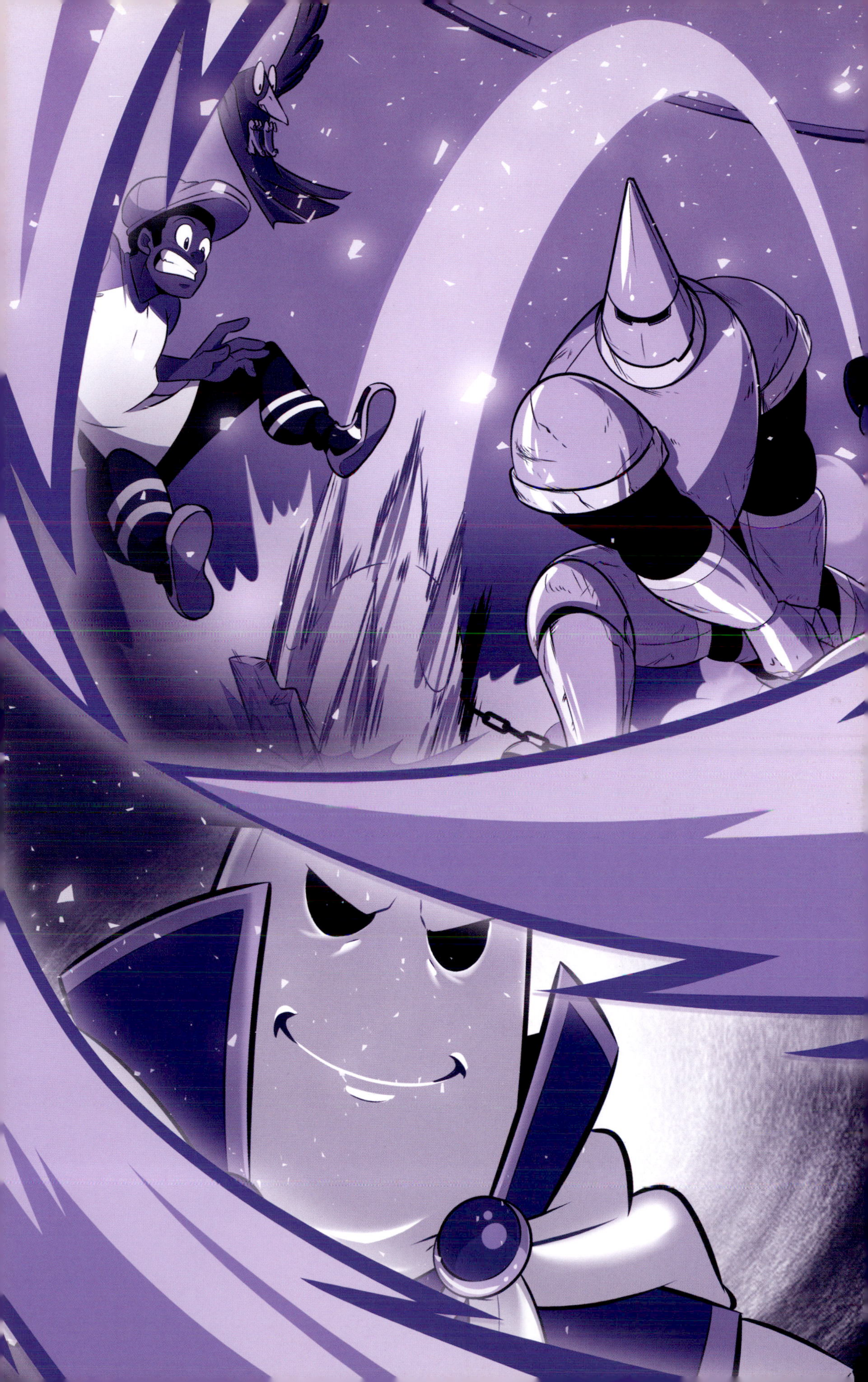

Chapter Three

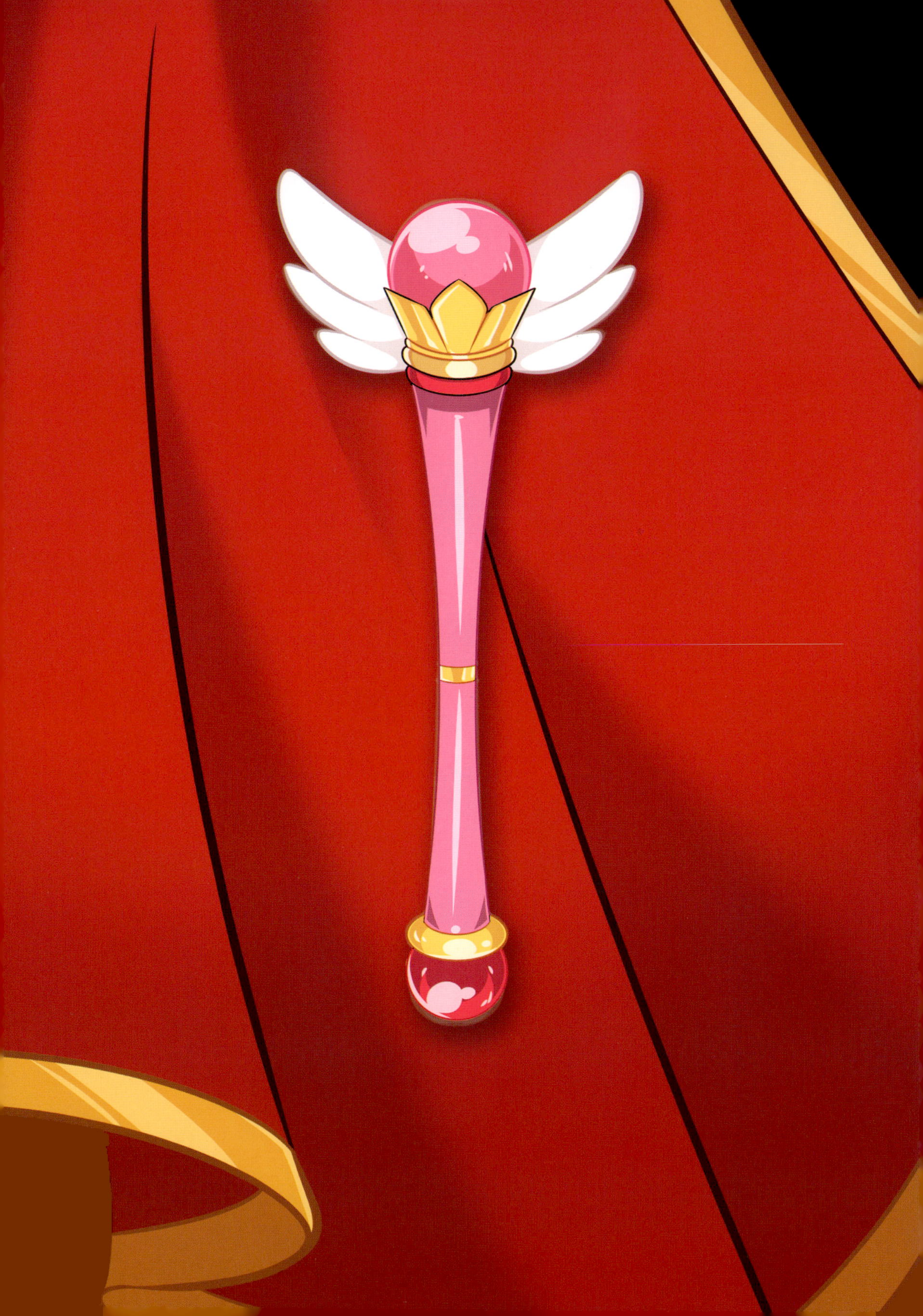

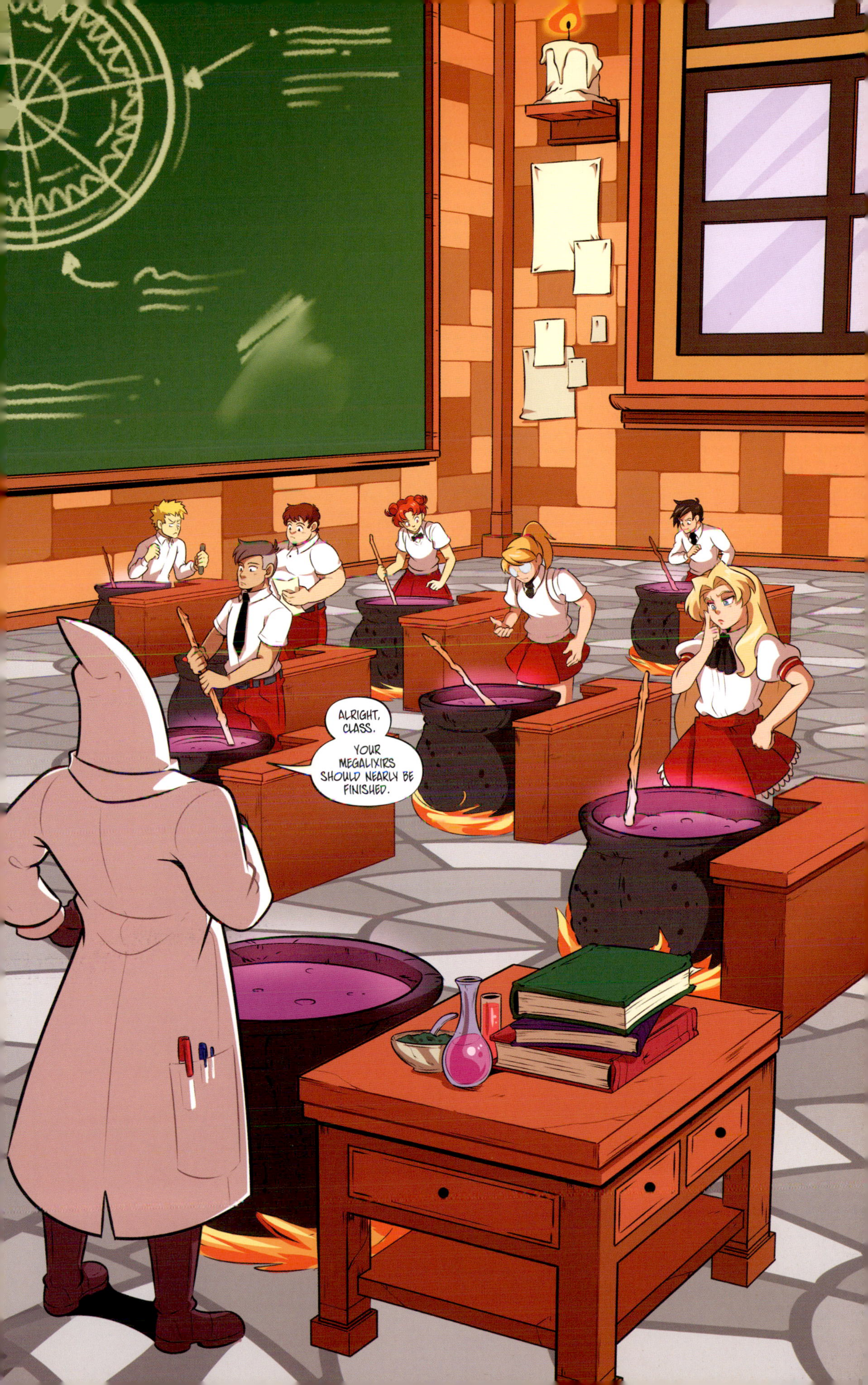
ALRIGHT, CLASS.
YOUR MEGALIXIRS SHOULD NEARLY BE FINISHED.

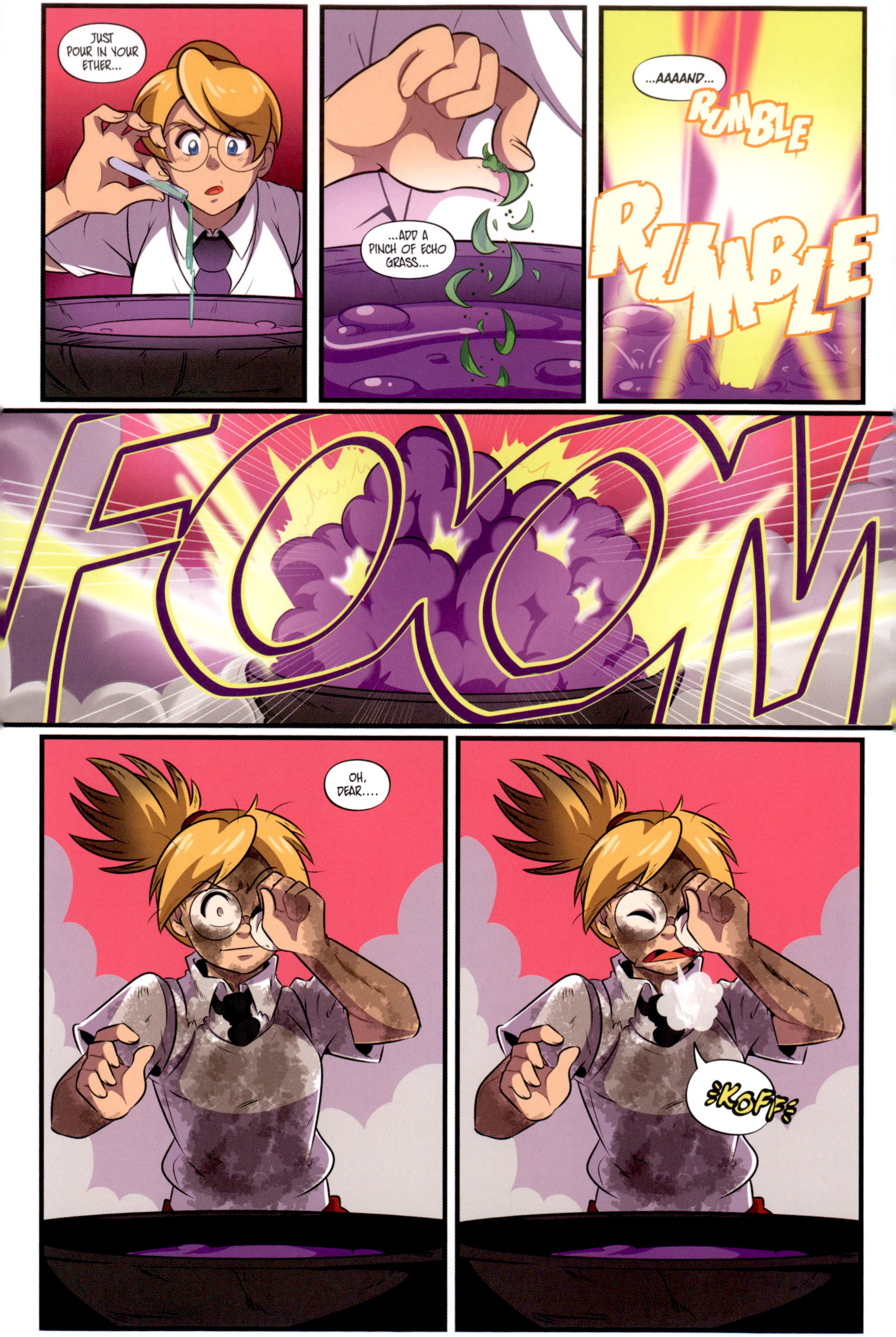
JUST POUR IN YOUR ETHER...
...ADD A PINCH OF ECHO GRASS...
...AAAAND...
RUMBLE
RUMBLE
FOOOM
OH, DEAR....
KOFF

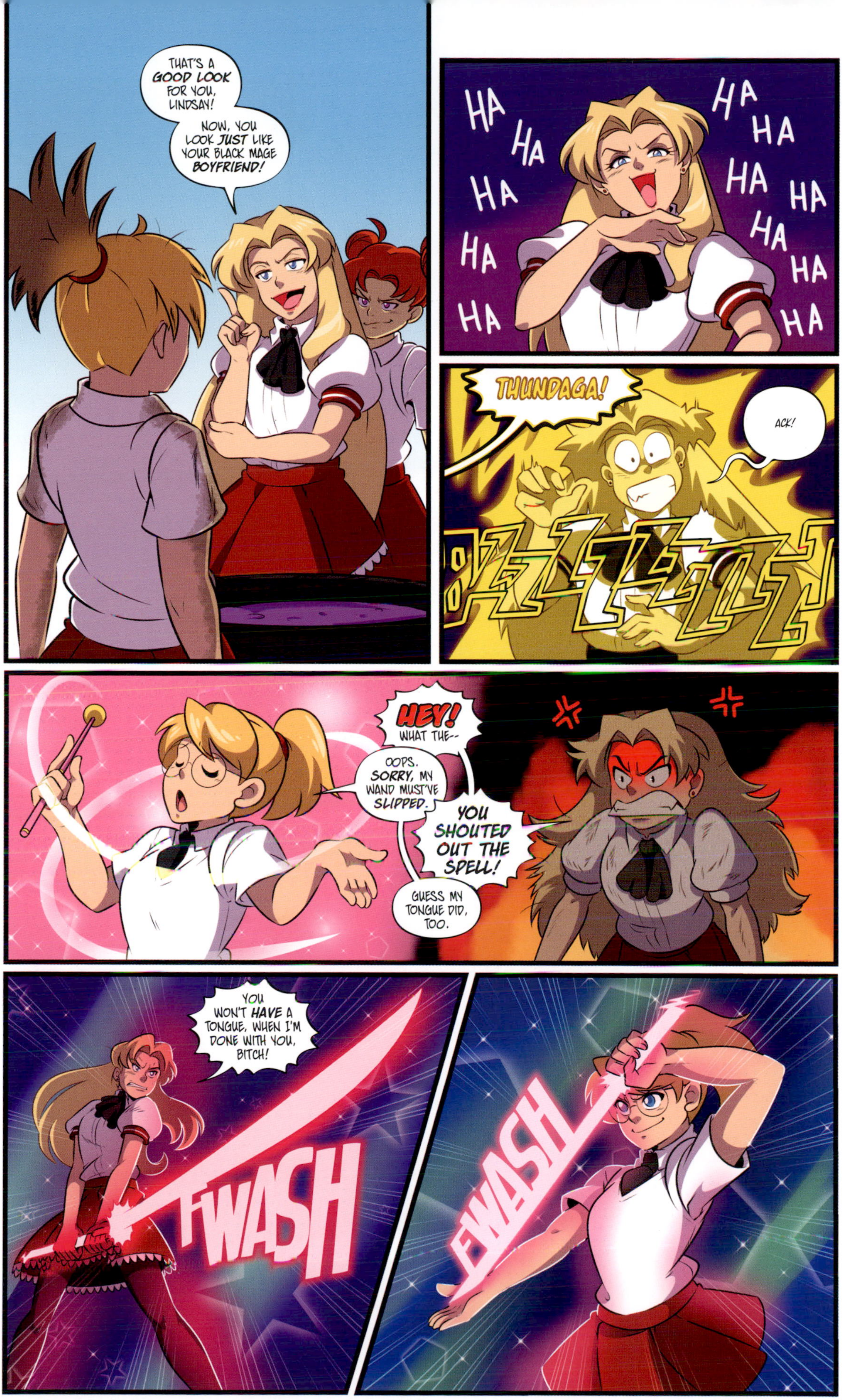
THAT'S A GOOD LOOK FOR YOU, LINDSAY!
NOW, YOU LOOK JUST LIKE YOUR BLACK MAGE BOYFRIEND!
HA HA HA HA HA HA HA HA HA HA HA HA
THUNDAGA!
ACK!
HEY! WHAT THE--
OOPS. SORRY, MY WAND MUST'VE SLIPPED.
YOU SHOUTED OUT THE SPELL!
GUESS MY TONGUE DID, TOO.
YOU WON'T HAVE A TONGUE, WHEN I'M DONE WITH YOU, BITCH!
FWASH
FWASH

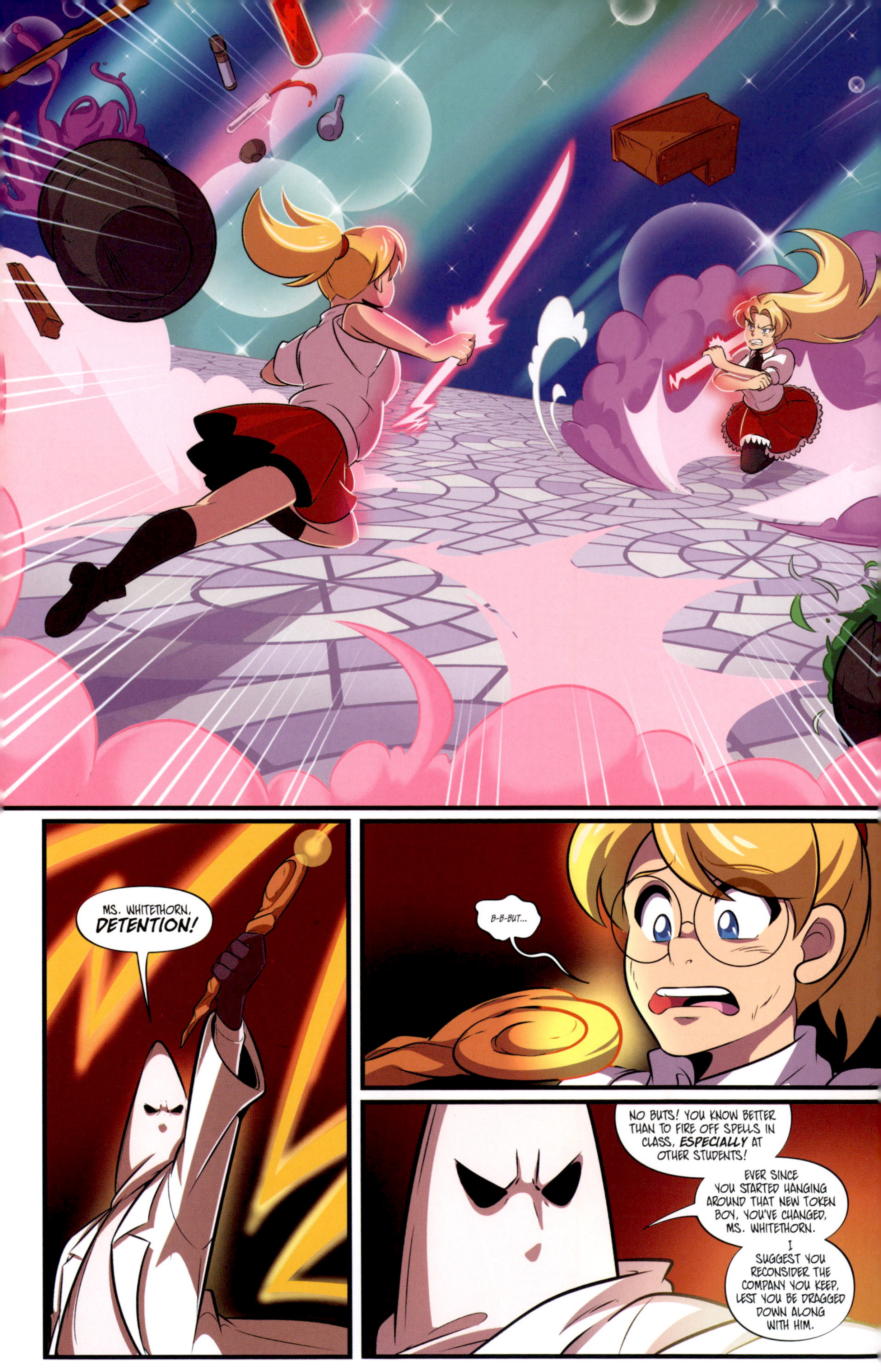
MS. WHITETHORN, **DETENTION!**
B-B-BUT...
NO BUTS! YOU KNOW BETTER THAN TO FIRE OFF SPELLS IN CLASS, **ESPECIALLY** AT OTHER STUDENTS!
EVER SINCE YOU STARTED HANGING AROUND THAT NEW TOKEN BOY, YOU'VE CHANGED, MS. WHITETHORN.
I SUGGEST YOU RECONSIDER THE COMPANY YOU KEEP, LEST YOU BE DRAGGED DOWN ALONG WITH HIM.

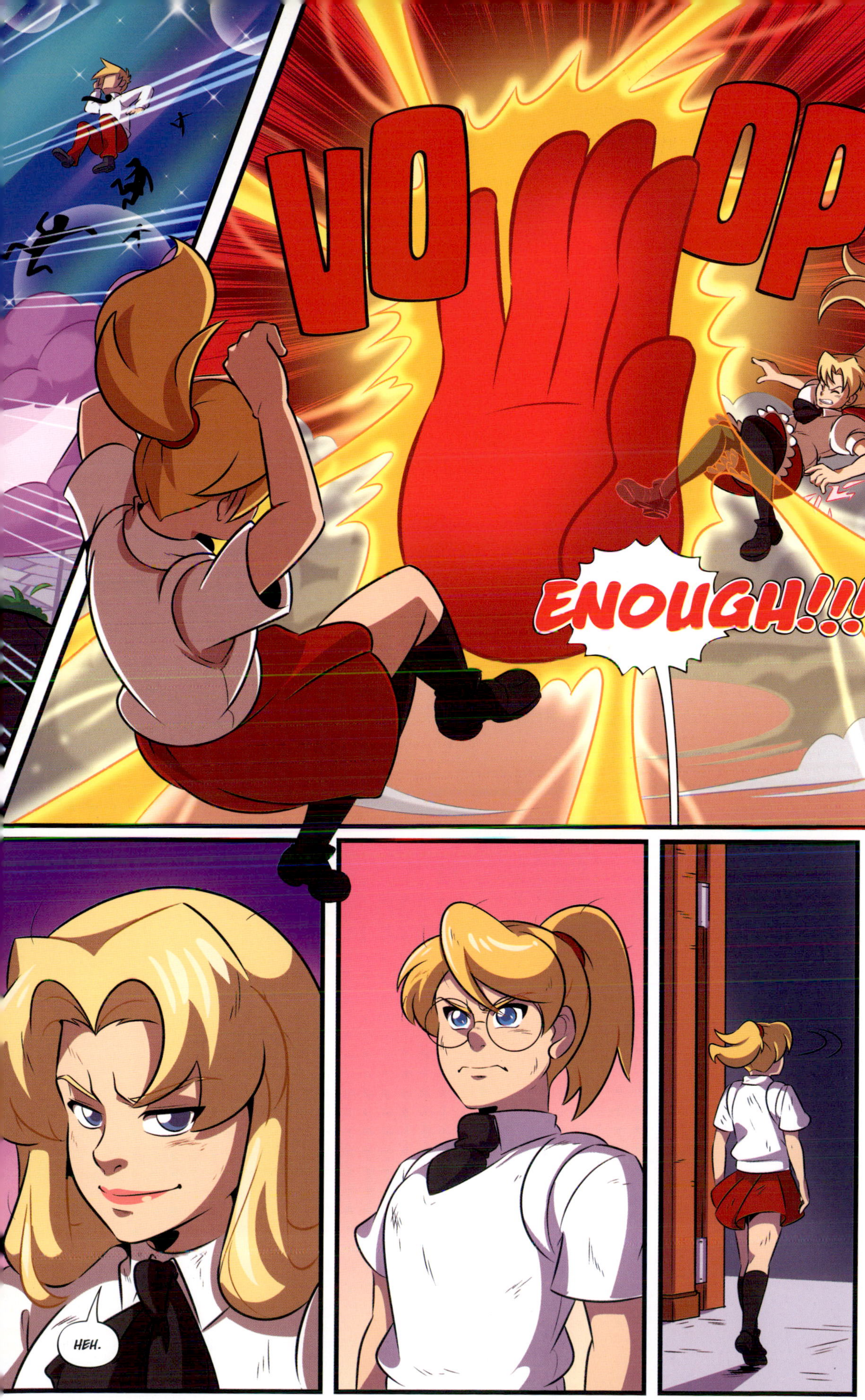
VOOOP
ENOUGH!!!
HEH.

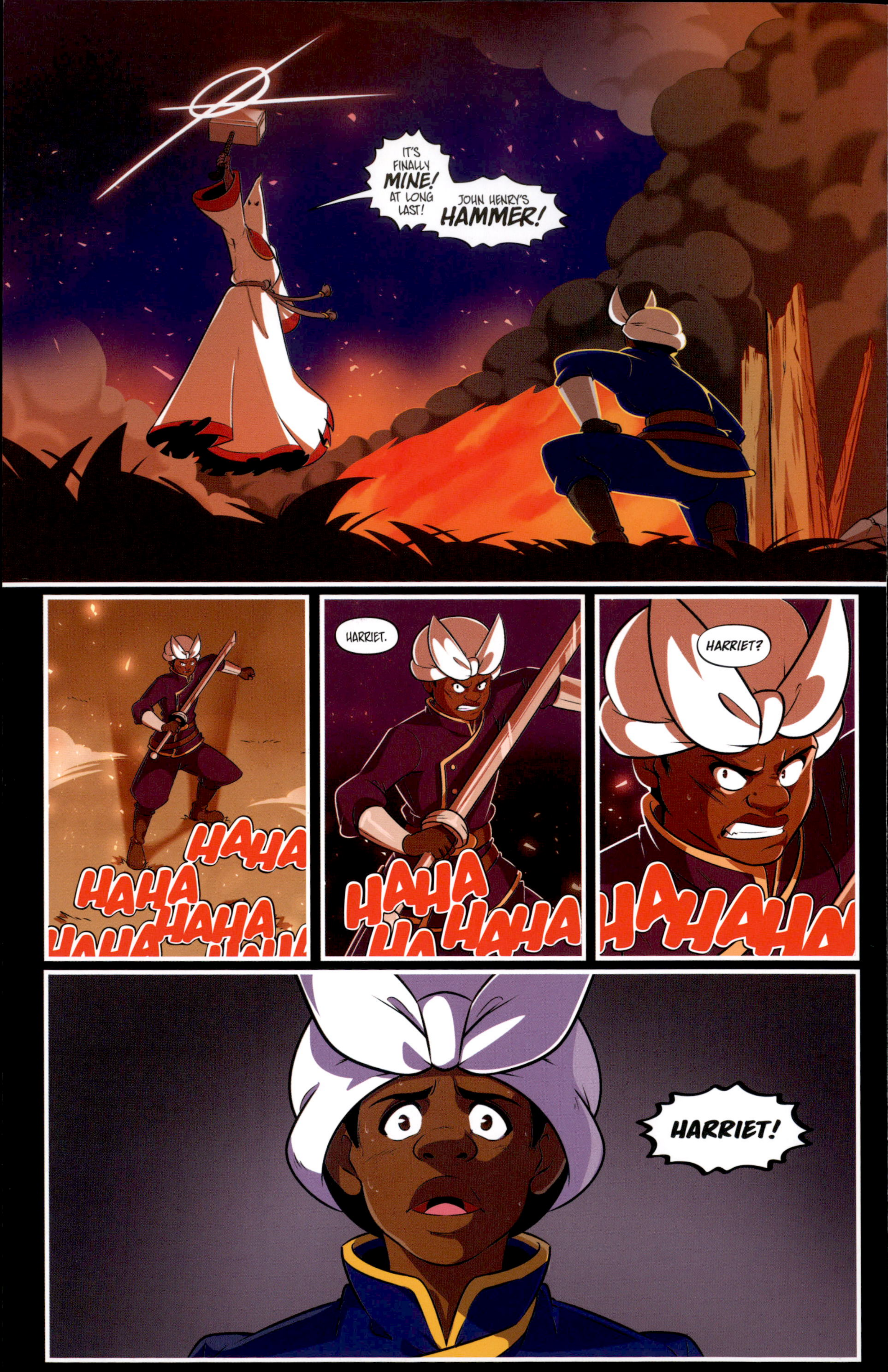
IT'S FINALLY MINE! AT LONG LAST!
JOHN HENRY'S HAMMER!
HARRIET.
HARRIET?
HAHA HAHA HAHA
HAHA HAHA
HAHAHA
HARRIET!

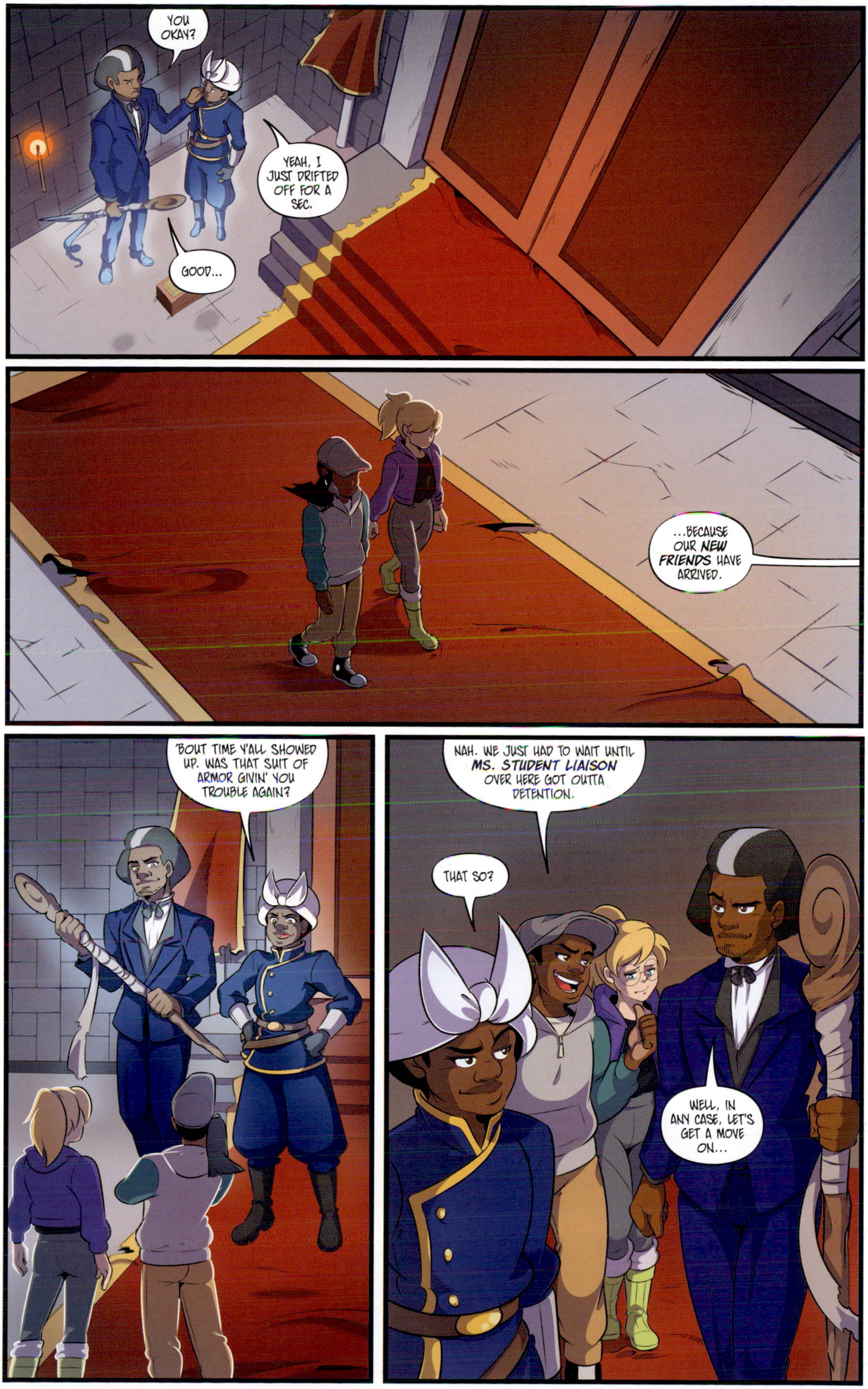

YOU OKAY?
YEAH, I JUST DRIFTED OFF FOR A SEC.
GOOD...
...BECAUSE OUR NEW FRIENDS HAVE ARRIVED.
'BOUT TIME Y'ALL SHOWED UP. WAS THAT SUIT OF ARMOR GIVIN' YOU TROUBLE AGAIN?
NAH. WE JUST HAD TO WAIT UNTIL MS. STUDENT LIAISON OVER HERE GOT OUTTA DETENTION.
THAT SO?
WELL, IN ANY CASE, LET'S GET A MOVE ON...

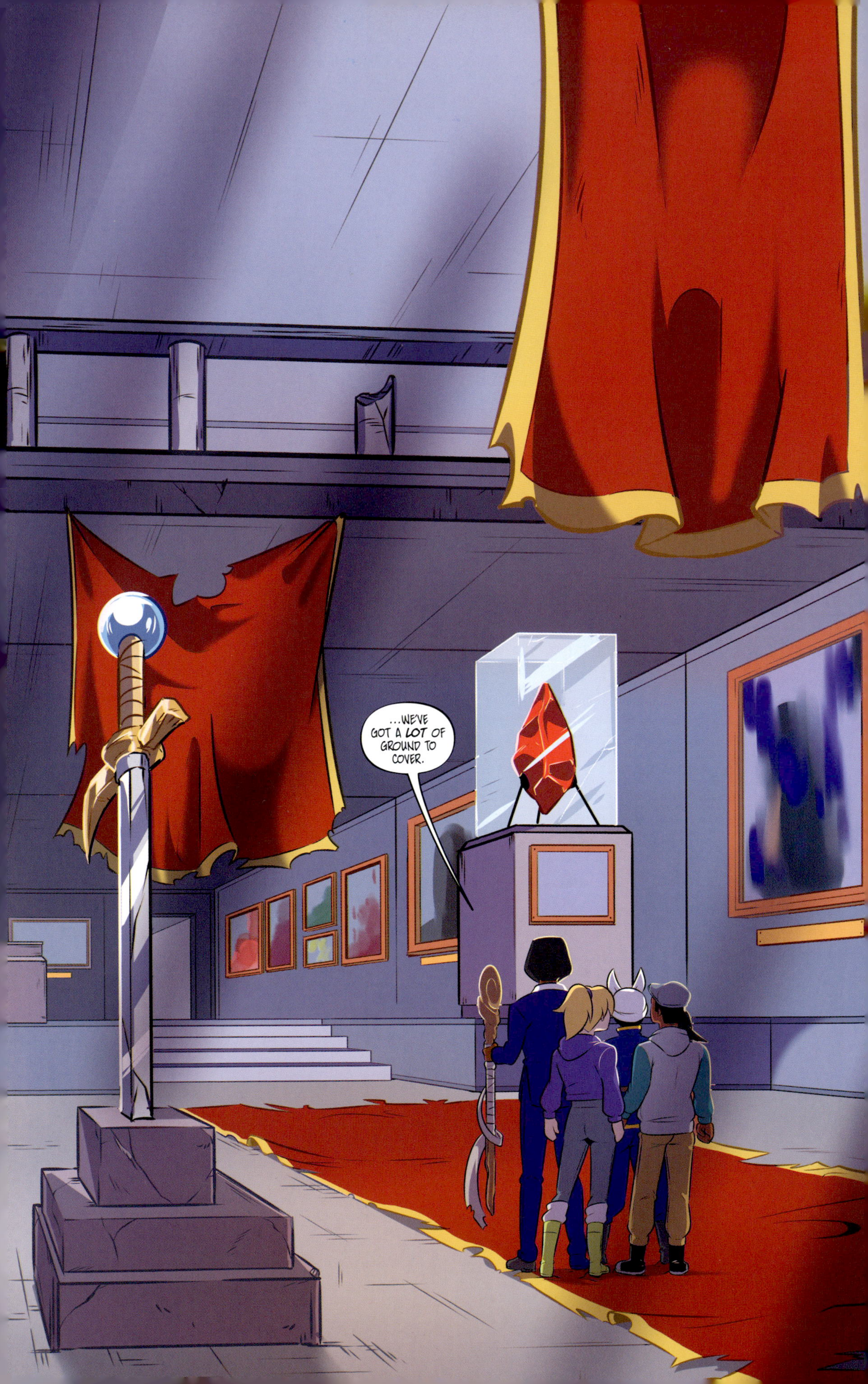
...WE'VE GOT A LOT OF GROUND TO COVER.

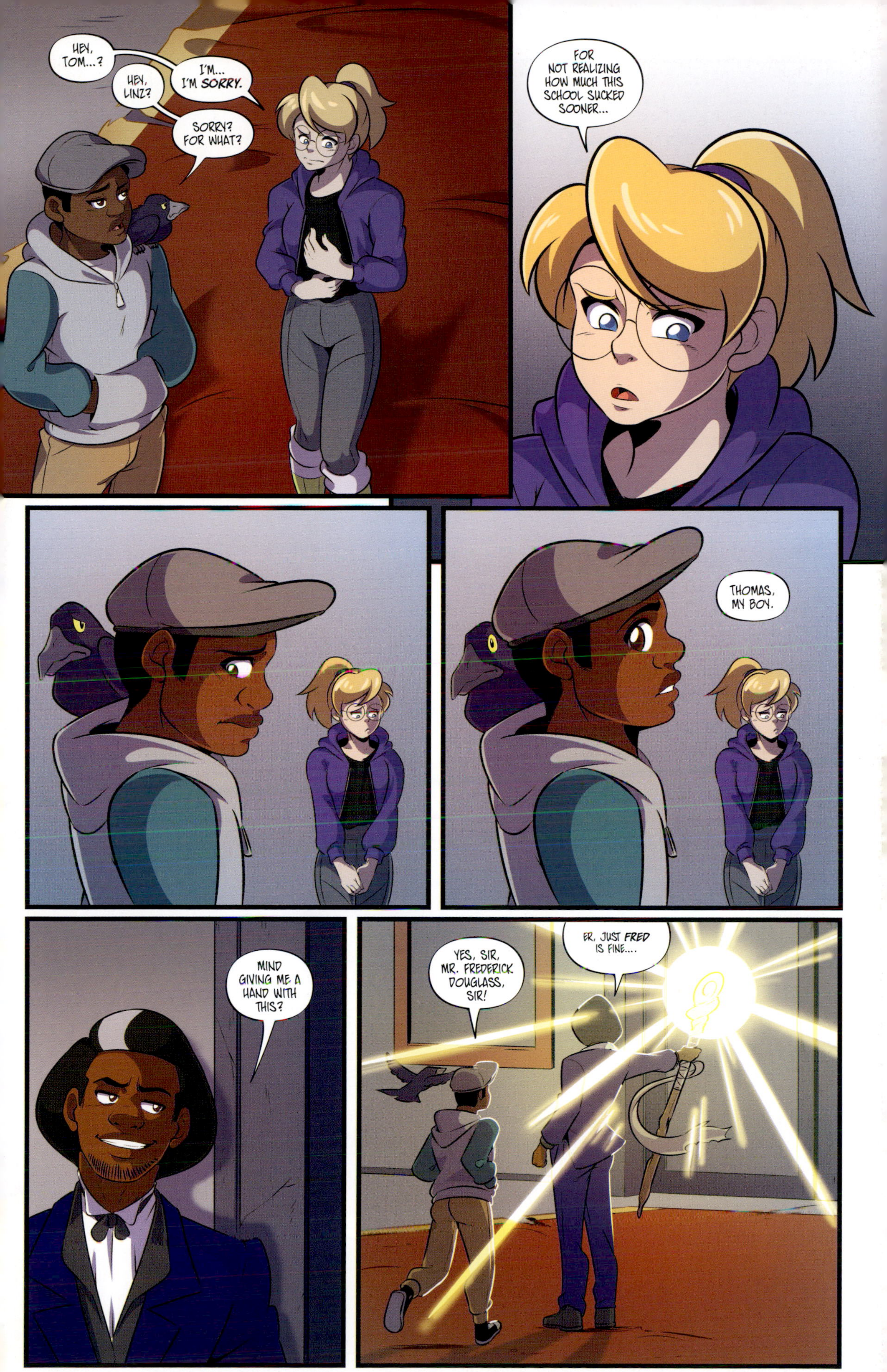
HEY, TOM...?
HEY, LINZ?
I'M... I'M **SORRY.**
SORRY? FOR WHAT?
FOR NOT REALIZING HOW MUCH THIS SCHOOL SUCKED SOONER...
THOMAS, MY BOY.
MIND GIVING ME A HAND WITH THIS?
YES, SIR, MR. FREDERICK DOUGLASS, SIR!
ER, JUST **FRED** IS FINE....

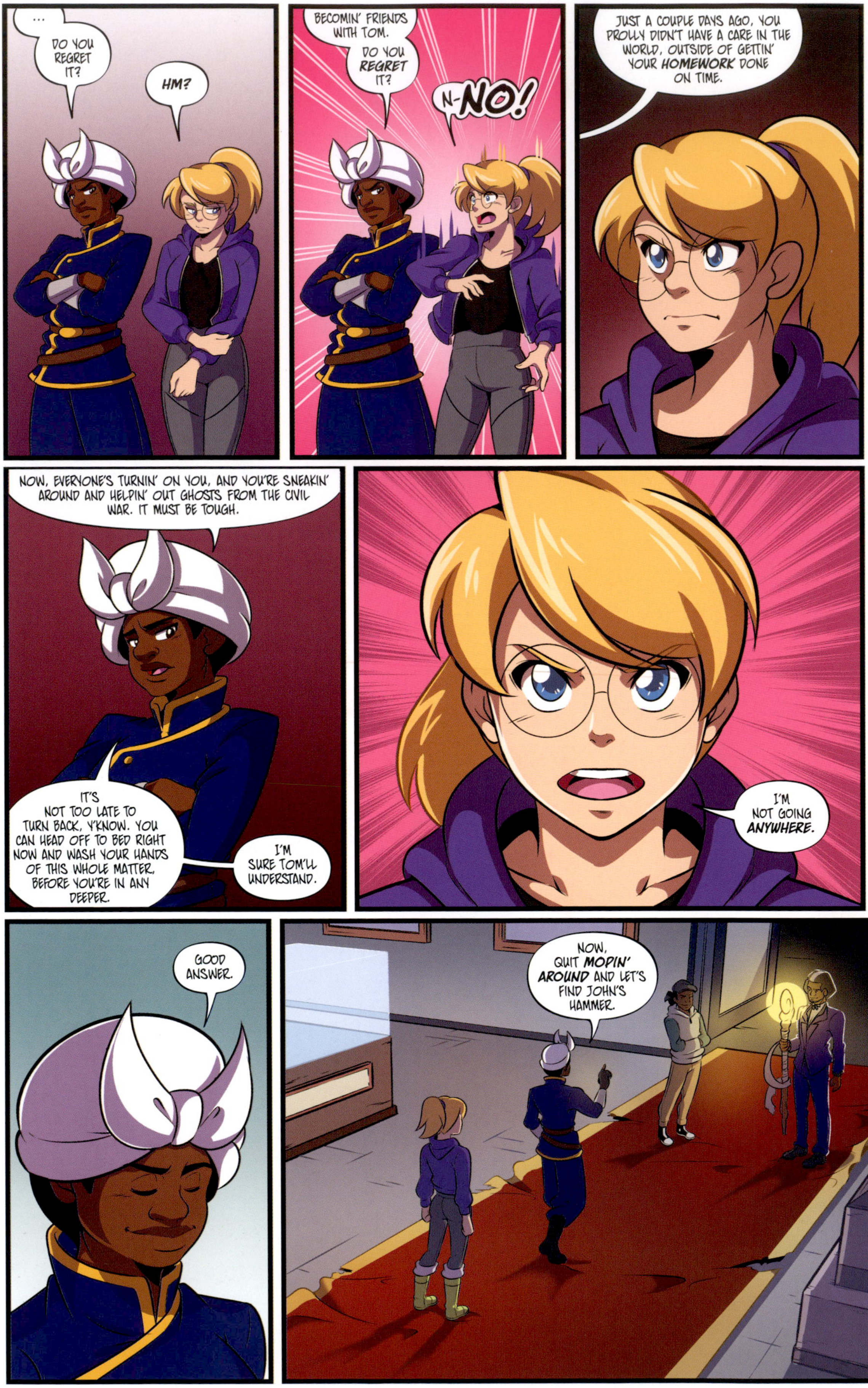
...
DO YOU REGRET IT?
HM?
BECOMIN' FRIENDS WITH TOM.
DO YOU REGRET IT?
N-NO!
JUST A COUPLE DAYS AGO, YOU PROLLY DIDN'T HAVE A CARE IN THE WORLD, OUTSIDE OF GETTIN' YOUR HOMEWORK DONE ON TIME.
NOW, EVERYONE'S TURNIN' ON YOU, AND YOU'RE SNEAKIN' AROUND AND HELPIN' OUT GHOSTS FROM THE CIVIL WAR. IT MUST BE TOUGH.
IT'S NOT TOO LATE TO TURN BACK, Y'KNOW. YOU CAN HEAD OFF TO BED RIGHT NOW AND WASH YOUR HANDS OF THIS WHOLE MATTER, BEFORE YOU'RE IN ANY DEEPER.
I'M SURE TOM'LL UNDERSTAND.
I'M NOT GOING ANYWHERE.
GOOD ANSWER.
NOW, QUIT MOPIN' AROUND AND LET'S FIND JOHN'S HAMMER.

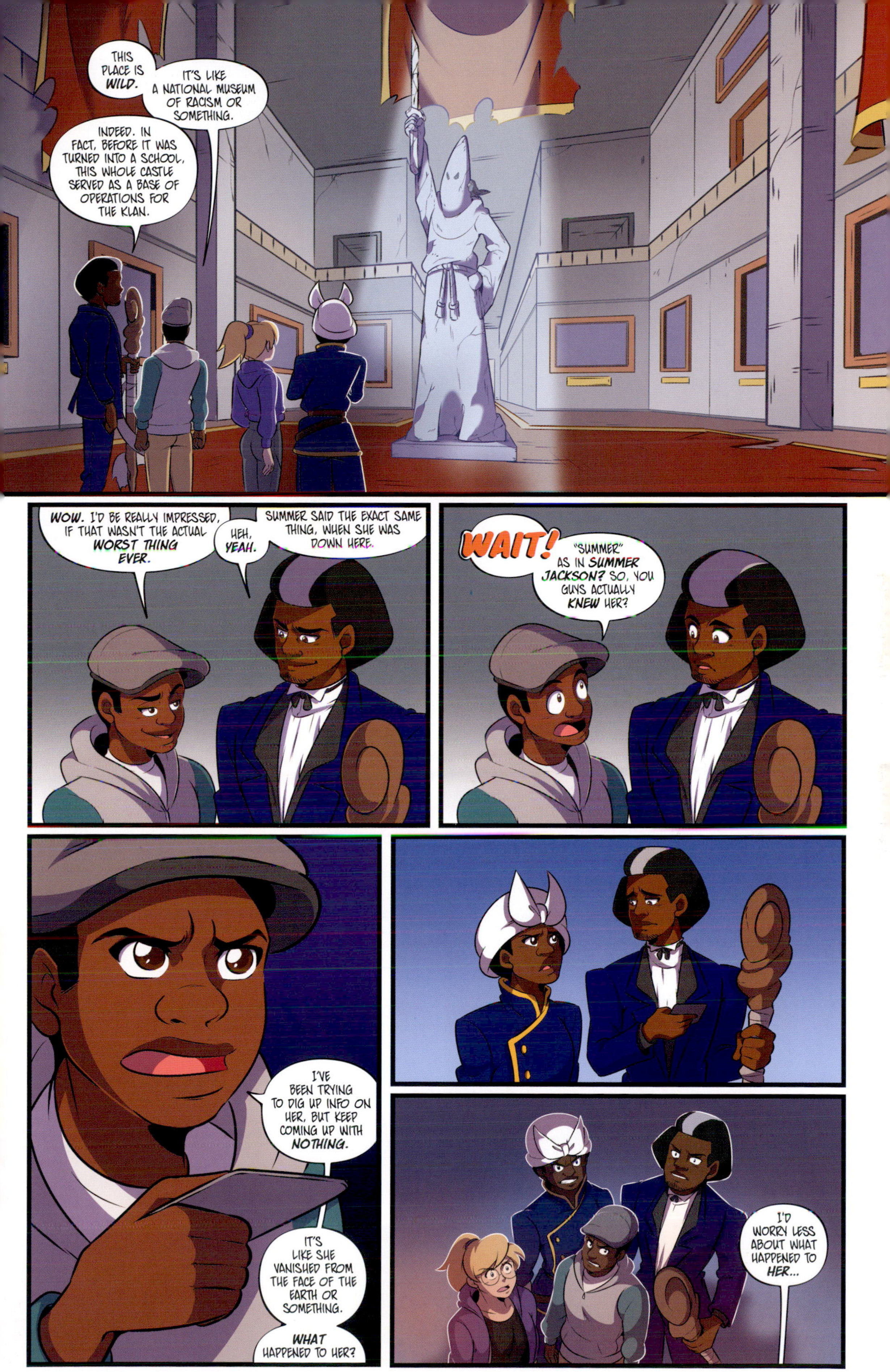

THIS PLACE IS WILD.
IT'S LIKE A NATIONAL MUSEUM OF RACISM OR SOMETHING.
INDEED. IN FACT, BEFORE IT WAS TURNED INTO A SCHOOL, THIS WHOLE CASTLE SERVED AS A BASE OF OPERATIONS FOR THE KLAN.
WOW. I'D BE REALLY IMPRESSED, IF THAT WASN'T THE ACTUAL WORST THING EVER.
HEH, YEAH.
SUMMER SAID THE EXACT SAME THING, WHEN SHE WAS DOWN HERE.
WAIT!
"SUMMER" AS IN SUMMER JACKSON? SO, YOU GUYS ACTUALLY KNEW HER?
I'VE BEEN TRYING TO DIG UP INFO ON HER, BUT KEEP COMING UP WITH NOTHING.
IT'S LIKE SHE VANISHED FROM THE FACE OF THE EARTH OR SOMETHING.
WHAT HAPPENED TO HER?
I'D WORRY LESS ABOUT WHAT HAPPENED TO HER...

...AND MORE ABOUT WHAT'S GONNA HAPPEN TO YOU.

HEY, IT'S THAT ONE GUY AGAIN! BLAKE!

MY NAME IS BRYCE!

WHATEVER.

WHAT ARE YOU EVEN DOING DOWN HERE, BRYCE? WHAT DO YOU WANT?

OH, IT'S NOT ABOUT WHAT I WANT...

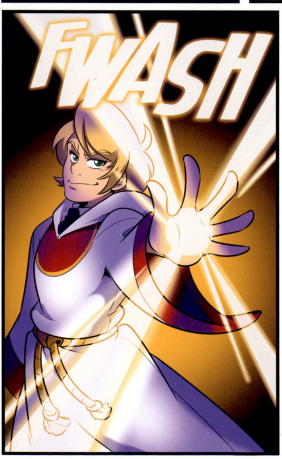

FWASH

...IT'S ABOUT WHAT YOU WANT.

THAT HAMMER DOESN'T BELONG TO YOU!
HAND IT OVER!
WHY DON'T YOU COME TAKE IT FROM ME?
HEHEHEHE
HEHEHEHE HEHE HEHE
WHOA.

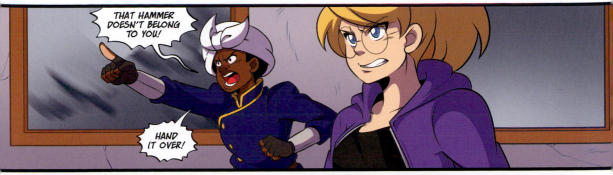

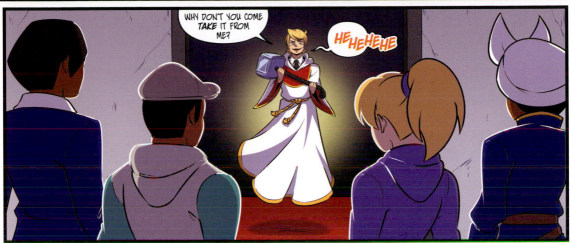

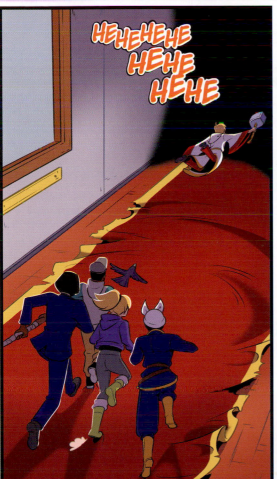

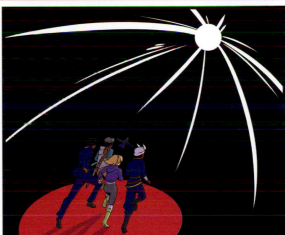

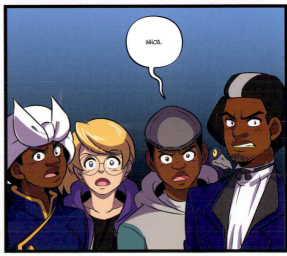

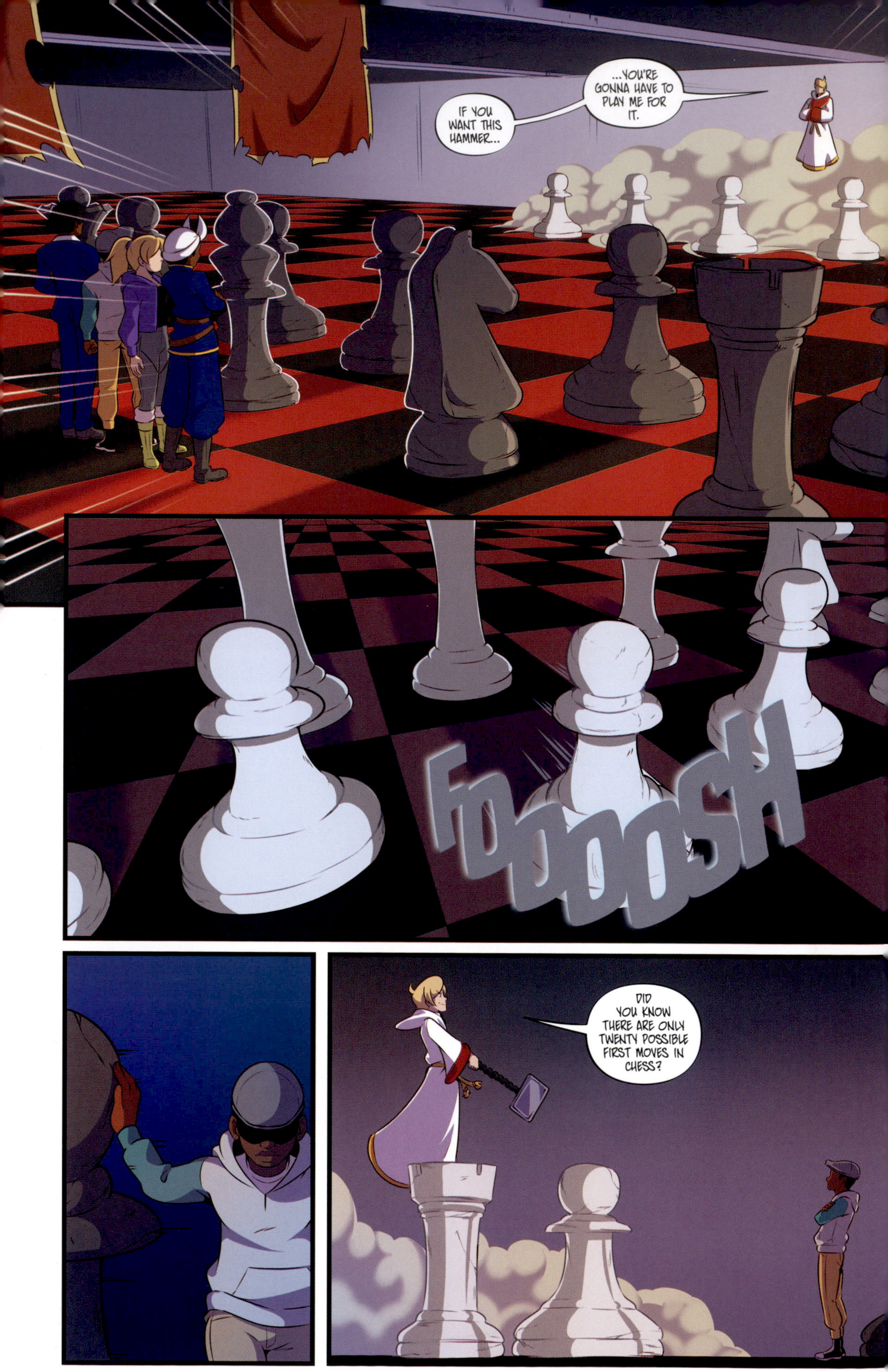
IF YOU WANT THIS HAMMER...
...YOU'RE GONNA HAVE TO PLAY ME FOR IT.
FOOOOSH
DID YOU KNOW THERE ARE ONLY TWENTY POSSIBLE FIRST MOVES IN CHESS?

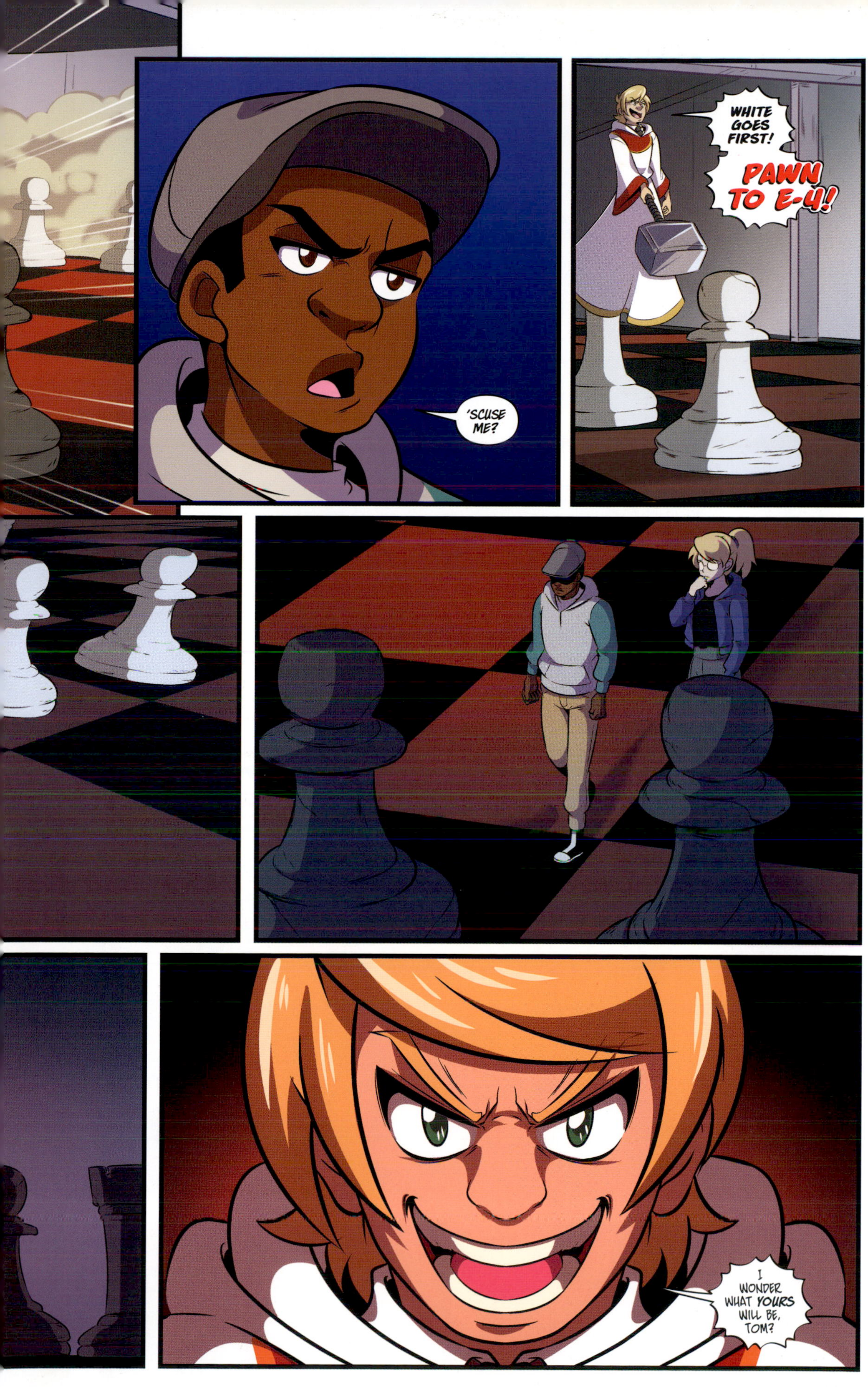
'SCUSE ME?
WHITE GOES FIRST!
PAWN TO E-4!
I WONDER WHAT YOURS WILL BE, TOM?

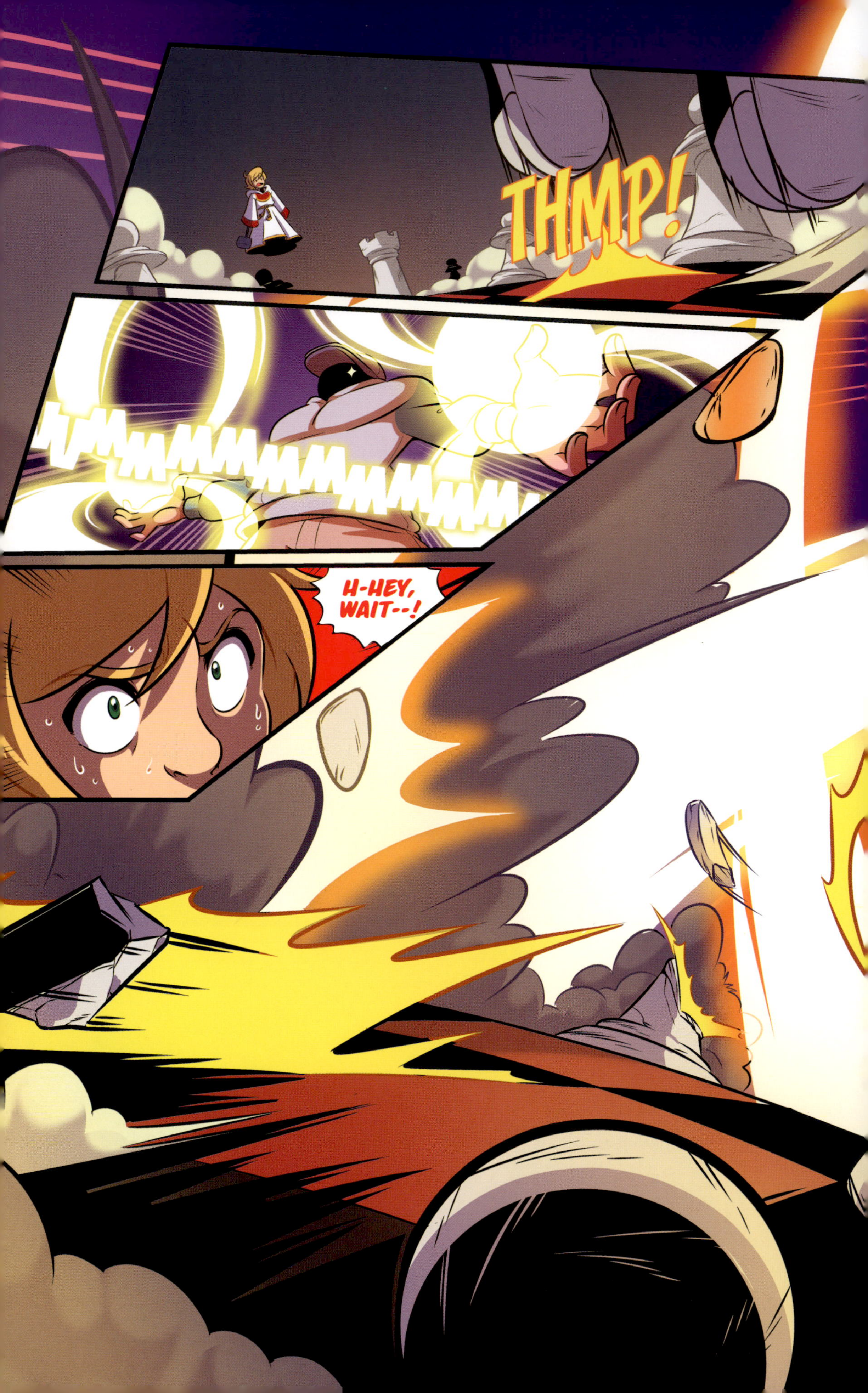
THMP!
MMMMMMMMMMMMMMMM
H-HEY, WAIT--!

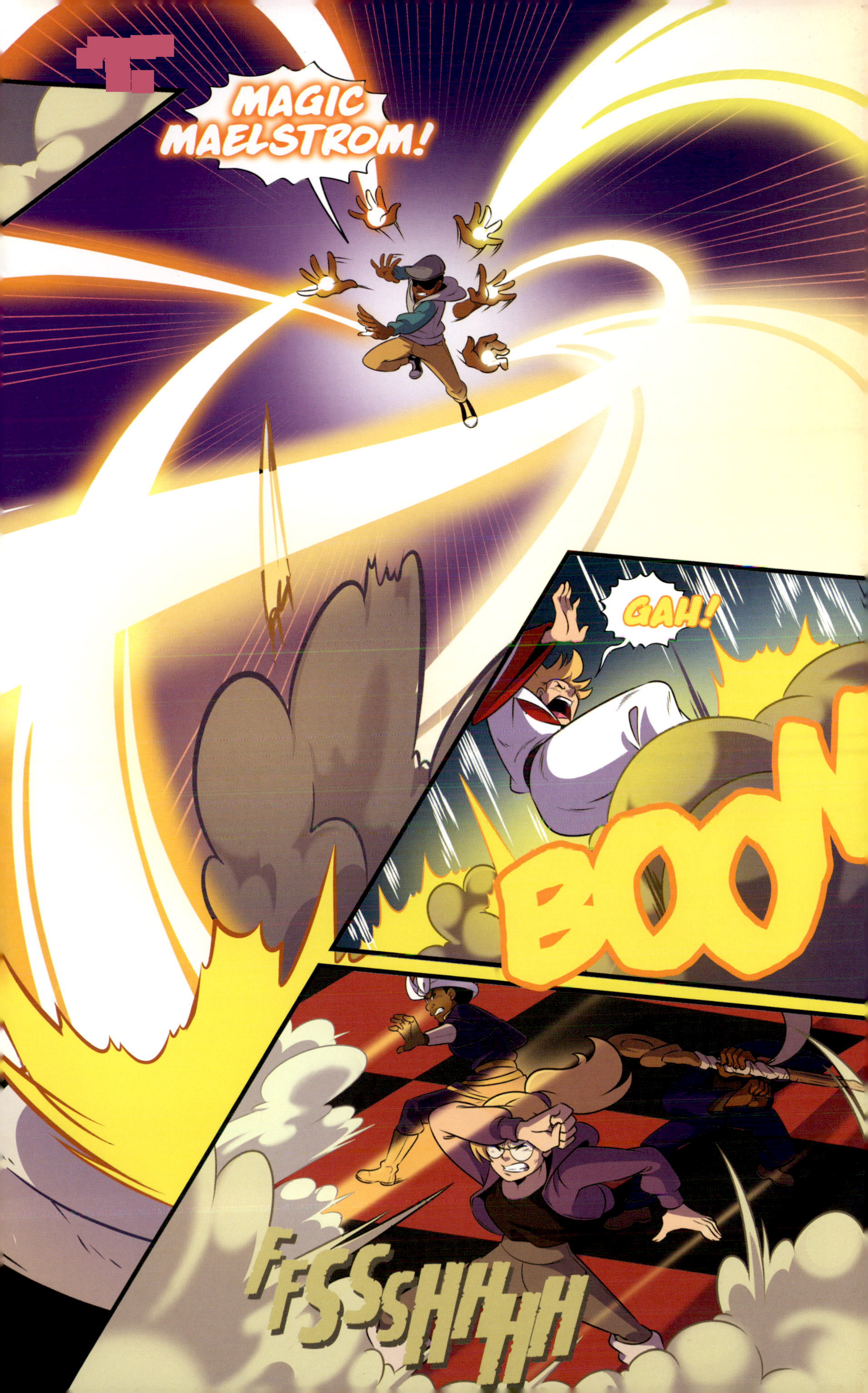
MAGIC MAELSTROM!
GAH!
BOOM
FFSSSHHHHH

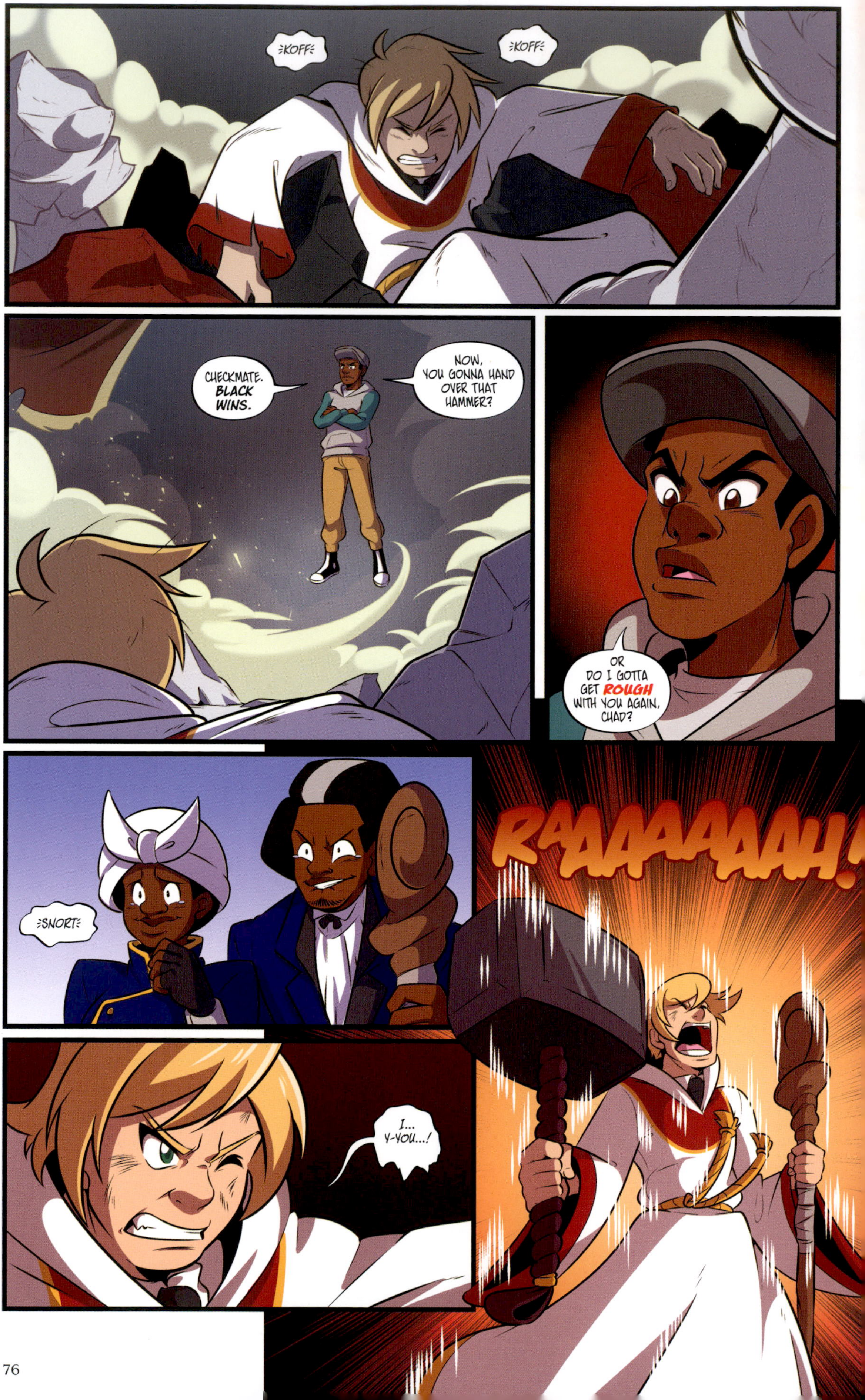

KOFF
KOFF
CHECKMATE. BLACK WINS.
NOW, YOU GONNA HAND OVER THAT HAMMER?
OR DO I GOTTA GET ROUGH WITH YOU AGAIN, CHAD?
SNORT
I... Y-YOU...!
RAAAAAAAH!

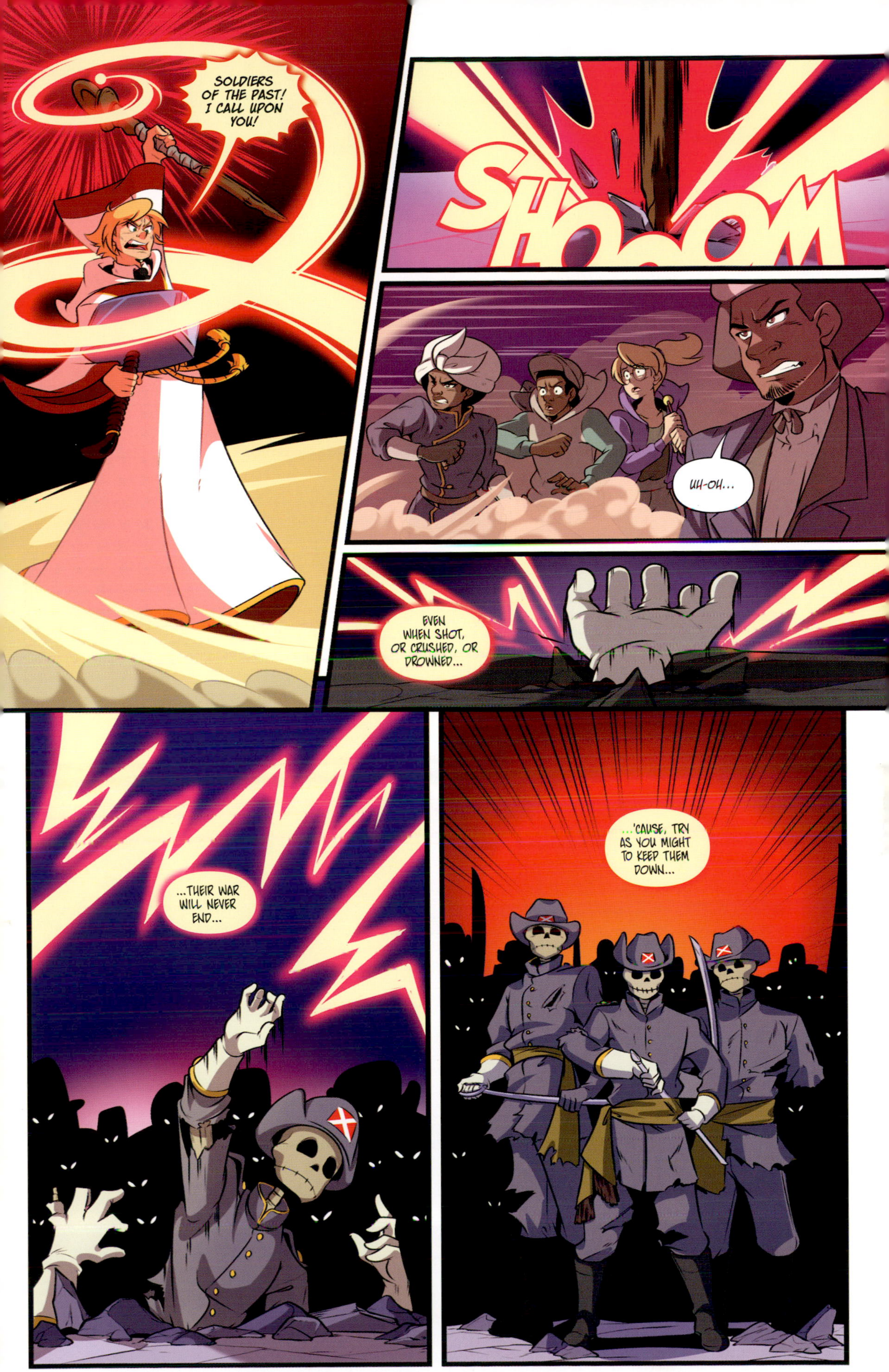
SOLDIERS OF THE PAST! I CALL UPON YOU!
SHOOOM
UH-OH...
EVEN WHEN SHOT, OR CRUSHED, OR DROWNED...
...THEIR WAR WILL NEVER END...
...'CAUSE, TRY AS YOU MIGHT TO KEEP THEM DOWN...

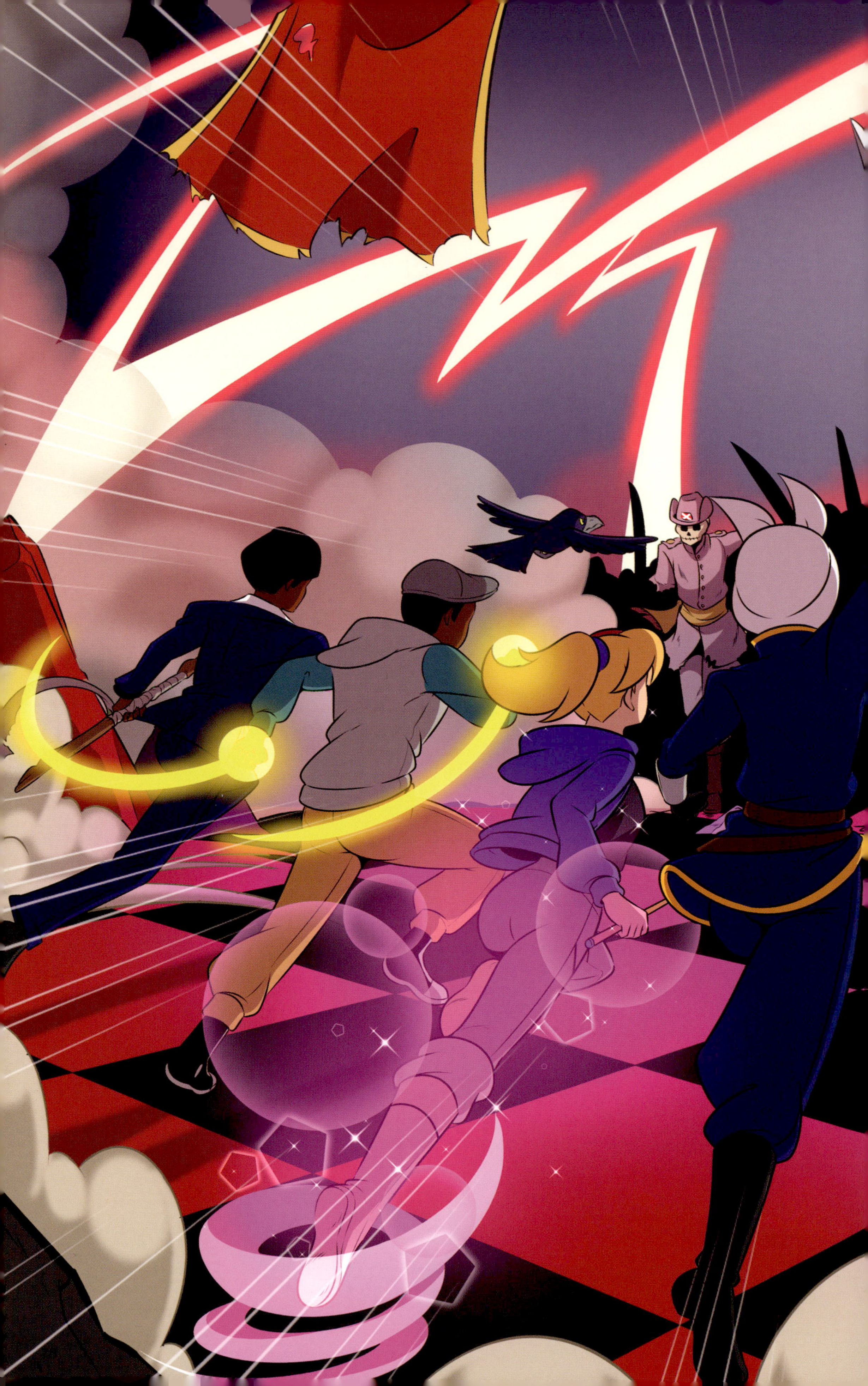

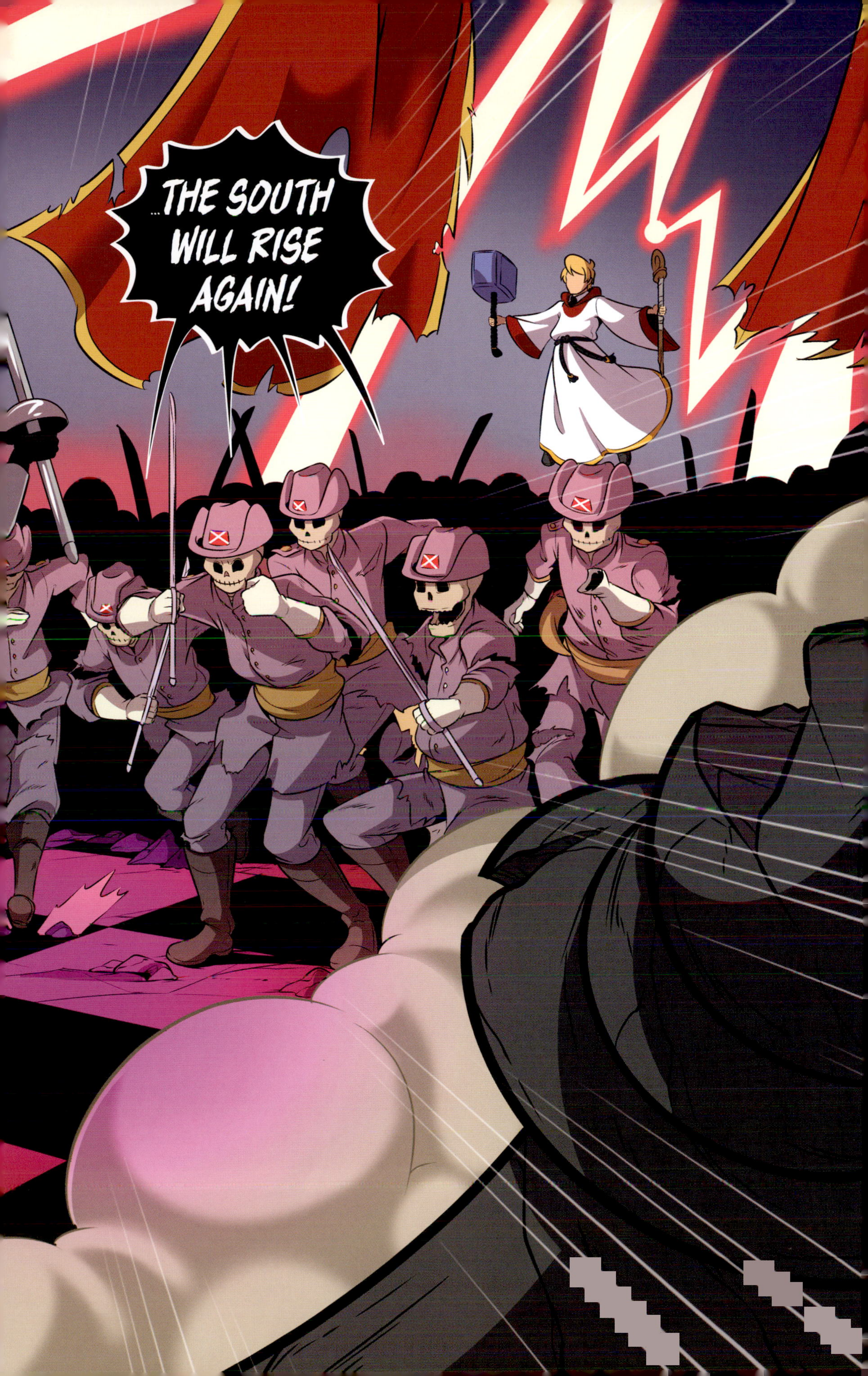
...THE SOUTH WILL RISE AGAIN!

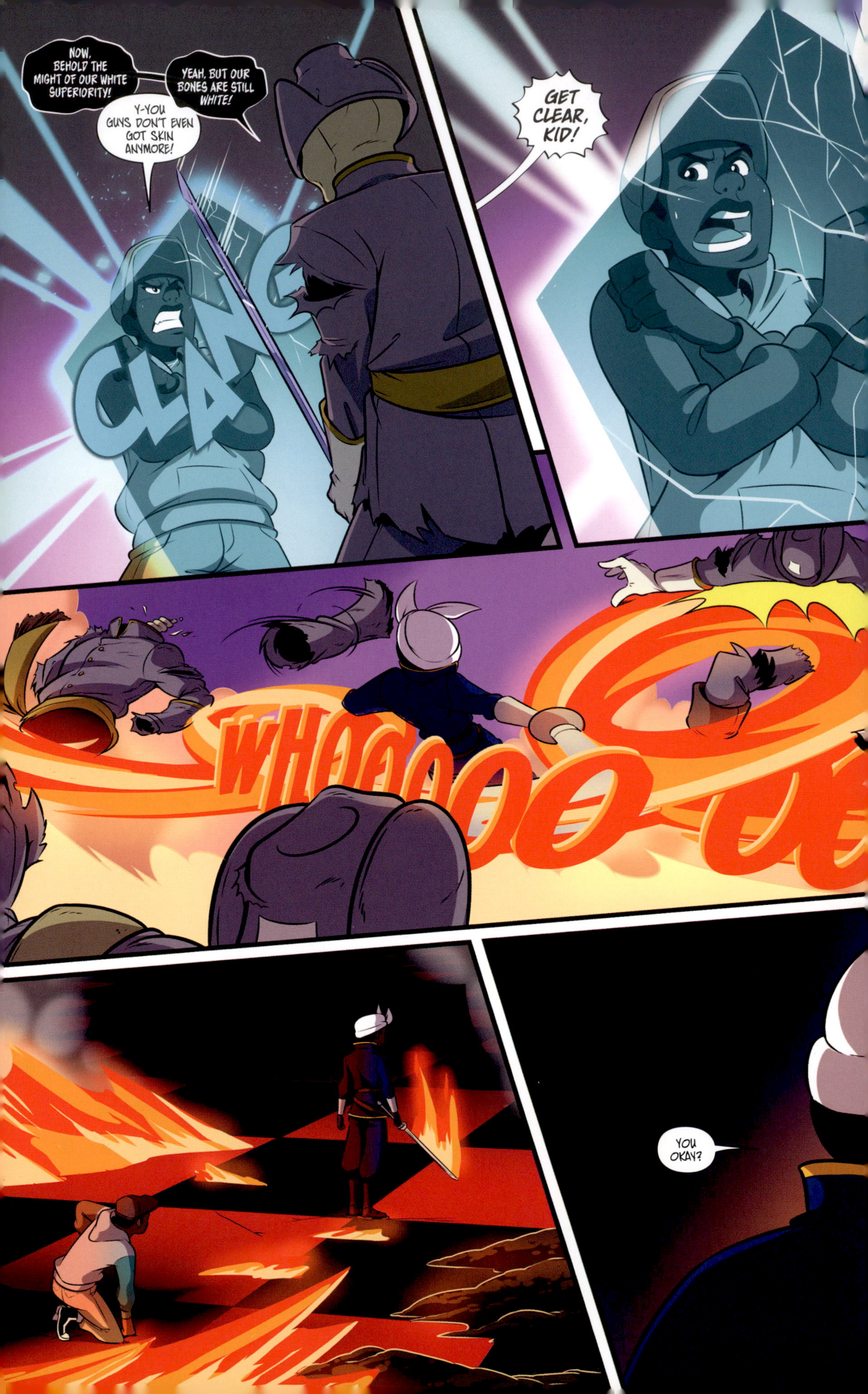
NOW, BEHOLD THE MIGHT OF OUR WHITE SUPERIORITY!
Y-YOU GUYS DON'T EVEN GOT SKIN ANYMORE!
YEAH, BUT OUR BONES ARE STILL WHITE!
CLANG
GET CLEAR, KID!
WHOOOOO-OO
YOU OKAY?

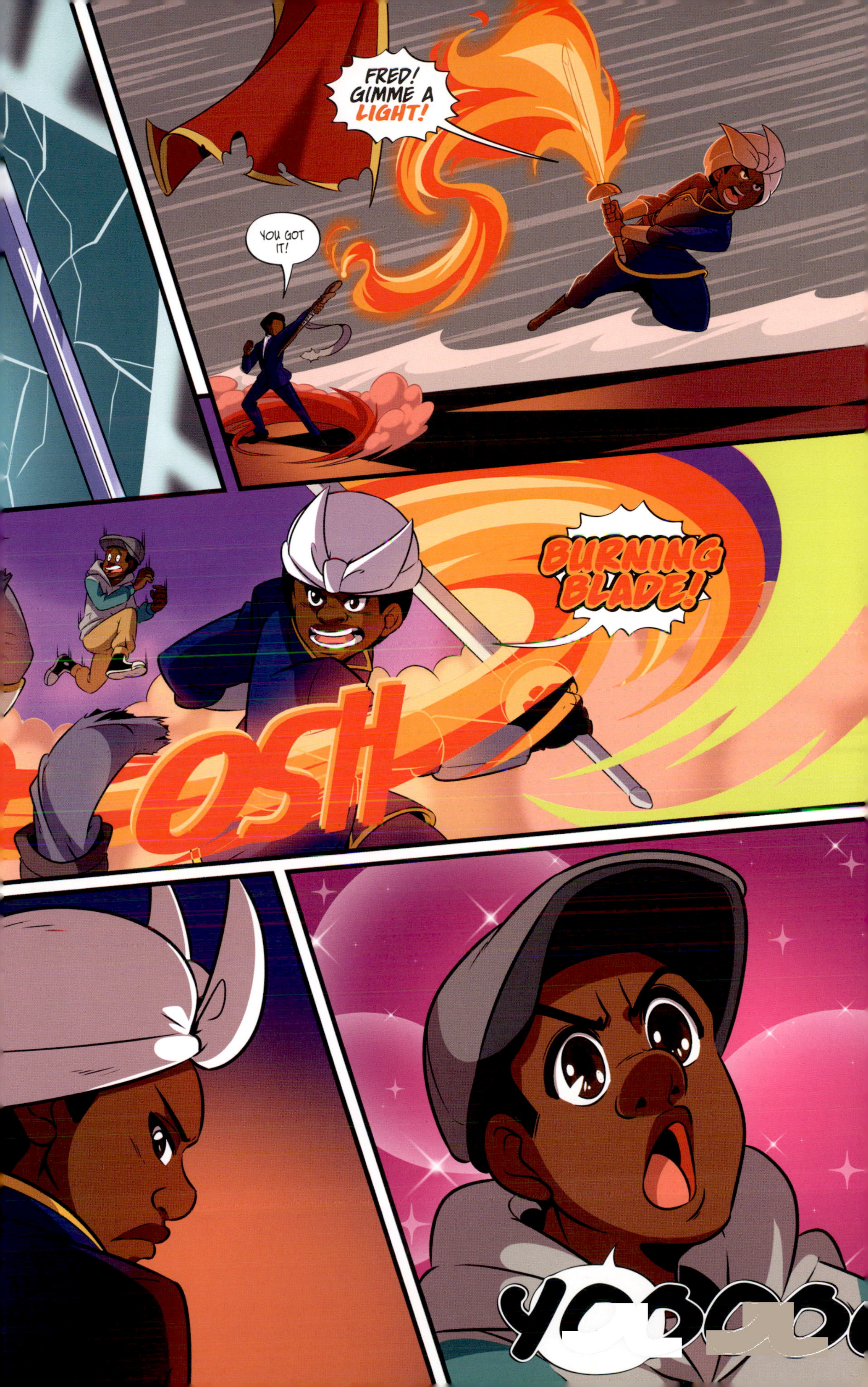
FRED! GIMME A LIGHT!
YOU GOT IT!
BURNING BLADE!
OSH

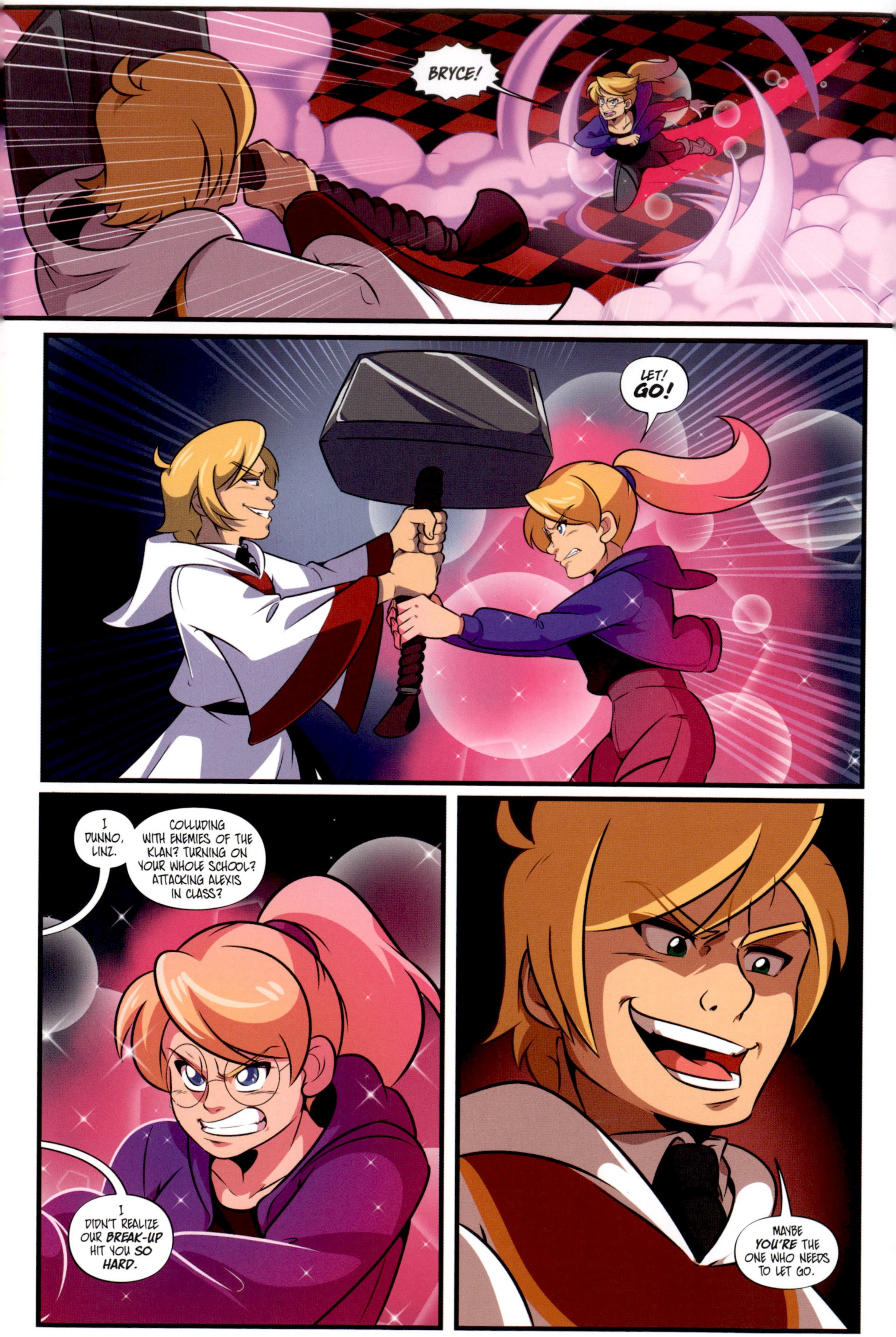
BRYCE!
LET! GO!
I DUNNO, LINZ.
COLLUDING WITH ENEMIES OF THE KLAN? TURNING ON YOUR WHOLE SCHOOL? ATTACKING ALEXIS IN CLASS?
I DIDN'T REALIZE OUR BREAK-UP HIT YOU SO HARD.
MAYBE YOU'RE THE ONE WHO NEEDS TO LET GO.

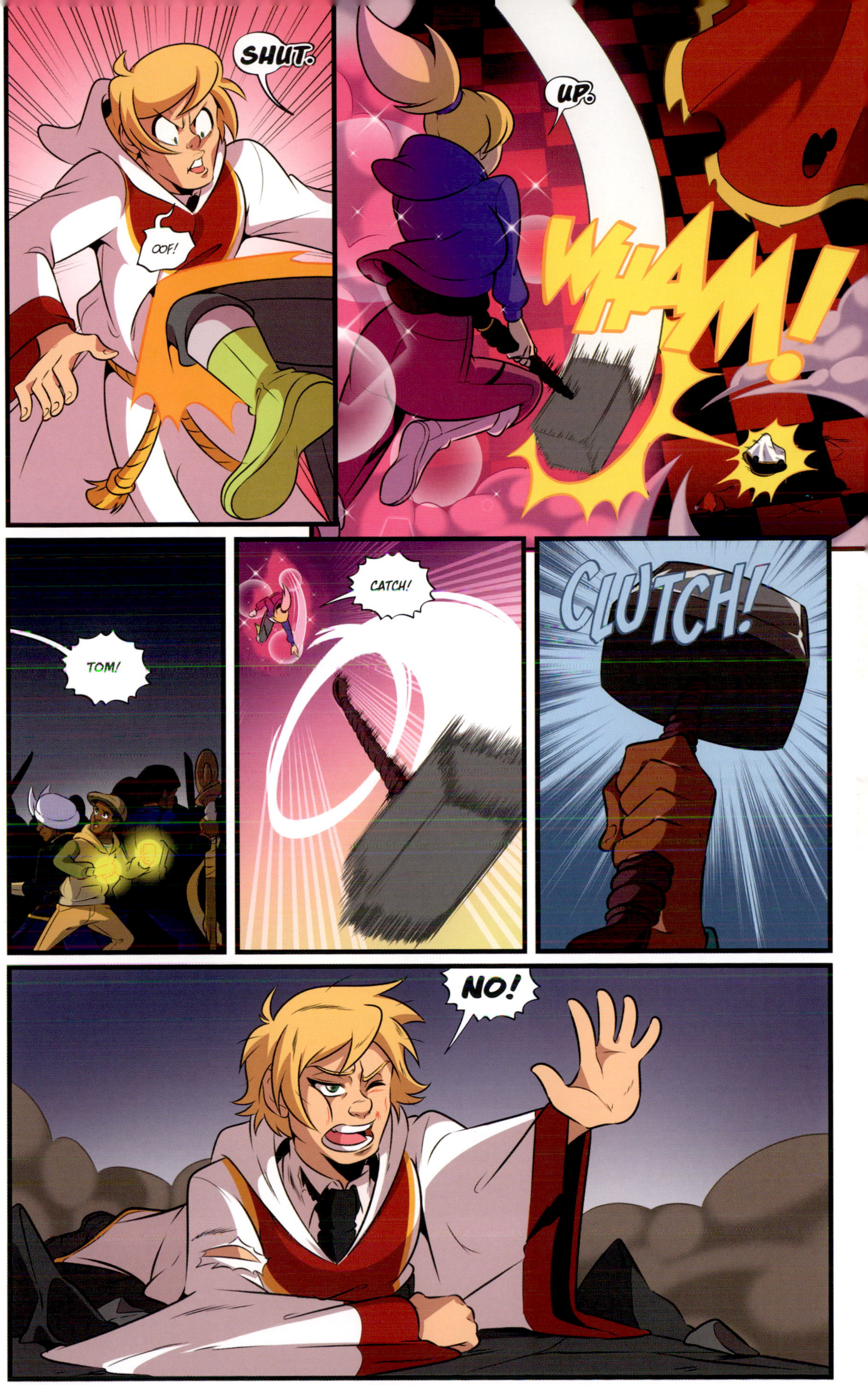
SHUT.
OOF!
UP.
WHAM!
TOM!
CATCH!
CLUTCH!
NO!

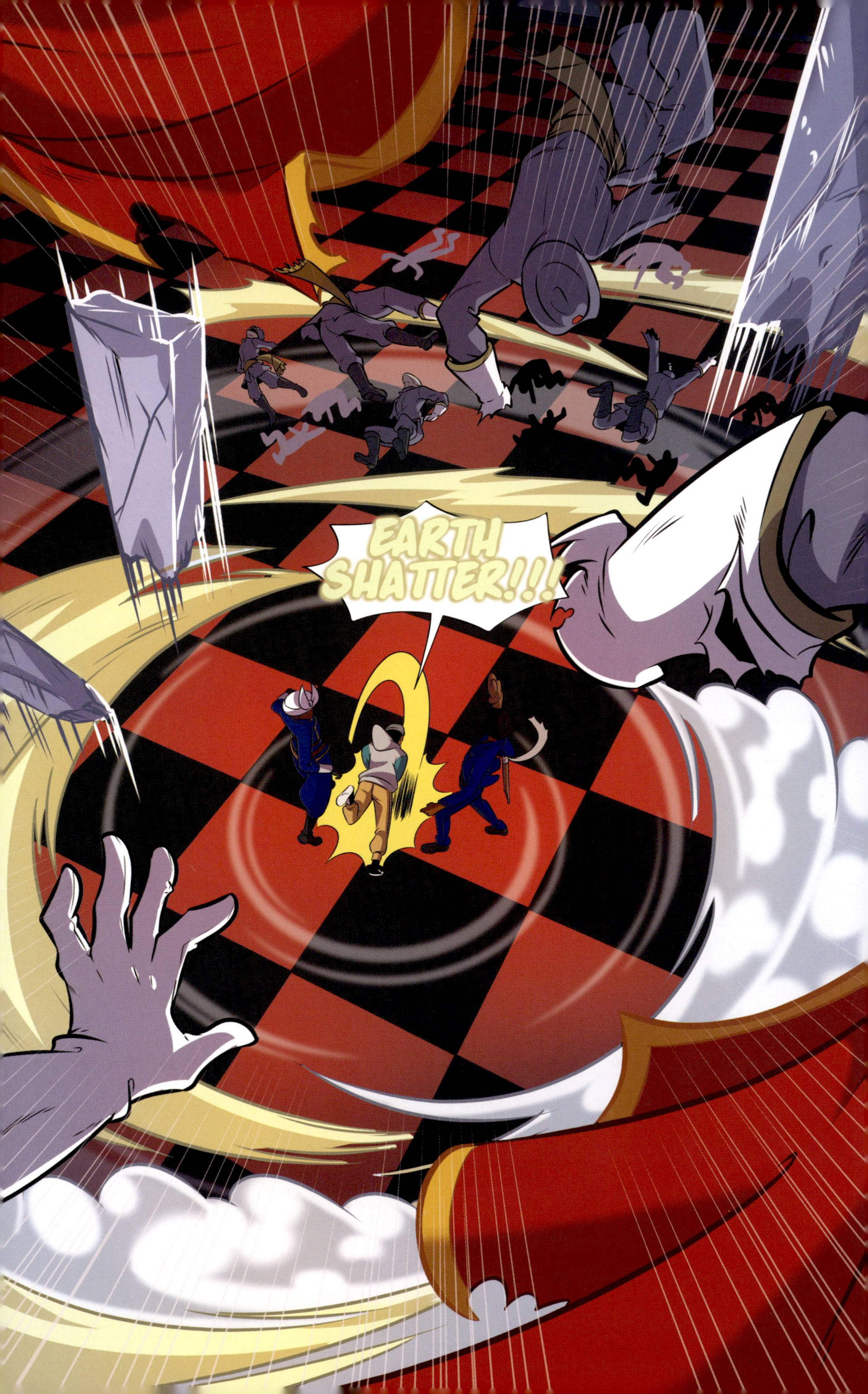
EARTH SHATTER!!!

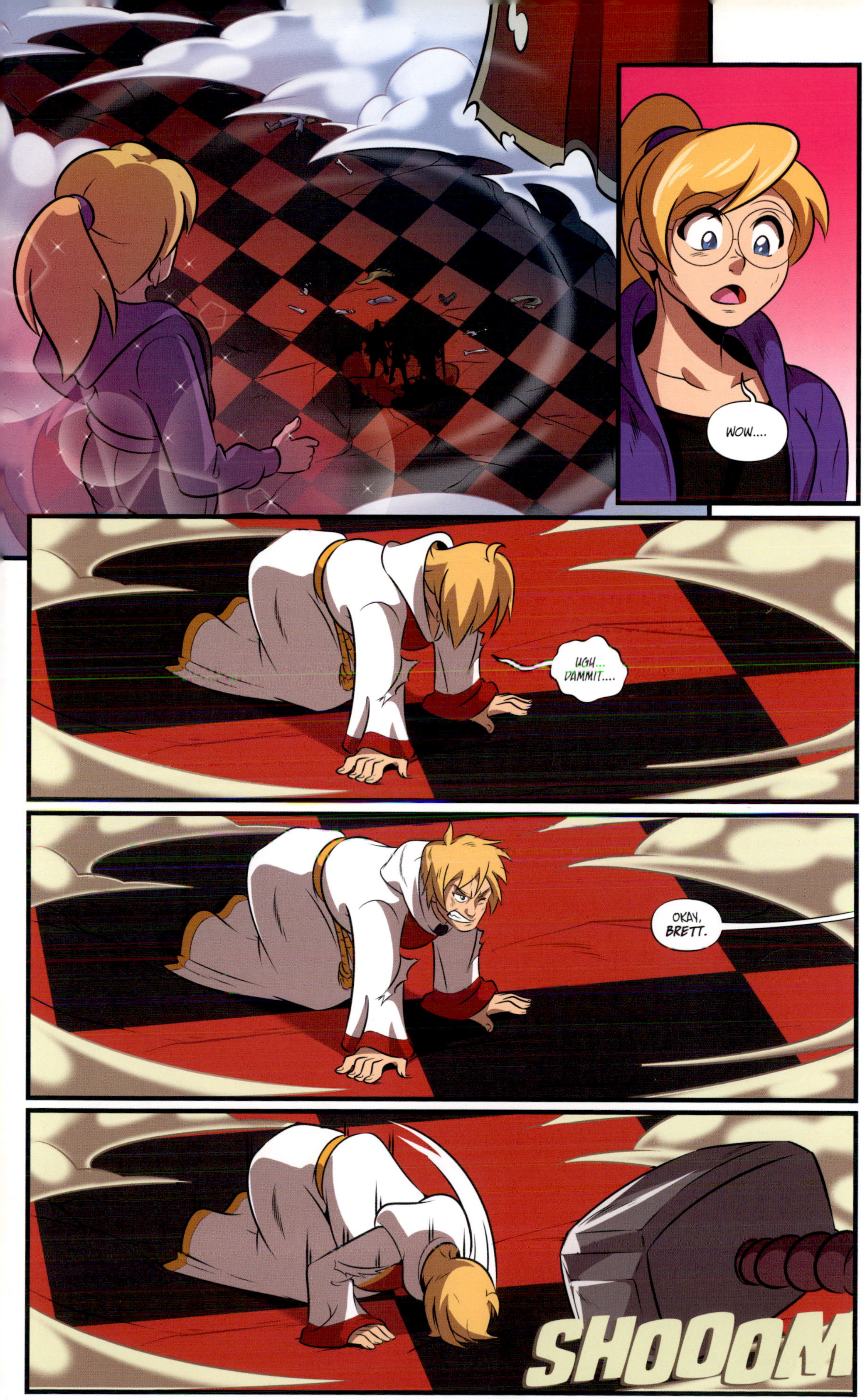

WOW....
UGH... DAMMIT....
OKAY, BRETT.
SHOOOM

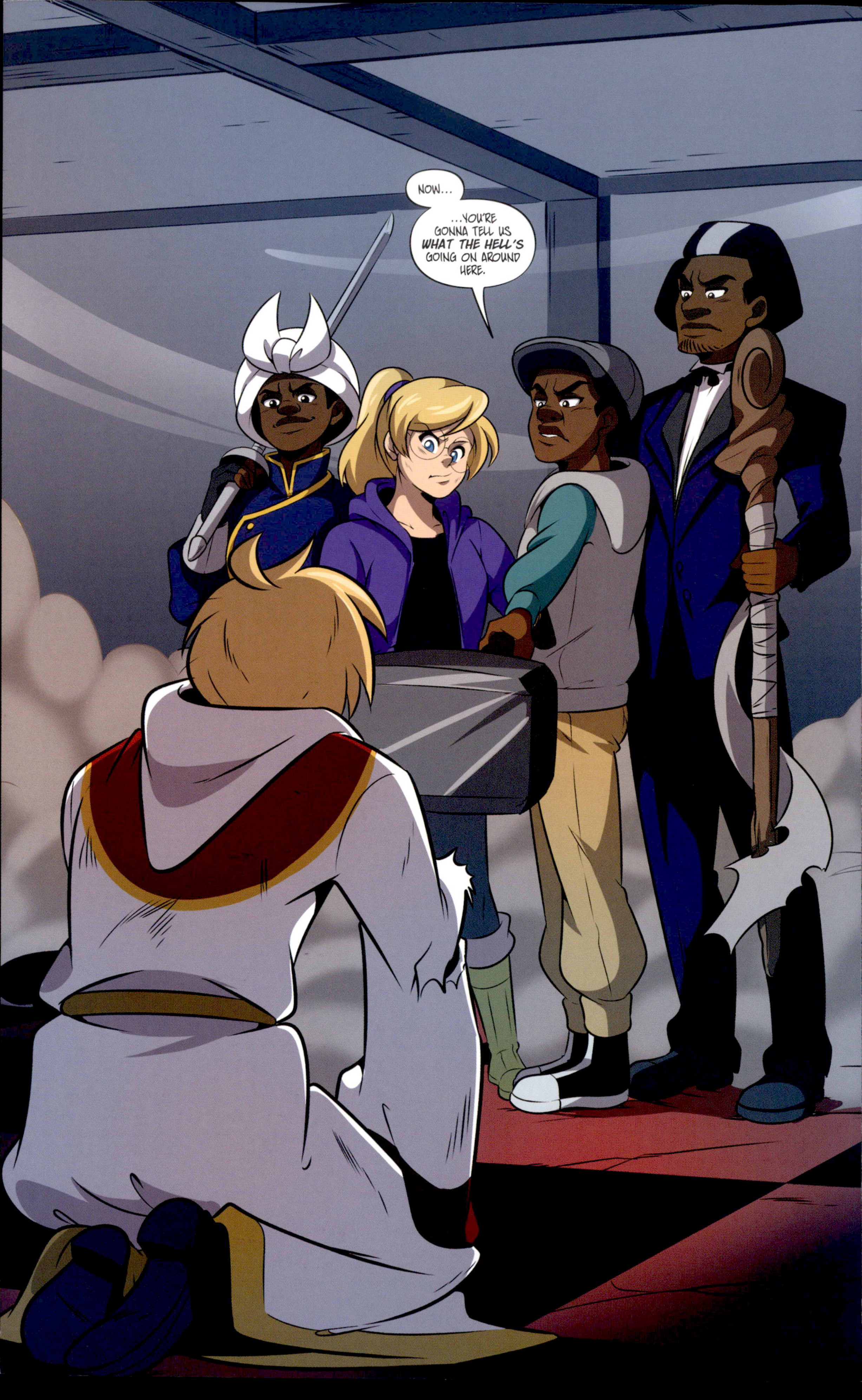
NOW...
...YOU'RE GONNA TELL US **WHAT THE HELL'S** GOING ON AROUND HERE.

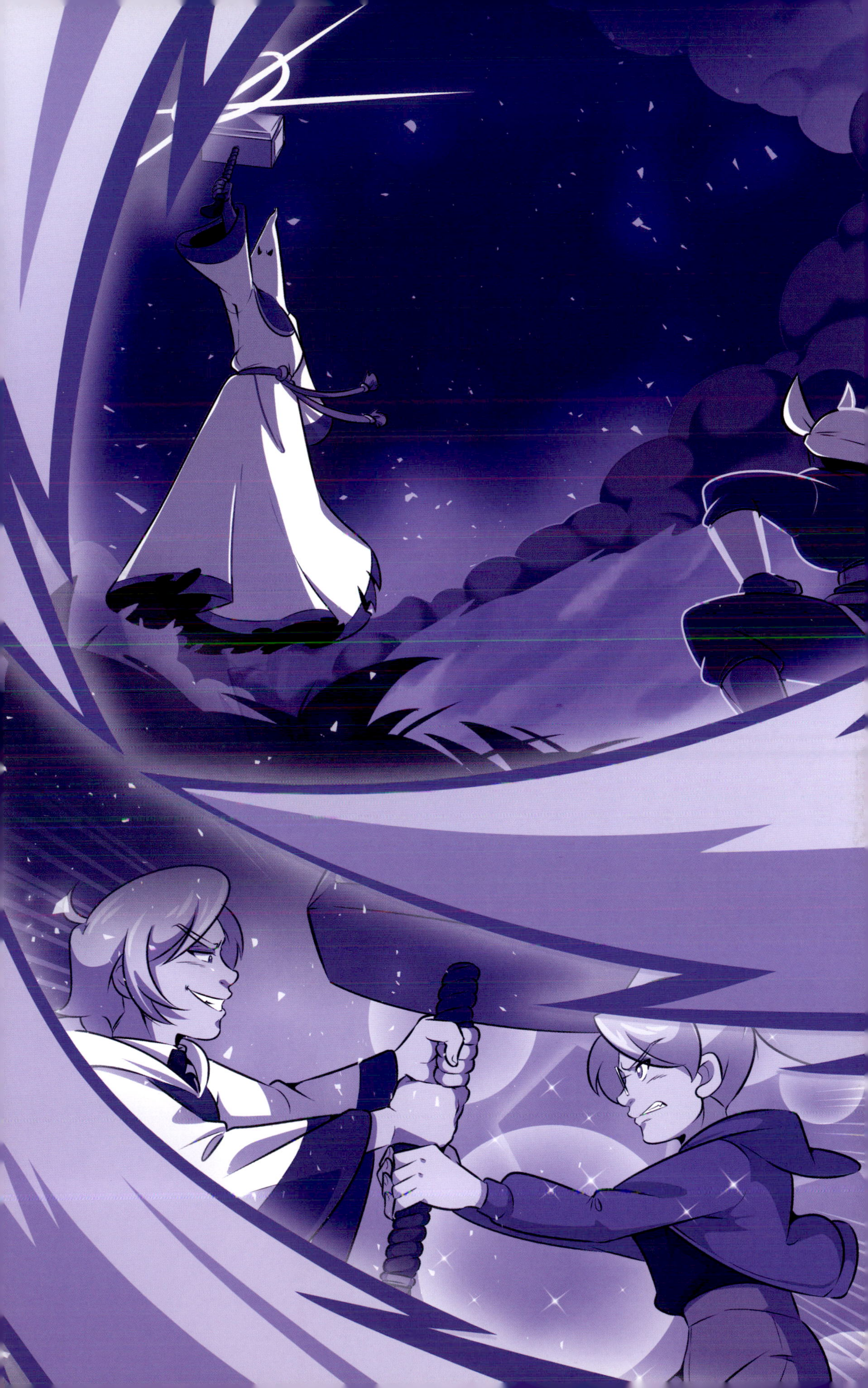

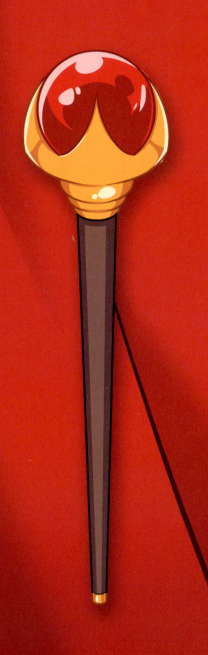

Chapter Four

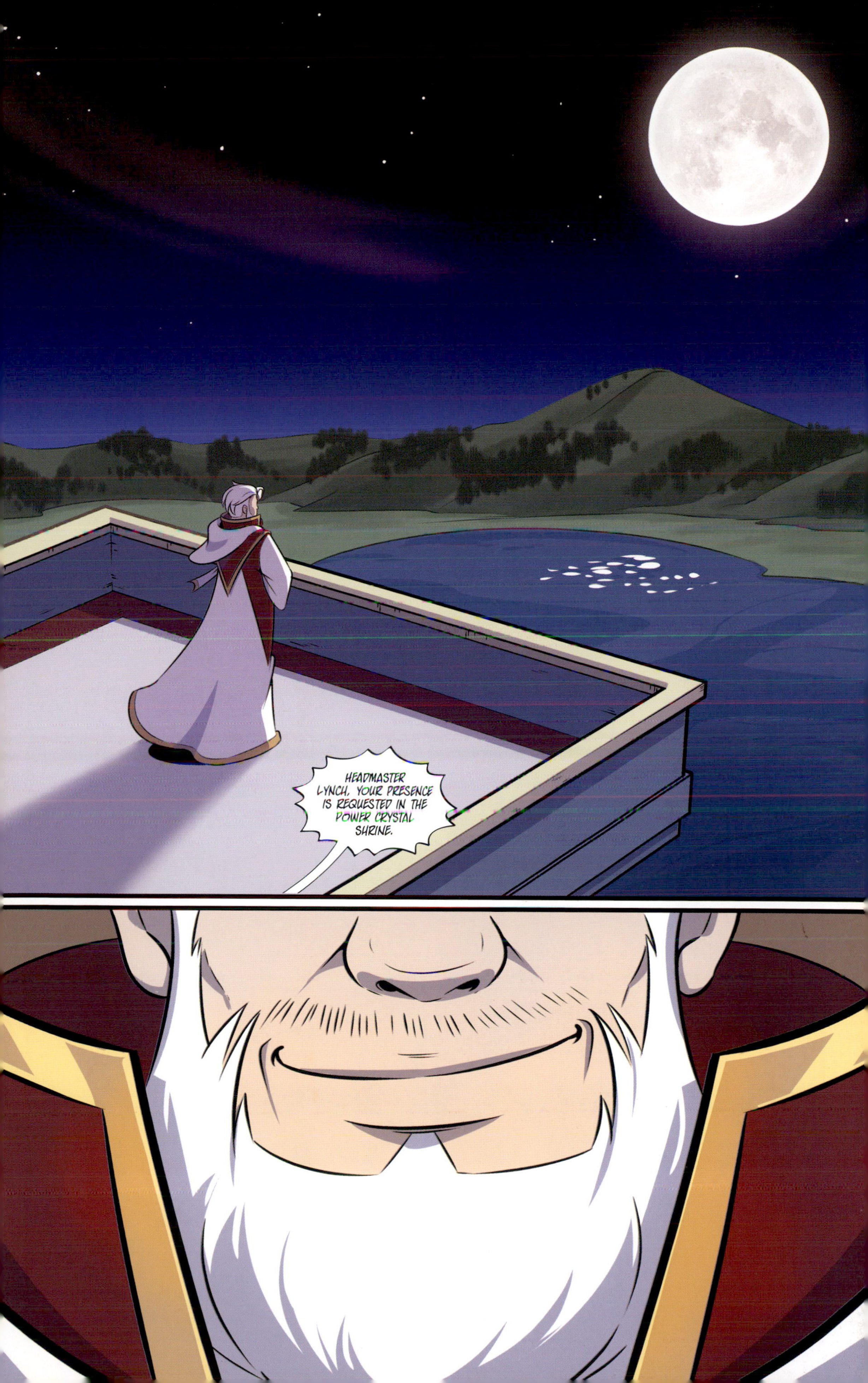
HEADMASTER LYNCH, YOUR PRESENCE IS REQUESTED IN THE POWER CRYSTAL SHRINE.

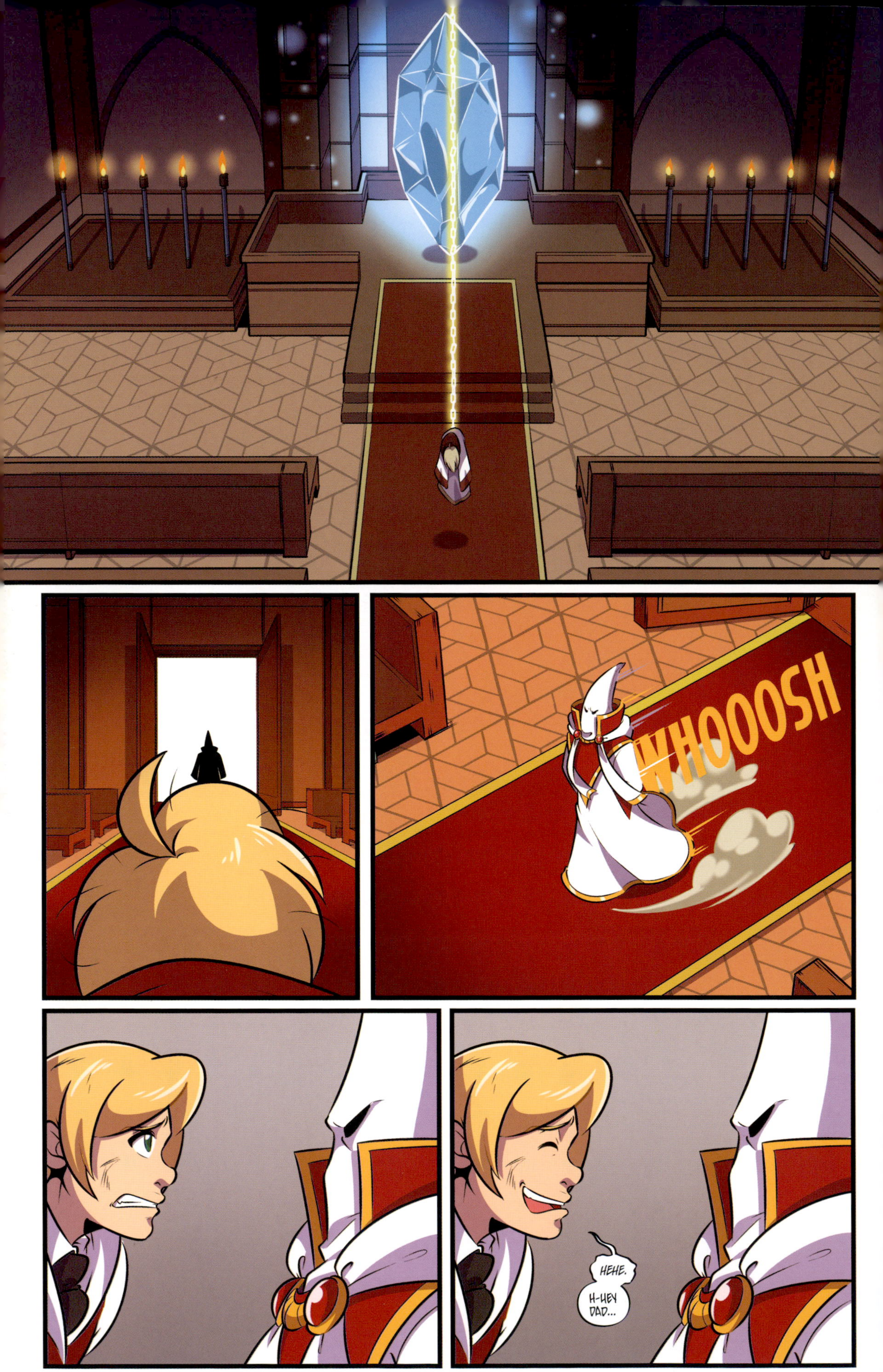
WHOOOSH
HEHE.
H-HEY DAD...

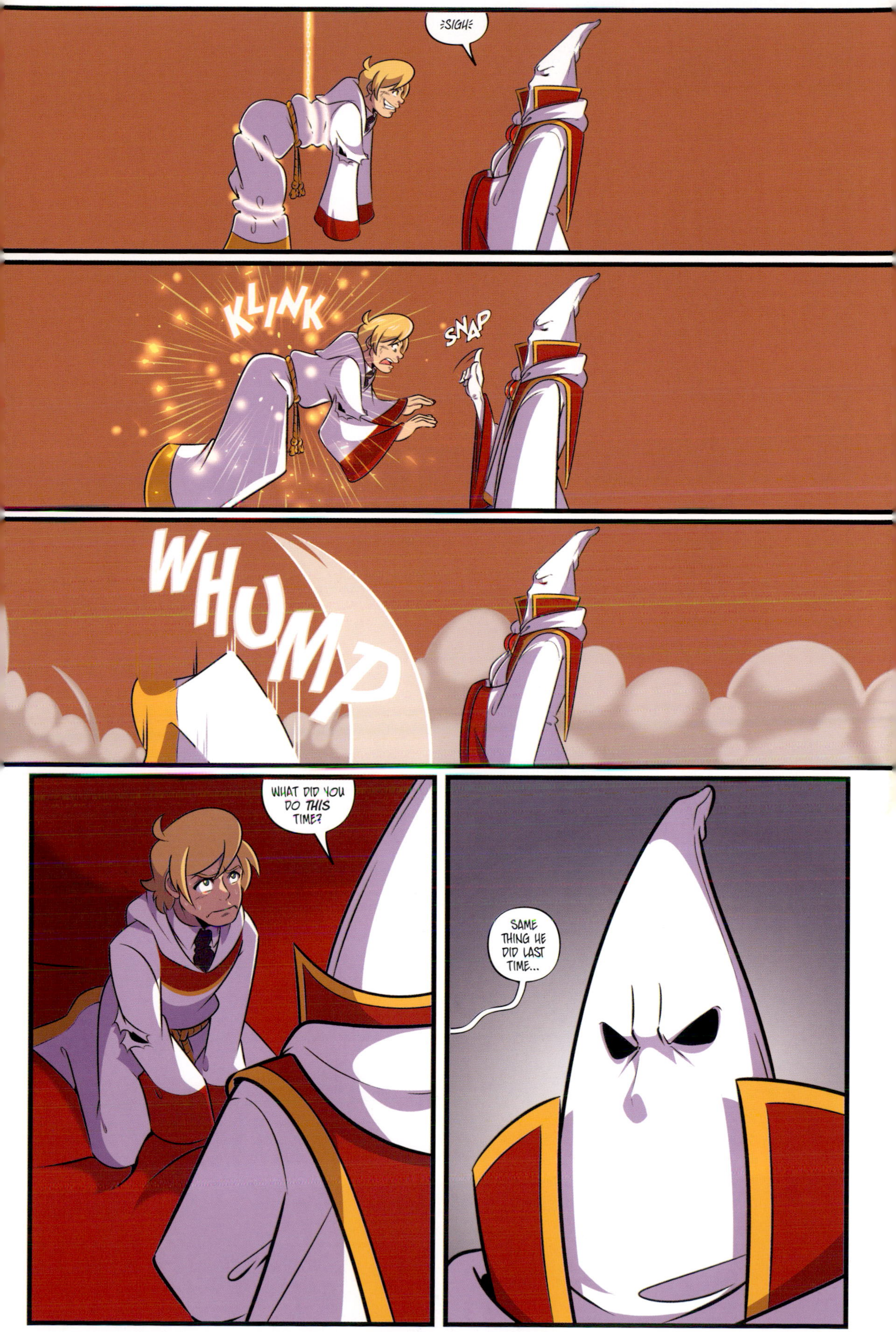

=SIGH=
KLINK
SNAP
WHUMP
WHAT DID YOU DO THIS TIME?
SAME THING HE DID LAST TIME...

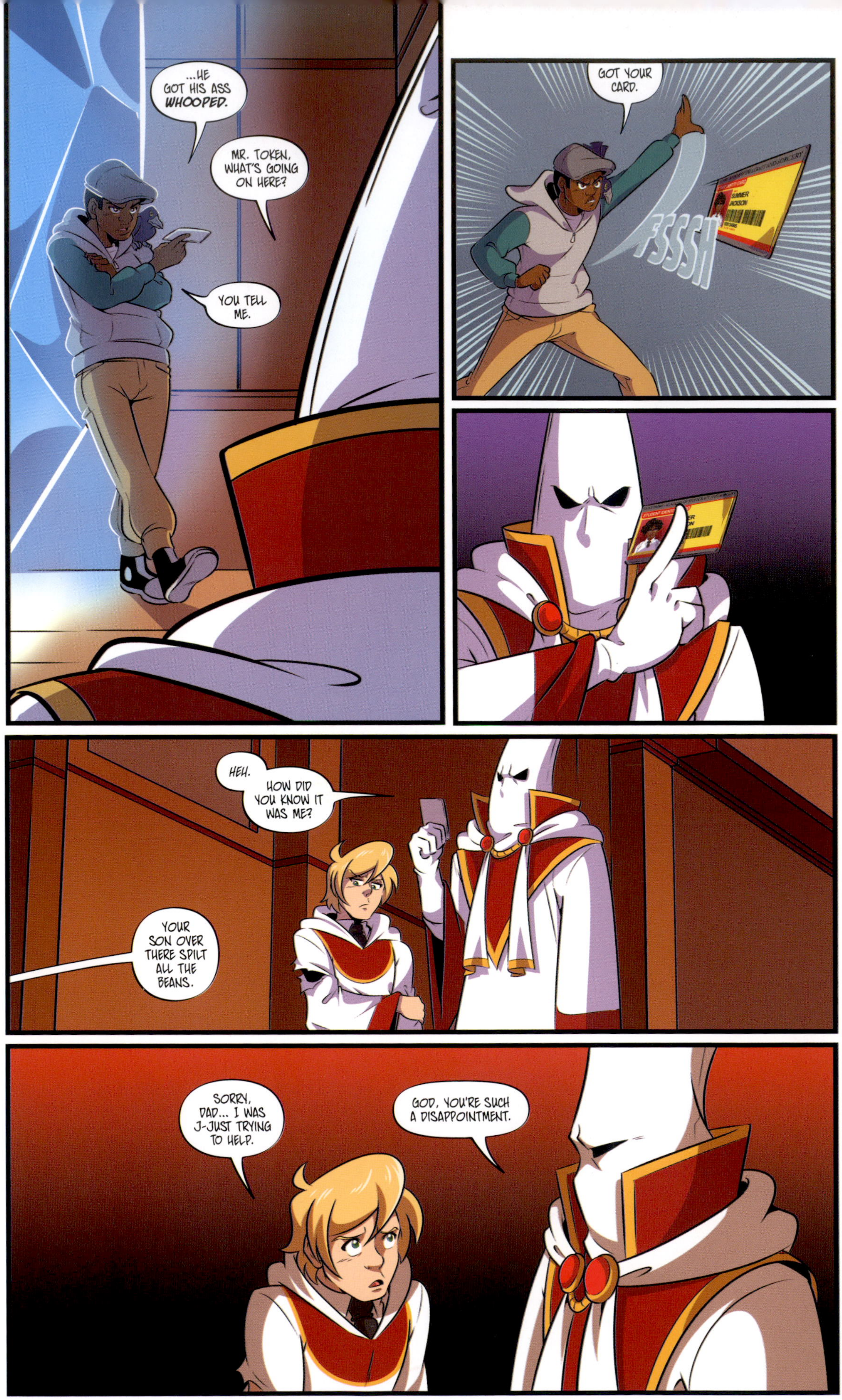
...HE GOT HIS ASS WHOOPED.
MR. TOKEN, WHAT'S GOING ON HERE?
YOU TELL ME.
GOT YOUR CARD.
FSSSH
HEH.
HOW DID YOU KNOW IT WAS ME?
YOUR SON OVER THERE SPILT ALL THE BEANS.
SORRY, DAD... I WAS J-JUST TRYING TO HELP.
GOD, YOU'RE SUCH A DISAPPOINTMENT.

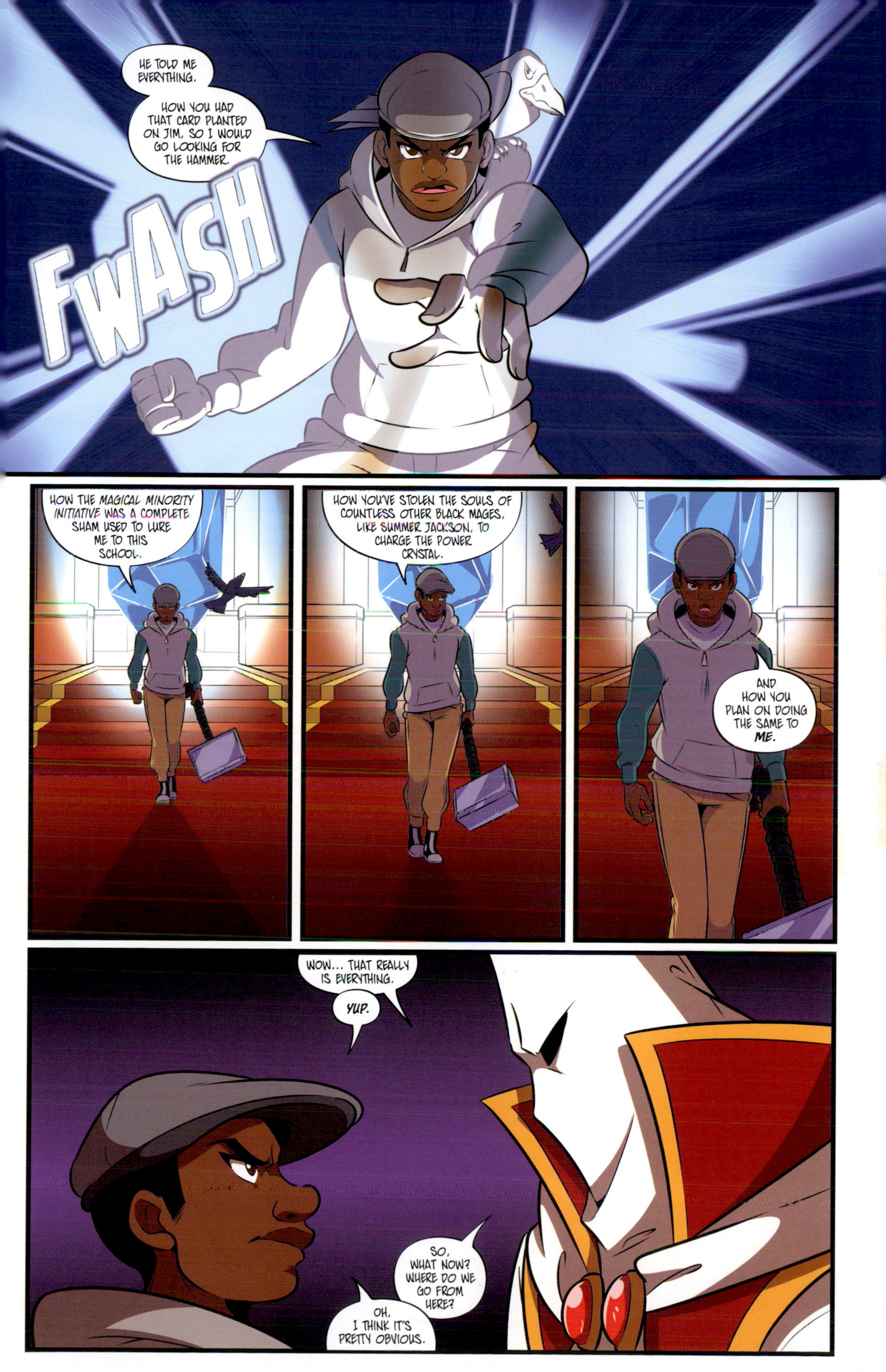
HE TOLD ME EVERYTHING.
HOW YOU HAD THAT CARD PLANTED ON JIM, SO I WOULD GO LOOKING FOR THE HAMMER.
FWASH
HOW THE *MAGICAL MINORITY INITIATIVE* WAS A COMPLETE SHAM USED TO LURE ME TO THIS SCHOOL.
HOW YOU'VE STOLEN THE SOULS OF COUNTLESS OTHER BLACK MAGES, LIKE SUMMER JACKSON, TO CHARGE THE POWER CRYSTAL.
AND HOW YOU PLAN ON DOING THE SAME TO **ME**.
WOW... THAT REALLY IS EVERYTHING.
YUP.
SO, WHAT NOW? WHERE DO WE GO FROM HERE?
OH, I THINK IT'S PRETTY OBVIOUS.

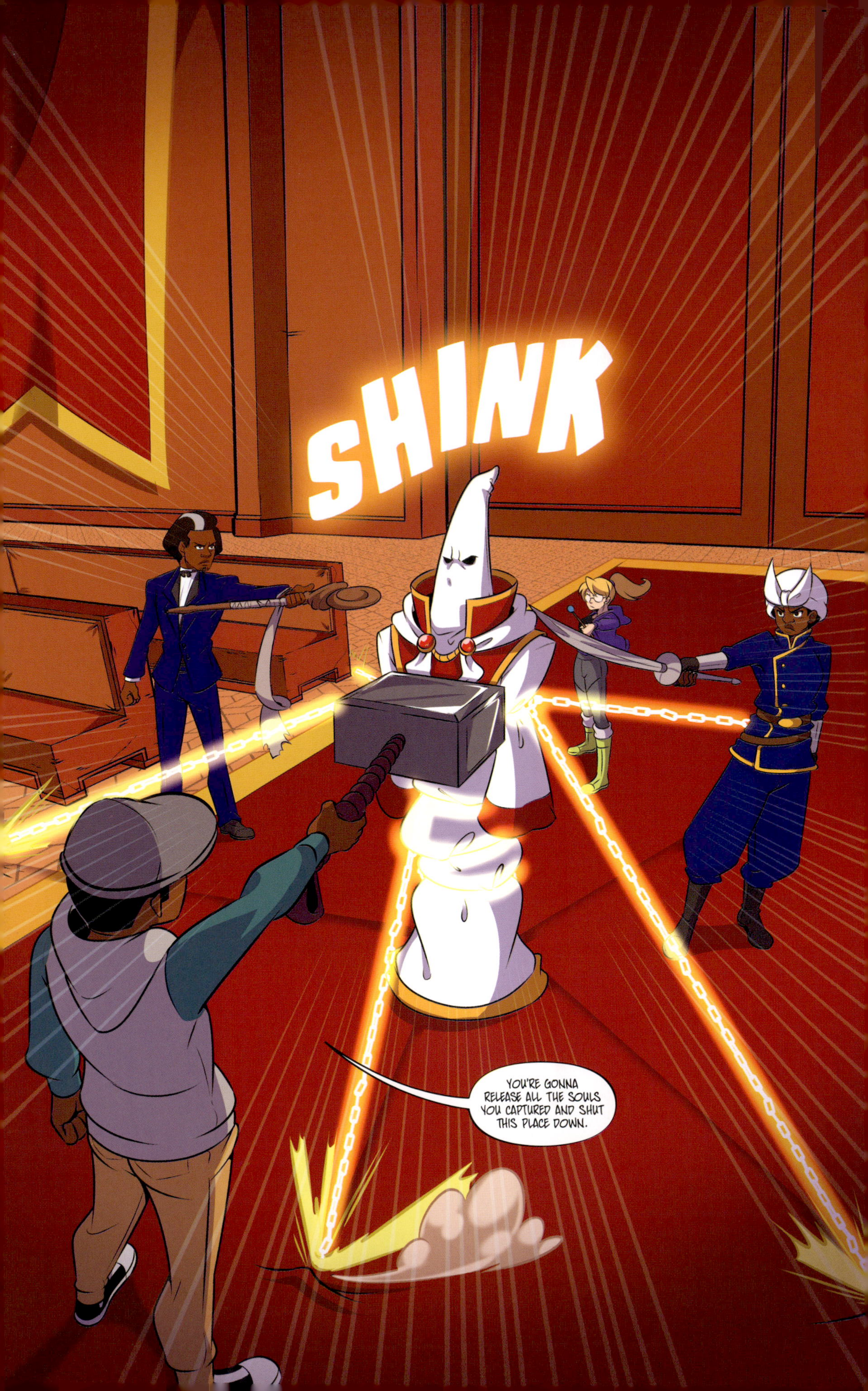
SHINK
YOU'RE GONNA RELEASE ALL THE SOULS YOU CAPTURED AND SHUT THIS PLACE DOWN.

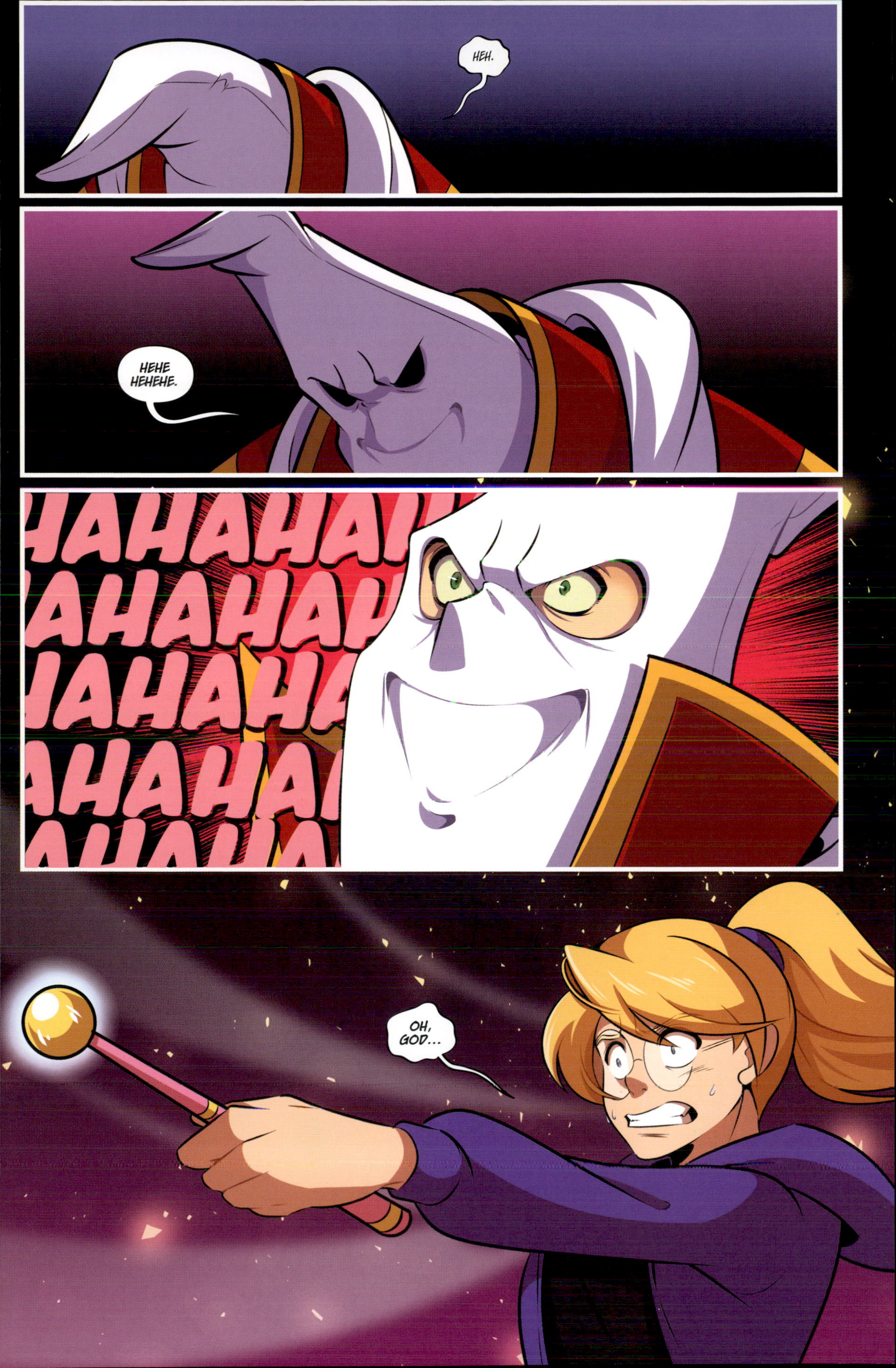
HEH.
HEHE HEHEHE.
HAHAHAHAHAHAHAHAHAHAHAHAHAHAHAHAHAHAHA
OH, GOD...

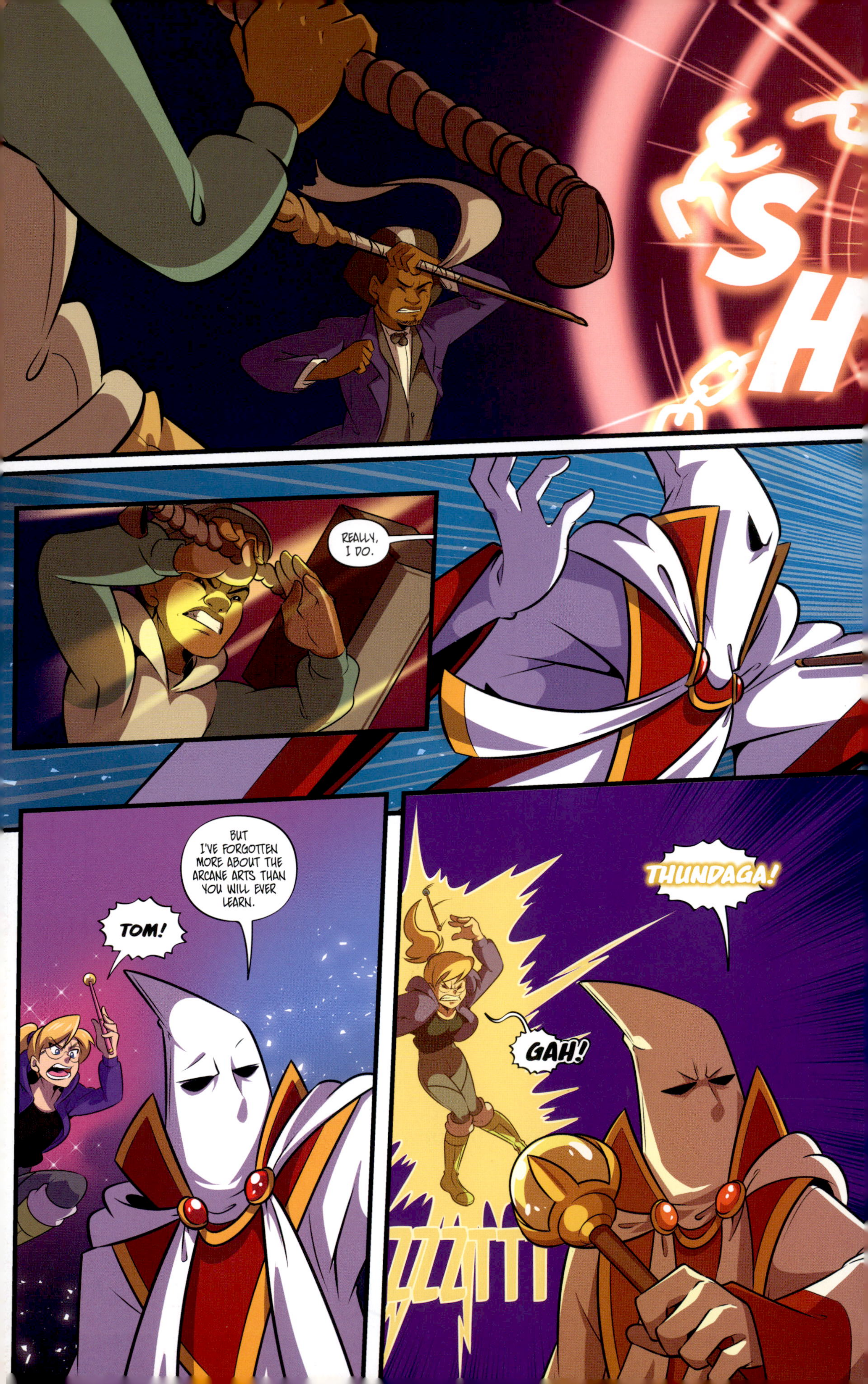
SH
REALLY, I DO.
BUT I'VE FORGOTTEN MORE ABOUT THE ARCANE ARTS THAN YOU WILL EVER LEARN.
TOM!
THUNDAGA!
GAH!
ZZZTTT

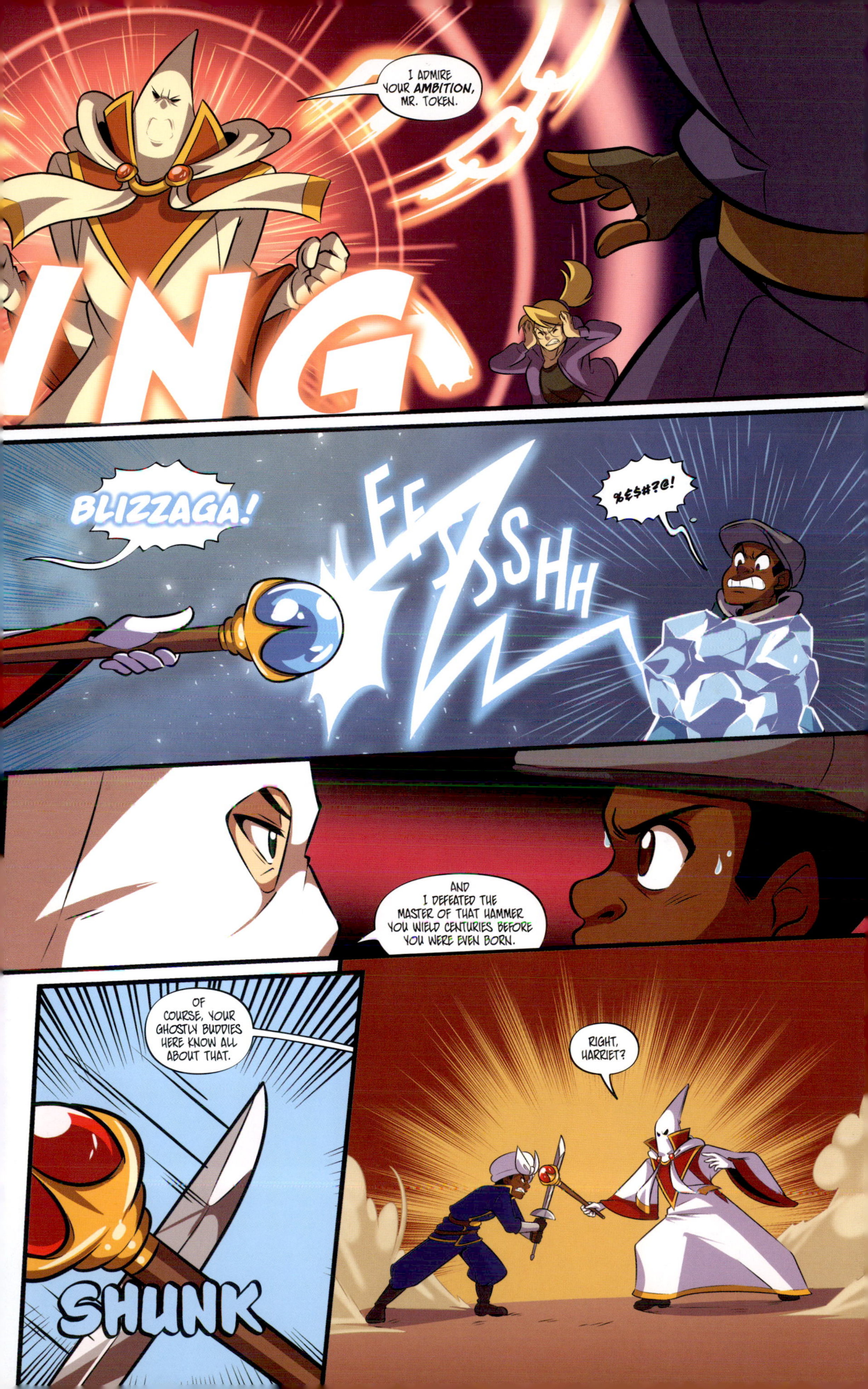

I ADMIRE YOUR AMBITION, MR. TOKEN.
ING
BLIZZAGA!
EEESSHH
%€$#?@!
AND I DEFEATED THE MASTER OF THAT HAMMER YOU WIELD CENTURIES BEFORE YOU WERE EVEN BORN.
OF COURSE, YOUR GHOSTLY BUDDIES HERE KNOW ALL ABOUT THAT.
SHUNK
RIGHT, HARRIET?

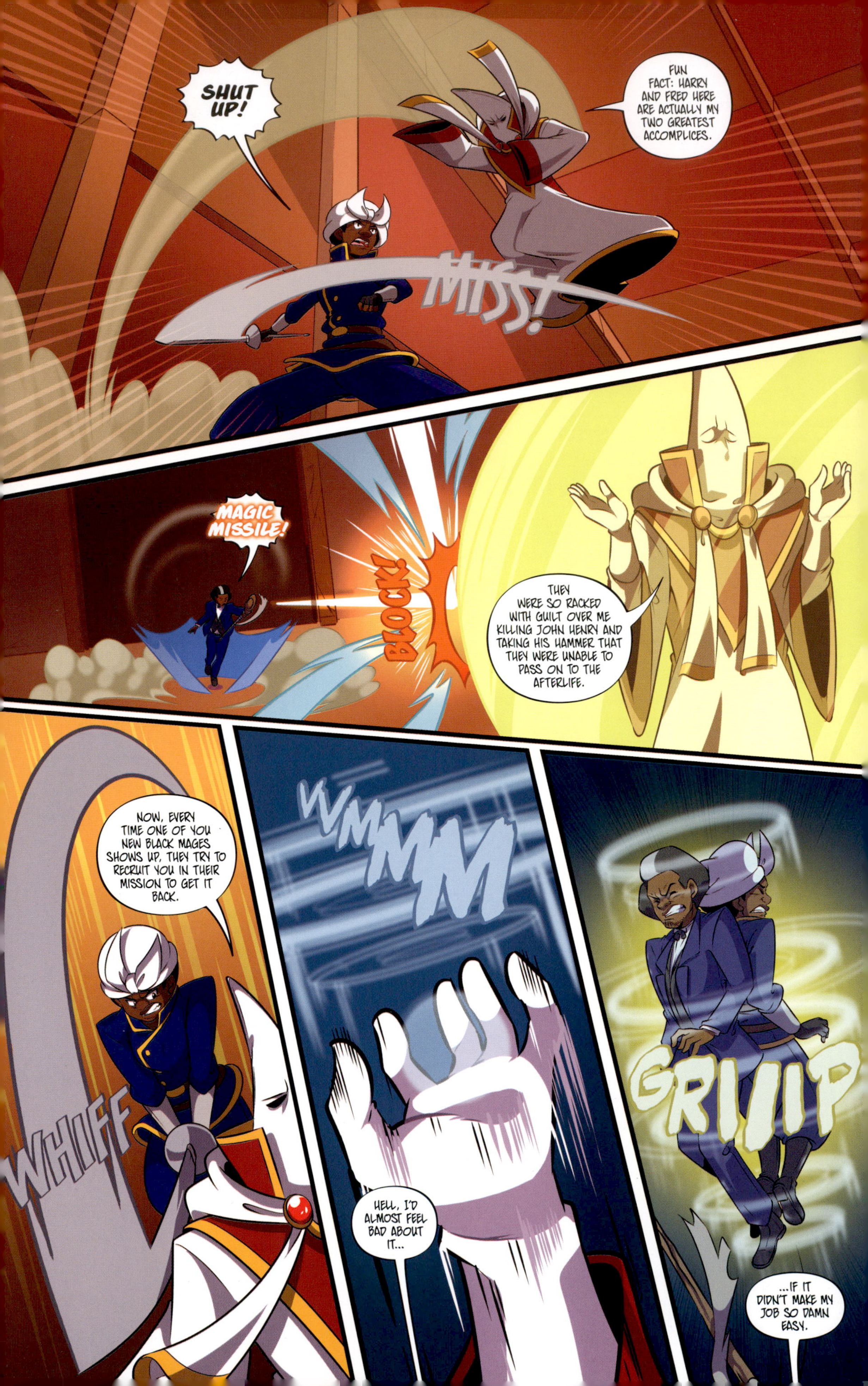
SHUT UP!
FUN FACT: HARRY AND FRED HERE ARE ACTUALLY MY TWO GREATEST ACCOMPLICES.
MISS!
MAGIC MISSILE!
BLOCK!
THEY WERE SO RACKED WITH GUILT OVER ME KILLING JOHN HENRY AND TAKING HIS HAMMER THAT THEY WERE UNABLE TO PASS ON TO THE AFTERLIFE.
NOW, EVERY TIME ONE OF YOU NEW BLACK MAGES SHOWS UP, THEY TRY TO RECRUIT YOU IN THEIR MISSION TO GET IT BACK.
WHIFF
VVMMMM
HELL, I'D ALMOST FEEL BAD ABOUT IT...
GRIIIP
...IF IT DIDN'T MAKE MY JOB SO DAMN EASY.

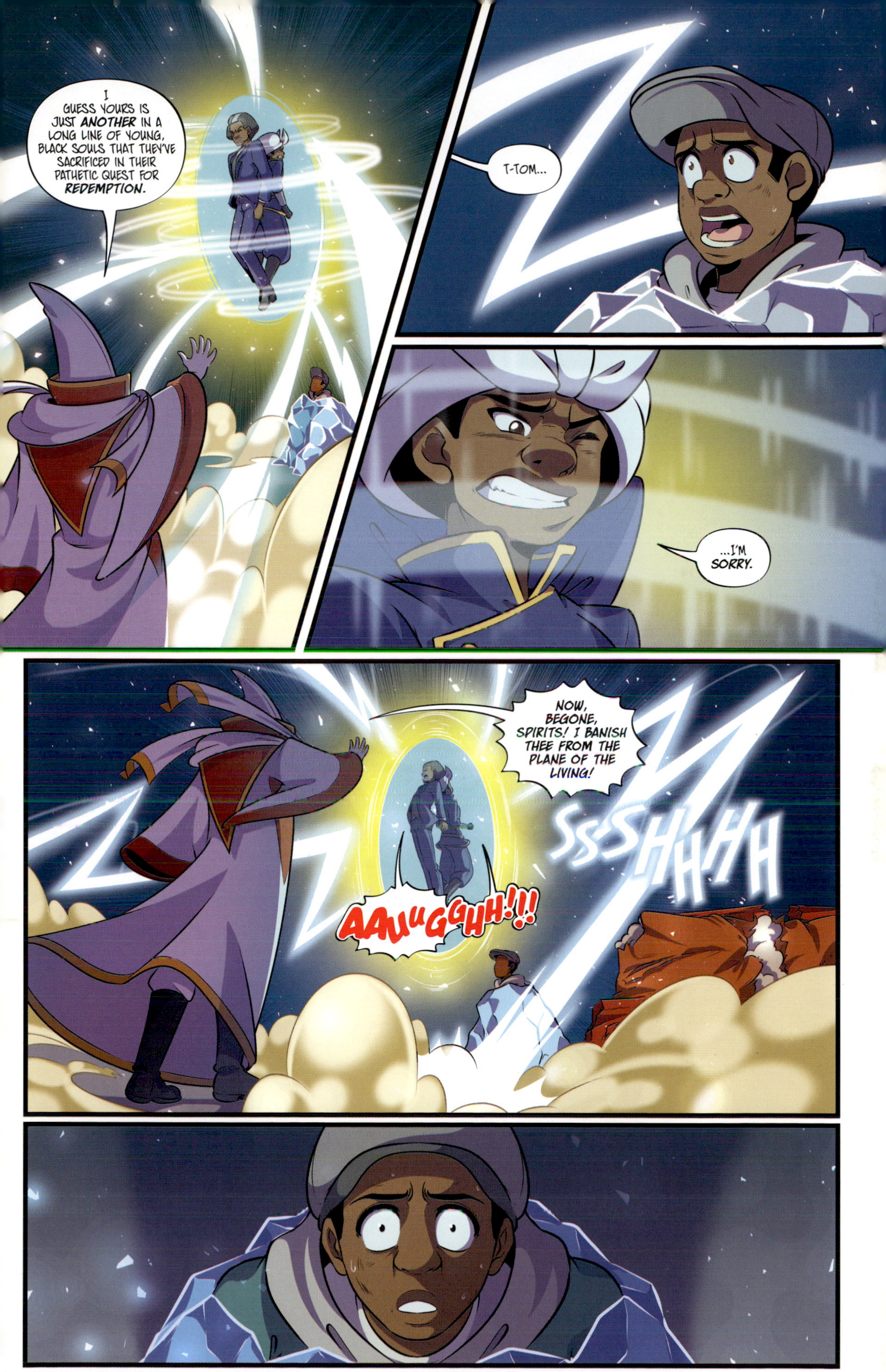
I GUESS YOURS IS JUST ANOTHER IN A LONG LINE OF YOUNG, BLACK SOULS THAT THEY'VE SACRIFICED IN THEIR PATHETIC QUEST FOR REDEMPTION.
T-TOM...
...I'M SORRY.
NOW, BEGONE, SPIRITS! I BANISH THEE FROM THE PLANE OF THE LIVING!
SS-SHHHHH
AAUUGGHH!!!

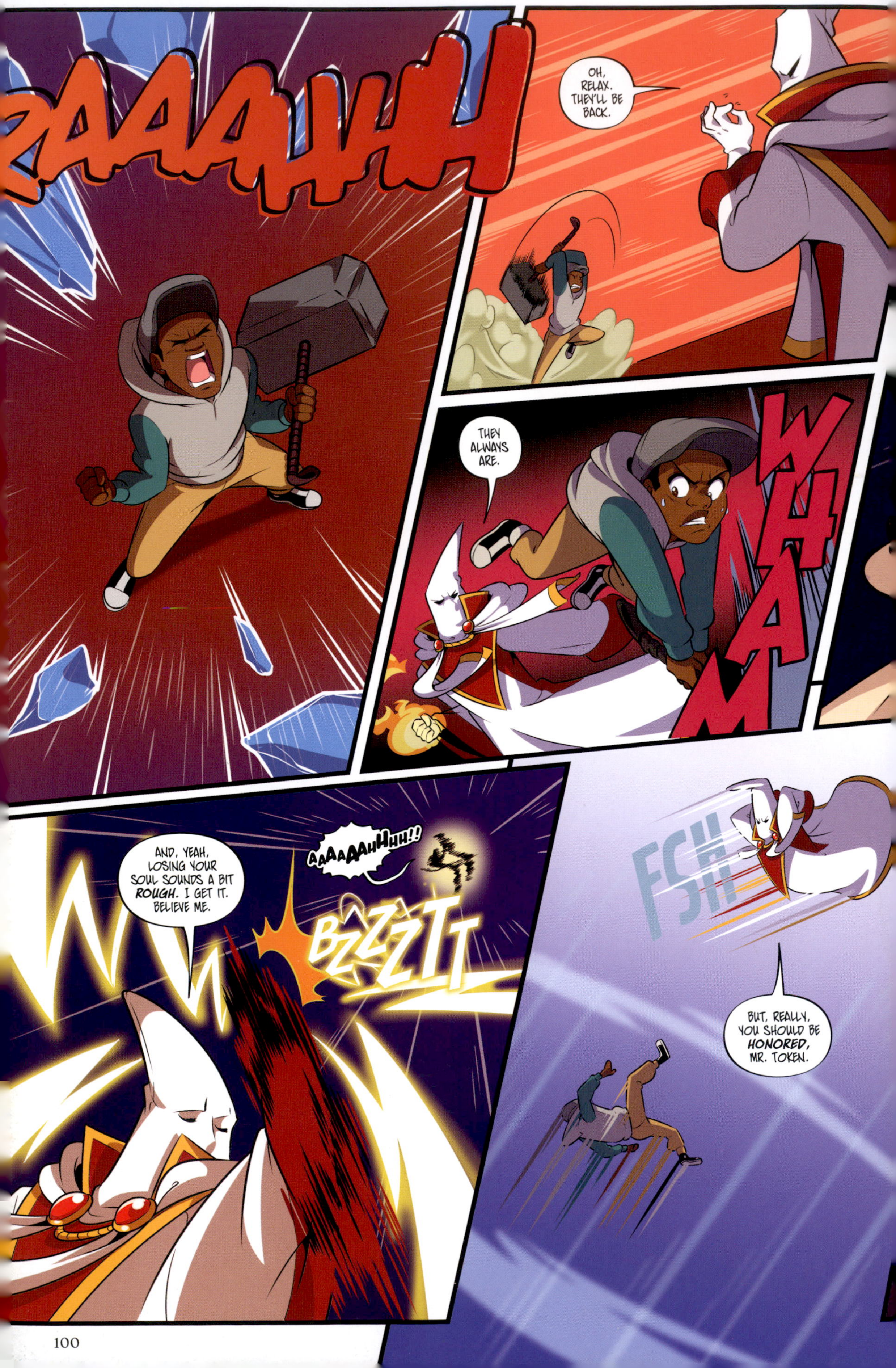
RAAAAHH
OH, RELAX. THEY'LL BE BACK.
THEY ALWAYS ARE.
WHAM
AND, YEAH, LOSING YOUR SOUL SOUNDS A BIT ROUGH. I GET IT. BELIEVE ME.
AAAAAHHHH!!
BZZZTT
FSH
BUT, REALLY, YOU SHOULD BE HONORED, MR. TOKEN.

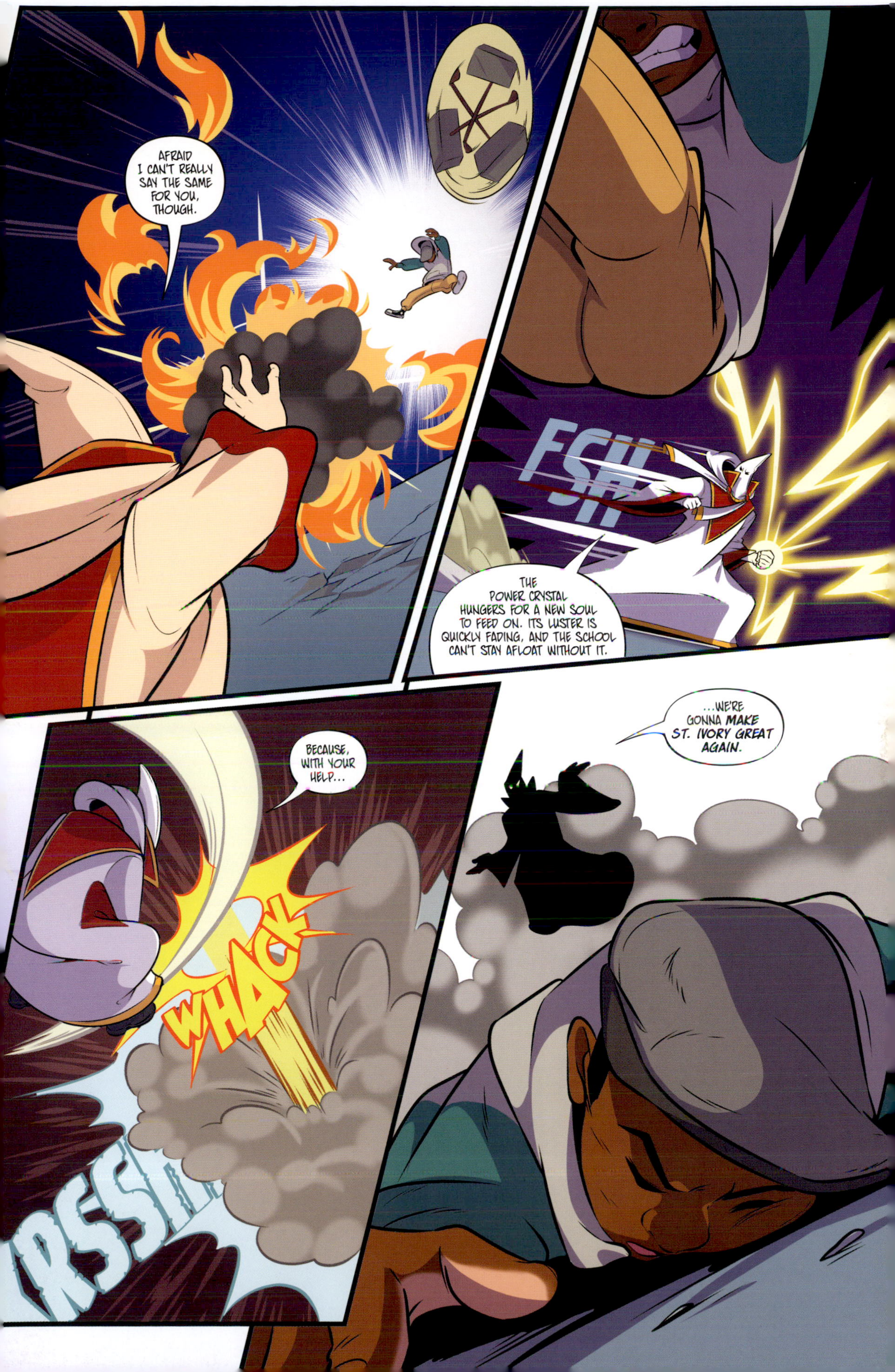
AFRAID I CAN'T REALLY SAY THE SAME FOR YOU, THOUGH.
FSH
THE POWER CRYSTAL HUNGERS FOR A NEW SOUL TO FEED ON. ITS LUSTER IS QUICKLY FADING, AND THE SCHOOL CAN'T STAY AFLOAT WITHOUT IT.
BECAUSE, WITH YOUR HELP...
WHACK
...WE'RE GONNA MAKE ST. IVORY GREAT AGAIN.

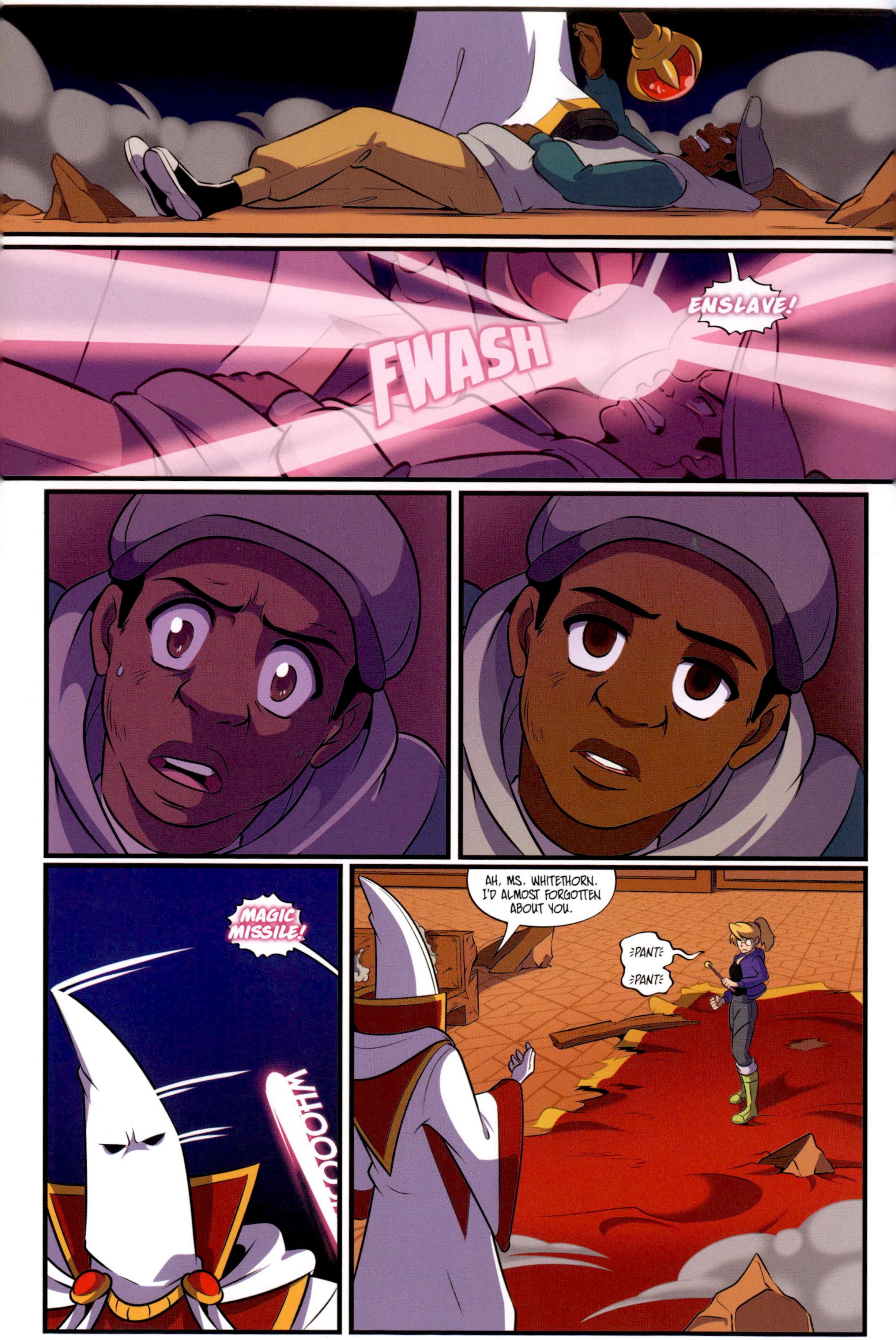
ENSLAVE!
FWASH
MAGIC MISSILE!
WHOOOOH
AH, MS. WHITETHORN. I'D ALMOST FORGOTTEN ABOUT YOU.
PANT
PANT

MR. TOKEN, TAKE CARE OF HER, PLEASE.

YES, MASSA...

T-TOM...?

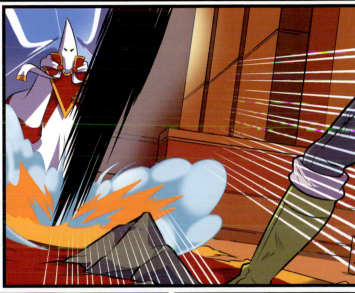

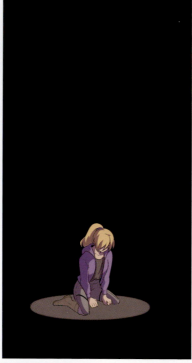

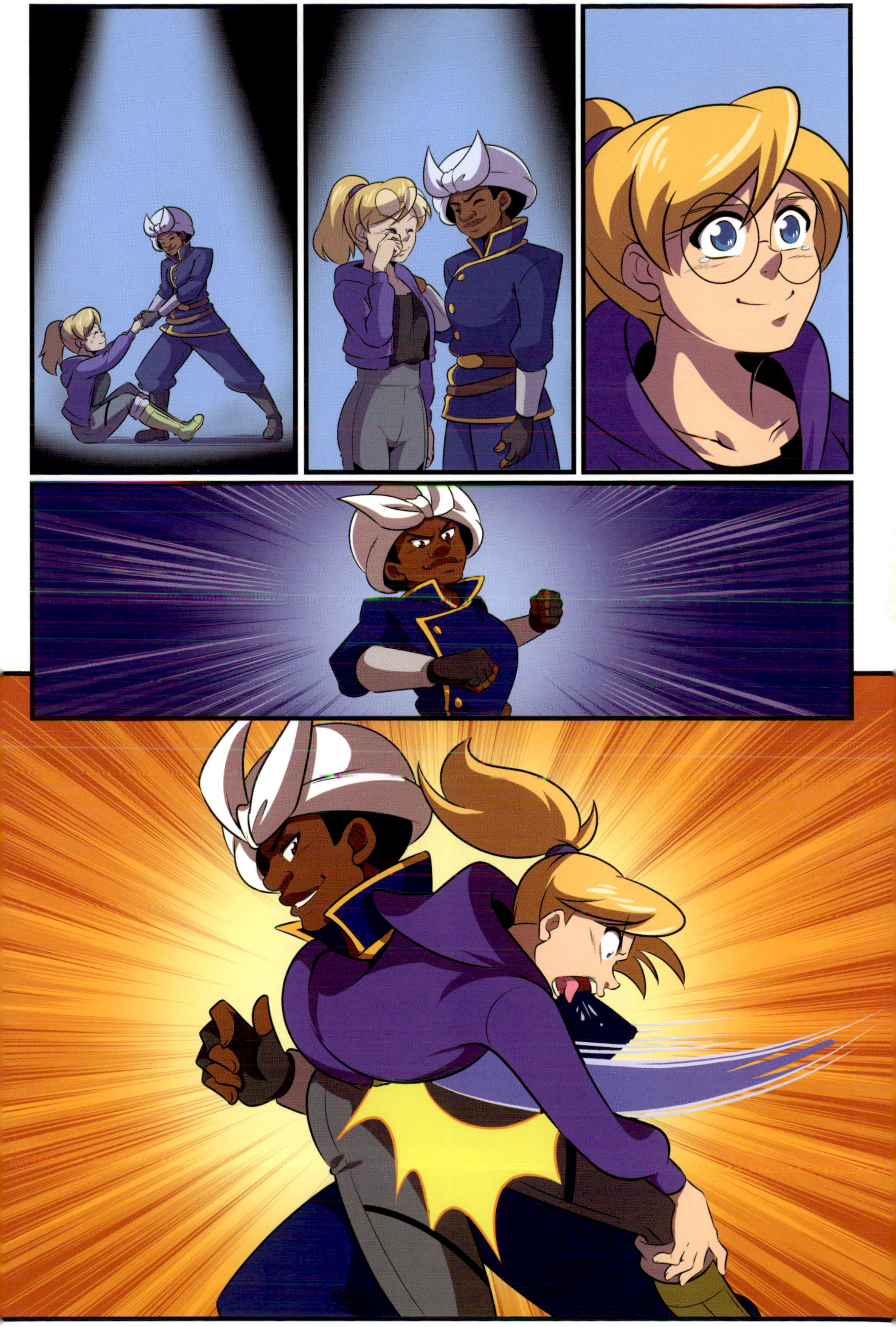

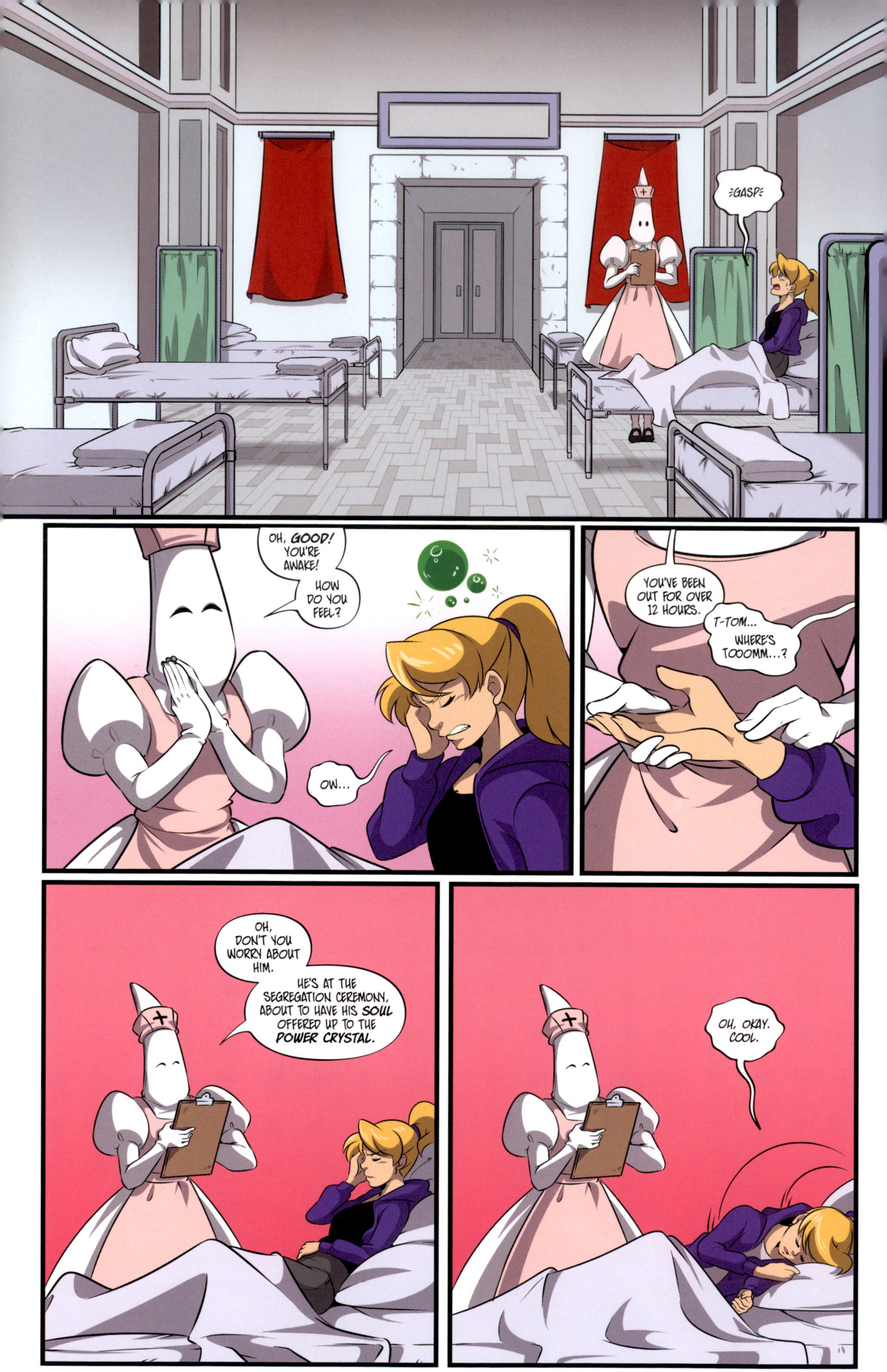

GASP
OH, GOOD! YOU'RE AWAKE!
HOW DO YOU FEEL?
OW...
YOU'VE BEEN OUT FOR OVER 12 HOURS.
T-TOM... WHERE'S TOOOMM...?
OH, DON'T YOU WORRY ABOUT HIM.
HE'S AT THE SEGREGATION CEREMONY, ABOUT TO HAVE HIS SOUL OFFERED UP TO THE POWER CRYSTAL.
OH, OKAY. COOL.

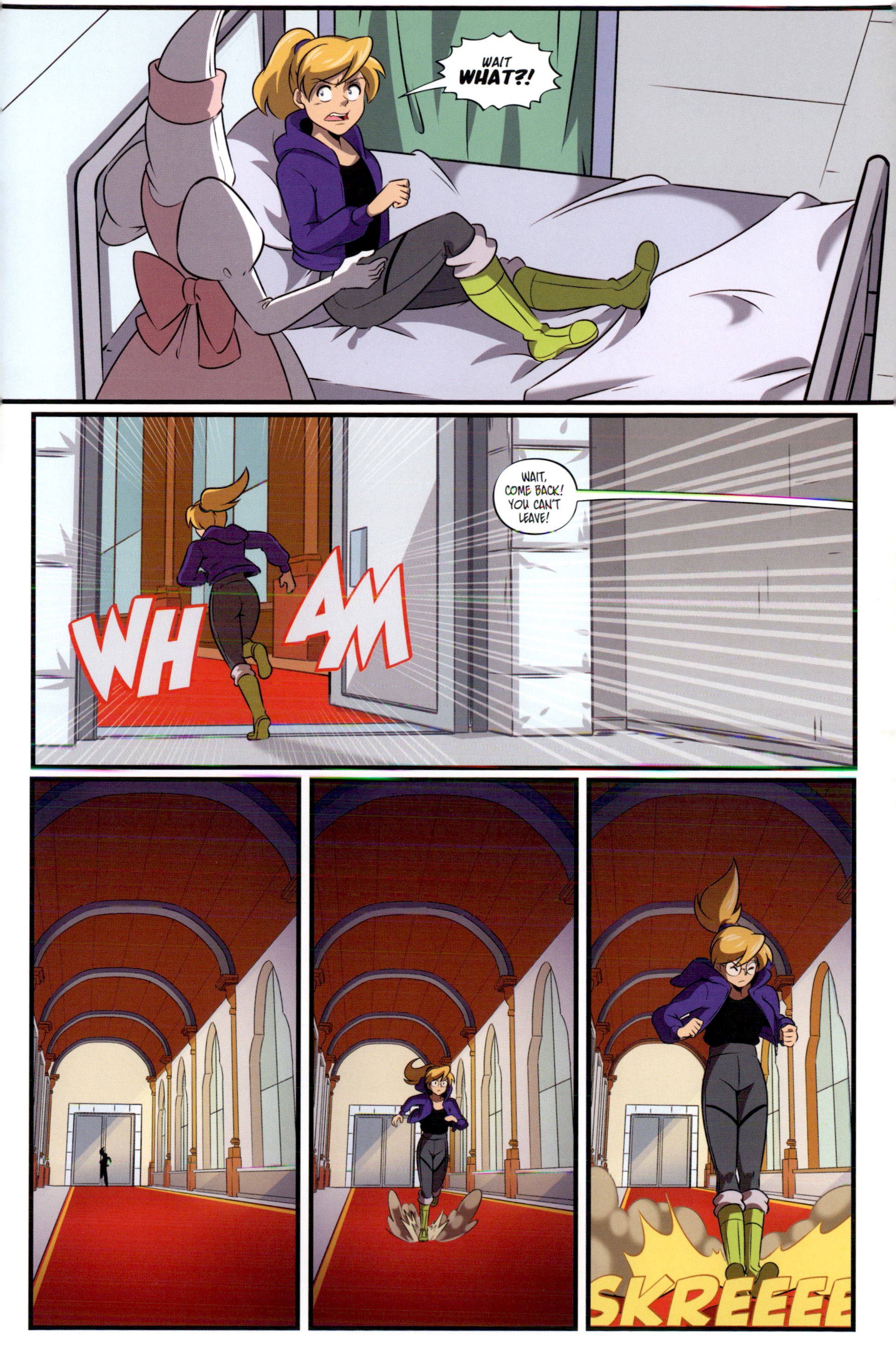
WAIT WHAT?!
WAIT, COME BACK! YOU CAN'T LEAVE!
WHAM
SKREEEE

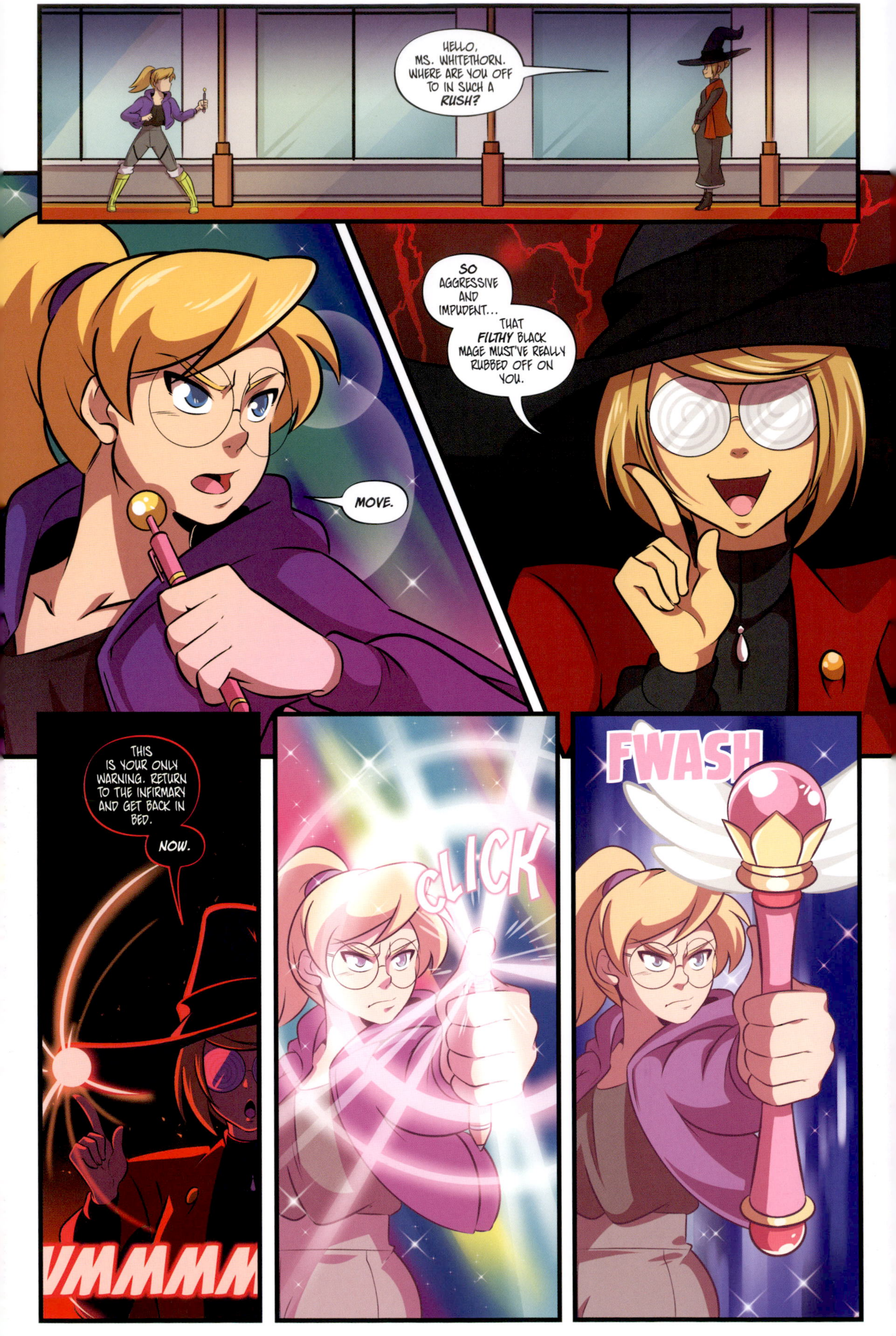
HELLO, MS. WHITETHORN. WHERE ARE YOU OFF TO IN SUCH A RUSH?
MOVE.
SO AGGRESSIVE AND IMPUDENT... THAT FILTHY BLACK MAGE MUST'VE REALLY RUBBED OFF ON YOU.
THIS IS YOUR ONLY WARNING. RETURN TO THE INFIRMARY AND GET BACK IN BED.
NOW.
VMMMM
CLICK
FWASH

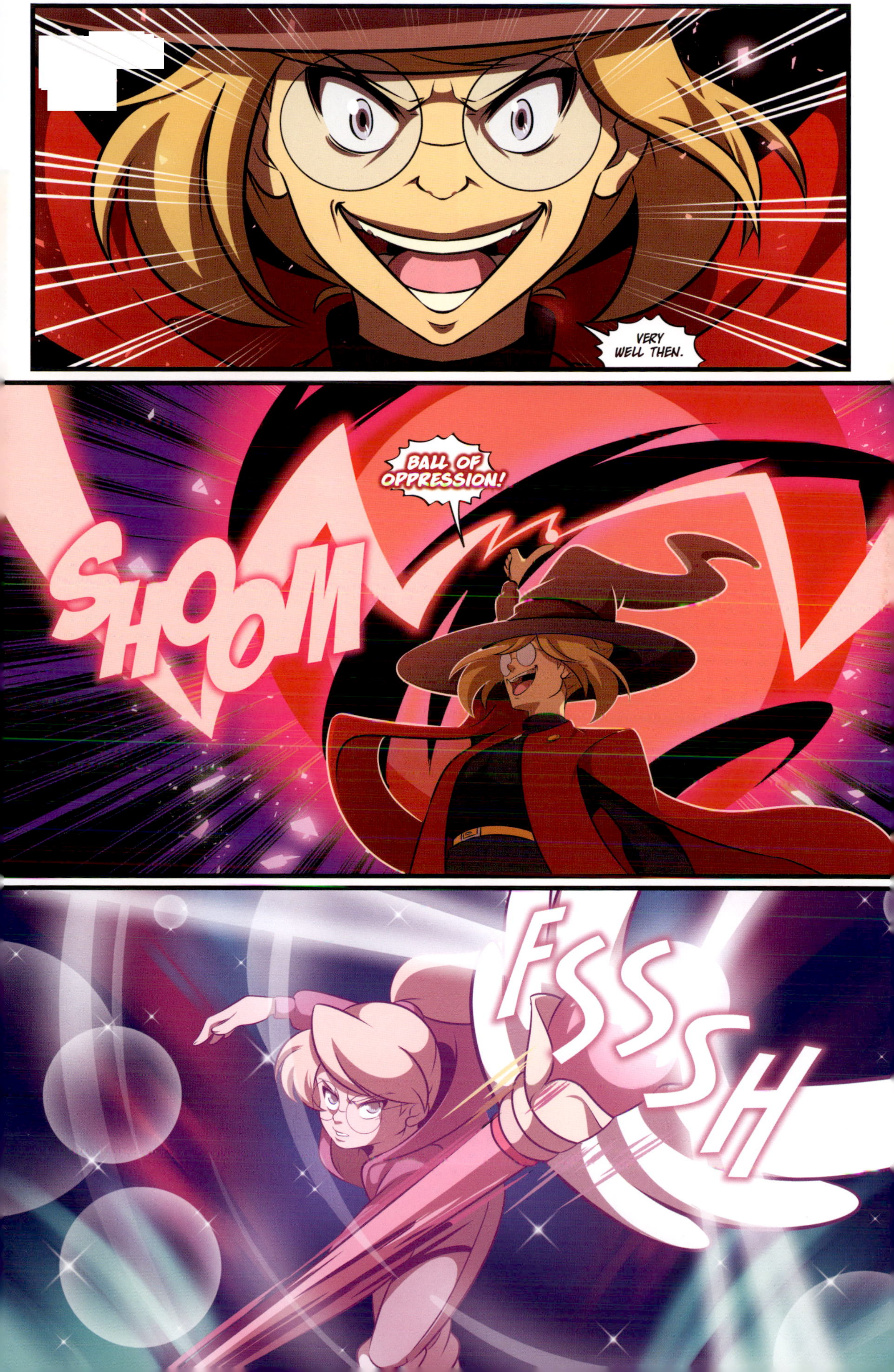
VERY WELL THEN.
BALL OF OPPRESSION!
SHOOM
FSSSH

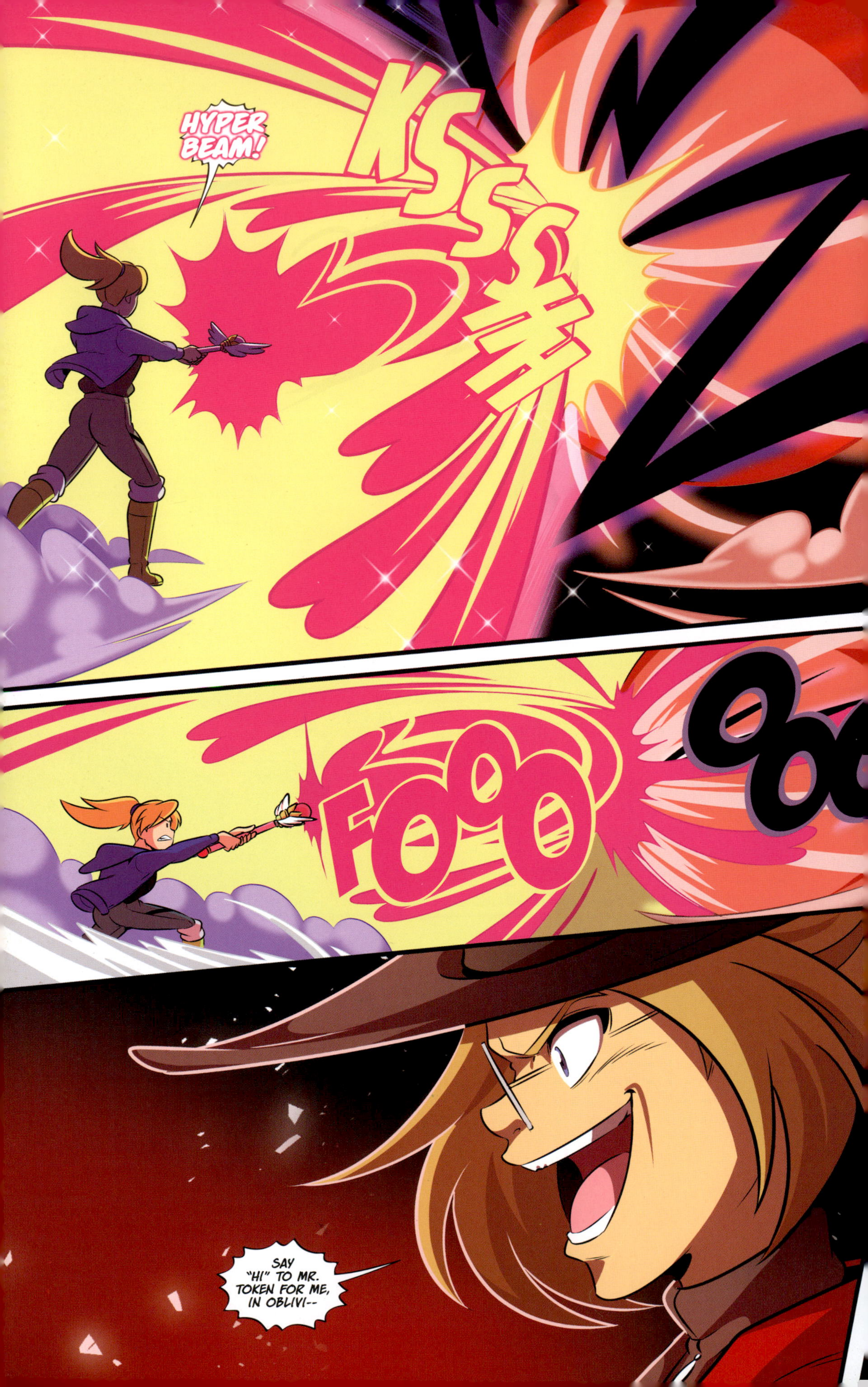
HYPER BEAM!
KSSSSH
FOOO
OOO
SAY "HI" TO MR. TOKEN FOR ME, IN OBLIVI--

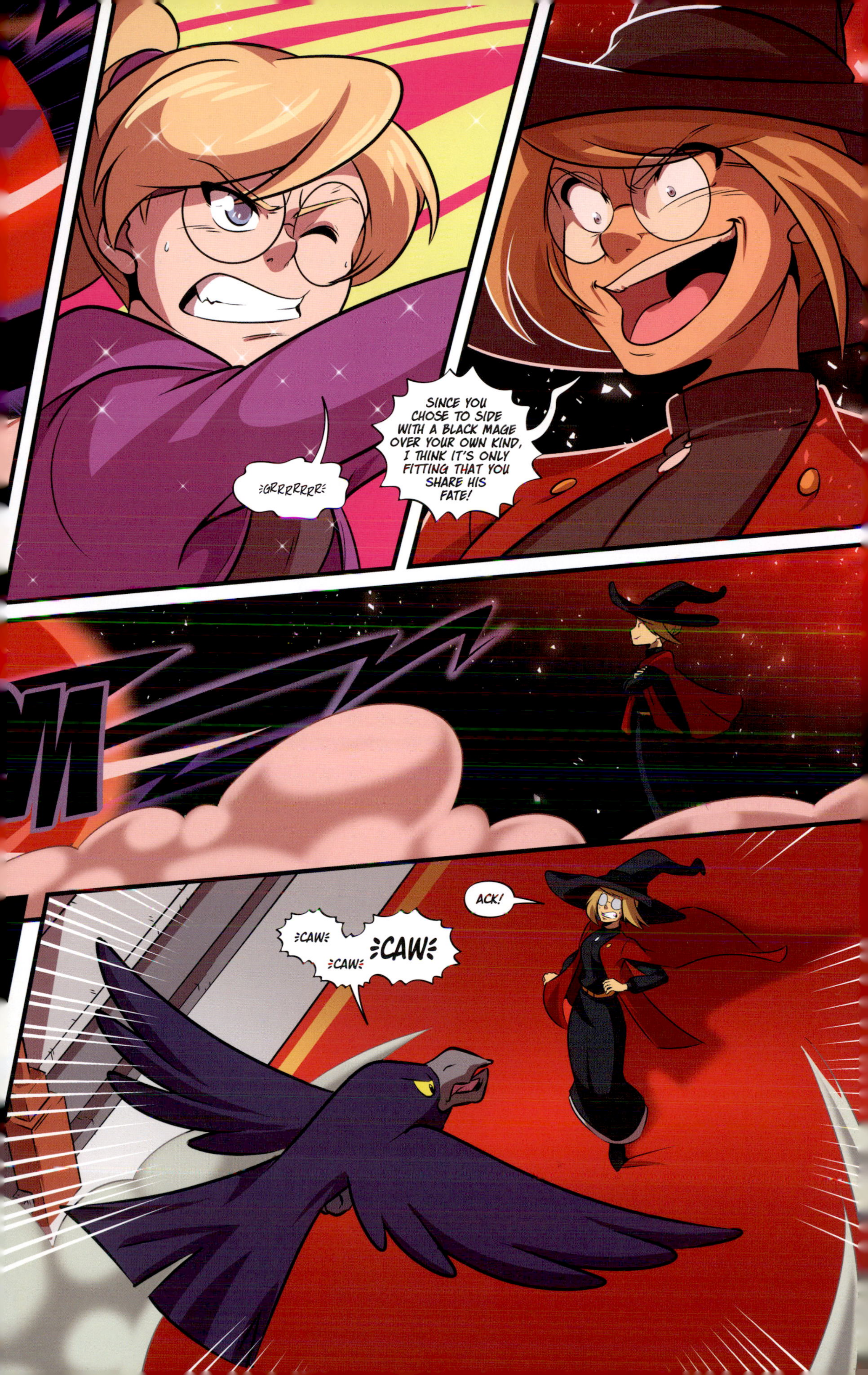

SINCE YOU CHOSE TO SIDE WITH A BLACK MAGE OVER YOUR OWN KIND, I THINK IT'S ONLY FITTING THAT YOU SHARE HIS FATE!
GRRRRRRR
ACK!
CAW
CAW
CAW

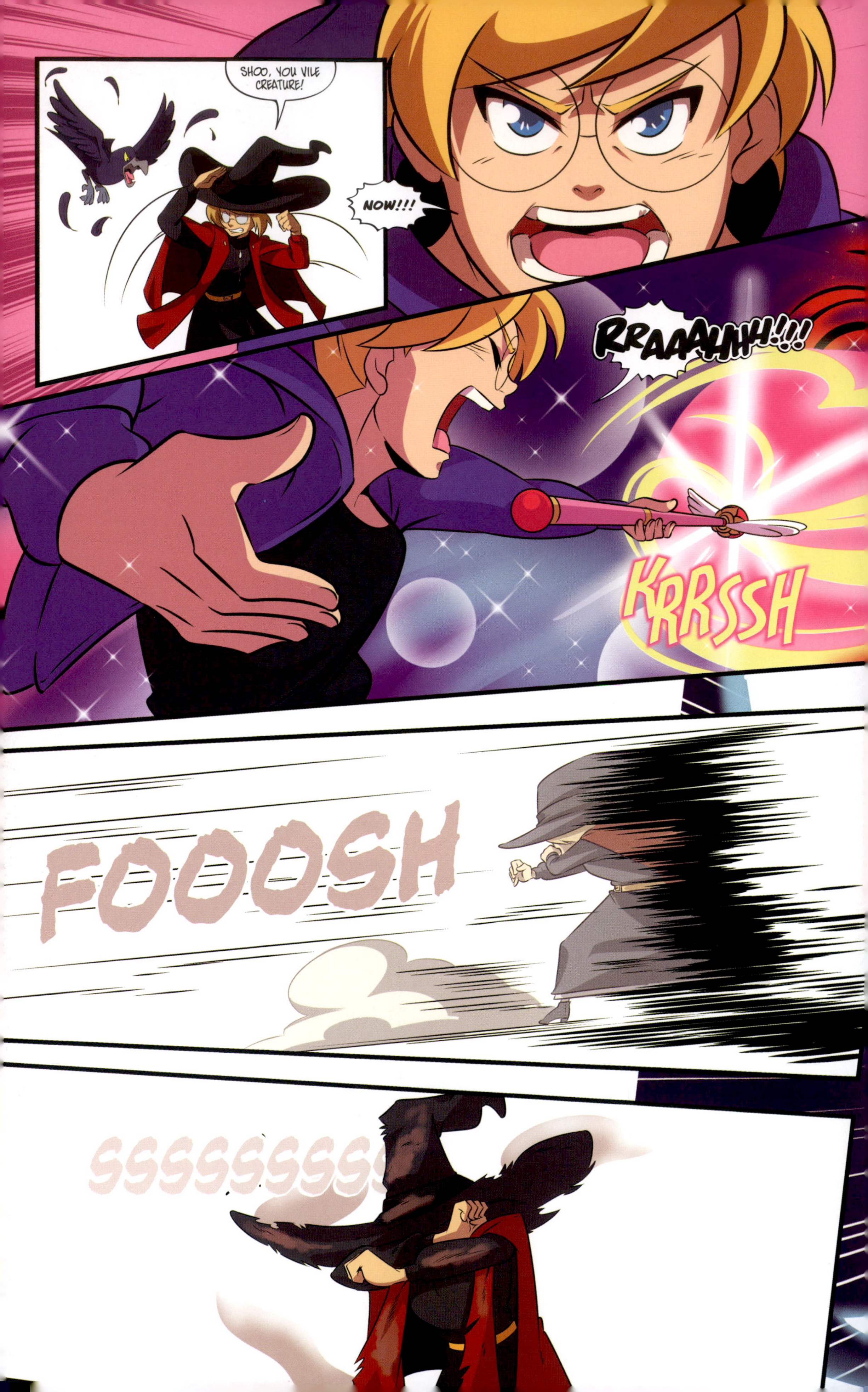
SHOO, YOU VILE CREATURE!
NOW!!!
RRAAAHHH!!!
KRRSSH
FOOOSH
SSSSSSSSSS

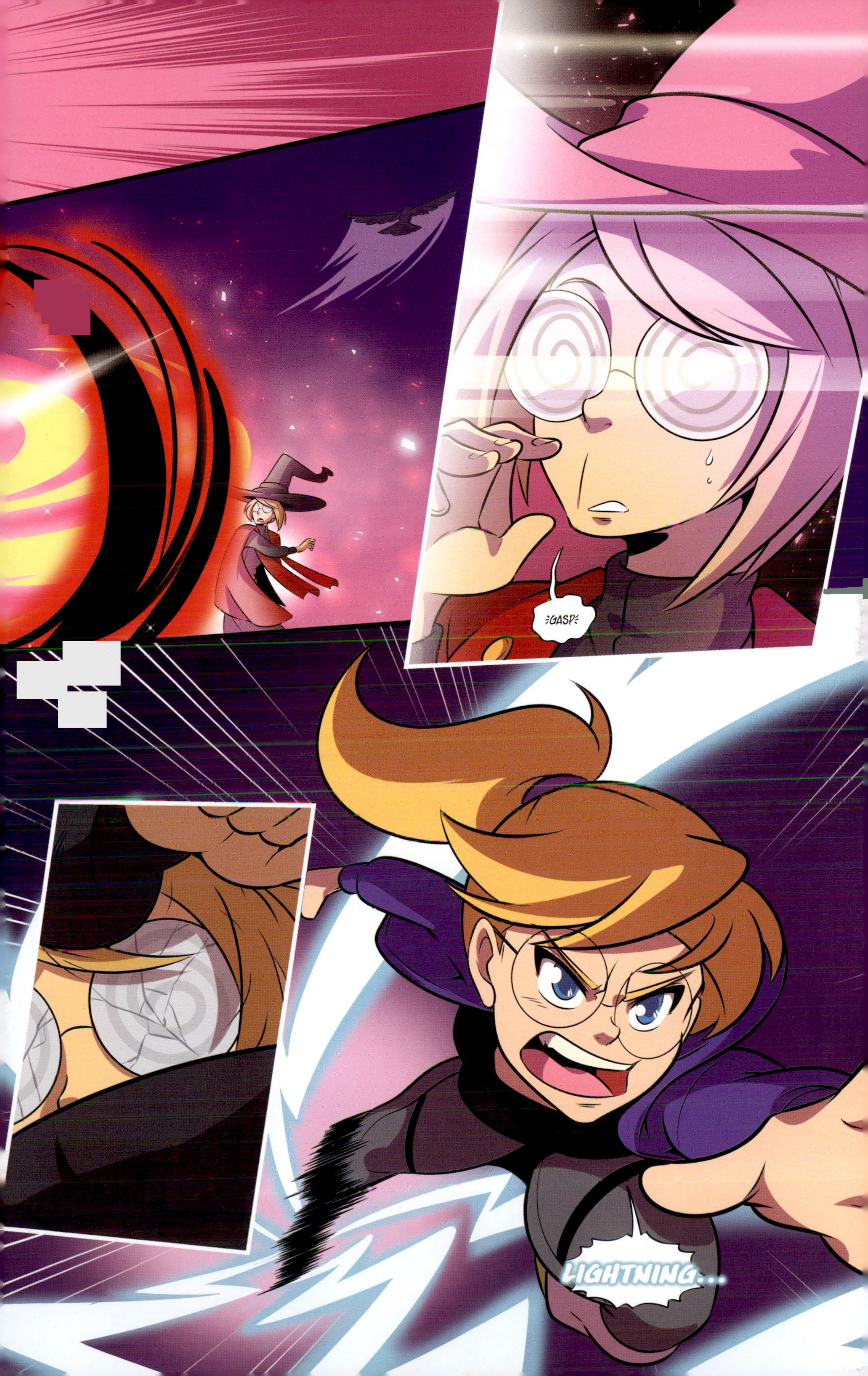
GASP
LIGHTNING...

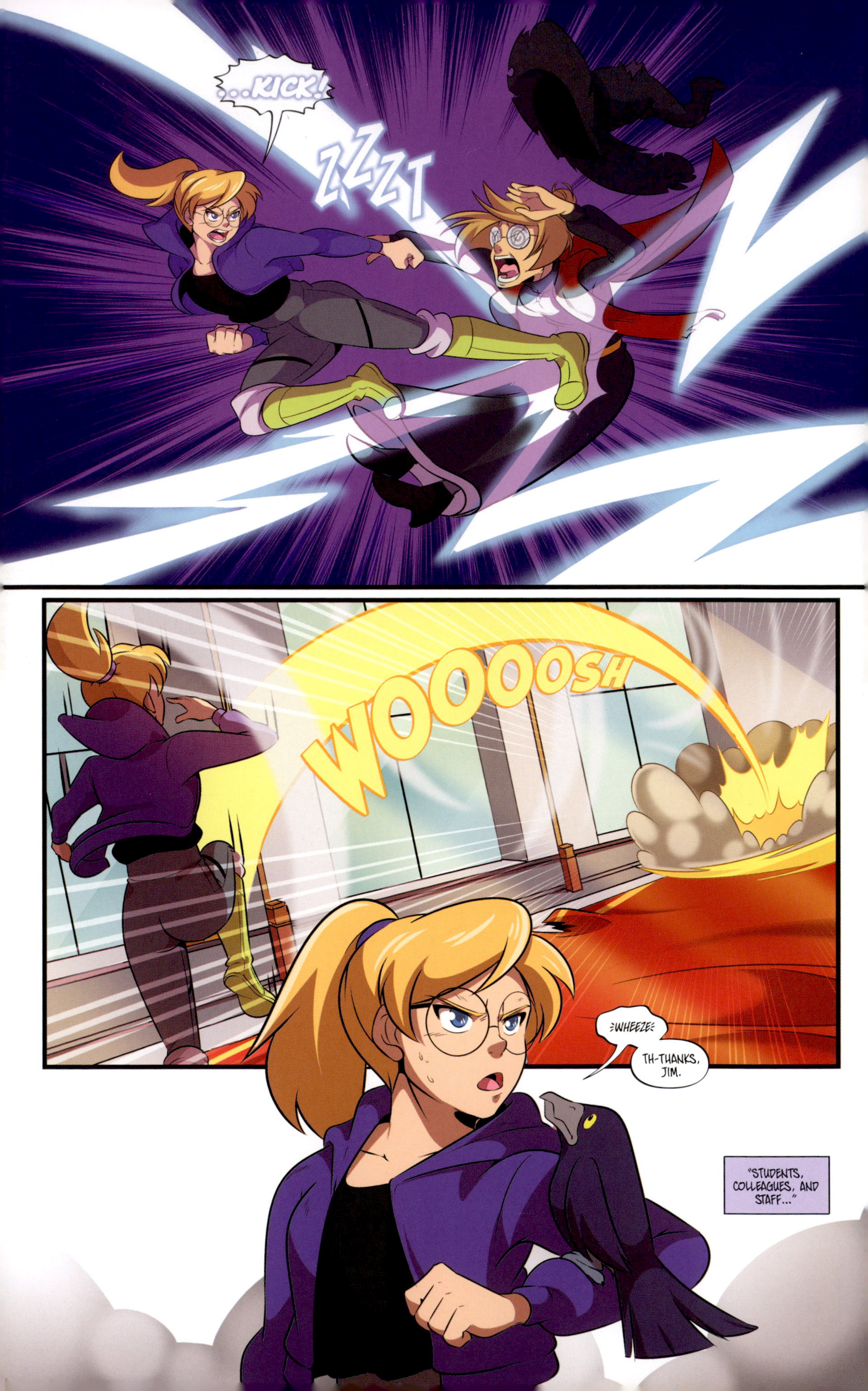
...KICK!
ZZZT
WOOOOSH
≡WHEEZE≡
TH-THANKS, JIM.
"STUDENTS, COLLEAGUES, AND STAFF..."

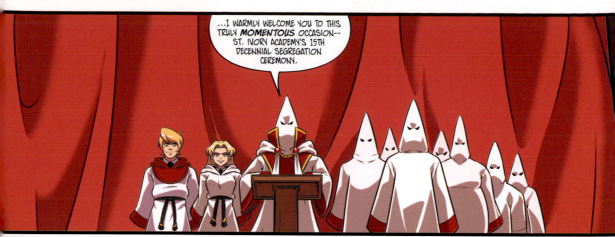

...I WARMLY WELCOME YOU TO THIS TRULY *MOMENTOUS* OCCASION-- ST. IVORY ACADEMY'S 15TH DECENNIAL SEGREGATION CEREMONY.

THE RITUAL YOU'RE ABOUT TO PARTAKE IN HAPPENS ONLY ONCE EVERY DECADE. YOU SHOULD ALL BE VERY PROUD.

TO PARTICIPATE IN SUCH AN IMPORTANT AND TIME-HONORED TRADITION IS A PRIVILEGE OF THE *HIGHEST CALIBER.*

THIS WILL BE A DAY THAT YOU SHALL REMEMBER FOR THE REST OF YOUR LIVES.

LONG AGO, THE LEGENDARY *TERRORIST*, JOHN HENRY, FORGED AN EXTREMELY POWERFUL MAGICAL WEAPON, IN A BID TO DESTROY THE KLAN AND ALL OF OUR GREAT WORKS.

THE MANA WITHIN THE SOUL OF THIS BLACK MAGE YOU SEE BEFORE YOU HAS NOW BEEN RIPENED TO *PERFECTION,* THANKS TO THAT WEAPON.

AND WITH IT, WE SHALL REJUVENATE OUR POWER CRYSTAL AND KEEP ST. IVORY AFLOAT FOR ANOTHER 10 YEARS.

JOHN HENRY SOUGHT TO *KILL US,* BUT THROUGH HIS DEFIANCE, WE SHALL BE *REBORN AGAIN...*

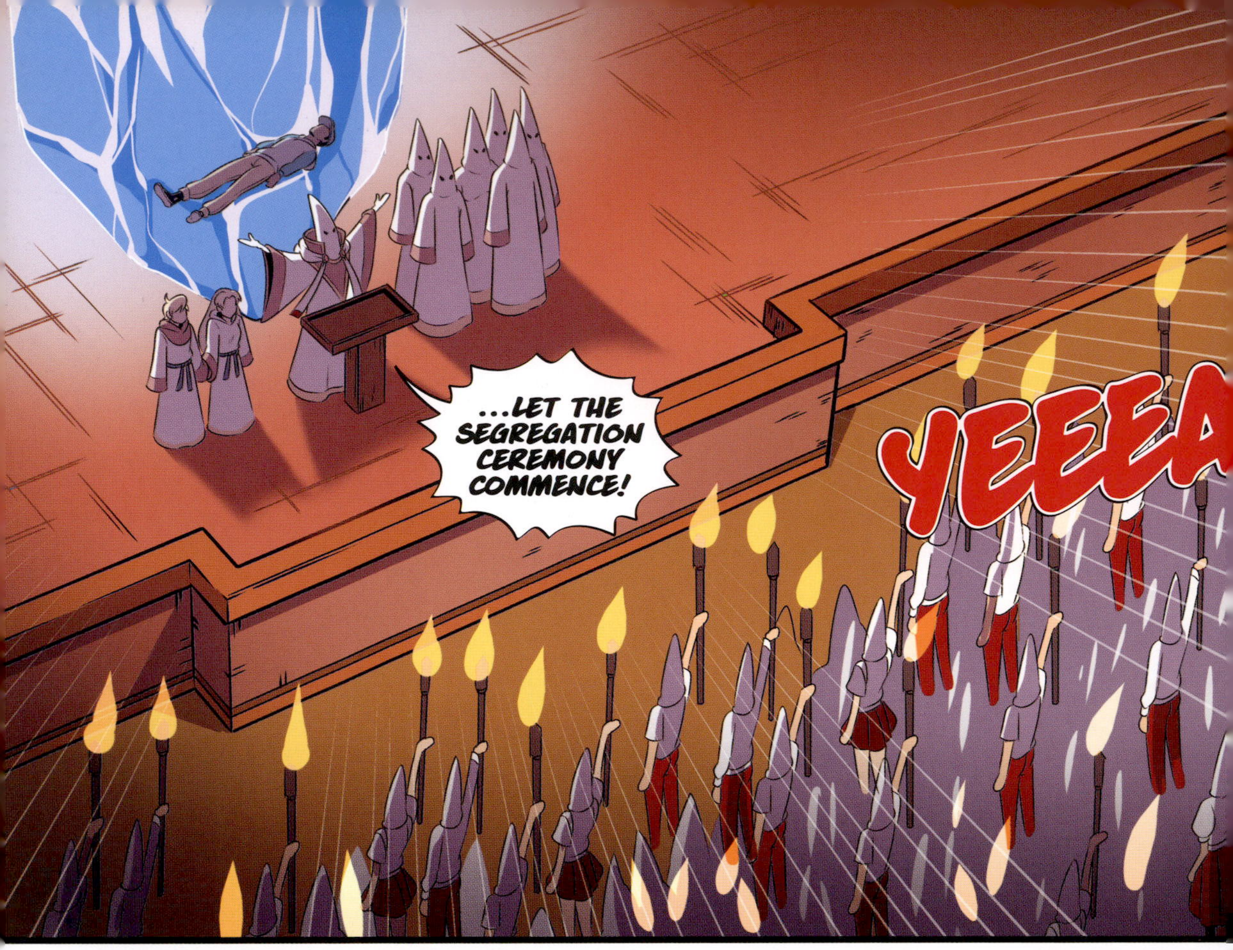
...LET THE SEGREGATION CEREMONY COMMENCE!
YEEEA

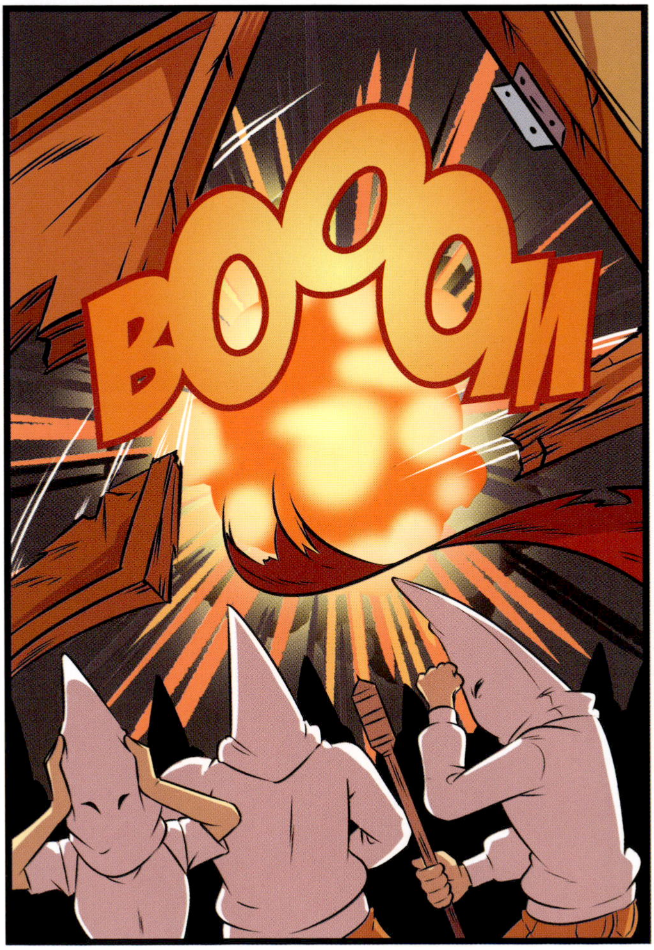
BOOOM

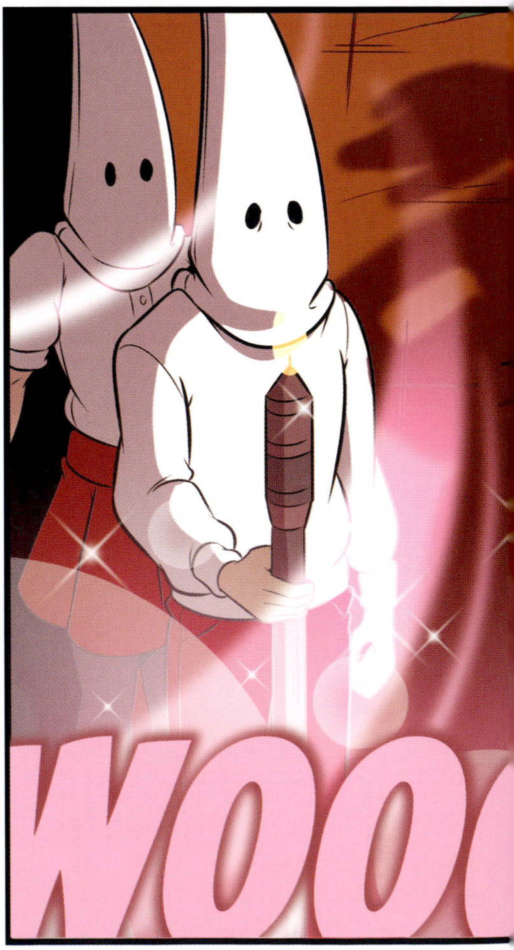
WOOO

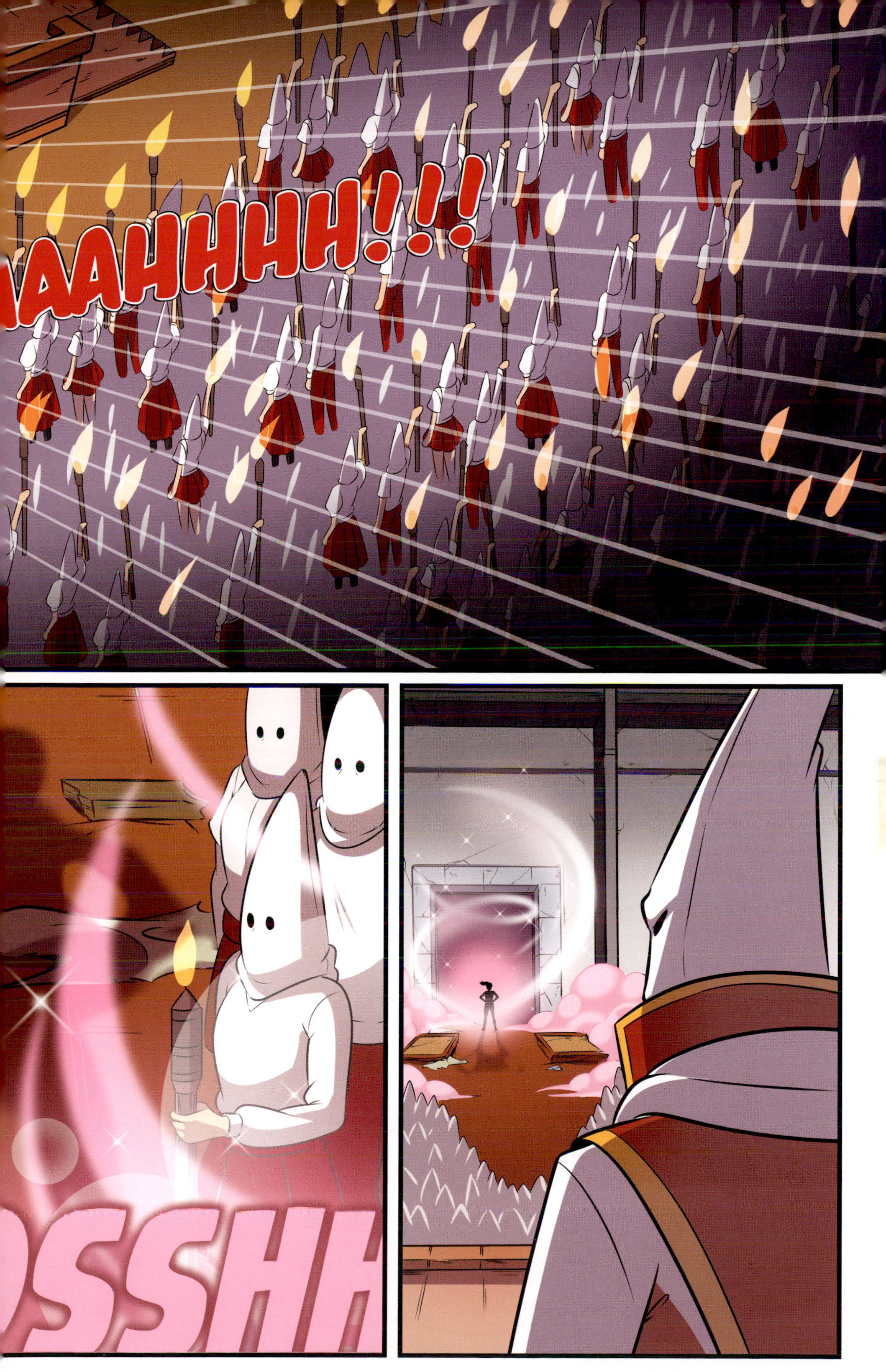
AAHHHH!!!
SSHH

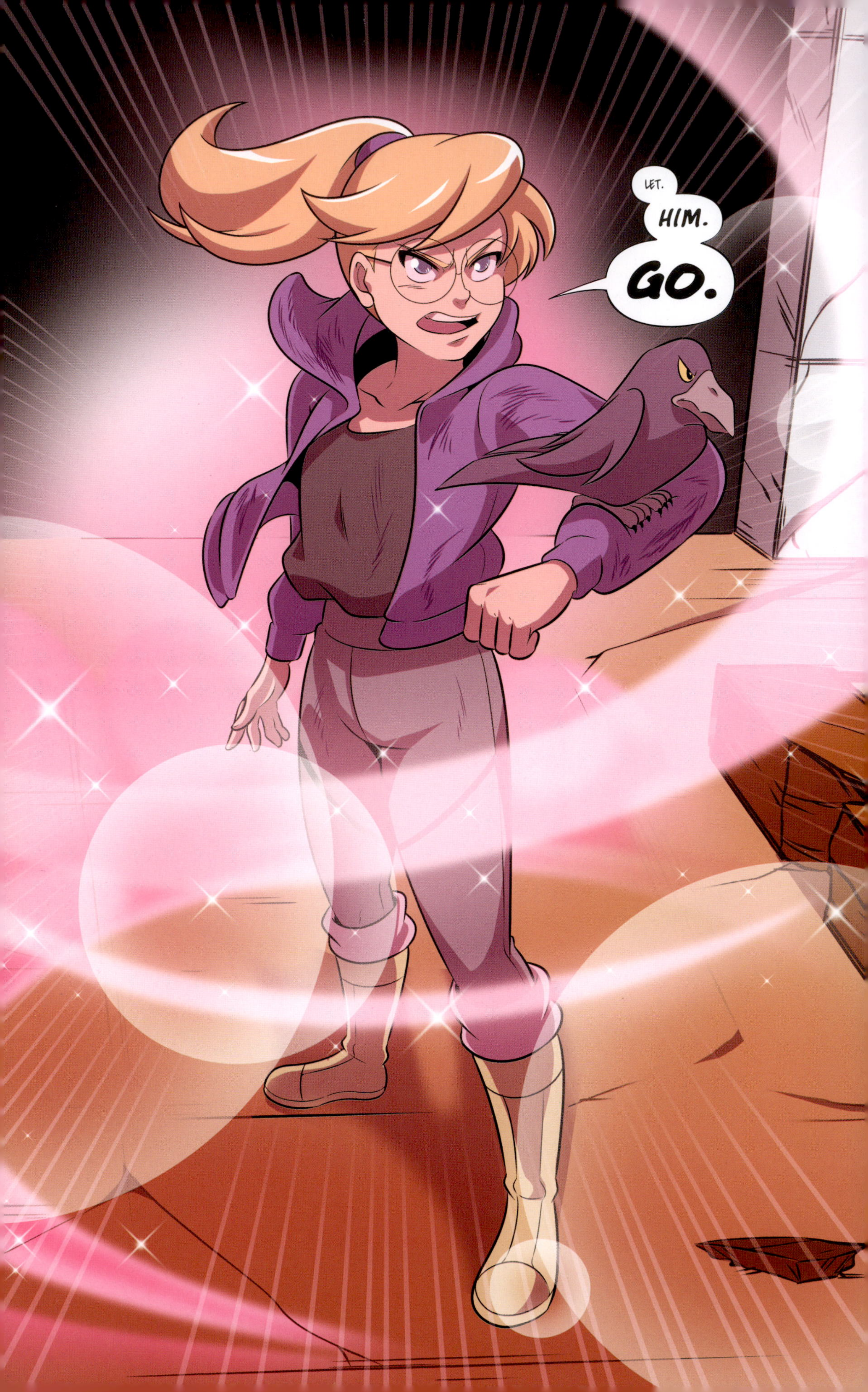
LET.
HIM.
GO.

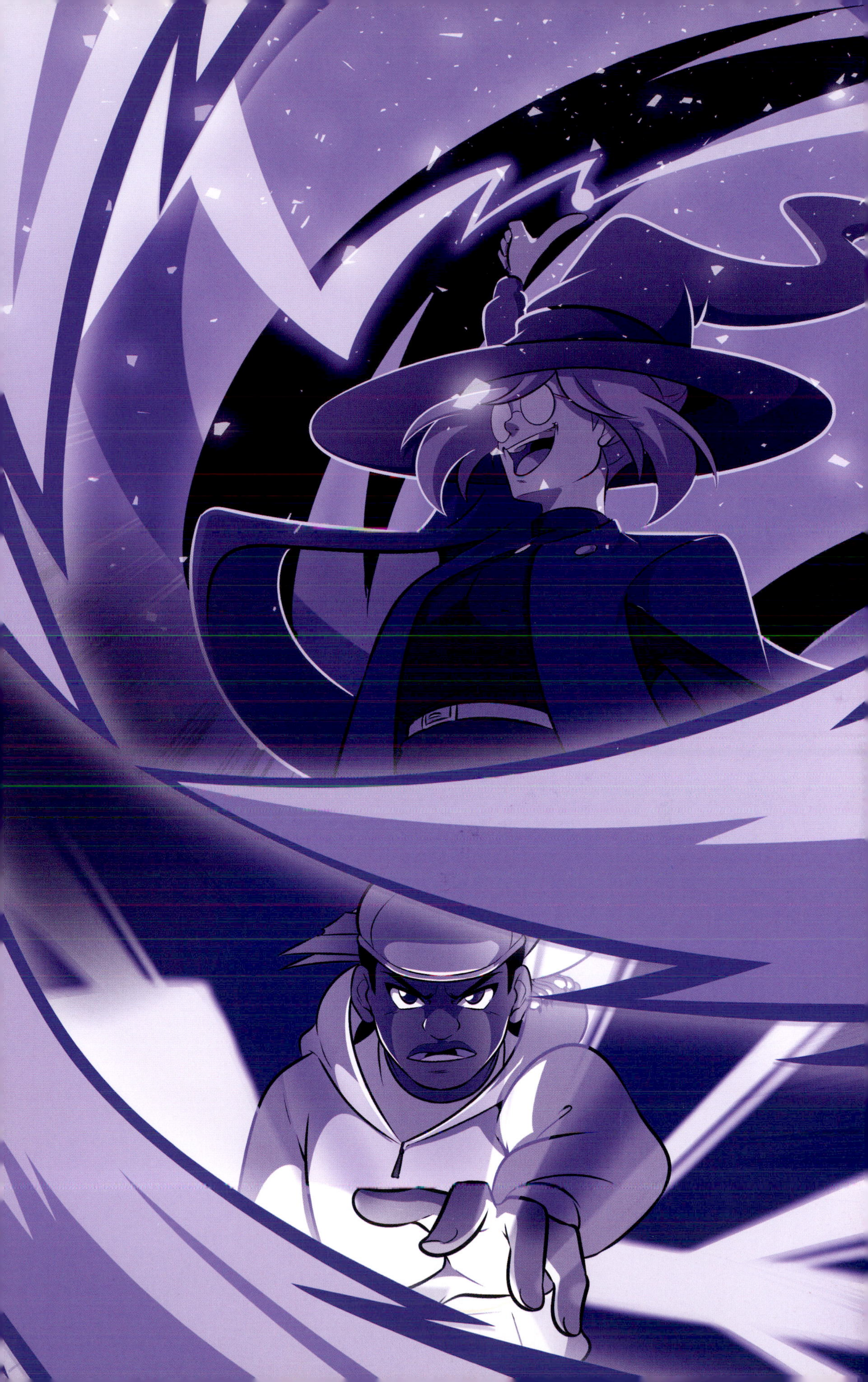

CHAPTER FIVE

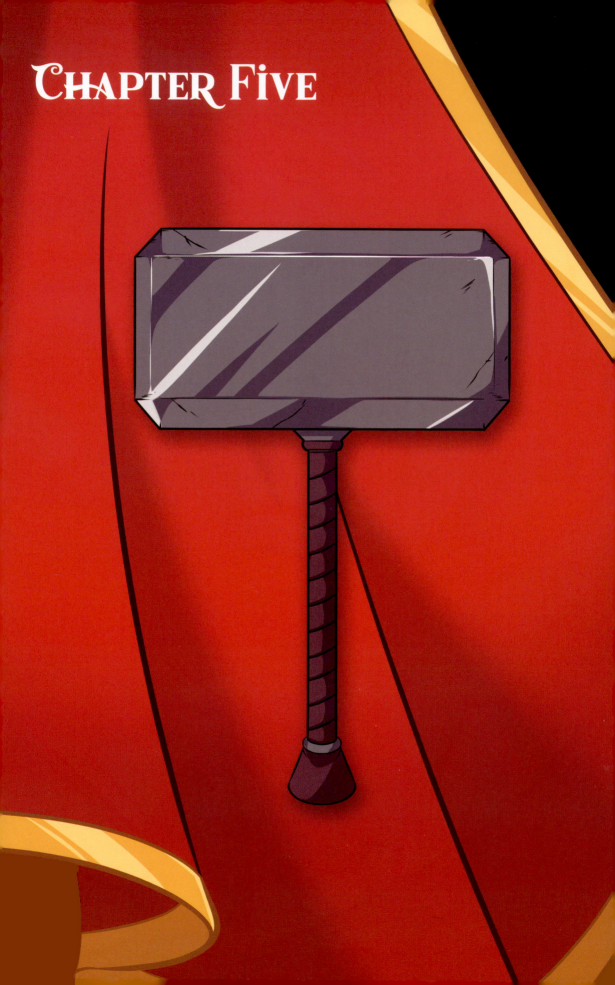

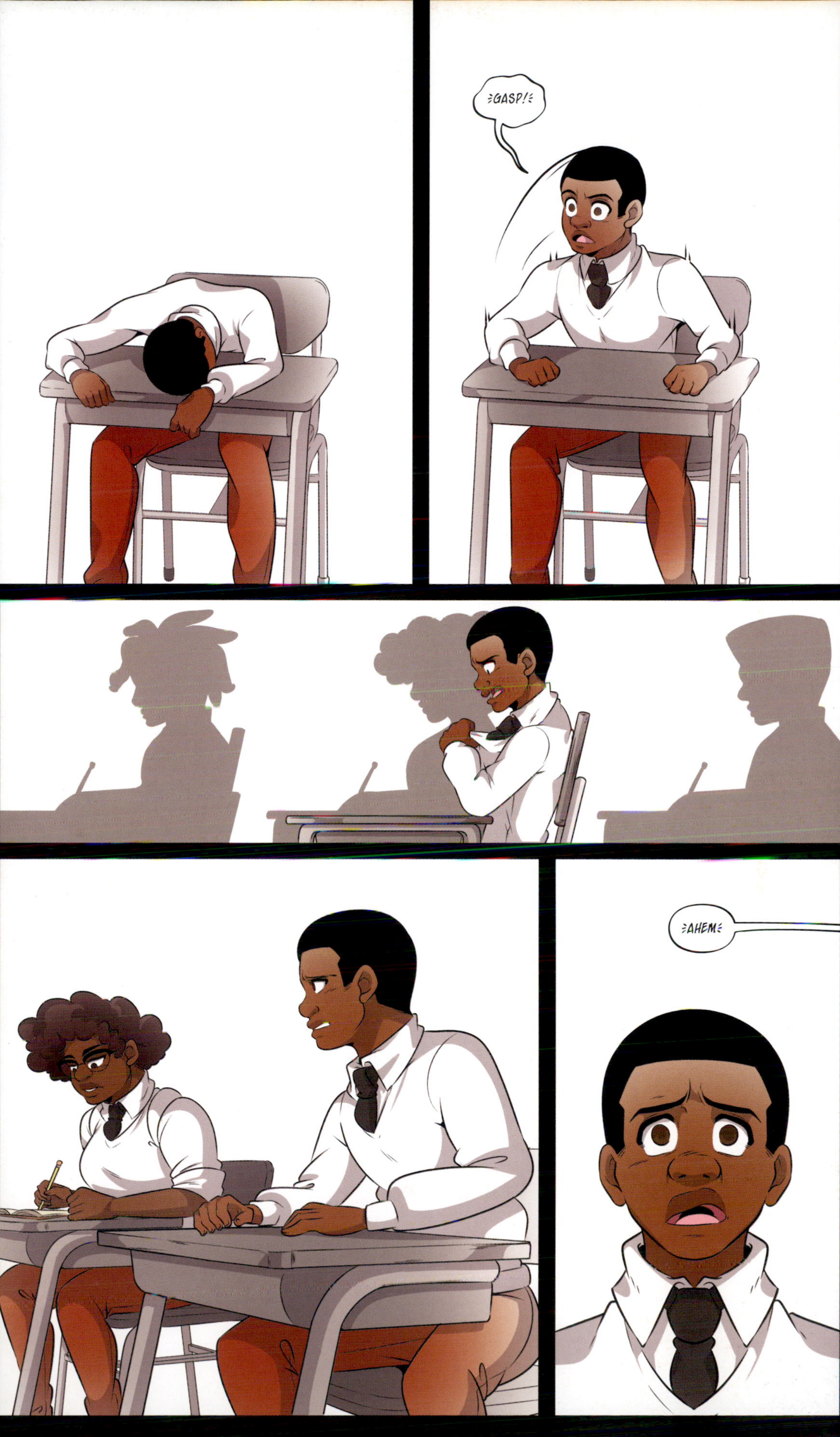
GASP!
AHEM

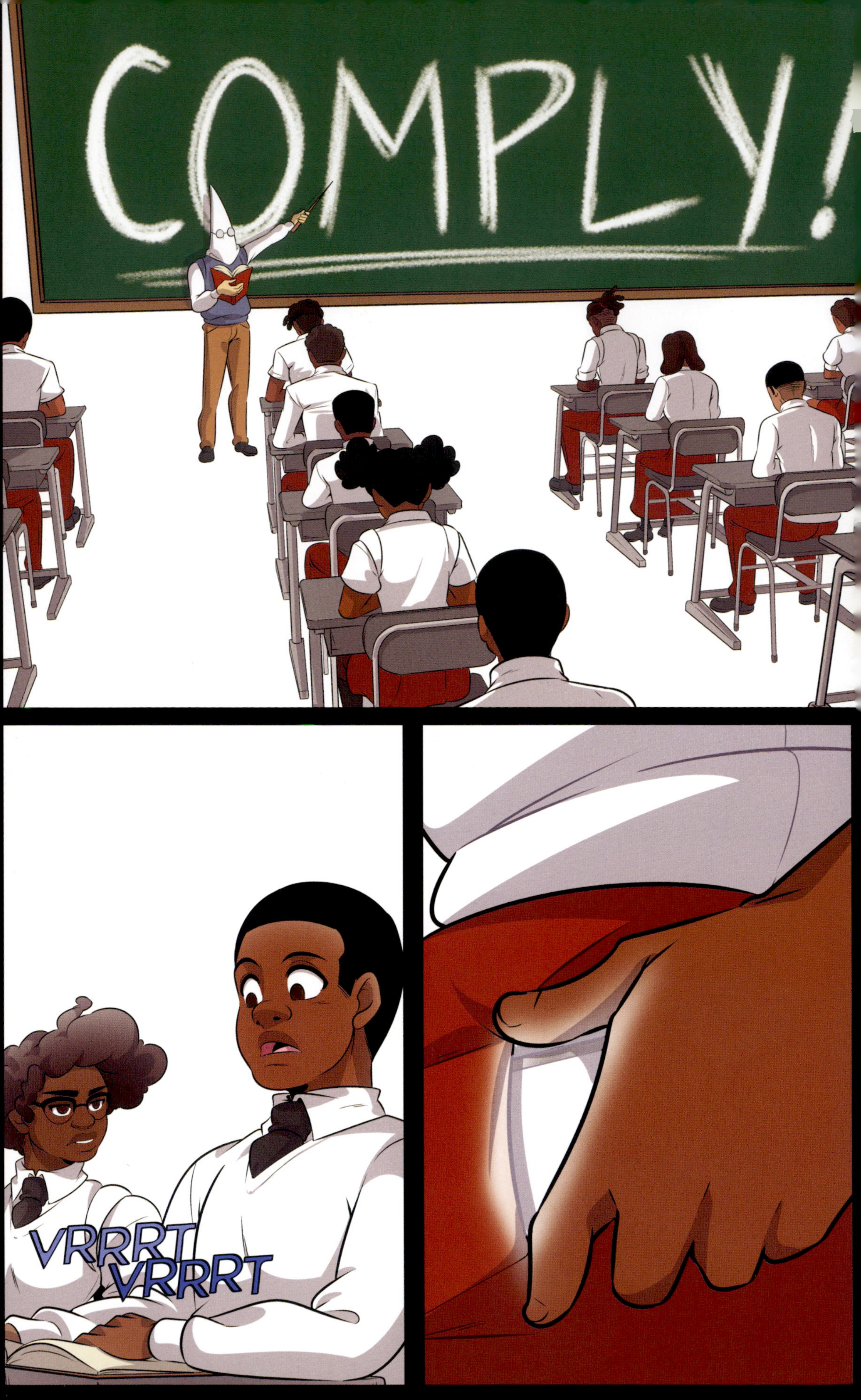
COMPLY!
VRRRT
VRRRT

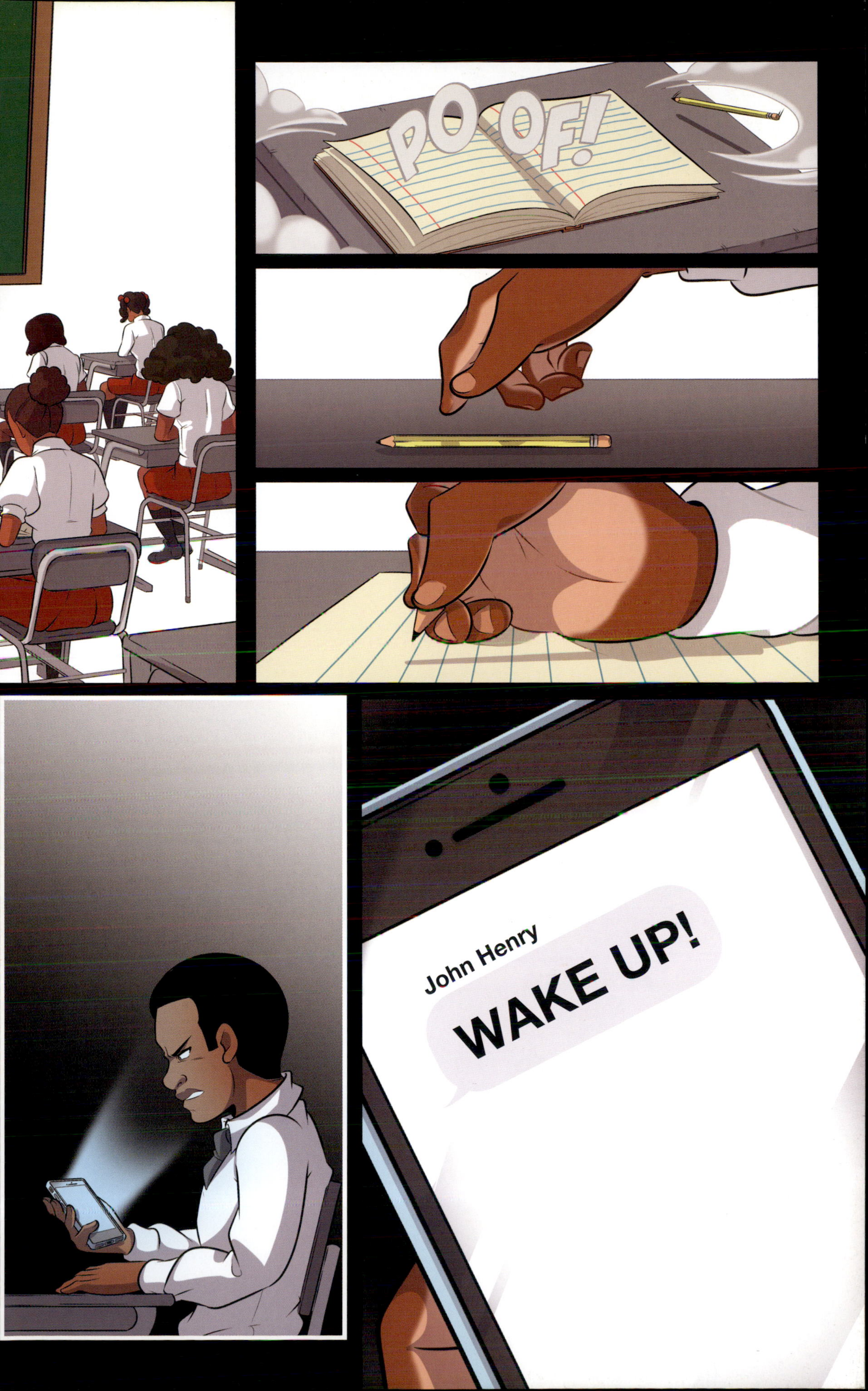
POOF!
John Henry
WAKE UP!

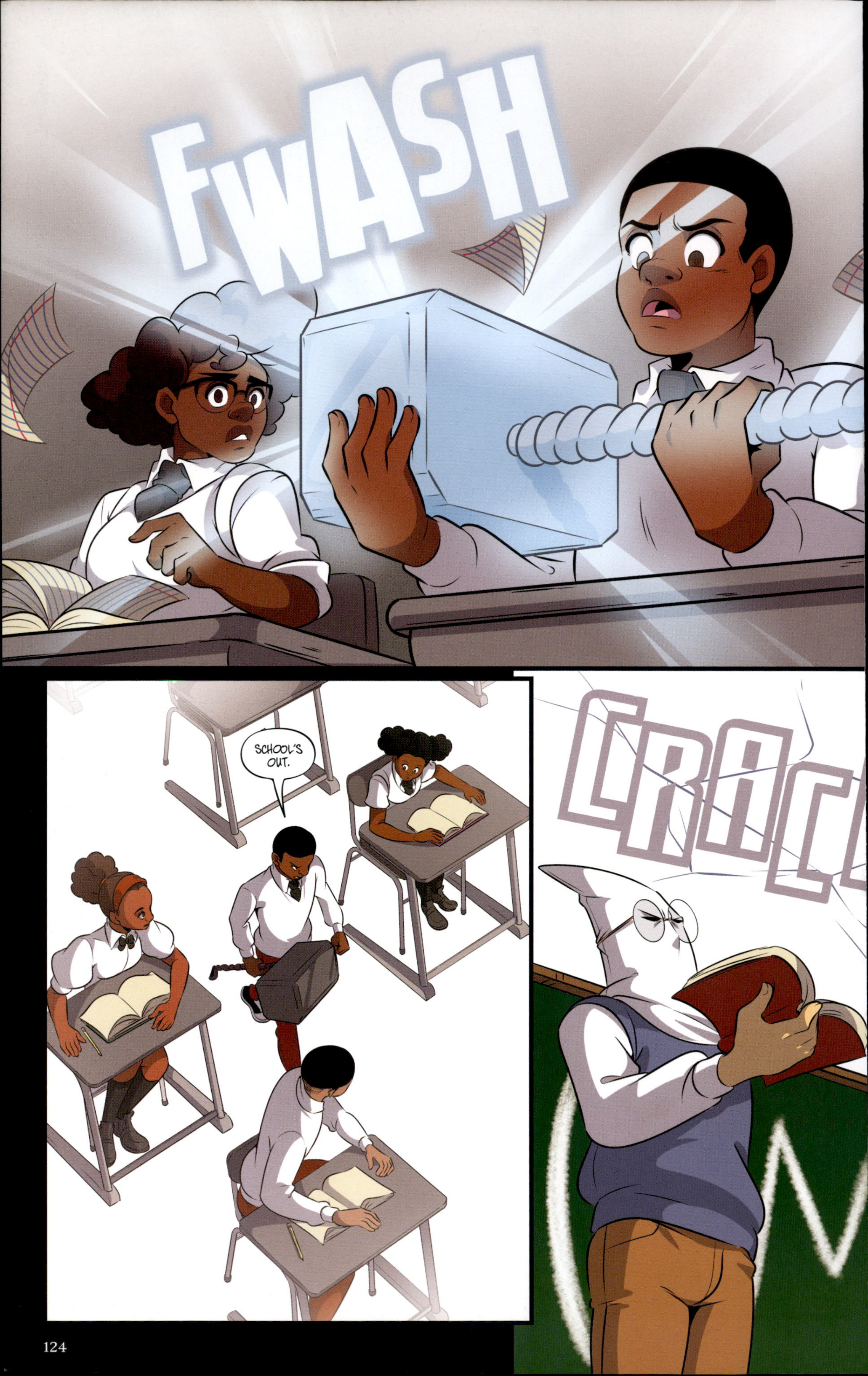
FWASH
SCHOOL'S OUT.
CRAC

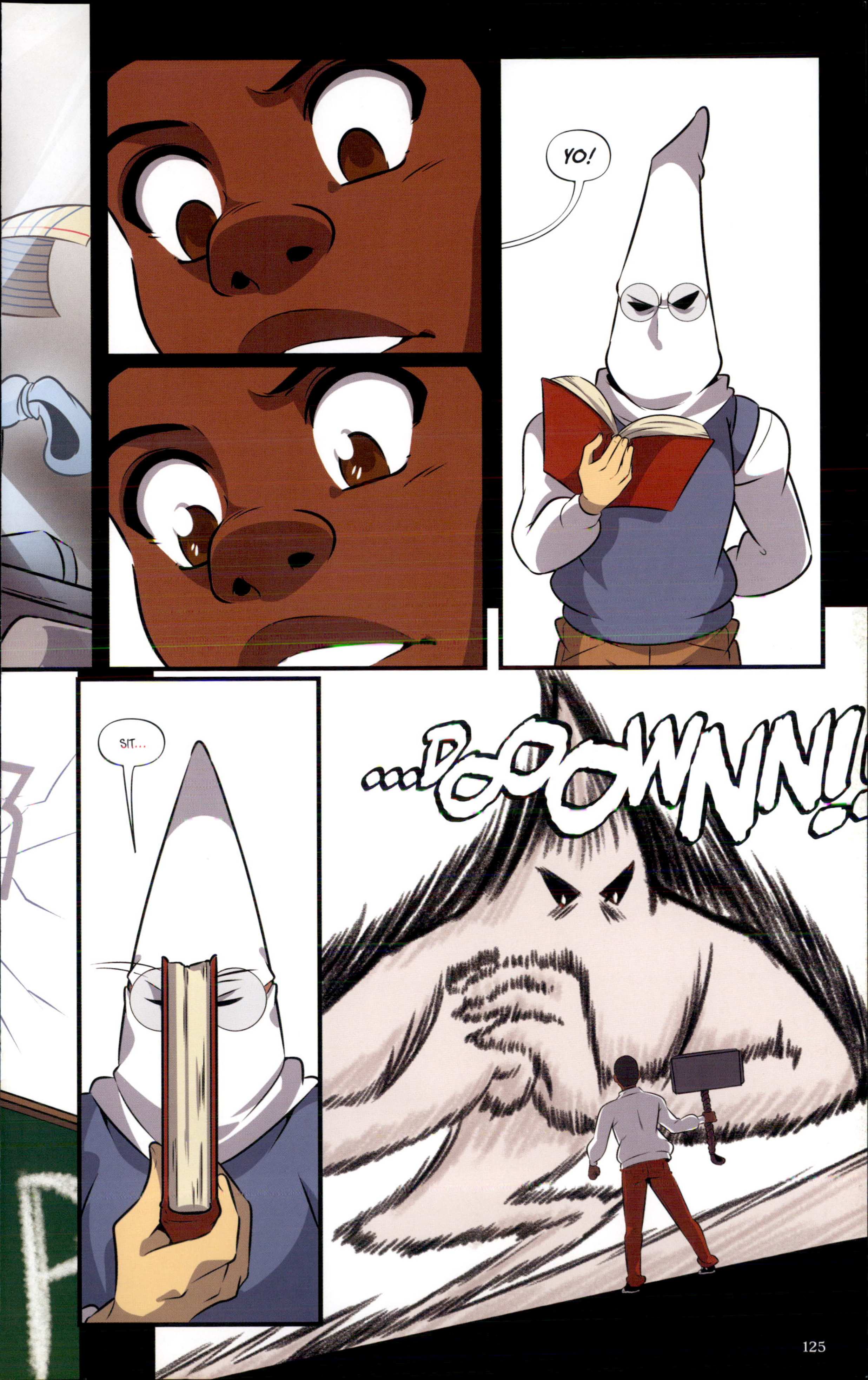
YO!
SIT...
...DOOOWNNN!!

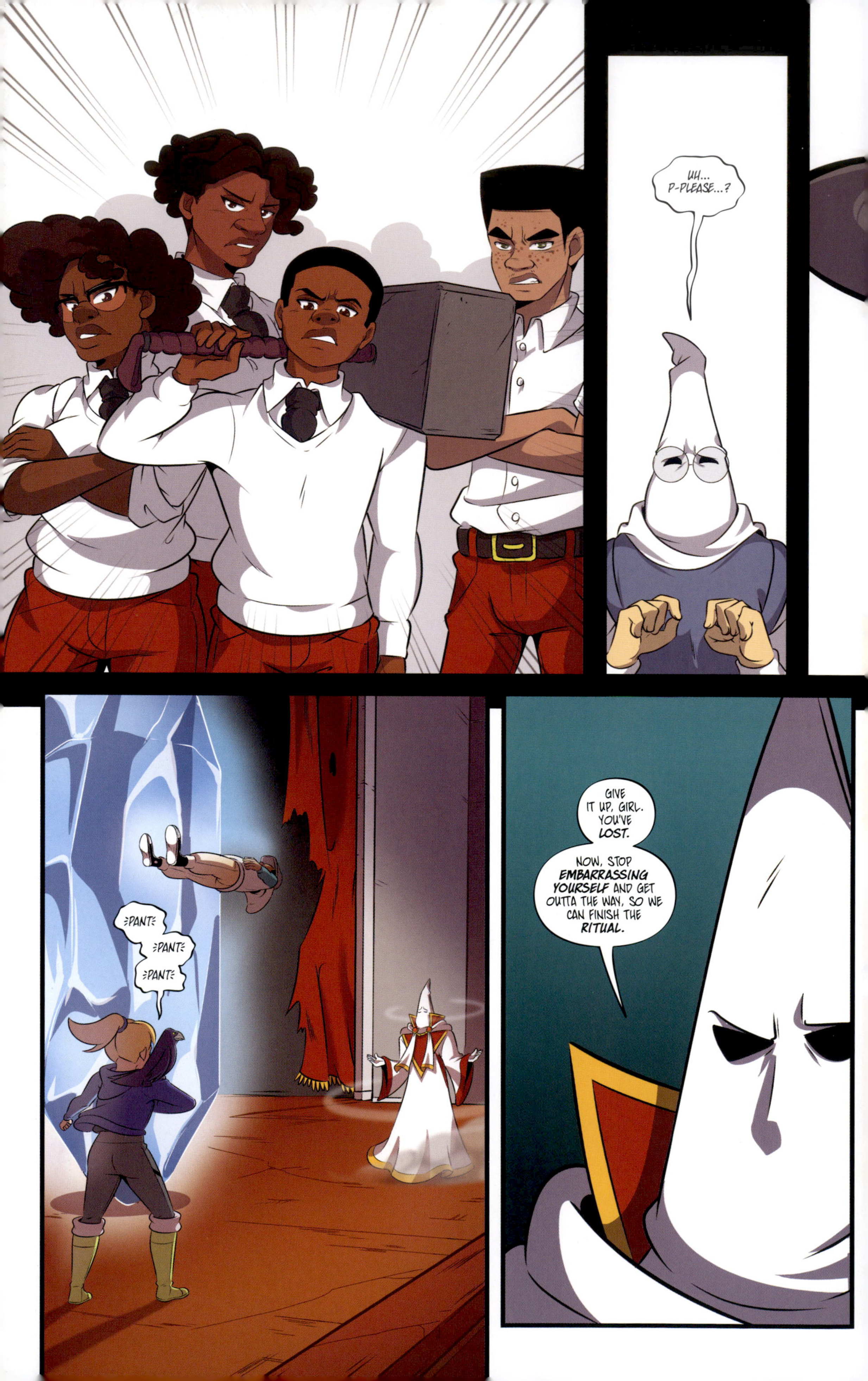
UH... P-PLEASE...?
PANT
PANT
PANT
GIVE IT UP, GIRL. YOU'VE LOST.
NOW, STOP EMBARRASSING YOURSELF AND GET OUTTA THE WAY, SO WE CAN FINISH THE RITUAL.

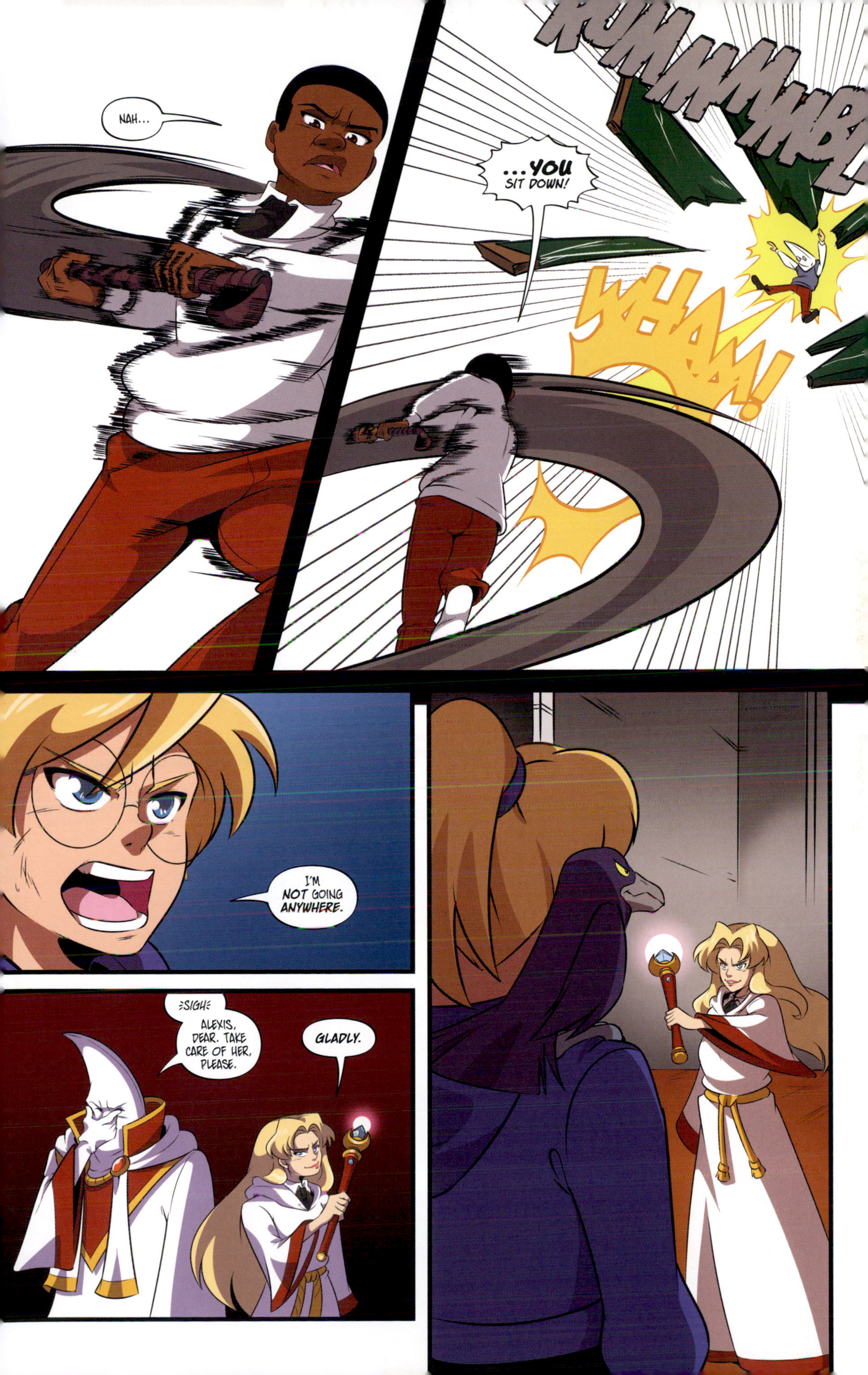
NAH...
...YOU SIT DOWN!
WHAM!
I'M NOT GOING ANYWHERE.
SIGH
ALEXIS, DEAR. TAKE CARE OF HER, PLEASE.
GLADLY.

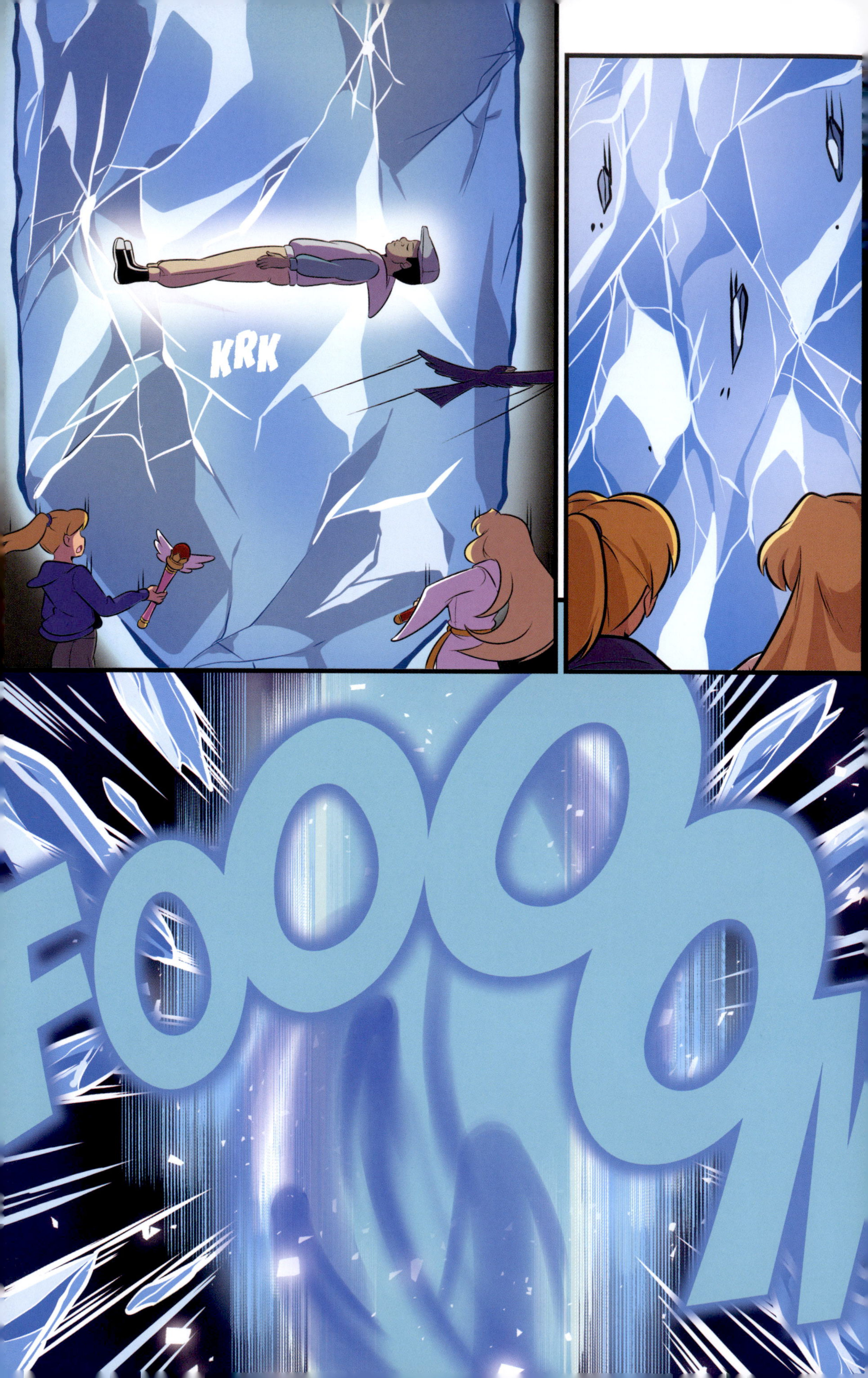
KRK
FOOOOM

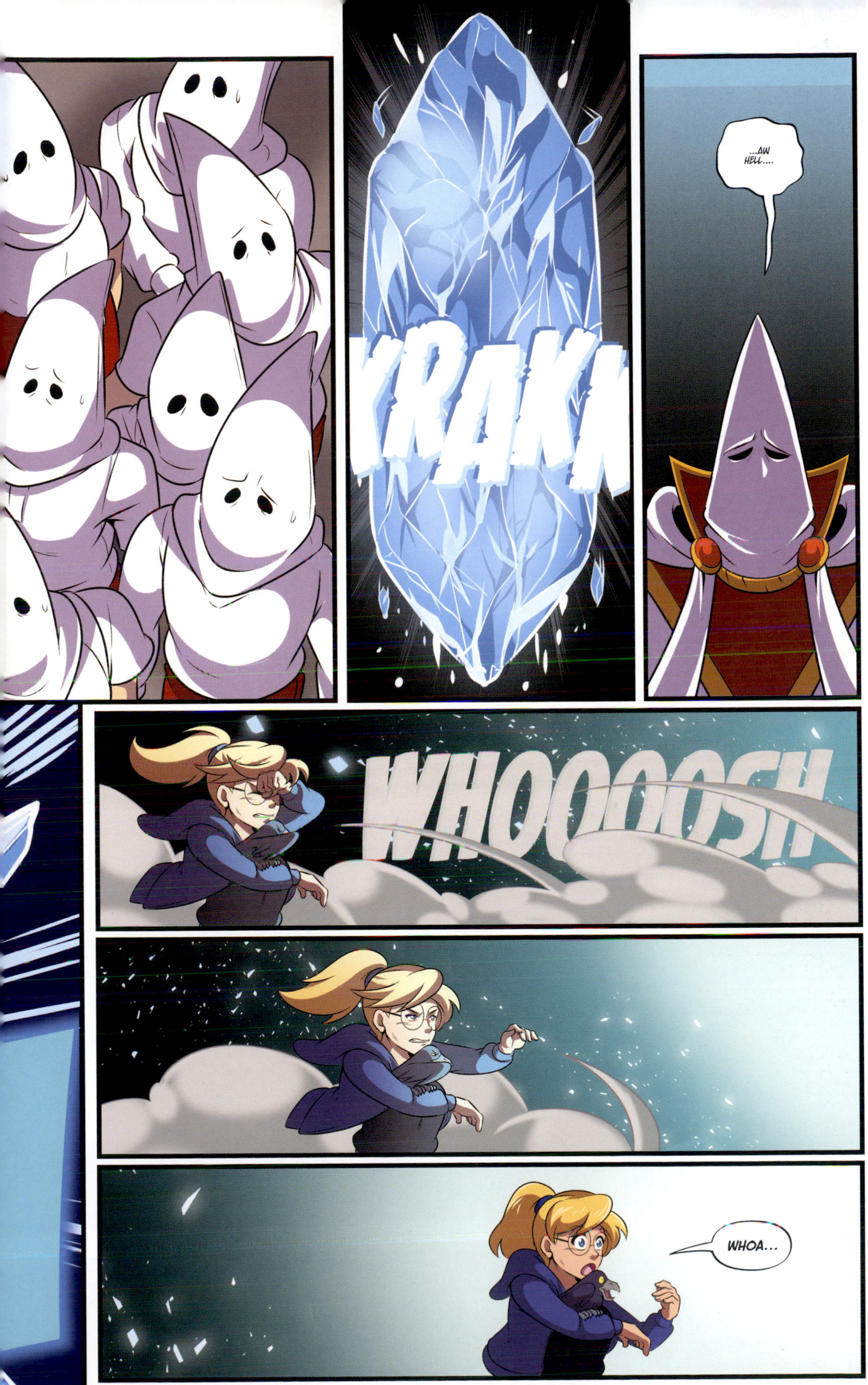
KRAKK
...AW HELL....
WHOOOOSH
WHOA...

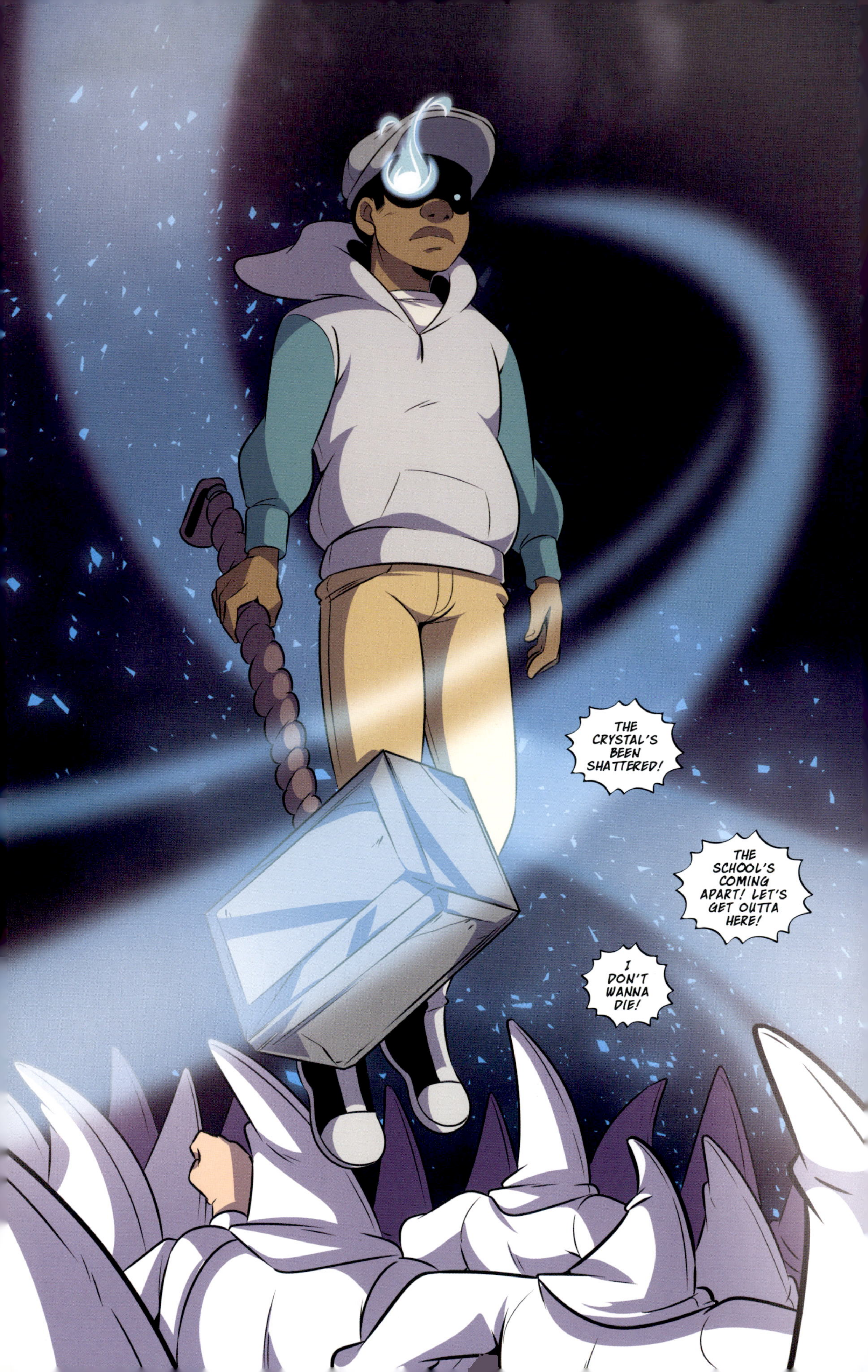
THE CRYSTAL'S BEEN SHATTERED!
THE SCHOOL'S COMING APART! LET'S GET OUTTA HERE!
I DON'T WANNA DIE!

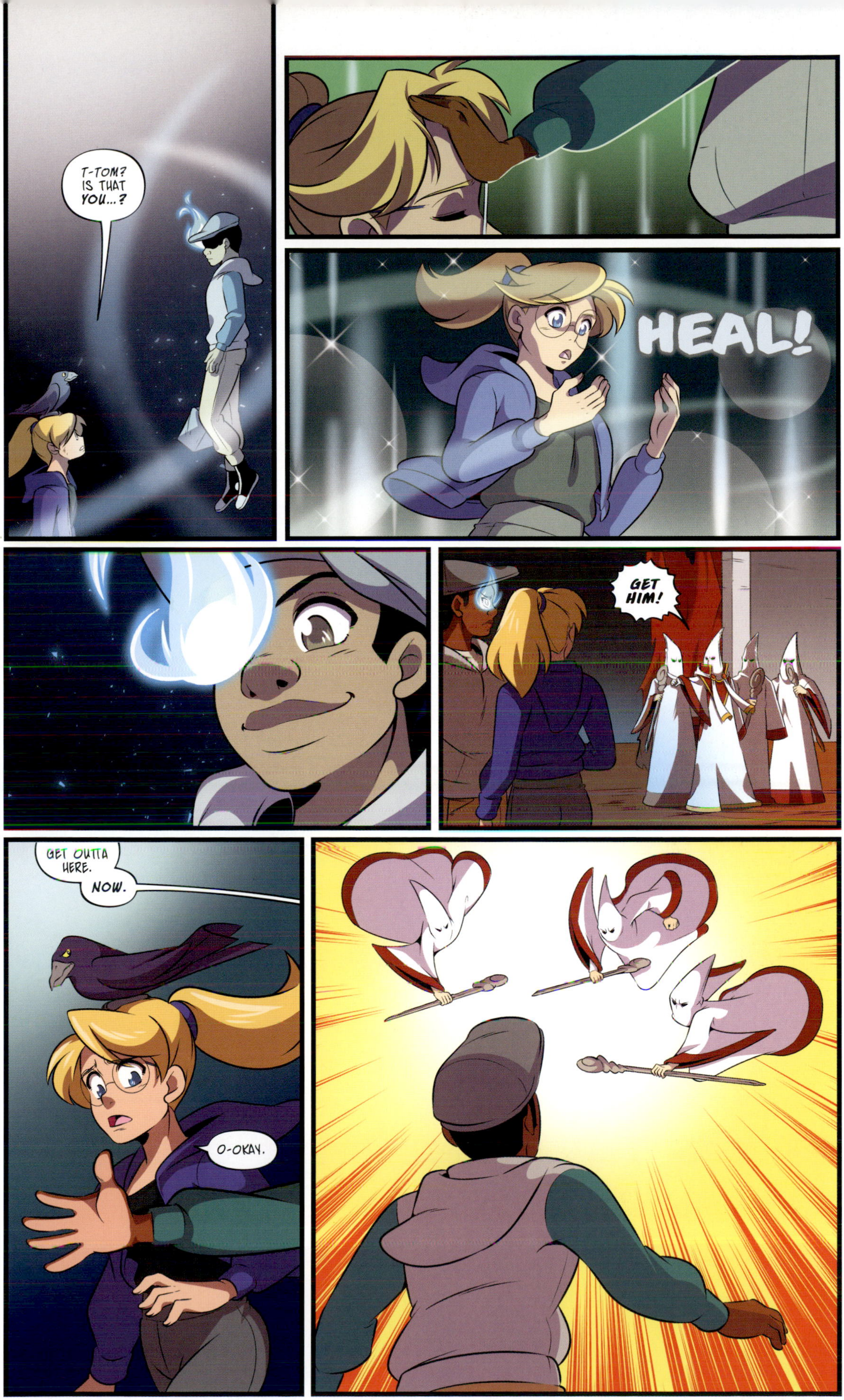
T-TOM? IS THAT YOU...?
HEAL!
GET HIM!
GET OUTTA HERE.
NOW.
O-OKAY.

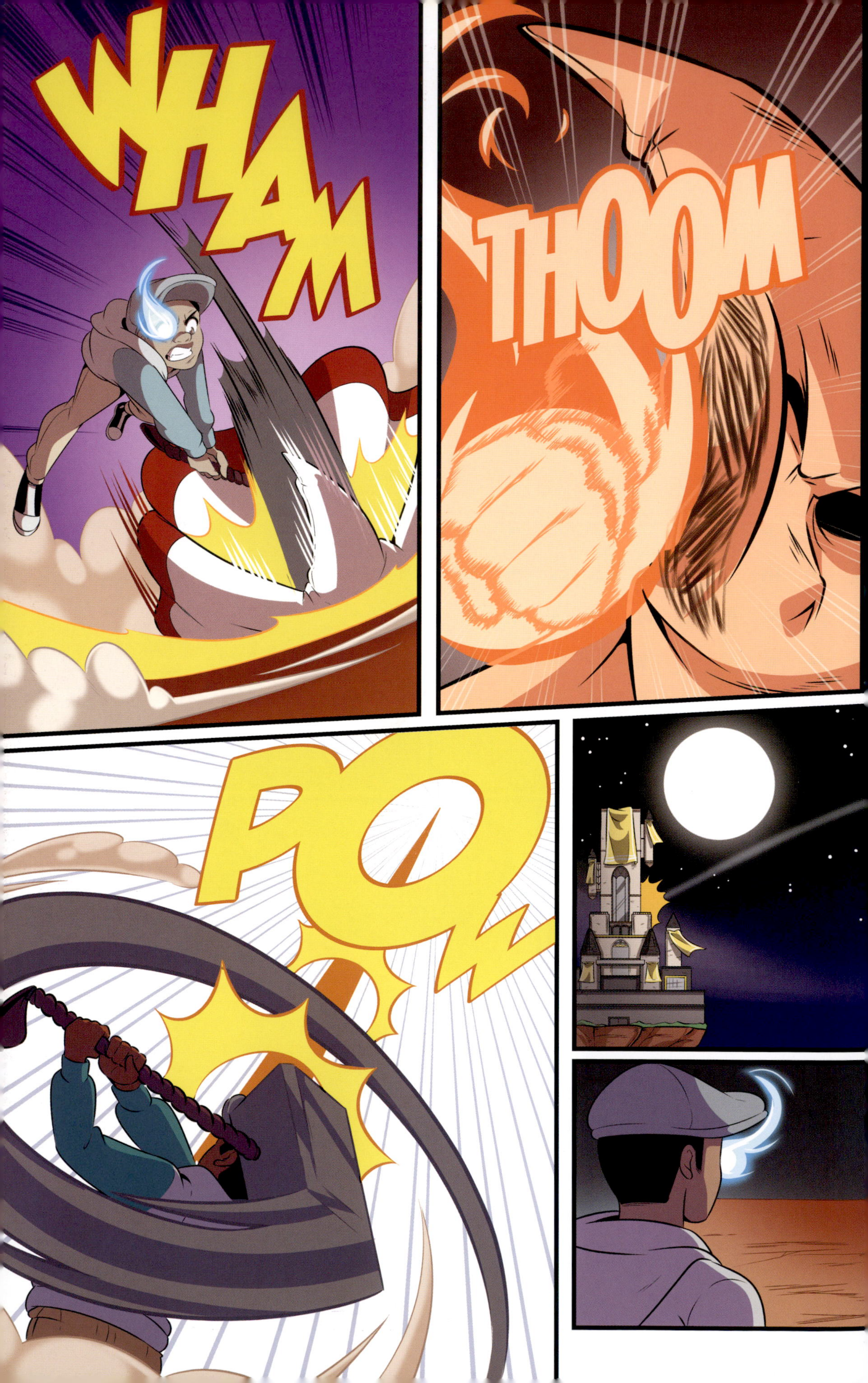
WHAM
THOOM
POW

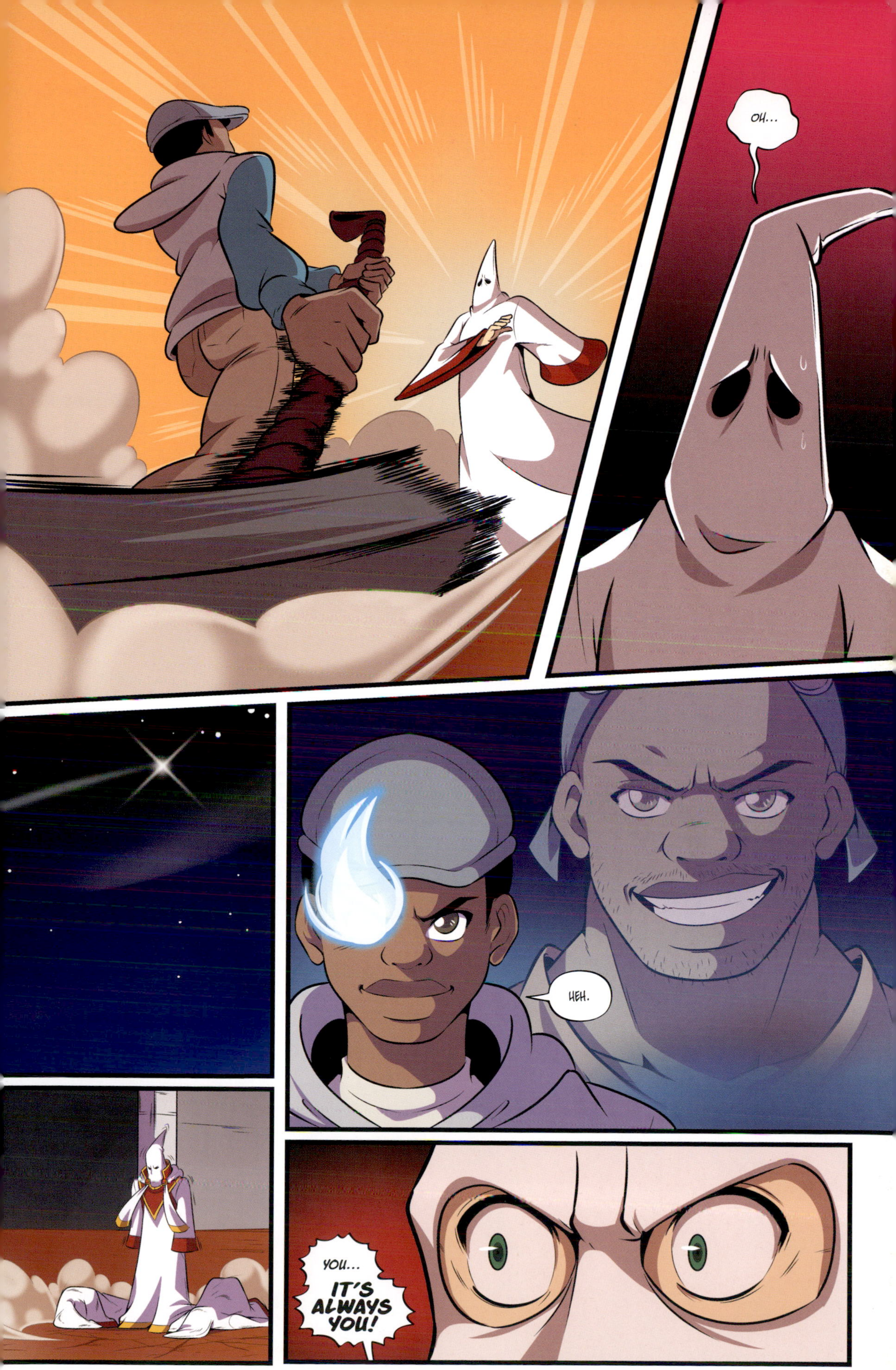
OH...
HEH.
YOU...
IT'S ALWAYS YOU!

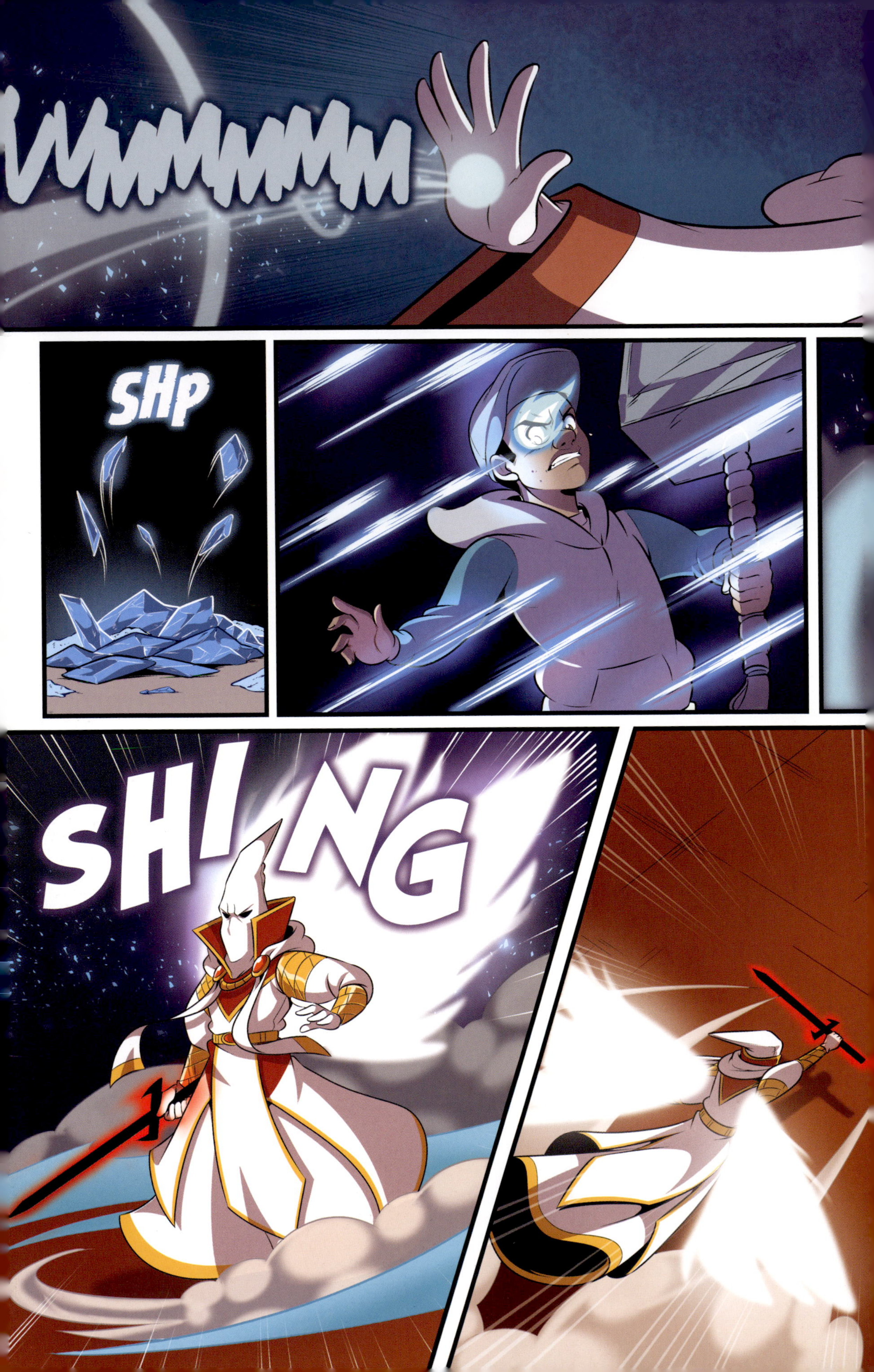
SHP
SHING

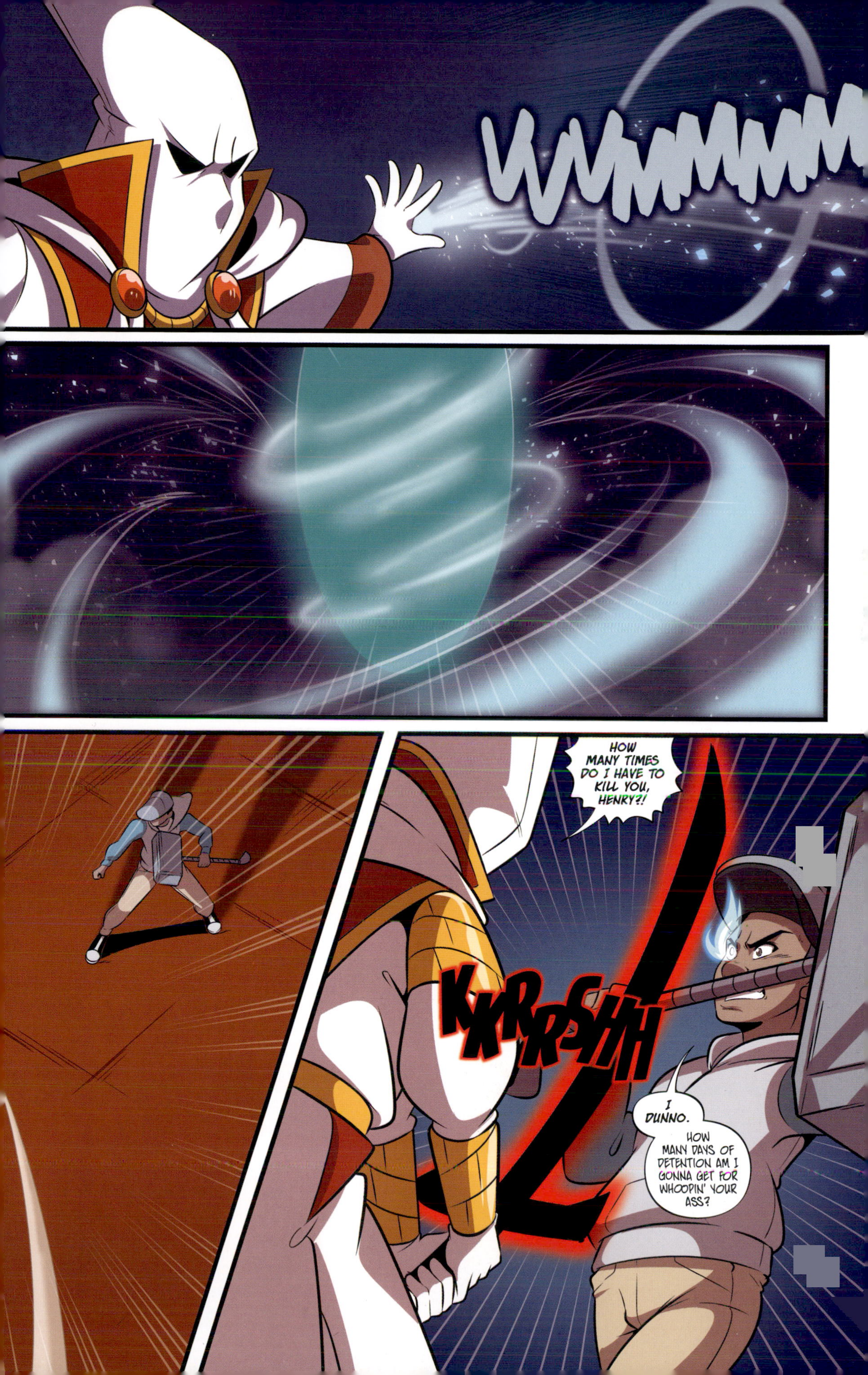
VVVMMMMM
HOW MANY TIMES DO I HAVE TO KILL YOU, HENRY?!
KKRRSHH
I DUNNO.
HOW MANY DAYS OF DETENTION AM I GONNA GET FOR WHOOPIN' YOUR ASS?

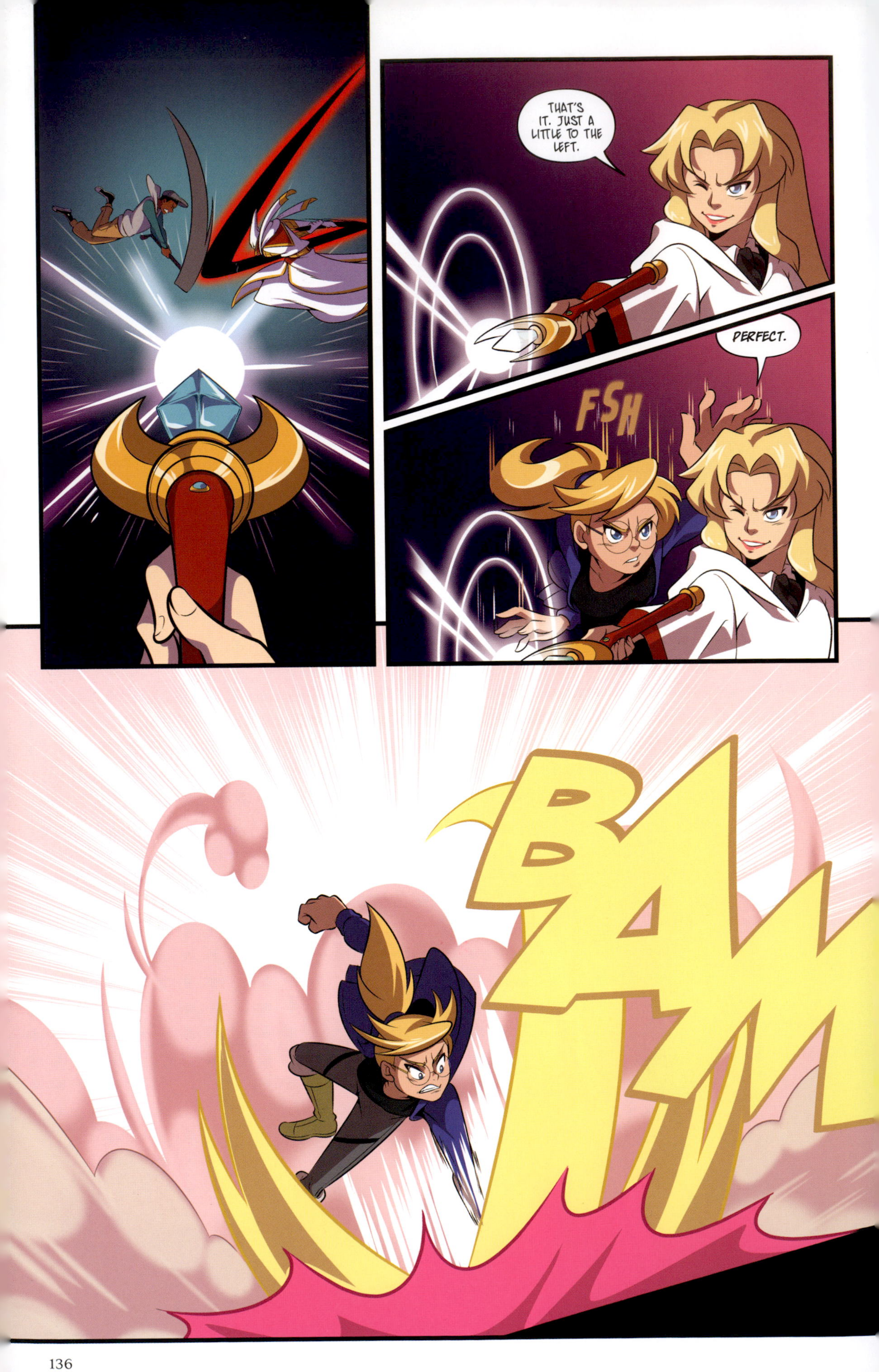
THAT'S IT. JUST A LITTLE TO THE LEFT.
PERFECT.
FSH
BAM

:SHUDDER:

:SHUDDER:

YOU! HELP ME CARRY YOUR GIRLFRIEND OUT.

I-I-I...

NOW!

Y-YES, MA'AM!

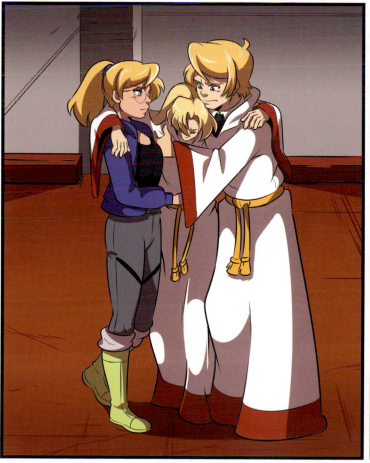

GET HIM, TOM.

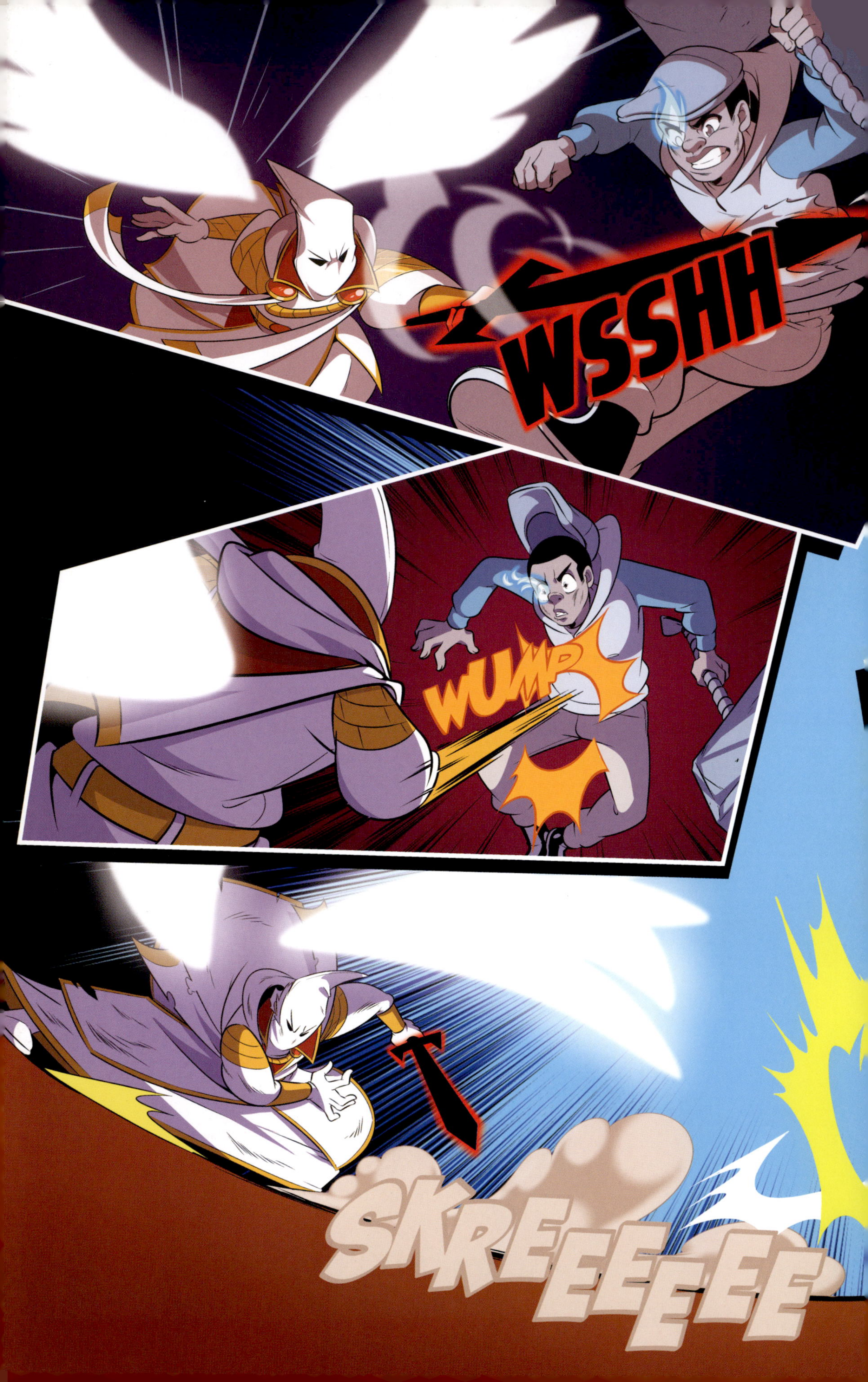
WSSHH
WUMP
SKREEEEEEE

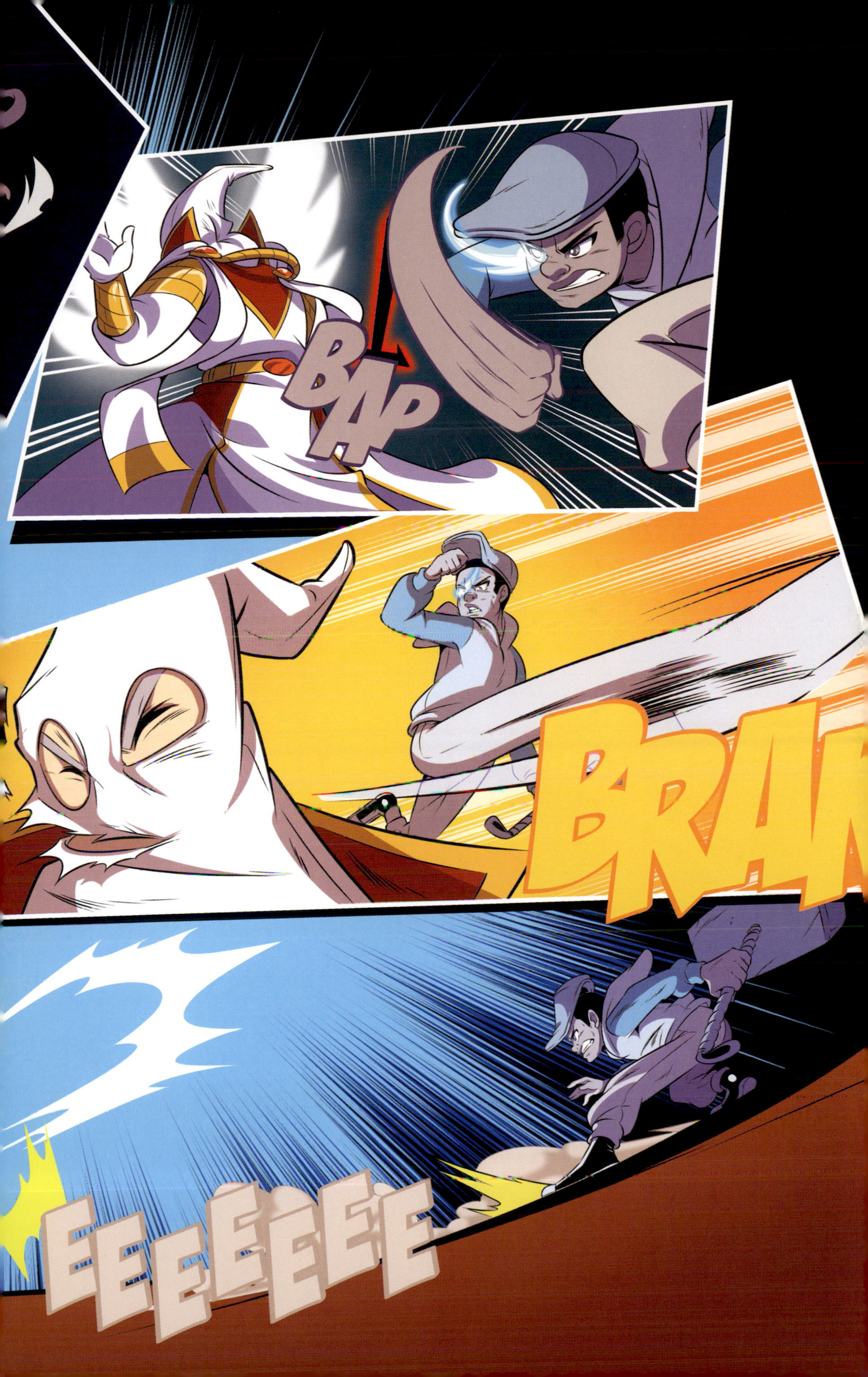
BAP
EEEEEEE

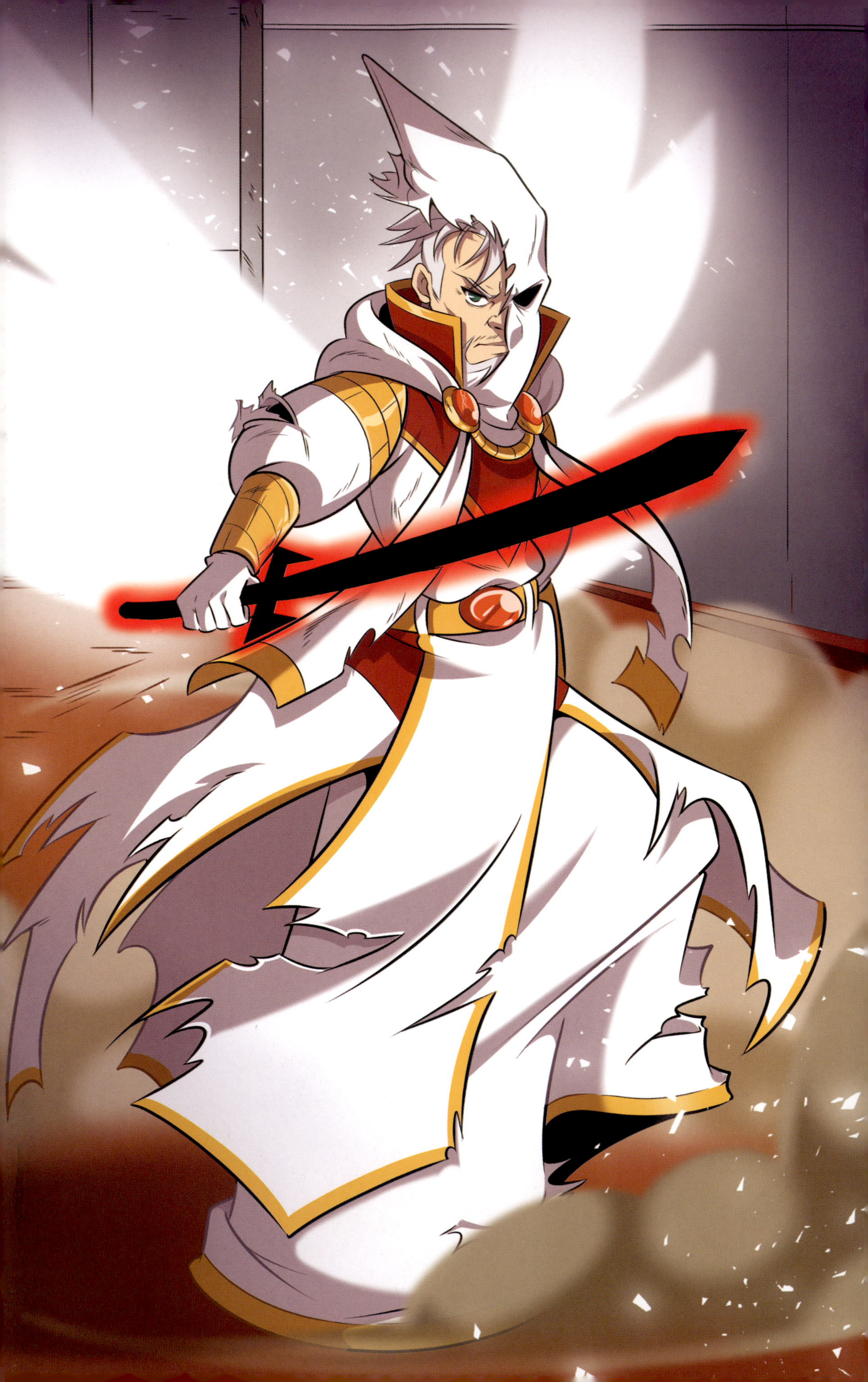

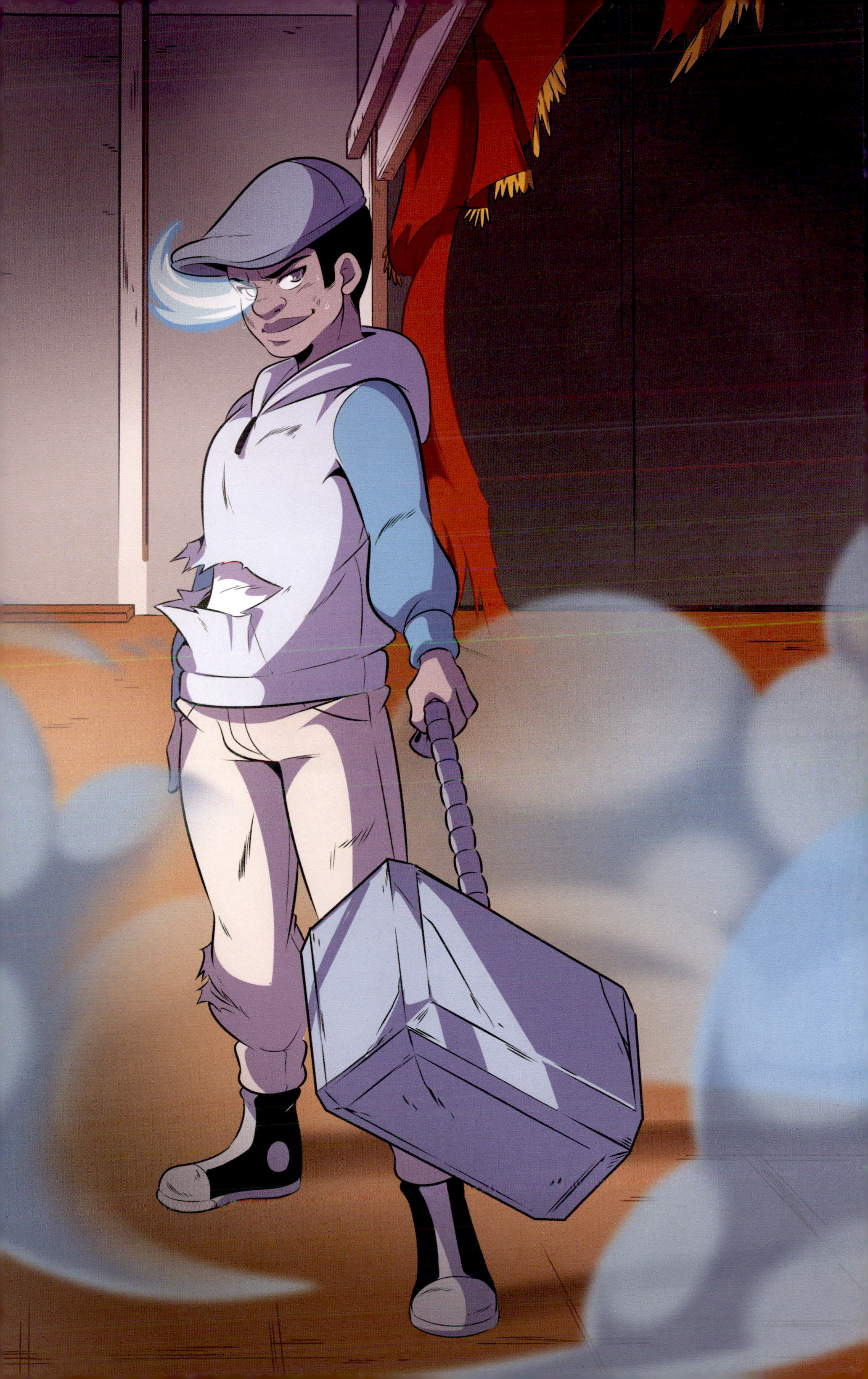

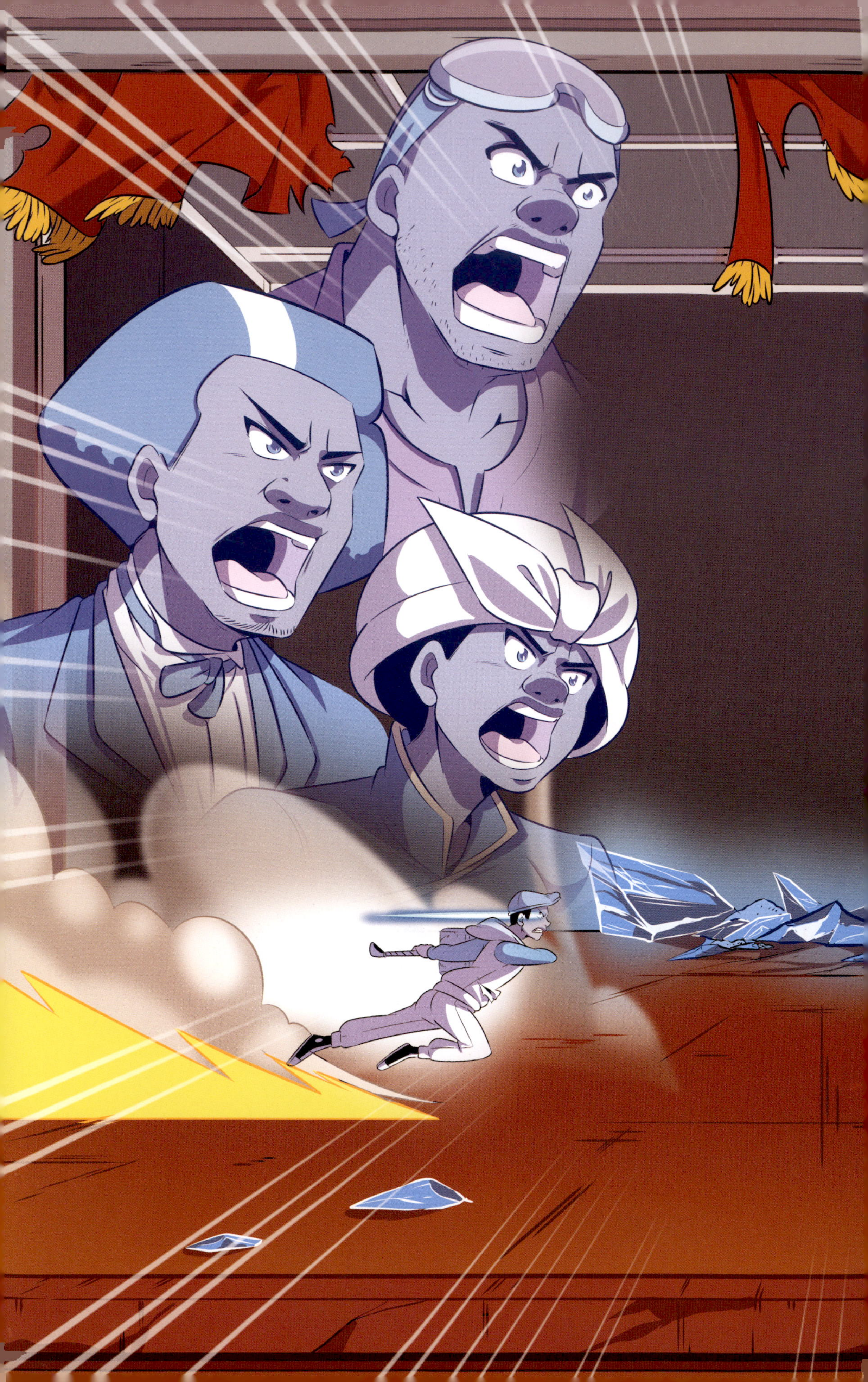

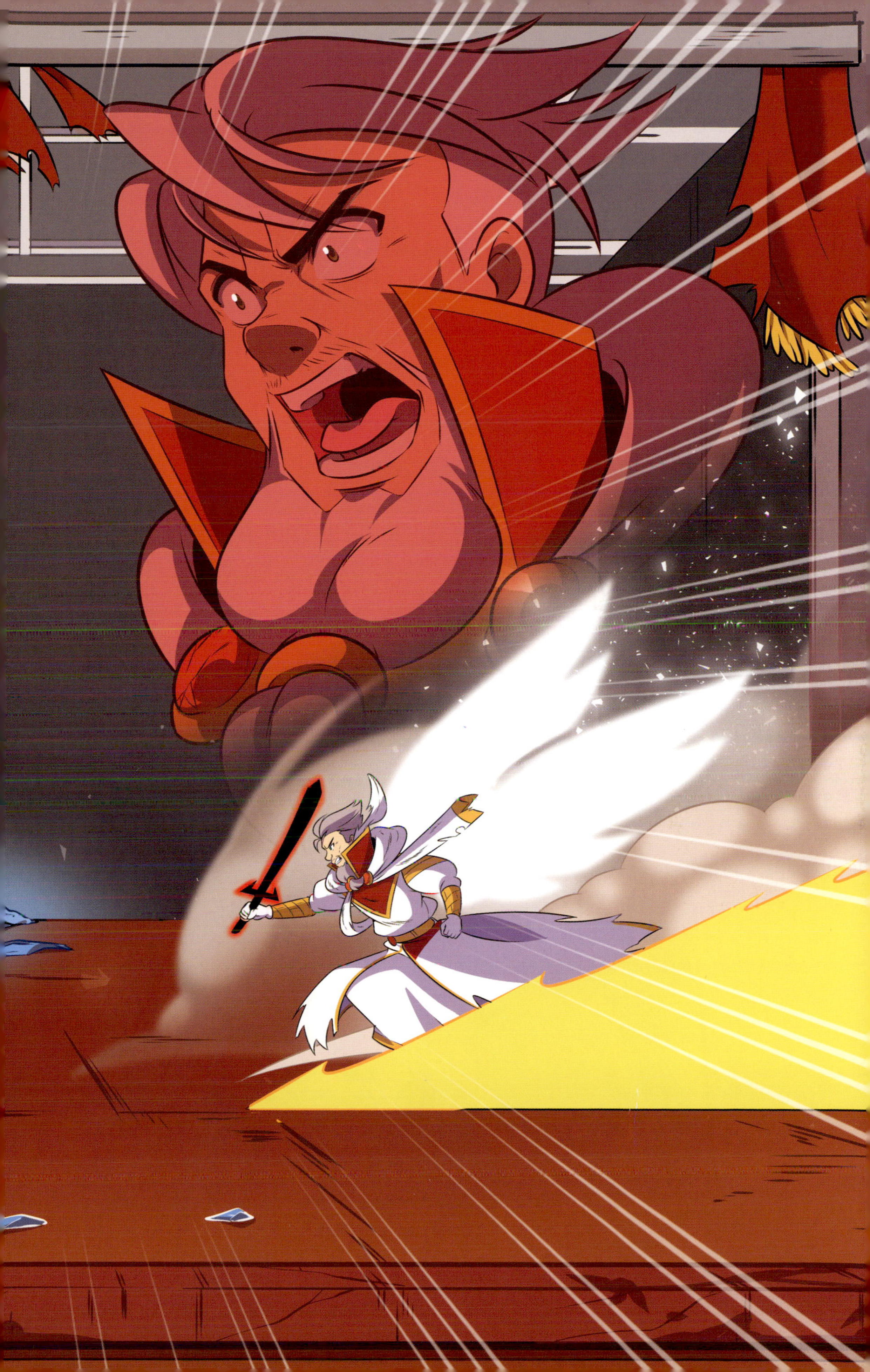

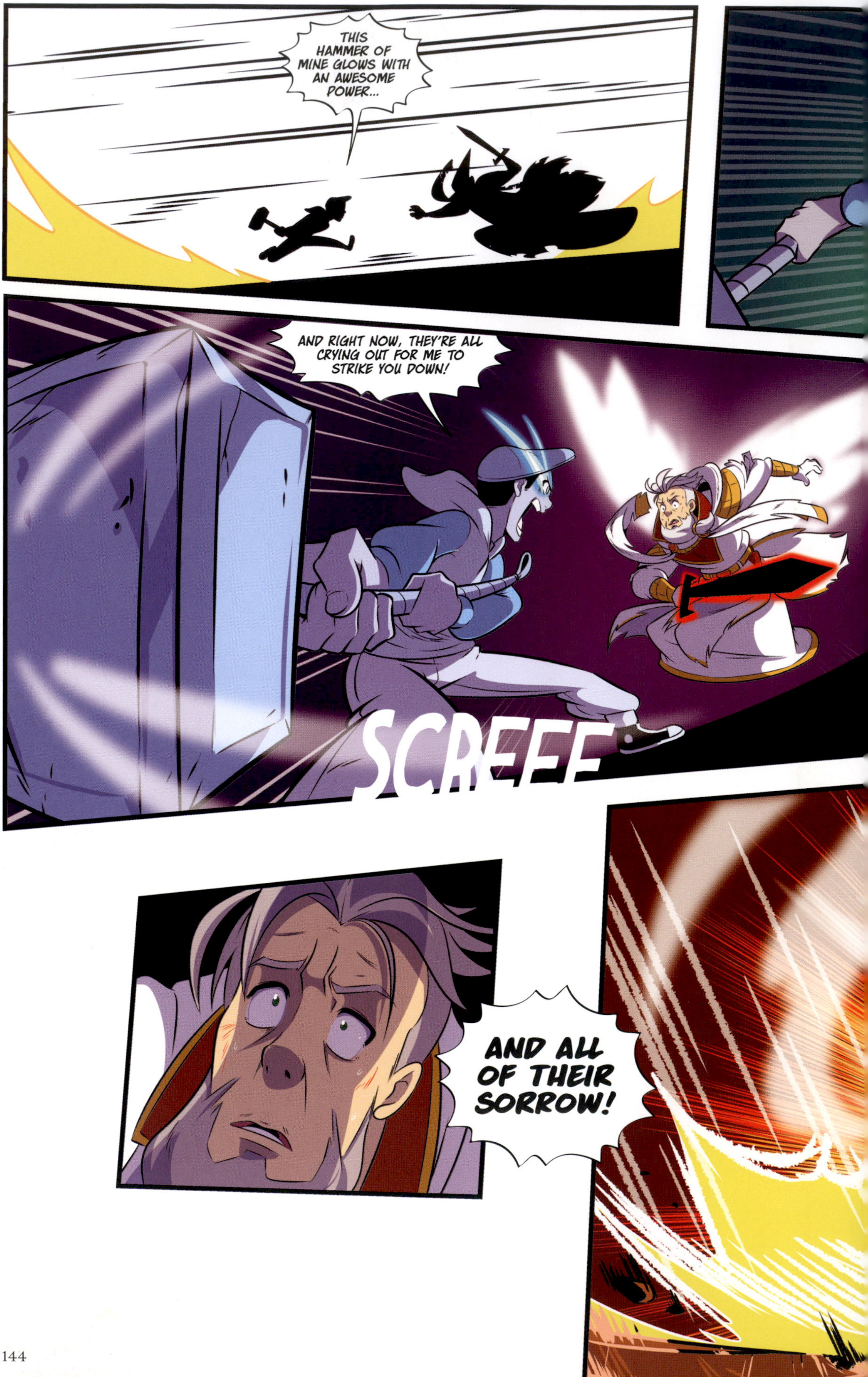
THIS HAMMER OF MINE GLOWS WITH AN AWESOME POWER...
AND RIGHT NOW, THEY'RE ALL CRYING OUT FOR ME TO STRIKE YOU DOWN!
SCREEE
AND ALL OF THEIR SORROW!

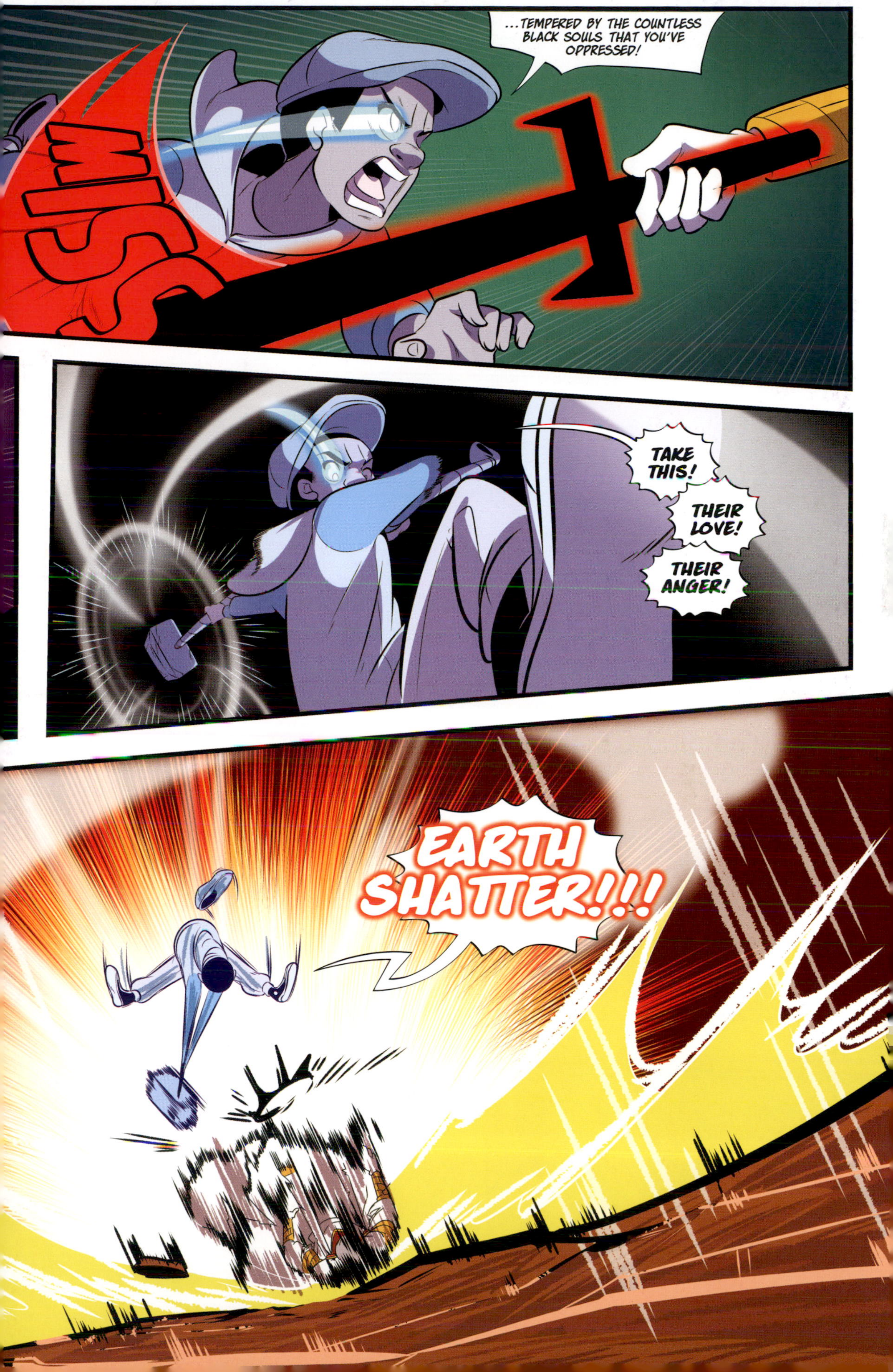
...TEMPERED BY THE COUNTLESS BLACK SOULS THAT YOU'VE OPPRESSED!
MISS
TAKE THIS!
THEIR LOVE!
THEIR ANGER!
EARTH SHATTER!!!

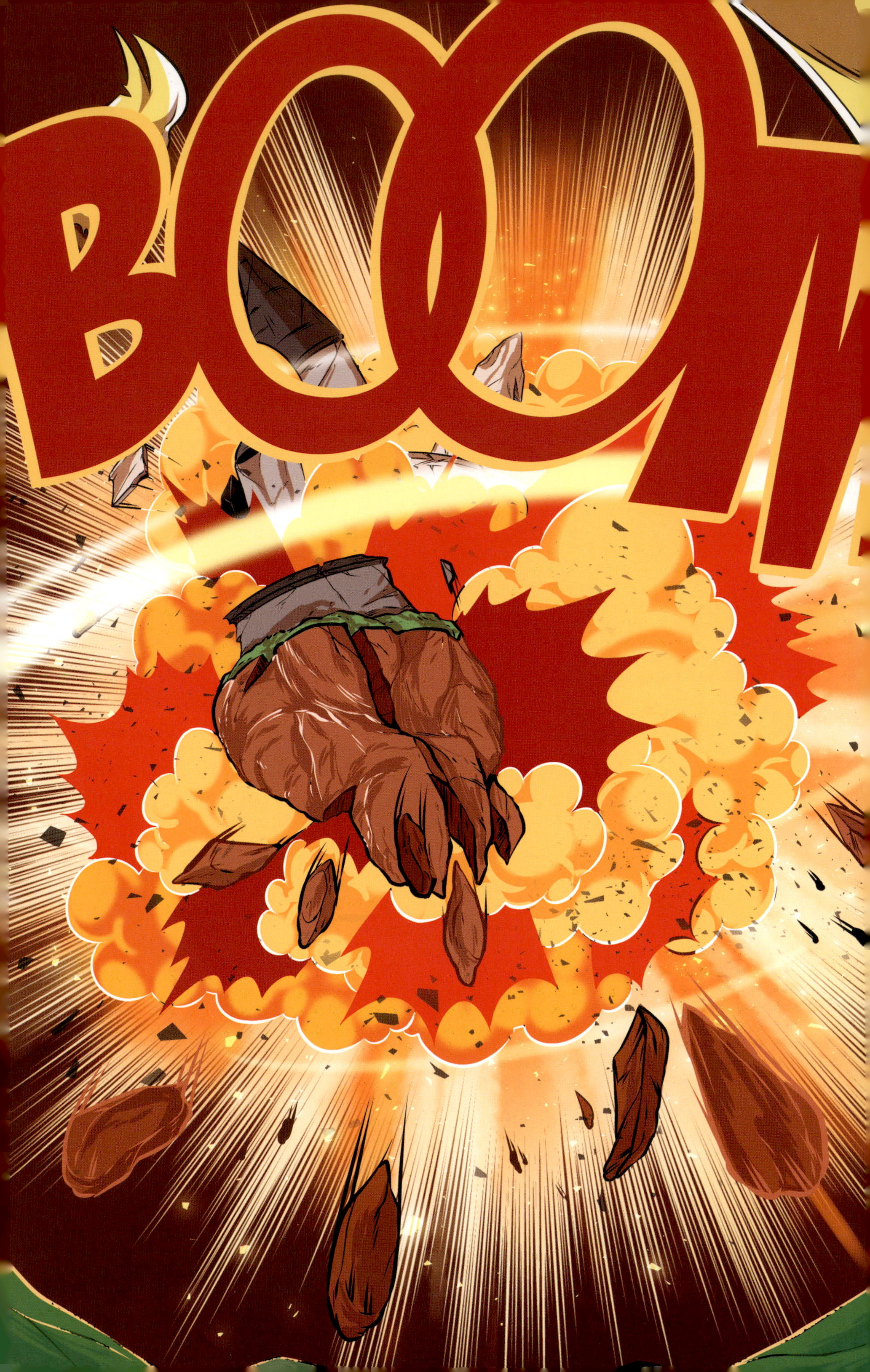
BOOM

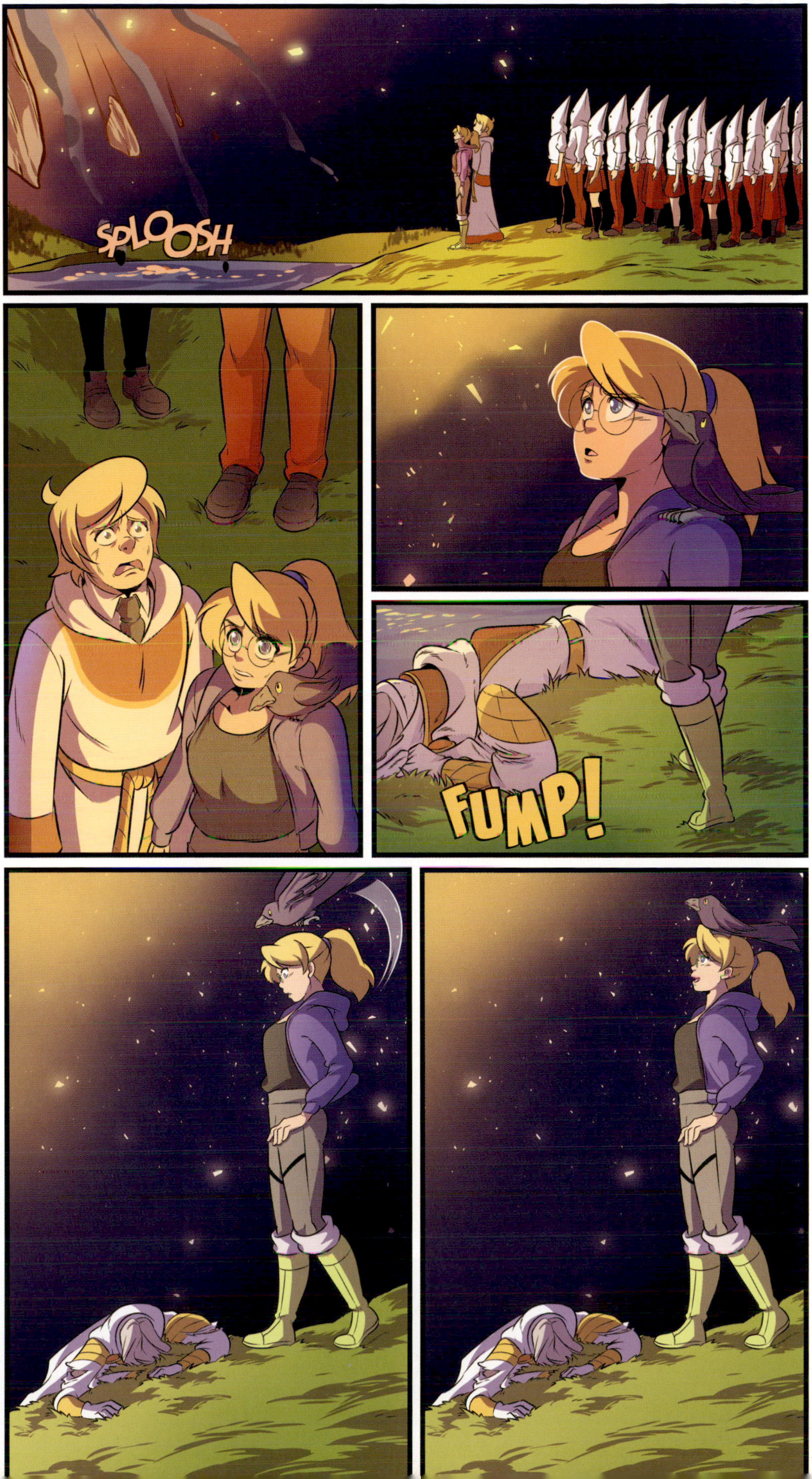
SPLOOSH
FUMP!

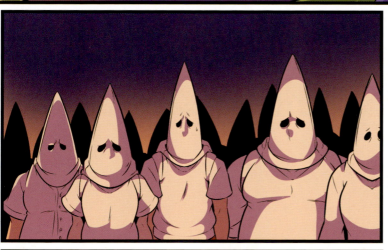

SHIFT

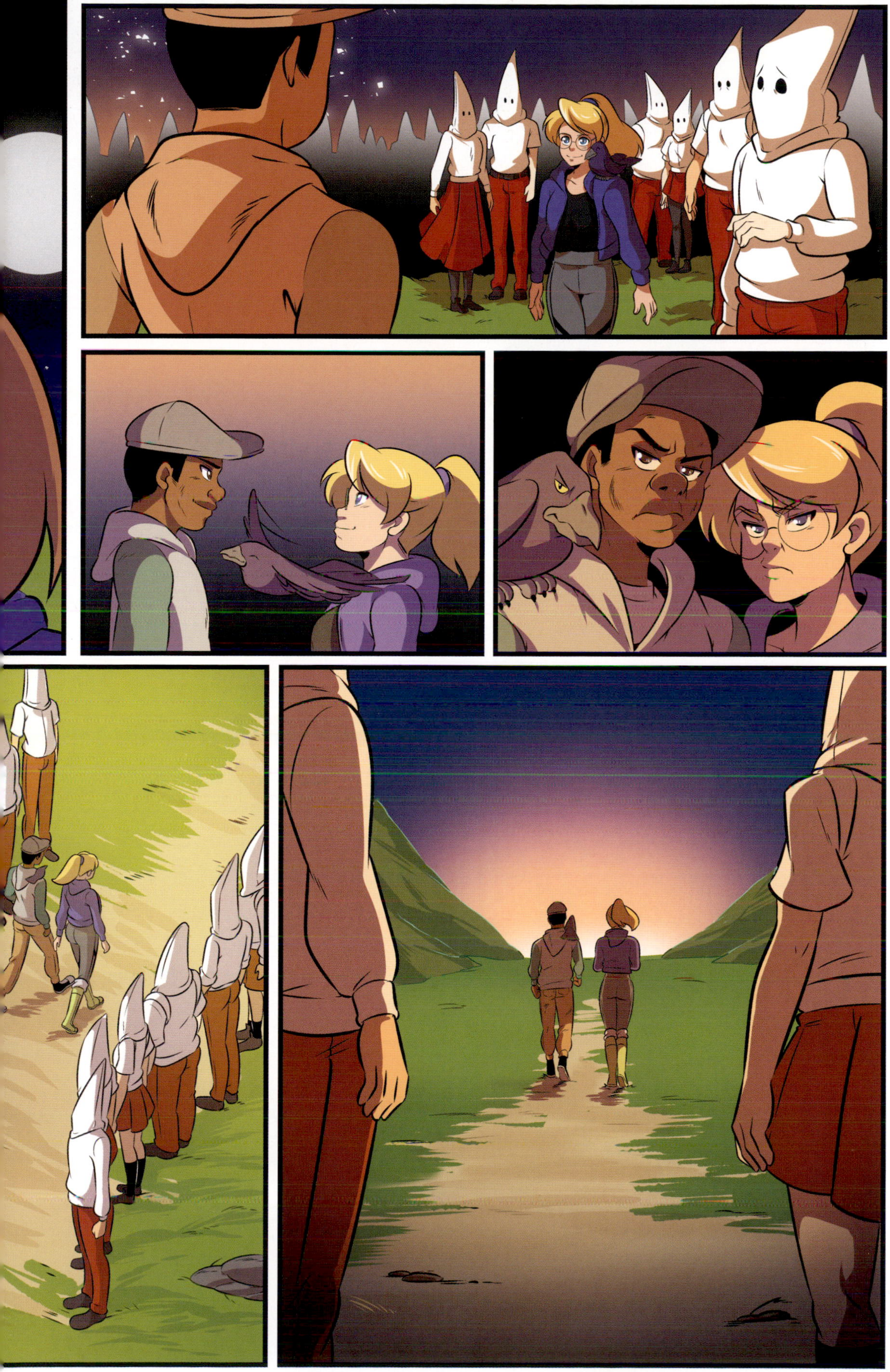

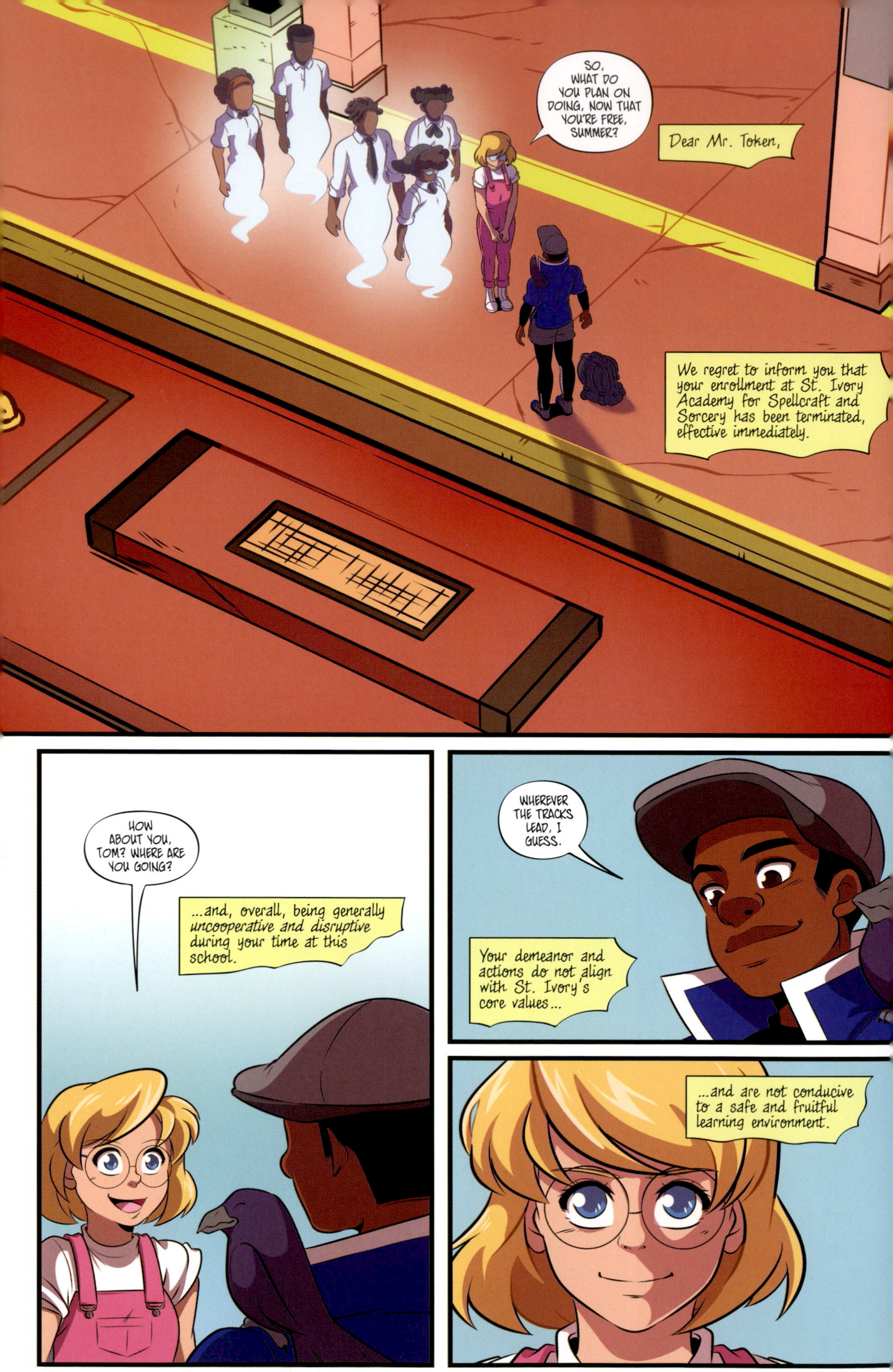
SO, WHAT DO YOU PLAN ON DOING, NOW THAT YOU'RE FREE, SUMMER?
Dear Mr. Token,
We regret to inform you that your enrollment at St. Ivory Academy for Spellcraft and Sorcery has been terminated, effective immediately.
HOW ABOUT YOU, TOM? WHERE ARE YOU GOING?
...and, overall, being generally uncooperative and disruptive during your time at this school.
WHEREVER THE TRACKS LEAD, I GUESS.
Your demeanor and actions do not align with St. Ivory's core values...
...and are not conducive to a safe and fruitful learning environment.

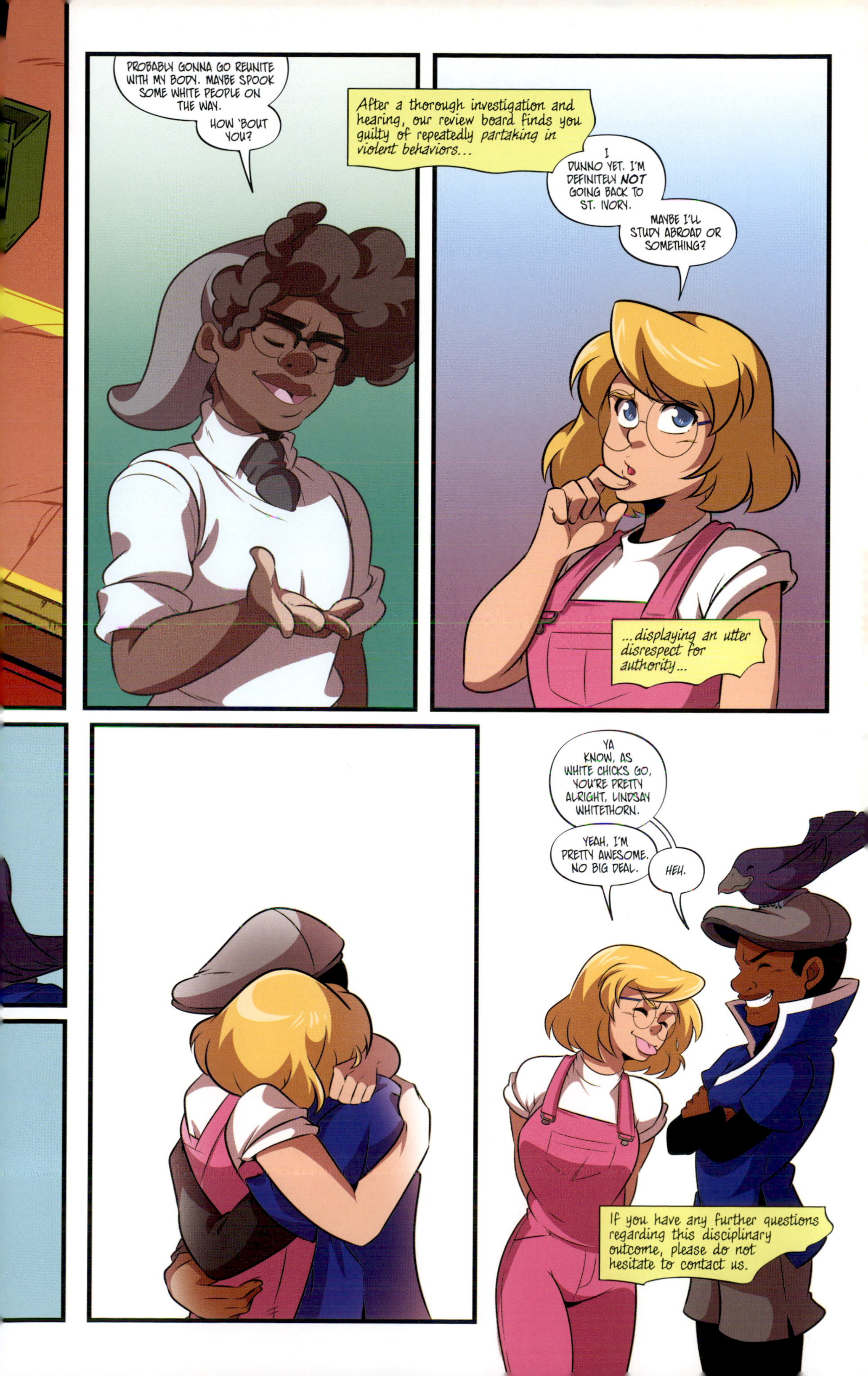
PROBABLY GONNA GO REUNITE WITH MY BODY. MAYBE SPOOK SOME WHITE PEOPLE ON THE WAY.
HOW 'BOUT YOU?
After a thorough investigation and hearing, our review board finds you guilty of repeatedly partaking in violent behaviors...
I DUNNO YET. I'M DEFINITELY NOT GOING BACK TO ST. IVORY.
MAYBE I'LL STUDY ABROAD OR SOMETHING?
...displaying an utter disrespect for authority...
YA KNOW, AS WHITE CHICKS GO, YOU'RE PRETTY ALRIGHT, LINDSAY WHITETHORN.
YEAH, I'M PRETTY AWESOME. NO BIG DEAL.
HEH.
If you have any further questions regarding this disciplinary outcome, please do not hesitate to contact us.

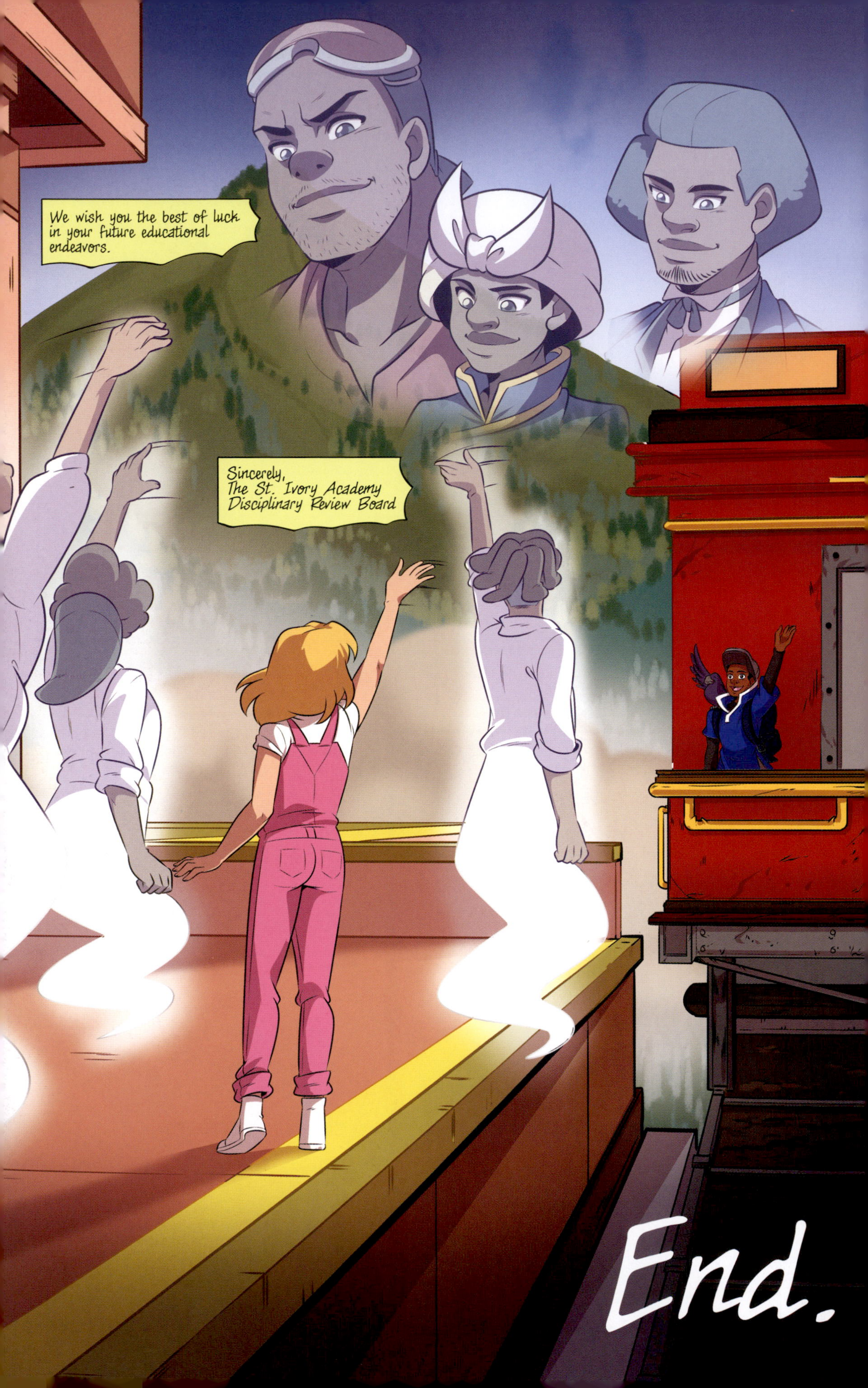
We wish you the best of luck in your future educational endeavors.
Sincerely, The St. Ivory Academy Disciplinary Review Board
End.

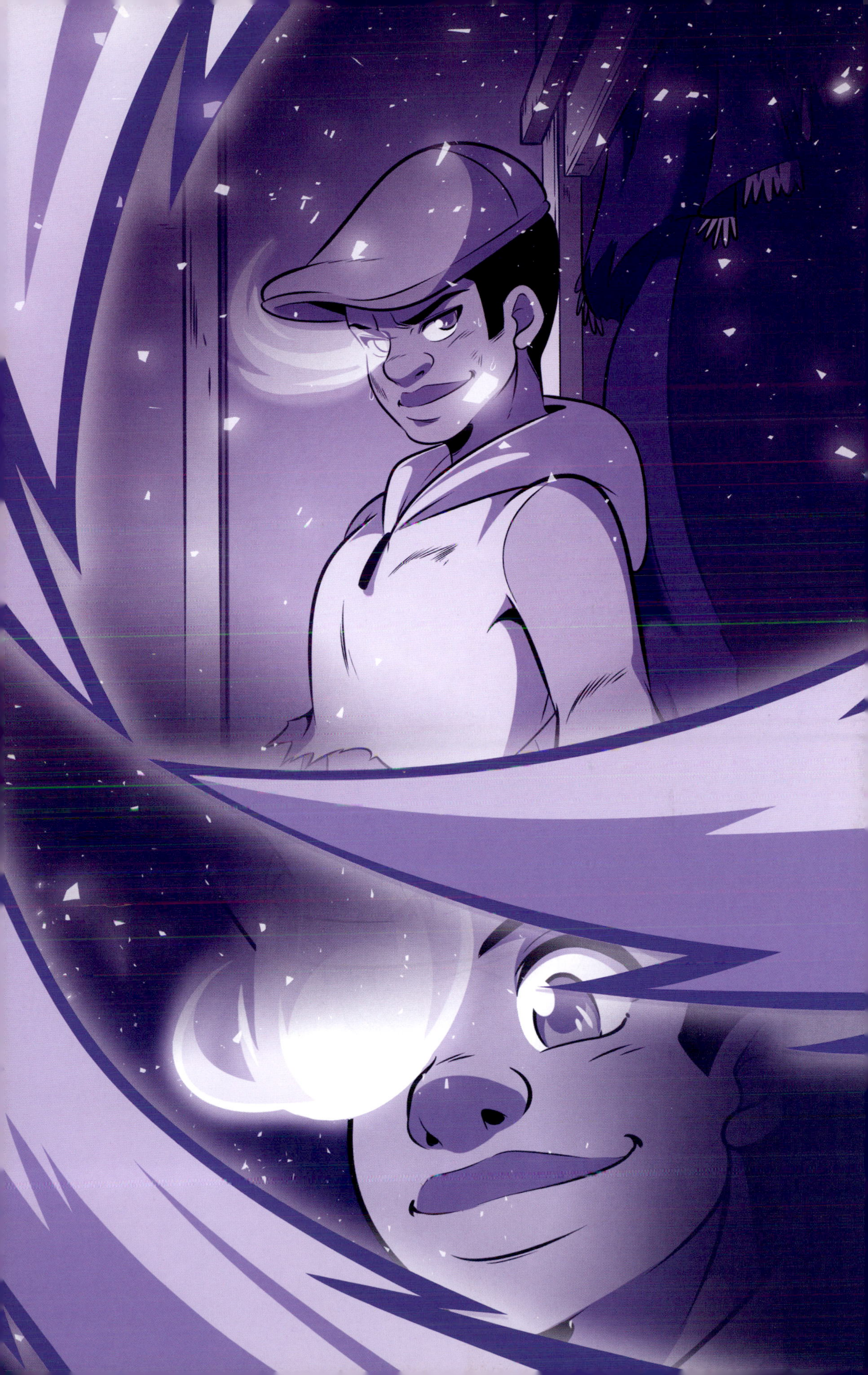

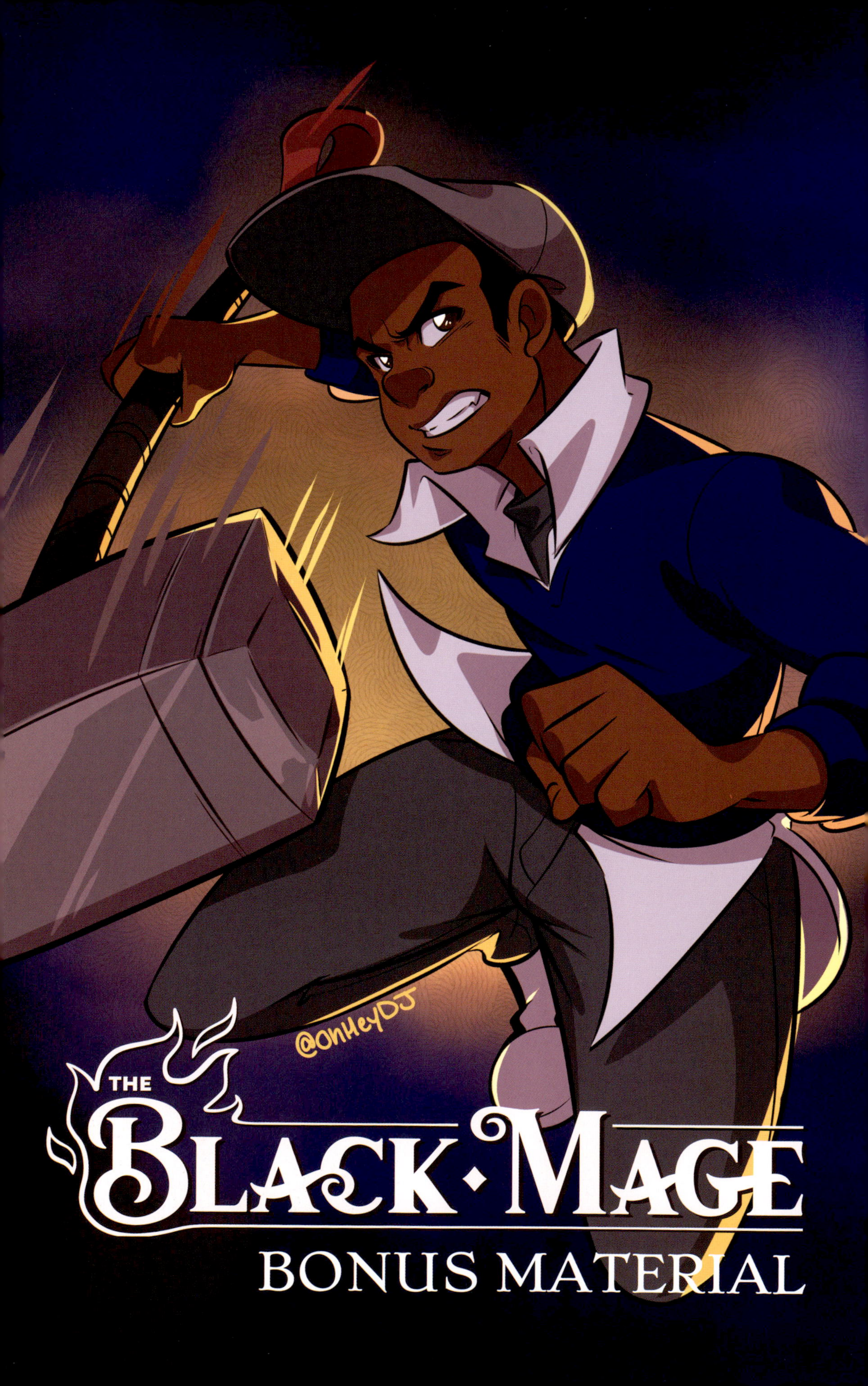
@OhHeyDJ
THE
BLACK·MAGE
BONUS MATERIAL

CHARACTER DESIGNS

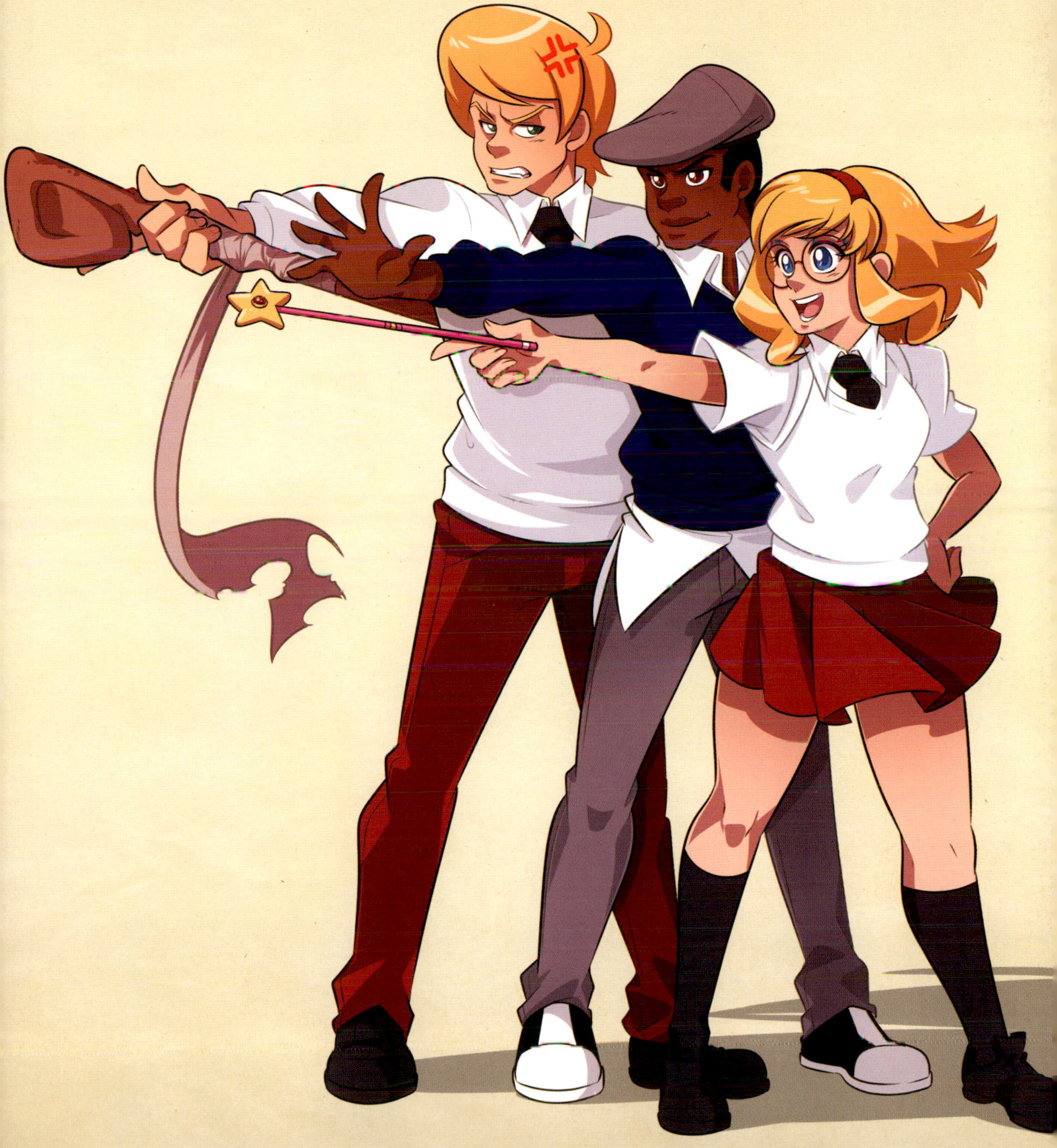

CHARACTER DESIGNS

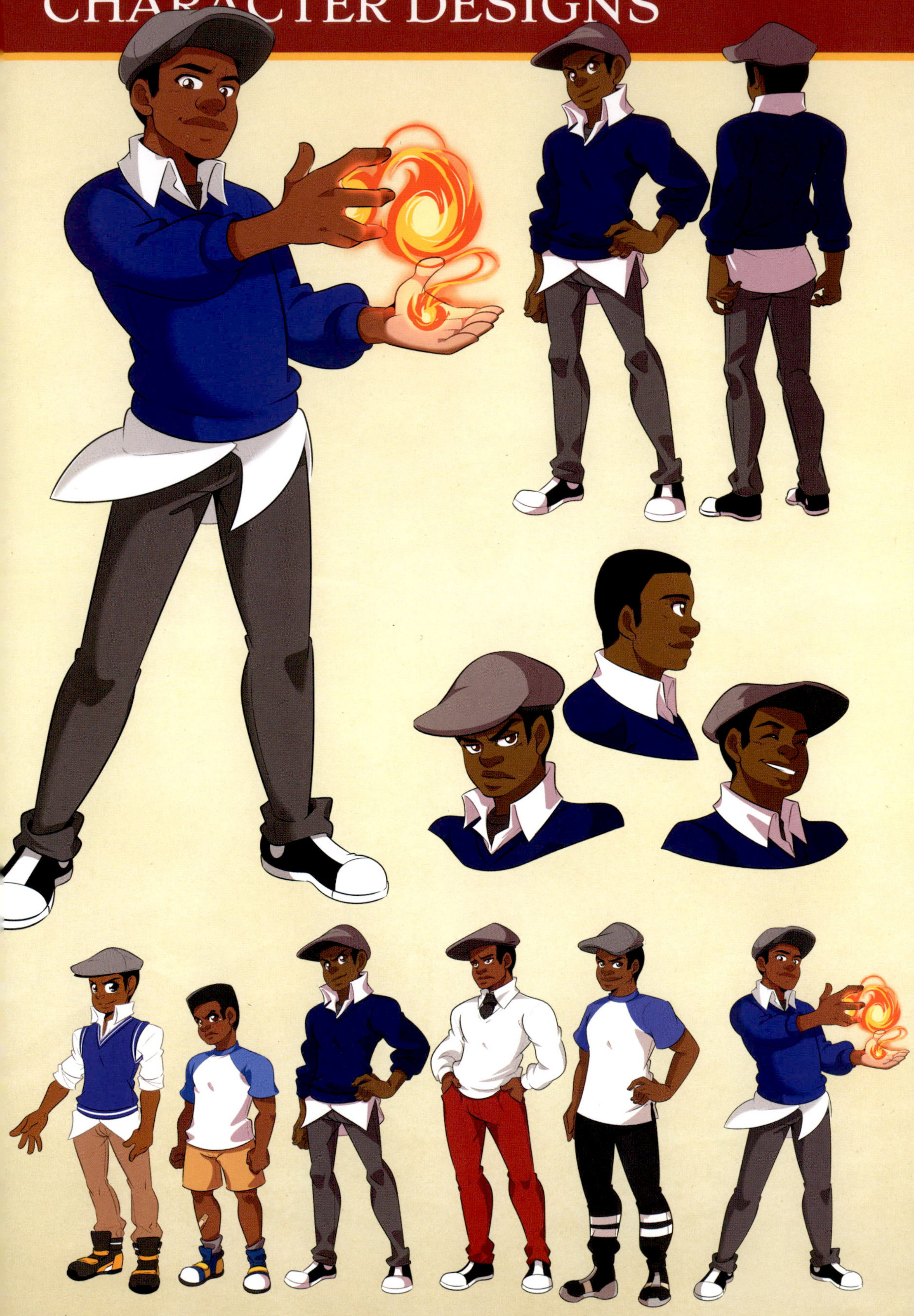

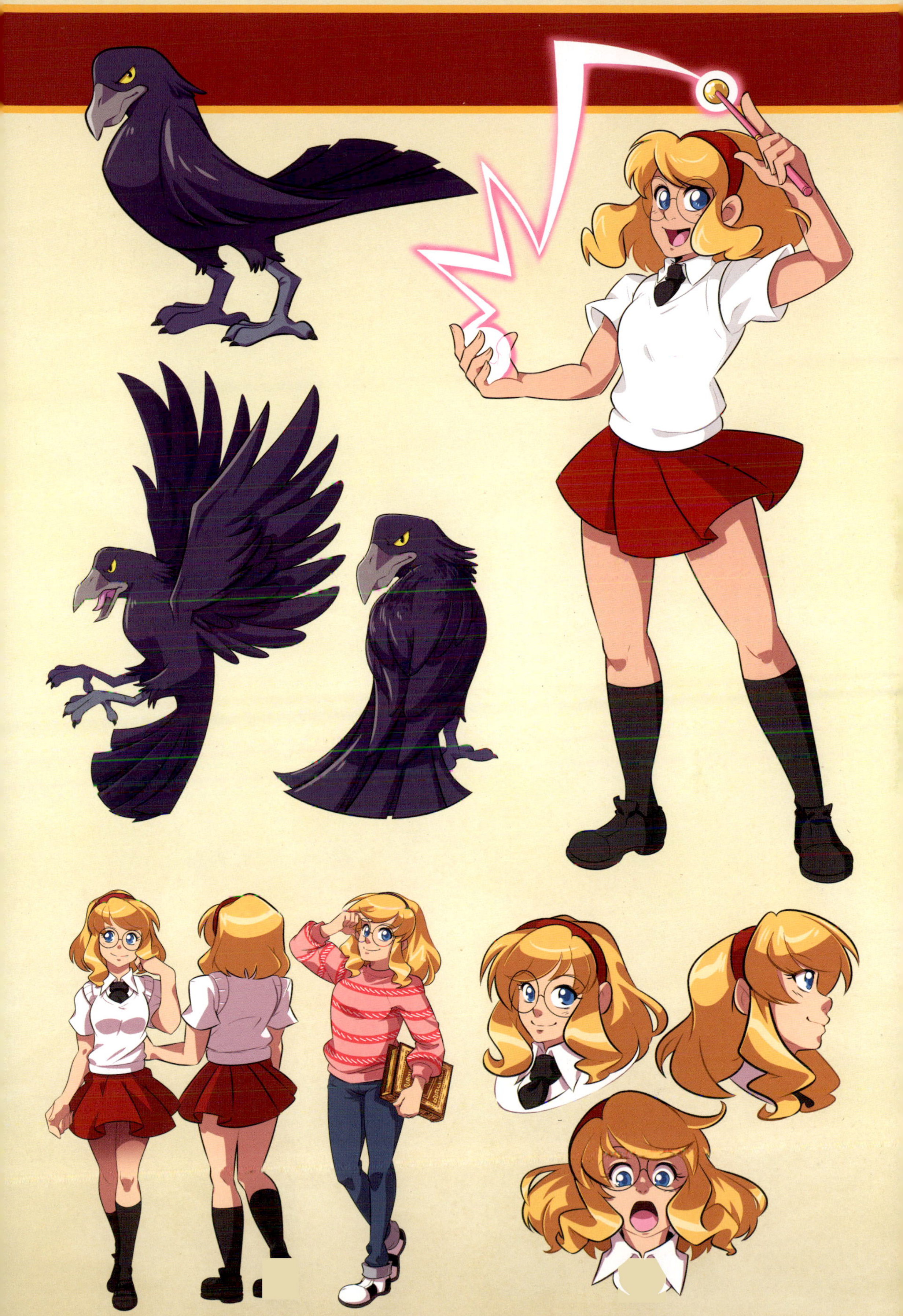

CHARACTER DESIGNS

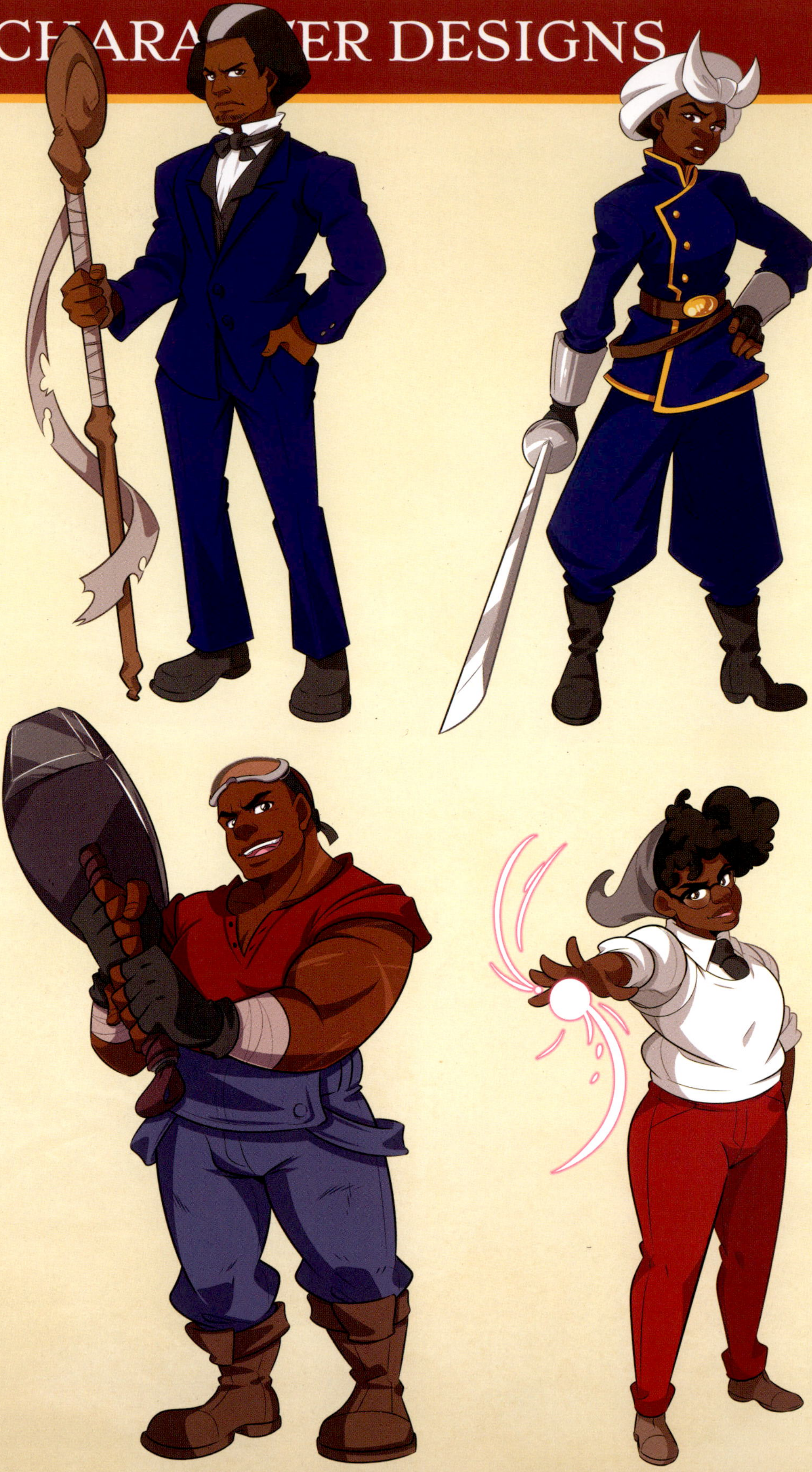

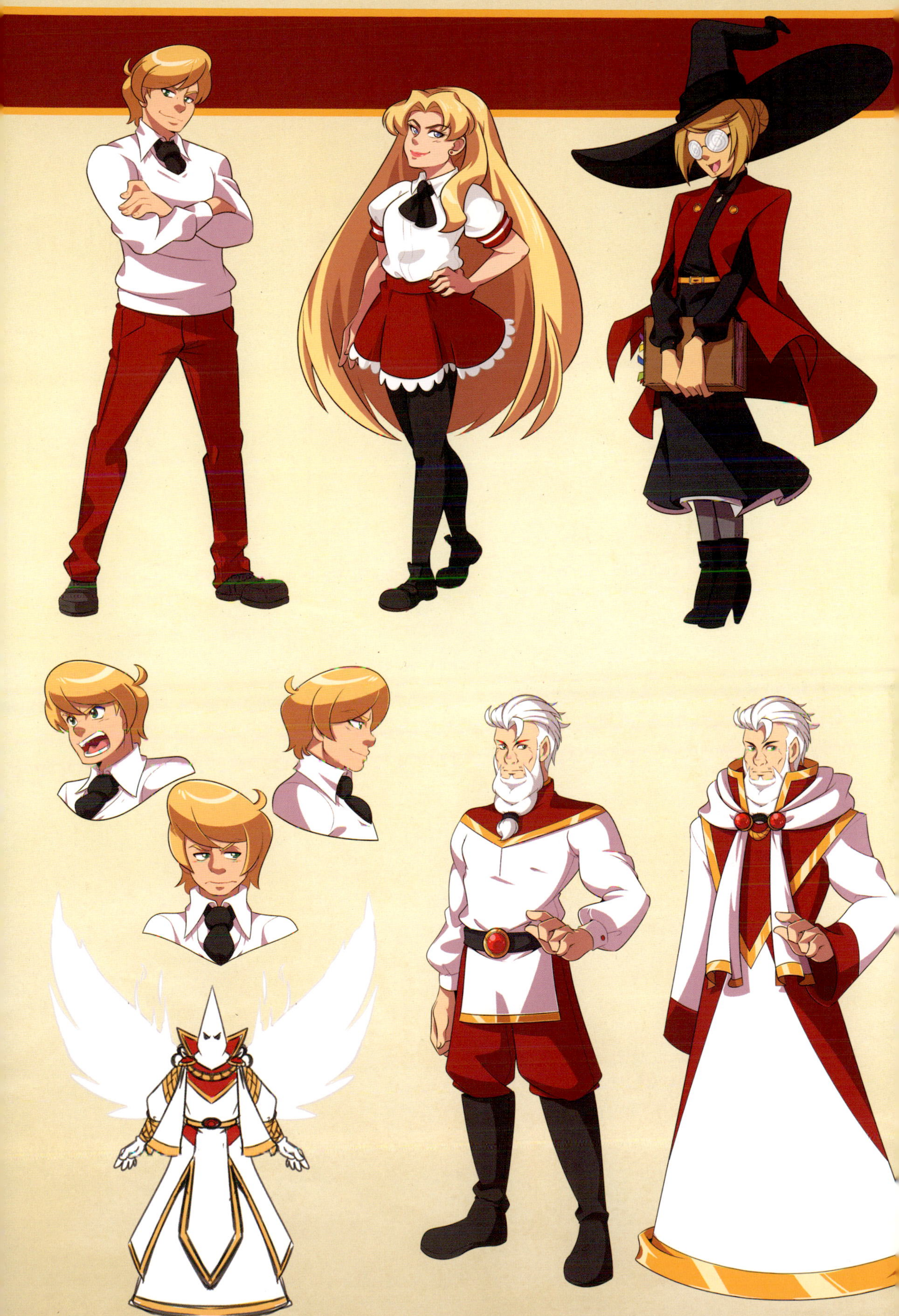

PIN-UP GALLERY

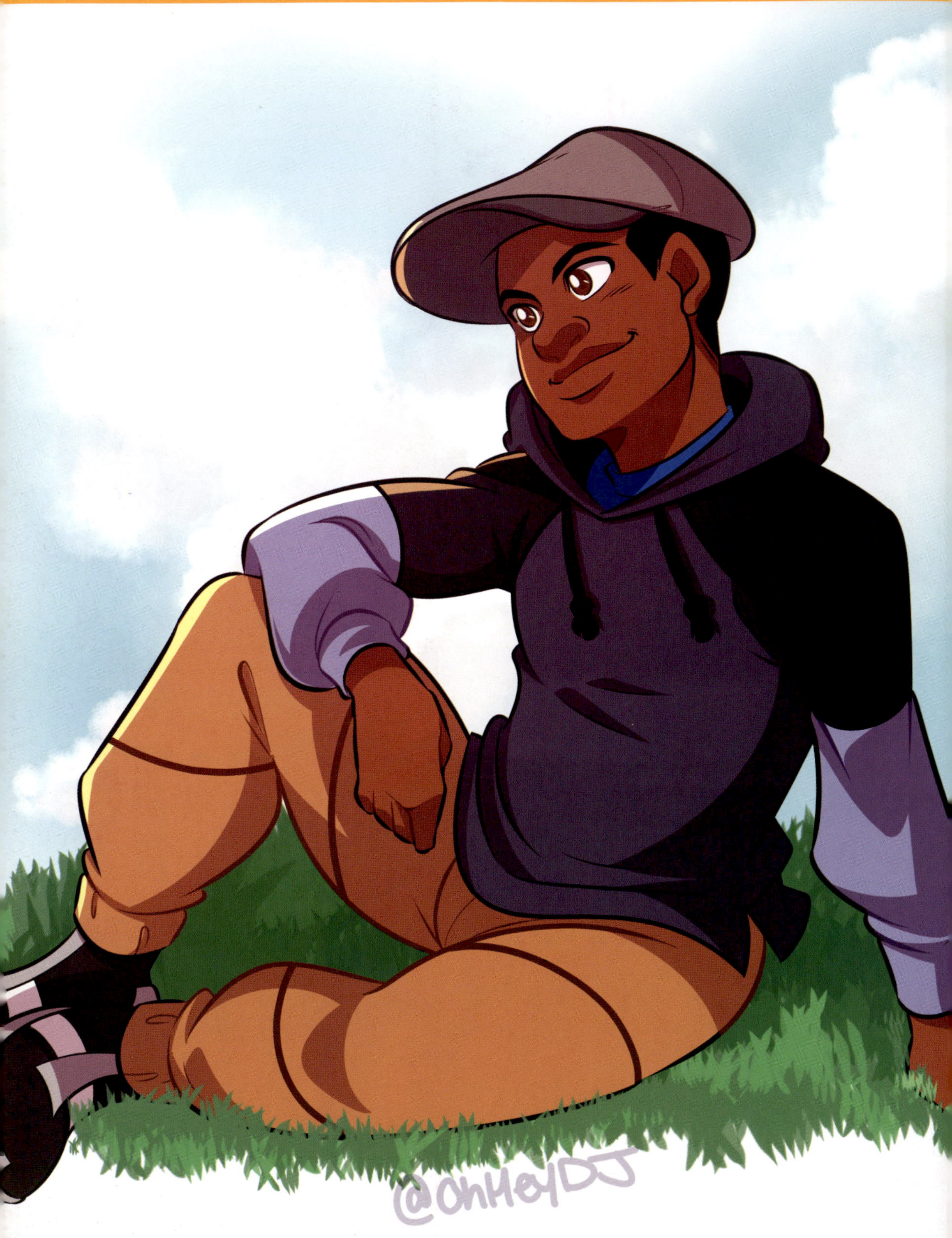
@OhHeyDJ

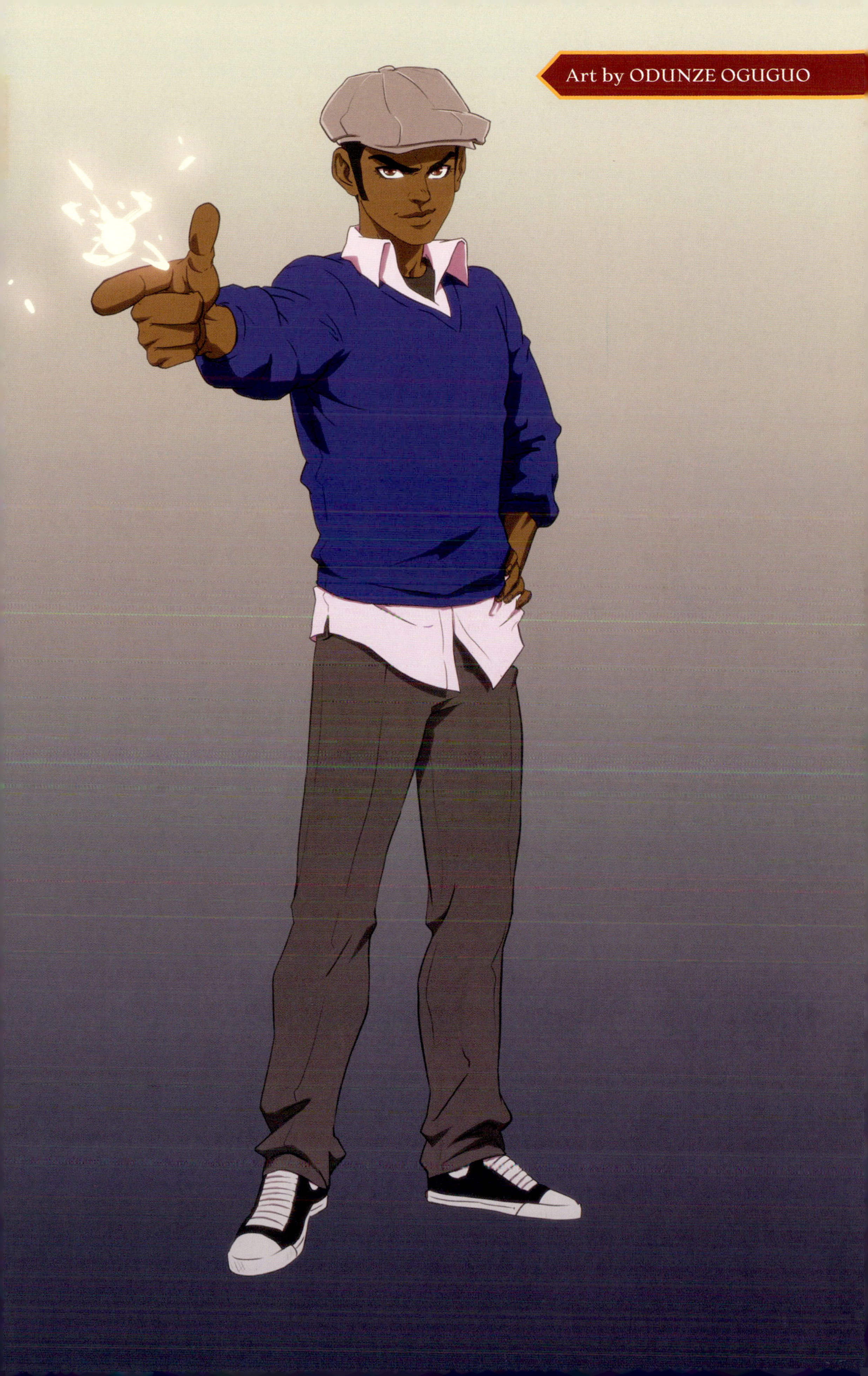

Art by ODUNZE OGUGUO

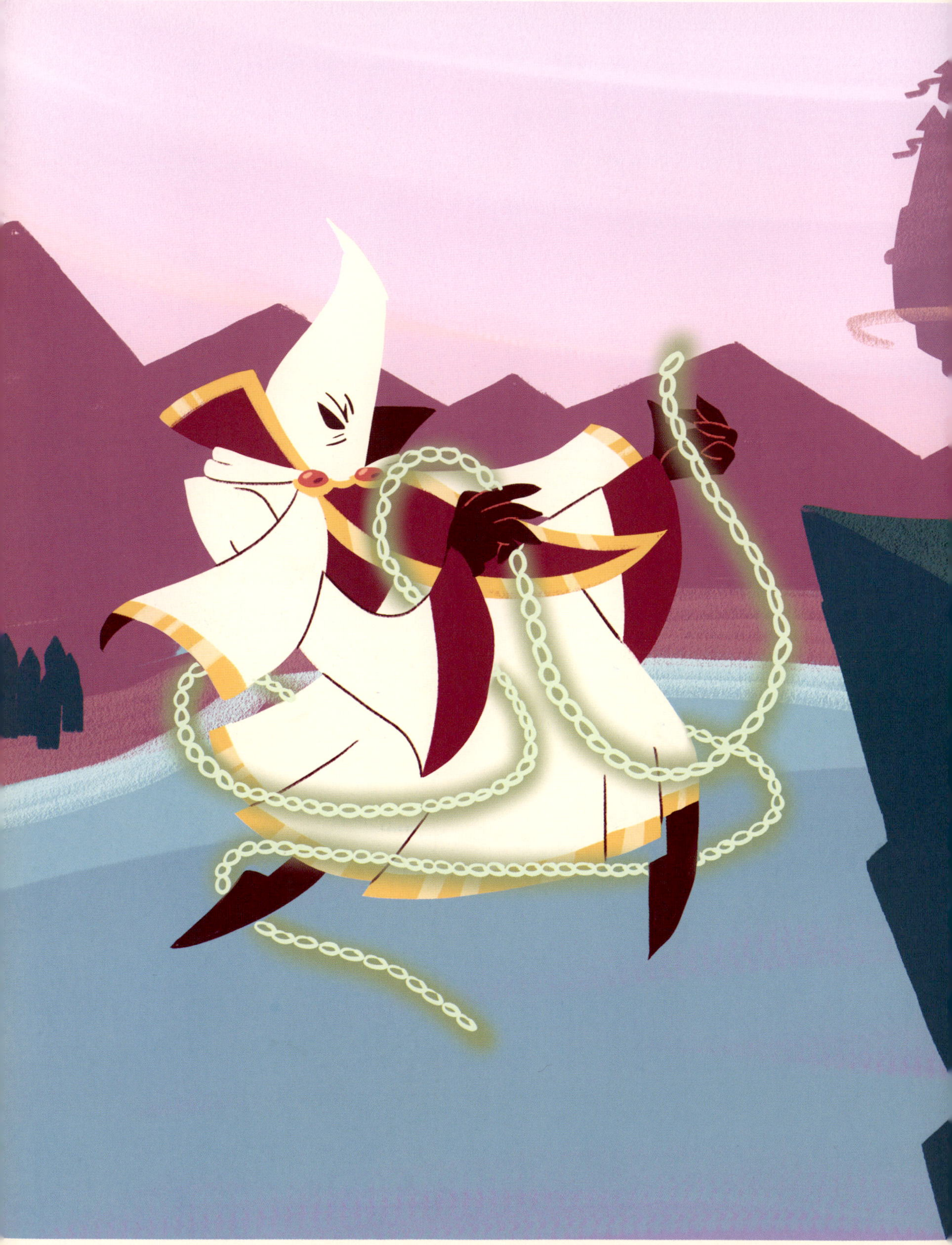

Art by JOHN-CHARLES HOLMES

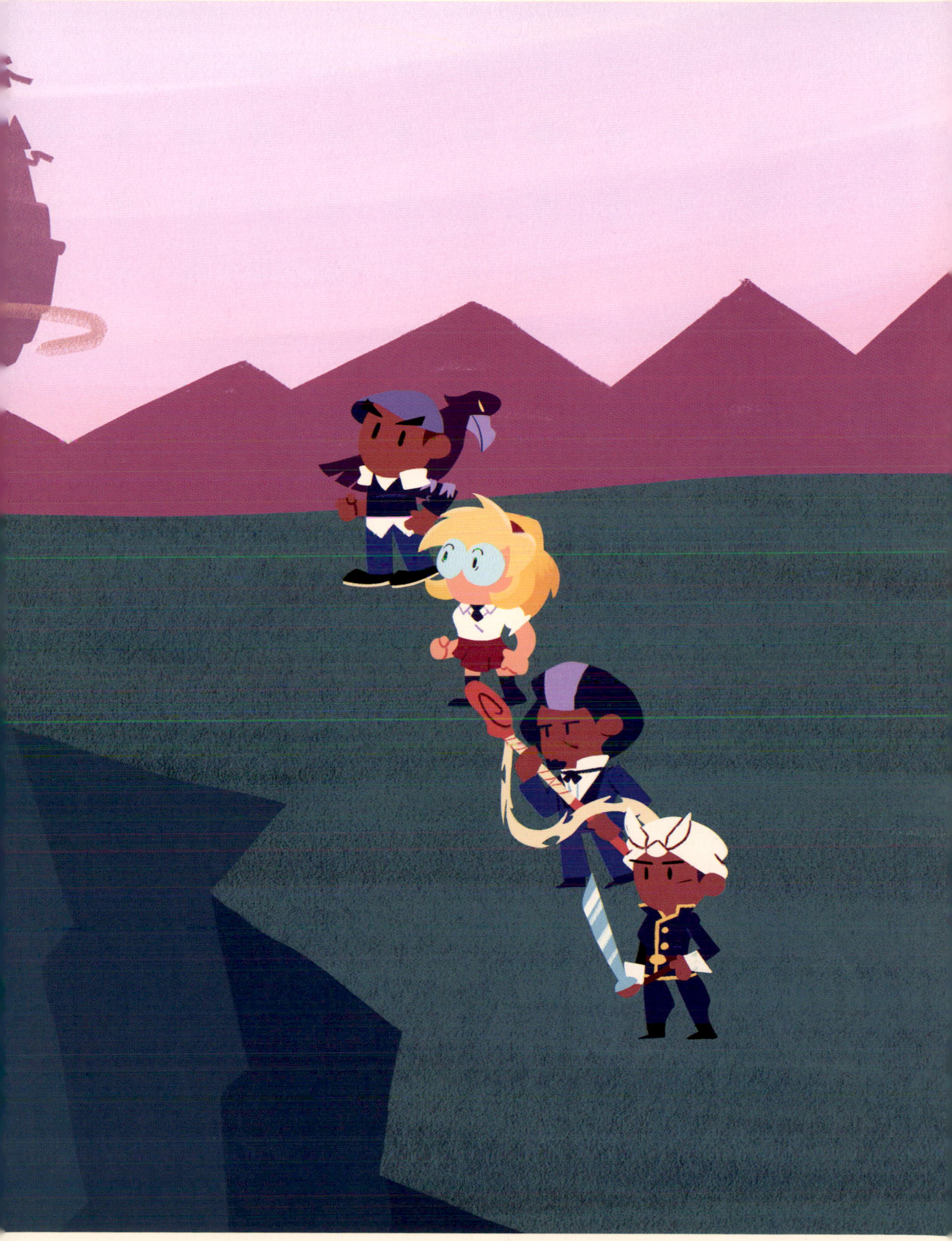

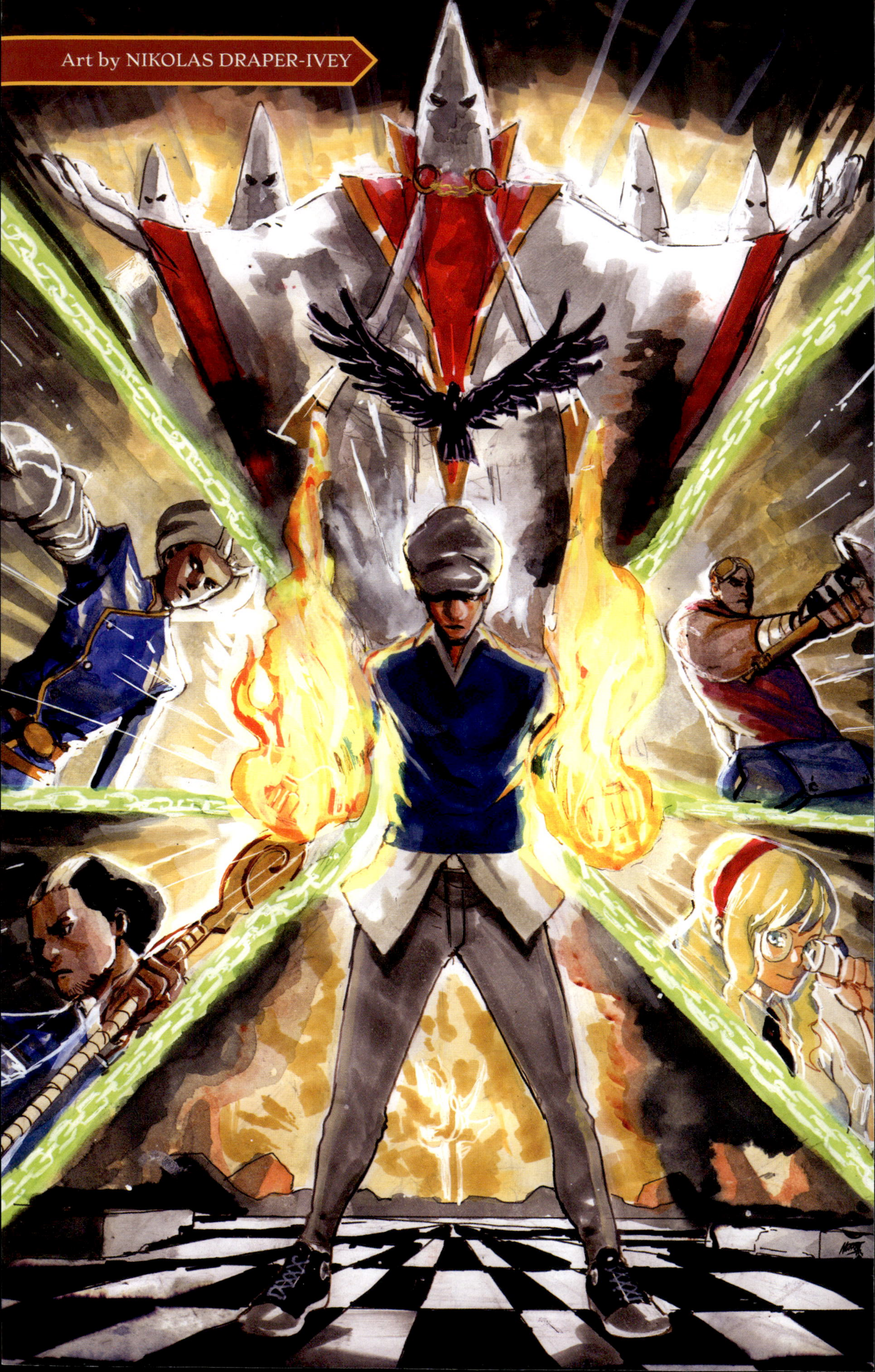

Art by NIKOLAS DRAPER-IVEY

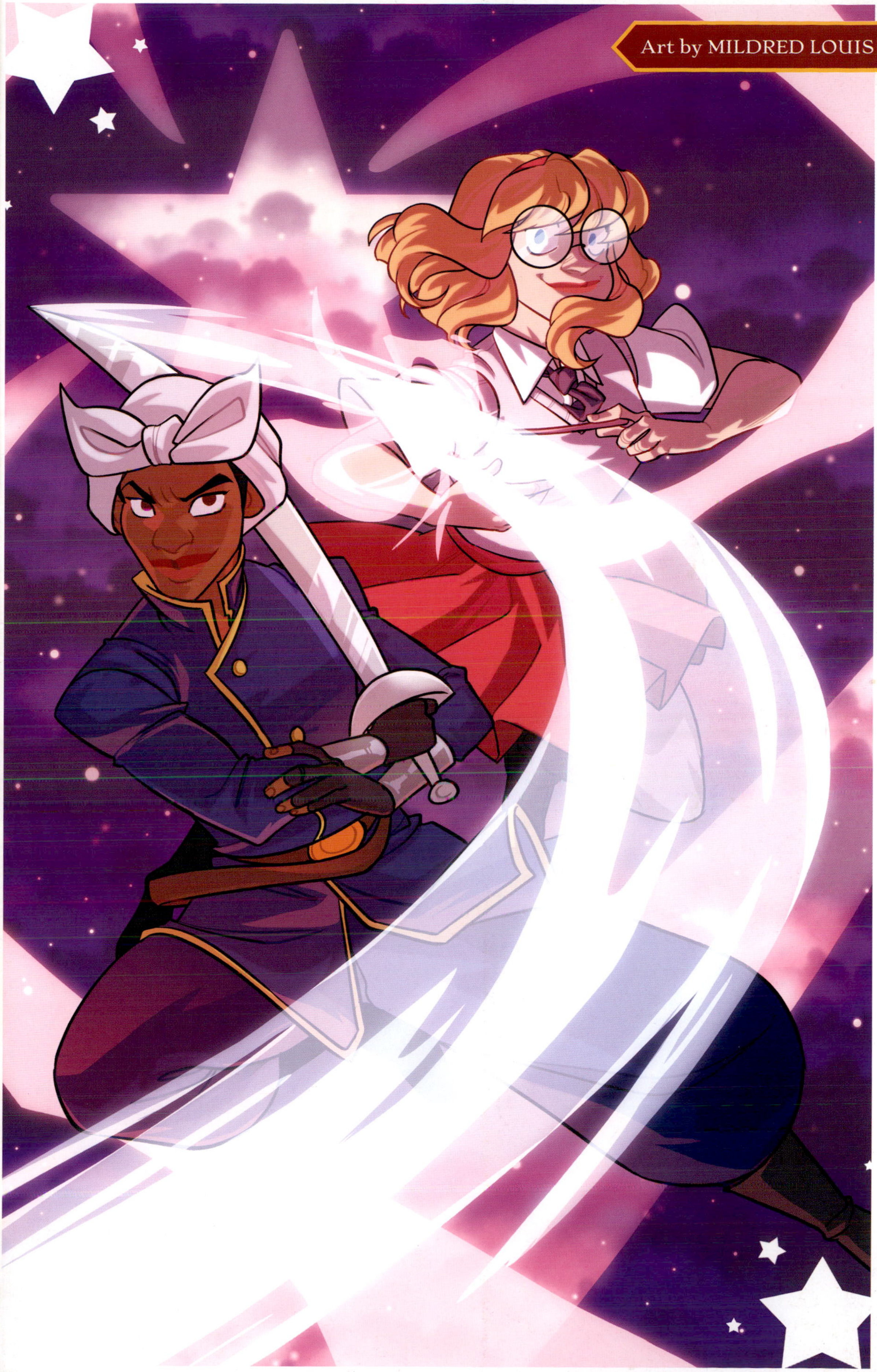
Art by MILDRED LOUIS

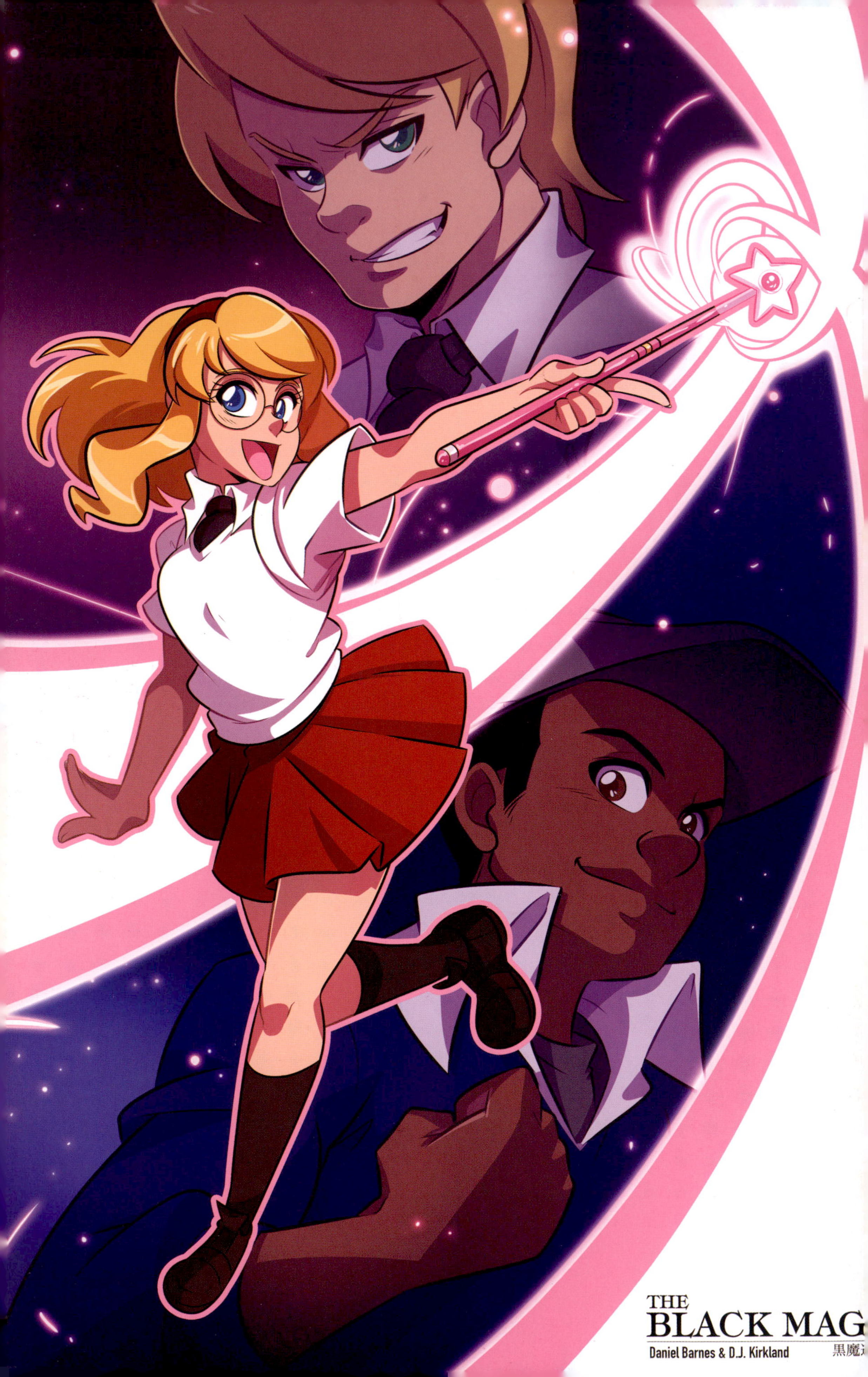
THE
BLACK MAG
Daniel Barnes & D.J. Kirkland
黒魔

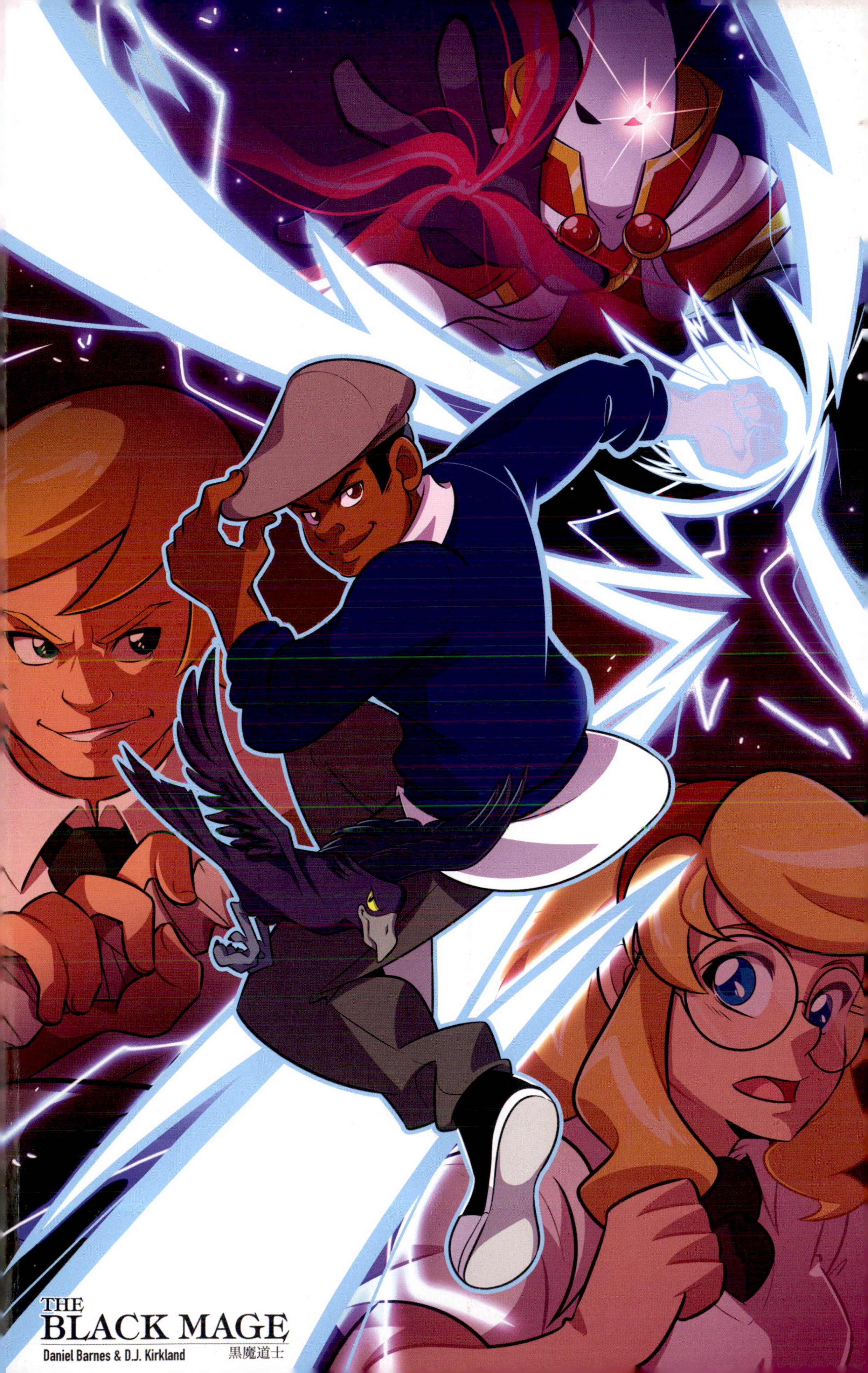
THE
BLACK MAGE
Daniel Barnes & D.J. Kirkland
黒魔道士

DANIEL BARNES is a writer from Fresno, CA. After serving in the U.S. Navy for four years, he enrolled in Academy of Art University, where he currently pursues a BFA in Animation Production. When he's not writing or procrastinating on his schoolwork, Daniel enjoys geeking out about Nintendo and being a weeb. He currently resides in San Francisco, CA.

D.J. KIRKLAND is a comic book artist from Charlotte, NC. He graduated from the Savannah College of Art and Design (SCAD) with a BFA in Sequential Art, which is just a fancy word for comic books. When he's not drawing comics, D.J. spends his time playing fighting games, streaming, and watching anime. D.J. now resides in Vallejo, CA.